For

Charles Ryan
Elinor Mavor
George Scithers
Pat Price
Kim Mohan
Gardner Dozois

Contents

REFLECTIONS AND REFRACTIONS

Thoughts on Science-Fiction,
Science, and Other Matters

REFLECTIONS AND REFRACTIONS

Thoughts on Science-Fiction, Science, and Other Matters

by

Robert Silverberg

Underwood Books
Grass Valley, California
1997

Reflections and Refractions
ISBN 1-887424-22-9 (trade paper)
ISBN 1-887424-24-5 (cloth)
ISBN 1-887424-23-7 (ltd. ed.)

Distributed by Publishers Group West
Manufactured in the United States of America
Cover design by Nora Wertz/Nora Wertz Design

FIRST EDITION
10 9 8 7 6 5 4 3 2 1

Library of Congress Cataloging-in-Publication-Data:
Silverberg, Robert.
Reflections and refractions: thoughts on science-fiction,
science, and other matters / by Robert Silverberg. --1st ed.
p. cm.
ISBN 1-887424-23-7 (ltd ed.). --ISBN 1-887424-24-5 (cloth). --
ISBN 1-887424-22-9 (pbk.)
1. Silverberg, Robert--Authorship. 2. Science fiction--History
and criticism--Theory, etc. 3. Science fiction--Authorship.
4. Literature and science. I. Title.
PS3569.I472Z474 1997
814.54--dc21   96-50494
                                                        CIP

Foreword: *Pontifications*

The Latin word for "bridge" is *pons* and a builder of bridges, in Latin, is a *pontifex*. *Pontifex* also was the term for a member of the college of Roman priests whose original responsibility was to see that the bridges were in good repair, and the chief priest of that group was known as the *Pontifex Maximus*. When Augustus, the first Roman emperor, consolidated all power into his hands by a process of having himself named to all the important governmental offices, he became, among many other things, the Pontifex Maximus; and all his successors on the imperial throne held that post after him.

Eventually the Empire was gone, but Rome itself, of course, remained, now under the control of the Bishop of Rome as head of the Catholic Church. During the Renaissance, amid a general revival of interest in classical antiquity, the old word *pontifex* began to come back into use as a way of referring to the local high priest, who by this time was, of course, the Catholic Bishop of Rome—that is, the Pope. Out of this usage comes our English word "pontiff" as a synonym for Pope; and, in the early nineteenth century, came by secondary derivation the word "pontificate," meaning "to issue dogmatic decrees." Anyone could pontificate, not just a Pope; all that was required was the possession of a few strongly held opinions and the willingness to speak out emphatically about them. That brings us a long way from bridge-building, but that's how languages operate.

We have, of course, plenty of such pontificators amongst us now. I am, I suppose, one of them, and I'm about to present you with an entire thick volume of my pontifications.

A little private joke is involved here, because I have on various occasions since about 1957 voiced a willingness to be named the actual Pope of Christendom whenever a vacancy has developed in the post. This irreverent fantasy of mine stems, I think, from my reading during my college days of Frederic Rolfe's famous novel *Hadrian the Seventh*, which is about an obscure English clergyman who through an astonishing sequence of unlikely but strangely plausible events *does* get to be Pope and sets about launching a furious campaign of ecclesiastical reform.

My own claim to the papacy is more tenuous even than that of Rolfe's Hadrian, since I am neither a Roman Catholic clergyman nor in fact a Christian at all (and am married, besides). But I did envision a process of investiture that would begin with my baptism at dawn, followed by my entry into Holy Orders and swift rise all morning through the ranks to the College of Cardinals, and my selection as Pope by nightfall, after which I would abolish priestly celibacy, welcome the Church of England and other separated groups back into the fold, appoint various science-fiction writers as Cardinals, and otherwise turn the venerable Catholic Church topsy-turvy. I would also have the pleasure of choosing my own regnal name. For a time I toyed with the notion of becoming Peter the Second, not just for the grandeur of the idea but because I was, like the original Peter, born a Jew; but then I decided that taking so lofty a name would be an act of *hybris*, or at least overweening *chutzpah*, and so I fixed on the idea of calling myself Sixtus the Sixth, there having been five previous Popes named Sixtus. (The fifth of them is the one responsible for the Sistine Chapel.)

Well, I never did become Pope, though I managed to have a robot Pope choose the name Sixtus VI in a story called "Good News from the Vatican," and I tipped my tiara to my old blasphemous ambition in my novel *Lord Valentine's Castle* by giving the title of Pontifex to the Emperor of Majipoor. But one thing I *have* done in my time is plenty of pontificating in the larger, metaphorical sense—spraying opinions far and wide on the subject I know best, which is science fiction.

Science-fiction readers, by and large, are ferocious pontificators. These days, I guess, most of them disseminate their views by electronic means, but long before the Internet was a reality, as far back, indeed, as the early 1930s, there was a network of low-circulation privately published little magazines—"fanzines"—in which any s-f aficionado who happened to own a typewriter felt empowered to cut loose with uninhibited blasts of opinion on all matters having to do with their favorite kind of reading matter. A few of these magazines, particularly at the beginning of the fanzine movement, were elegantly printed from hand-set type; but most were crudely produced items reproduced by such methods, largely obsolete today, as mimeography, hektography, and dittography. I know. I published one of them myself, an effusion called *Spaceship*, between 1949 and 1955, abandoning it only when I moved over from the pontificating side of things to the productive side and became a professional science-fiction writer.

The vehemence with which I expressed my pontifical opinions, in my days as a science-fiction fan, sometimes proved a little embarrassing later on. For example, I have here the Fall-Winter 1952 issue of *Fantastic Worlds*, one of the more attractive fanzines of its era (it was produced by the relatively costly photo-offset process) in which I hold forth about a new professional science-fiction magazine called *Fantastic* and its editor, Howard Browne. My piece begins:

"How Howard Browne has been able to reconcile his career-long ambition to edit a top-quality science-fiction magazine, one which will rank with the best in tone, format, and content, with his career-long profession of editing the two poorest (and admitted so by Browne himself) professional magazines of the field, will long remain one of publishing's greatest mysteries."

After flaming Browne up and down and sideways for his poor editorial performance, I go on to discuss his new magazine *Fantastic* and I express my astonishment that this time he had actually done something worthwhile. I end my little essay with the magnanimous hope that *Fantastic* would prosper and thrive, but since the whole thrust of my remarks was surprise that Browne had turned out to be capable of producing a magazine that intelligent adults would want to read (I was 17 at the time), he was hardly likely to have been flattered by my appended praise and good wishes.

Nor was he. In that very same issue of *Fantastic Worlds* appeared Browne's reply to my strictures. He began by quoting a Mid-western newspaper editor who, when under attack, replied, "These jackals grow too bold." Point by point he refuted my various impugnings of his prior editorial performance. Then he added, "Mr. Silverberg's almost ecstatic reaction to the first two issues of *Fantastic*, our new digest-sized publication, is gratifying. But I have no illusions because of it. That segment of fandom which writes most of the letters to editors, puts out fanzines, and joins fan clubs is famous for building heroes one day and tearing them down the next—both with little justification. When this group discovers that the second issue of *Fantastic* contains a long suspense story containing not one bit of fantasy or science, I shall probably be damned as a traitor to the field." And so on, in a good-humored way that made it clear that Browne didn't give a damn what science-fiction fandom in general, or Bob

Silverberg in particular, thought of any of his magazines: his goal was simply to find a format that would sell a lot of copies each month.

Well, so be it, I thought, flattered that my little article had elicited Browne's attention, and went on with my life. It never occurred to me that he might actually have been stung, at least for a moment or two, by my words.

Three years later—an endless span of time, for the adolescent that I was—I made the transition from fan to writer, partly as a result of a scathing review of a science-fiction novel that I did for my high-school newspaper, which brought me to the attention of the publisher of that novel and led to my getting a book contract from that publisher. One sale led to another and before long I was getting my stories published all over the place; and one of the people with whom I found myself doing business, eventually, was Howard Browne, the editor of *Fantastic* and its companion magazine, *Amazing Stories*. I had forgotten all about my denunciation of Browne by that time. But Browne hadn't.

He had known all along, from the first moment that I came to him with my stories, that I was the kid who had written that brash 1952 fanzine article. But he bided his time, while over a period of six months or so I sold him story after story. Then, one day early in 1956 when I showed up at Browne's Manhattan office to deliver my latest mediocre-but-acceptable offering, he had that copy of *Fantastic Worlds* on his desk. He grinned and pushed it across to me while I reddened in chagrin. "Remember this?" he said. He wondered if I still thought so little of his editorial abilities, now that he was buying material so frequently from me.

I stammered something about the impetuousness of youth, and he forgave me for my adolescent indiscretion and went on buying stories from me, quite a few, for the rest of his editorial career. A less magnanimous man would have tossed me out of his office the first time I dared to turn up there; but Howard was a gentleman and a pro. He didn't quite cure me of pontificating, of course. But he did teach me to be a little less exuberant in my self-righteous belligerence, and thus helped me to become the mild-mannered man I am today.

During the first decade of my career as a professional writer I wrote, as a sideline activity, a fair number of reviews of my colleagues' new books—not for fanzines, any more, but for such professional magazines of the time as *Infinity* and *Science Fiction Stories*. In the main I was more generous to them than I had been earlier to Howard Browne, because I knew that my colleagues were, like me, hapless mortal beings struggling to do their best. I preferred to praise books rather than slam them, and even when I did slam one I tried to find something to praise ("But yet one live, quivering story right in the middle of all this pretentious claptrap and pastiche bears witness to the fact that X *can* write, and write superbly....") Eventually, though, I came to feel uncomfortable about the whole process of passing judgment on the work of my peers, and stopped doing book reviews altogether, with just a few rare exceptions, somewhere about 1970.

But that doesn't mean I ceased to have opinions—about the books I was reading, about the most effective methods of telling a story, about literary style, about the policies of publishers, about political leaders, about society in general. Instead of expressing them in cogent little pieces for mimeographed fanzines or second-rank newsstand magazines, though, I uttered them to my wife, my friends, my cat, my houseplants, or any other reasonably willing auditor; and so a lot of really dogmatic Silverbergian pontification was forever lost to the world in the years between, approximately, 1965 and 1978.

Charlie Ryan put a stop to that.

He was the editor, then, of a sprightly science-fiction magazine called *Galileo*, which then was making a game attempt to establish itself in competition with much more securely financed publications. In May, 1978 he wrote to me and said, "I'd like to tempt you....I'd like you to consider writing a column for us, on a regular basis, on s-f, its strengths and weaknesses." And suggested a few topics for me to deal with: "Is the fact many authors are writing one, two, and in many cases more books on contract resulting in lesser quality?...Is there too much s-f being written for anyone to read it all? How do you balance a literary s-f story with the expected sense of adventure and wonder?"

At that time I had been absent from the science-fiction world for about four years, going through what was (I'm still not sure) either an extended vacation or a long period of writer's block or a virulent midlife crisis. But in the spring of 1978 I resolved to return—that was when I agreed to write *Lord Valentine's Castle*—and Charlie Ryan's offer of a bi-monthly column struck me as a good way to re-establish my visibility in the field. I was eager to re-establish my connection with the field of fiction that had been the center of my imaginative experience since my boyhood. The truth was that I missed science fiction and the conspicuous role that I had since the mid-1960s in shaping it. So I accepted *Galileo*'s invitation to do a regular commentary piece gladly and eagerly, and indeed with some relief; and for the next couple of years held forth with might and main in *Galileo*'s pages on this subject and that, to the edification and, I hope, delight of Charlie's unfortunately rather modest number of readers.

The realities of publishing economics did *Galileo* in with its sixteenth issue, which was dated January, 1980. By then I had done six columns for it—you will find some of them reprinted here—and I was definitely back in harness with the bit between my teeth. Scarcely had *Galileo* been laid to rest but I had an offer from Elinor Mavor, then the editor, at several levels of succession from Howard Browne, of the venerable *Amazing Stories*, to move my column to her magazine. Which I did, beginning with the May, 1981 *Amazing*; and there I held forth for thirteen years, through one change of publisher, three changes of editor (Mavor to George Scithers to Pat Price to Kim Mohan), one change in the column's name (from "Opinion" to "Reflections") and a total transformation of the magazine's physical appearance. There I was, spouting off on any topic that happened to interest me that month, for more than a hundred columns.

Amazing too went the way of all magazines in 1994, two years short of its seventieth birthday. Caught without a podium for my orations and thoroughly accustomed now to orating, I adroitly transferred the site of my column to the monthly magazine *Asimov's Science Fiction*, which had emerged in the 1980s as the dominant s-f publication of its era and now, under the inspired editorship of Gardner Dozois, was essential reading for anyone interested in the state of the science-fiction art. Isaac Asimov, the guiding spirit of the magazine, had written its editorial column every issue since the magazine's inception, but his death in June, 1992 had left the slot for that column vacant, and editor Dozois was troubled by the loss of continuity and personality that the end of Isaac's column had caused. So I was gladly welcomed to fill those gigantic shoes; and I was glad enough to do it. *Asimov's*, which everybody in the field read with care, was the perfect place to pontificate from, and I have happily contributed dozens of essays to its pages over the past three years, with, I hope, many more to come.

The present fat book, then, has been in the making, essentially, for nearly fifty years—from my first smartass comments on science fiction in the smudgy mimeographed fanzines of the late 1940s to last month's column in *Asimov's*. What I have brought together here is most of my columns from *Galileo*, *Amazing Stories*, and *Asimov's Science Fiction Magazine*, along with occasional pieces written for other publications and some essays originally intended as introductions to new editions of my own books. They cover a span of thirty years or so of my life. The tone of my essay-writing has changed, somewhat, during my five-decade evolution from wiseacre brat to somber and weary *eminence grise*. But certain positions remain consistent.

From start to finish, for example, these essays are grounded in my belief that the world we inhabit and the universe that contains it are intensely interesting places full of wonders and miracles, and that one way we can bring ourselves closer to an appreciation, if not an understanding, of those wonders and miracles is through reading science fiction. There is also—consistently—the recognition that not all science fiction is equally valuable for that purpose, that in fact a lot of it is woeful junk; and I can be seen, again and again, expressing the same kind of displeasure with mediocre, cynical, or debased science fiction that I was voicing when I sounded off at Howard Browne in 1952.

Which is not to say that I haven't written plenty of stories myself over those forty years that fail to live up to my own lofty standards of execution, some because my skills have not been equal to my vision, and some because circumstances (like the need to pay the rent) led me to knock out some quick piece of formula prose instead of taking the time to turn out another award-winning classic. I am as human as the next guy, after all.

But my own literary sins, and they are numerous, haven't kept me from crying out in the public square against those who, for the sake of a dollar or two, would transform science fiction into something less than it can be. I know how the finest s-f can pry open the walls of the universe for an intelligent and inquisitive reader, for it has done that for me since I was ten or eleven years old, and it angers me to see writers and editors and publishers refusing even to make the attempt. In my own best fiction I have tried to achieve for other readers what H.G. Wells and Jules Verne and Robert A. Heinlein and Isaac Asimov and Jack Vance and A.E. van Vogt and Theodore Sturgeon and fifty other wonderful writers achieved for me ever since the time I first stumbled, wide-eyed and awe-struck, into the world of science fiction. And in many of the essays in this book I try, perhaps with the same naive idealism that I aimed at poor Howard Browne in 1952, to advocate the creation of more science fiction of that high kind and to urge the spurning the drab simple-minded stuff that leads us away from the real exaltation that an intense encounter with the fabric of space and time can provide.

There are also some essays here examining the foibles and oddities of the present-day world. I have to confess that even the best of science-fiction writers have no more access to the secret recesses of space and time than you do; the sources of their fiction lie in part in their own souls, in part in the reading and studying that they do, and in part in their observation of the world around them. I do plenty of observing, and plenty of rueful shaking of my head; and because I am a man of profound common sense (or, as some might say, a man of increasingly crotchety prejudices) I deplore a lot of what I see. Since I have a thousand words a month at my disposal in which to express my thoughts, I often tell my readers about those deplorable things, perhaps with some hope of winning allies in my lifelong crusade against idiocy and irrationality, or—perhaps—just to get some things off my chest.

My basic attitude in these essays, I suppose, can be called libertarian/conservative, though a lot of people nowadays who call themselves libertarians or conservatives often say things that appall me. (I am not such a doctrinaire libertarian that I favor the abolition of government inspection of food products or an end to government regulation of the manufacturers of medicines; I am not such a doctrinaire conservative that I look kindly on governmental attempts to legislate personal morality, or favor mandatory religious instruction in state schools. And so forth.)

Very likely you will find me advocating a number of positions with which you disagree. It would surprise me if you didn't. If we all held the same set of beliefs on everything, the world would be a dreary thing indeed, and so would this book. Grant me, as a minimum, that in all my thinking I am trying to grope my way toward sane answers to crazy problems, and if I come to conclusions that you don't share, it's not because I'm a black-hearted villain or an eager oppressor of the unfortunate but because—having spent a lot of my life imagining myself living a million light-years from Earth or a million chronological years from the present day—I've come to feel that a lot of what goes on all around me in the actual world I inhabit doesn't make a lot of sense, and, because I have the privilege of saying so in print, I do say so, with the small and faint hope that I am thereby nudging the world a little closer to rationality.

And, finally, there are some pieces in here that deal with my long career as a science-fiction writer: editors I have dealt with, writers I have known, events in my writing life, commentary on my own books and stories. Whatever else the life of a professional writer can sometimes be—exhausting, frustrating, bewildering, even frightening—it is rarely dull; and it has been my great good luck to spend nearly half of this rapidly expiring twentieth century right in the midst of that strange and wonderful literary microcosm called science-fiction publishing. I've known almost everyone involved in it, and experienced just about everything that an s-f writer can experience, and I have a lot of tales to tell about those experiences, some of which—just a few—I tell here. It's as close to a formal autobiography as I'll ever write, I suspect.

I offer these reminiscences and self-referential essays without apology, not only because I enjoyed writing them but also because I think you'll find them of interest. (Modesty is not a trait widely found among writers. The successful ones are those who are convinced, at least while they're actually at work, that what they're writing, whatever it may be, is inherently interesting to other people and will find an immediate, eager, happy audience. Without that conviction, I imagine it would be very hard for writers to push themselves all the way from the first page of a story to the last.)

So, then. Herewith a bunch of essays on science-fiction, science, and various other matters, written by someone who has very gradually grown old and gray dreaming about far galaxies and other dimensions and somehow still keeps at it, writing stories about people and places who never existed. Being a professional science-fiction writer is, I have to admit, a very peculiar way to have spent your whole adult life. But so be it; that is the choice I made, unhesitatingly, a long time ago; and here are some of the thoughts that have occurred to me along the way.

—Robert Silverberg
Oakland, California
April, 1996

ONE

SCIENCE FICTION:
SOME GENERAL THOUGHTS

Enwonderment

Enwonderment.

It's an awful word. It's mine. I literally dreamed it up.

One night I was addressing some congregation of teachers in my sleep—the keynote speaker at an imaginary academic hoedown that I must have conjured out of too much Nepalese lamb curry, or was it the appetizer of baked spleen at that Lebanese restaurant that did it to me?—and I heard myself telling the assembled educators that it was important for them to foster a state of "enwonderment" in their pupils. It was, I suppose, some sort of cockeyed linguistic analogy with "empowerment," which everybody is talking about these days, or perhaps the root word was "enrichment," which I gather is still one of the big academic buzzwords.

You know how a dream can be so horrible that it wakes you up? You're in a natural history museum, say, and suddenly the fossil dinosaurs start snorting and snuffling and chasing you through the halls like a bunch of velociraptors out of *Jurassic Park*. Or you're arriving at the hotel where the World Science Fiction Convention is about to take place and just as you enter the crowded lobby you notice that you've forgotten to put your clothes on that morning. The alarms go off in your dreaming mind, and you find yourself wide awake, sweating and muttering, reassuring yourself as best you can that whatever it was you dreamed is in fact not happening to you at all.

That's how it was with me and "enwonderment." A really gross linguistic construction upsets me the way getting chased around a museum by velociraptors would upset most other people. And so I awakened with the nasty sound of that word still ringing in my mind, and the recollection that it was I, the urbane and literate Robert Silverberg, who had uttered it in front of an audience of professional educators.

[*Asimov's Science Fiction*, September 1994]

1

And yet—and yet—

Forget about what a klutzy-sounding word it is. Indigestion or not, I think my dreaming mind may have been on to something. For is it not true that one of the primary things we science-fiction writers try to accomplish is to bring a note of, well, enwonderment to our readers' minds—to startle and delight and astonish them with miraculous and magical visions of wondrous things?

I say *one of* the primary things because there are many sorts of science fiction, and many different things that people look for in the particular kind of s-f they read. Some like to read about clever gadgets and their applications to tough problems. Some are after sociological or technological or political speculations about the near future. Some are turned on by social satire (which usually means that they like reading stories that make fun of things they don't like.) Some have an inexhaustible appetite for grand epics of future galactic empires built on analogies with Rome and Byzantium, and others prefer trips back to Rome or Byzantium themselves. Some want to get embroiled in a futuristic mystery; some like tales of heroic Schwarzeneggeresque action involving lots of splashy weapons; some—

Different folks, different strokes. There's enough s-f around for everyone's tastes.

My own s-f reading over the past five decades has embodied some of all of the above. The names of the magazines I read in my youth indicate the range: *Astounding Science Fiction* one day, for the gadgetry and sociological speculations; *Planet Stories* the next for the ray-gun and spaceship stuff; *Famous Fantastic Mysteries* for the trips back in time to lost empires. But what I was really searching for most of the time, and what I have tried to embody above all else in my own writing since I made the big shift from consumer of science fiction to creator of it about forty years ago, is passages that give me the verbal equivalent of what I feel when I stare up at the stars in the night sky, or peer into the eyepiece of a microscope at a drop of water teeming with protozoa, or walk the columned aisles of a Roman or Egyptian temple thousands of years old. Passages like these:

"When at last the time for migration was approaching, a specially designed vegetation was shipped to Neptune and established in the warm area to fit it for man's use. Animals, it was decided, would be unnecessary. Subsequently a specially designed human species, the Ninth Men, was transported to man's new home. The giant Eighth Men could not themselves inhabit Neptune. The trouble was not merely that they could scarcely support their own weight, let alone walk, but that the atmospheric pressure on Neptune was unendurable. For the great planet bore a gaseous envelope thousands of miles deep. The solid globe was scarcely more than the yolk of a huge egg...."

"In my mundane consciousness I could never have imagined the existence, anywhere in this universe, of this thousand-peaked range of glistening black and bloodred rock, bordering a steaming sea of dull silver under a sky that was not blue but that consisted of unbearably blinding mother-of-pearl and opal fish scales, behind which lurked the blackness of space."

"It had not been fear of physical menace that had shaken his reason, nor the appearance of the creature—he could recall nothing of how it looked. It had been a feeling of sadness infinitely compounded which had flooded through him at the instant, a sense of tragedy, of grief insupportable and unescapable, of infinite weariness. He had been flicked with emotions many times too strong for his spiritual fiber and which he was no more fitted to experience than an oyster is to play a violin.

"He felt that he had learned all about the High Ones a man could learn and still endure. He was no longer curious. The shadow of that vicarious emotion ruined his sleep, brought him sweating out of dreams."

"I cannot convey the sense of abominable desolation that hung over the world. The red eastern sky, the northward blackness, the salt Dead Sea, the stony beach crawling with these foul, slow-stirring monsters, the uniform poisonous-looking green of the lichenous plants, the thin air that hurts one's lungs; all contributed to an appalling effect. I moved on a hundred years, and there was the same red sun—a little larger, a little duller—the same dying sea, the same chill air, and the same crowd of earthy crustacea creeping in and out among the green weed and the red rocks. And in the westward sky I saw a curved pale line like a vast new moon."

"Worlds young....warm....volcanic and steaming....the single cell emerging from the slime of warm oceans to propagate on primordial continents....other worlds, innumerable....life divergent in all branches from the single cell....amorphous

globules....amphibian....crustacean....reptilian....plant....inse
ct....bird....mammal....all possible variations of combina-
tions....crystalline beings sentient and reasoning.....great
shimmering columnar forms, seemingly liquid, defying gravity by some strange power of cohesion...."

"I talked with the mind of Yiang-Li, a philosopher from
the cruel empire of Tsan-Chan, which is to come in 5,000
A.D; with that of a general of the great-headed brown people
who held South Africa in 50,000 B.C.; with that of a twelfth-
century Florentine monk named Bartolomeo Corsi; with that
of a king of Lomar who ruled that terrible polar land one
hundred thousand years before the squat, yellow Inutos
came from the west to engulf it."

These are quotes from *The Time Machine*, by H.G. Wells, "He Who
Shrank," by Henry Hasse, *Last and First Men*, by Olaf Stapledon, "By
His Bootstraps," by Robert A. Heinlein, "The Shadow Out of Time,"
by H.P. Lovecraft, and *Star of the Unborn*, by Franz Werfel. These are
some of the passages that did it for me, forty-odd years back, when I
was first being exposed to the incurable science-fiction virus. I'm not
going to tell you which comes from what. If science fiction means half
as much to you as it does to me, you already know. And if you don't
know, I suggest that you check out all the items I've mentioned and
find out for yourself. You have a treat coming.

Of course, these are *my* enwonderment texts—a few of them,
anyway—passages that mean more to me, in a specifically science-fictional way, than any quantity of clever plotting or depth of character
analysis or elegance of literary style. For such commodities as those,
I can always turn to John Le Carre or Thomas Mann or John Updike,
or Shakespeare and Proust and Joyce, or a lot of other people who
never wrote for *Astounding Science Fiction*. As I've noted, my quota-
tions go back some decades, and then some—as do I. I'd be interested
in seeing little excerpts from *your* reading lists—passages from the s-f
books or stories of recent years (whatever seems recent to you— 1970,
1980, 1990)—that have kindled in you that sense of—yes, enwonderment—which is, I believe, the highest achievement of science fiction.

Bat Durston's Blasting Jets

Almost thirty-five years ago, on the back cover of the first issue of his extraordinary new science fiction magazine *Galaxy*, the brilliant editor H.L. Gold offered this pair of opening paragraphs from two stories that *Galaxy* did not plan to publish:

> "Jets blasting, Bat Durston came screeching down through the atmosphere of Bblizznaj, a tiny planet seven billion light years from Sol. He cut out his super-hyper-drive for the landing...and at that point, a tall, lean spaceman stepped out of the tail assembly, proton gun-blaster in a space-tanned hand.
>
> " 'Get back from those controls, Bat Durston,' the tall stranger lipped thinly. 'You don't know it, but this is your last space trip!"

> "Hoofs drumming, Bat Durston came galloping down through the narrow pass at Eagle Gulch, a tiny gold colony only 400 miles north of Tombstone. He spurred hard for a low overhang of rimrock...and at that point a tall, lean wrangler stepped out from behind a high boulder, six-shooter in a sun-tanned hand.
>
> " 'Rear back and dismount, Bat Durston,' the tall stranger lipped thinly. 'You don't know it, but this is your last saddle-jaunt through these here parts.' "

Gold's target in this clever (and instantly famous) bit of prose was a kind of story all too common in the pulp-magazine science fiction of the 1940's—the transplanted western, in which venerable storytelling cliches were given a flashy new life by substituting Mars for Arizona, gzlploks for horses, and Greenskins for Redskins. Writers who used to earn a penny a word banging out the stuff for *Enthralling Western* found it no great trick to expand their markets a little by turning out similar commodities for *Stupefying Science Tales*. But that wasn't really what most science fiction readers past the mental age of ten were hoping to find in the magazines, and Gold, a vigorous and uncompromising iconoclast, served notice right away that his magazine was not going to publish Bat Durston epics. (He also warned prospective contributors not to waste postage sending him stories in which the characters turned out to be Adam and Eve at the end, or the one about the alien life-force eater hidden in the Andes, or the one

[*Amazing Stories*, November 1984]

in which the characters travel to a hideous alien world that we finally find out is Earth—all of them well-worn cliches by the time *Galaxy* was launched in 1950.)

Cliches, it should be noted, are items that once had real value, In nineteenth-century printing terminology, a cliche was a readymade stereotype block that could easily be inserted ("clicked") into a printer's plate. But by 1892 it was being used in metaphorical extension to mean a commonplace phrase that could be inserted without the trouble of thought into a piece of writing; and in further extension it has come to mean any excessively worn concept. What began as a time-saver evolved into a time-waster, devoid of useful content. (Information, remember, is novelty.)

Gold, an acutely intelligent man, was more demanding than most s-f editors, but even he was not incapable of making use of cliches. In place of the transplanted western, he eventually gave us the transplanted slick story—what James Blish used to call the "call the rabbit a smeerp" story, in which a cocktail party becomes a vilbar party and the rest of the story proceeds precisely as it might have done in *Cosmopolitan* or *Redbook*. That kind of stuff was more sophisticated than transplanted westerns, but hardly more nourishing to the real s-f reader.

And now, many literary revolutions later, the old cliches are ostensibly gone, but a bunch of new ones have crept into science fiction. These are just a few:

• *The female villain.* In the bad old days we used to find stories full of sinister Saturnian dope peddlers, nasty asteroid-belt mining tycoons, quick-on-the-blaster bounty hunters, and other mustache-twirling scoundrels. They were all male, of course. *All* the characters in the s-f stories were male, except for the scientist's delicate daughter and the crusading newspaperwoman. We are in an age of liberation, now, and so we find stories populated by *female* dope peddlers, tycoons, and bounty hunters, just as villainous, or even more so. Most of this space-opera junk is written by women, who evidently feel they are just as entitled to crank out formula pulp stuff as men are. Indeed they are: but junk is still junk, no matter what the sex of the author or her characters. (Some men are writing this stuff too, to show how enlightened they are. I can't find any excuse for them at all.)

• *The trilogy.* C. S. Lewis and J. R. R. Tolkien, long ago, found themselves possessed by fantasy themes so immense that they needed three volumes to tell the tale. Isaac Asimov, also long ago, had an epic science fiction theme that couldn't readily fit into a single volume. They had good reasons for writing trilogies. Nowadays, though, ideas that wouldn't ordinarily serve to pad out a novelet are routinely spun into tripledecker sets because some publishers noticed that the Lewis and Tolkien and Asimov trilogies had won big audiences. A lot of the new trilogies sell very well too, alas. But that doesn't entirely justify filling three volumes with a story that wasn't worth one.

• *Celtic lore.* There's a lot of lovely stuff in the Arthurian legends, the *Mabinogion*, the Cuchulain cycle, and so forth. It was nicely plundered by a good many gifted fantasists of the nineteenth and early twentieth centuries, and it is getting plundered all over again today. I guess it sells pretty well too. Although I tend to write science fiction myself, I have always found fantasy just as enjoyable—but I long ago reached my saturation point with Cuchulain and Taliesin and Mordred and that crowd. Will the upcoming fantasy writers please start looting the Vedas or the Eddas instead, for a while?

• *False honorifics.* A minor point. But it seems that every science fiction novel I open nowadays is stocked with characters named Vaskar piBrell and Lompoc syMethicone and Dilvibong vorVorkish. Those capital letters in the middle of names are starting to get to me. I think the problem is that it's one more aspect of the Graust-ark/Ruritania syndrome in modern science fiction—the adoption of the cliched paraphernalia of the nineteenth-century middle-European romance novel, which I think deserves lengthier analysis on its own another time. Too many books are full of bemedalled noblethings with fake post-Napoleonic titles, strutting around pretending to be aliens. I think I'd prefer Bat Durston.

Dumbing Down

Some time back—it was in the November, 1984 issue—I wrote a piece inveighing against the new cliches now prevalent in science fiction, and one that I cited was the female villain: the nasty, snarling space pirate, bounty hunter, narcotics peddler, or whatever, who in the bad old days of pulp-magazine fiction was always a man and who now, in the bad new days of junky paperback s-f, has better than a fifty-fifty chance of being a woman.

Which led a reader named Robert Nowall to take me to task in the letter column of the March, 1985 issue. "In his discussion of the female villain," he writes, "[Silverberg] appears to be implying that no woman can be a villain under any circumstances. Why can't women be villains? Don't they have as much right as men to be nasty and evil (or just to oppose the hero, in more sophisticated science fiction)?"

I don't actually think reader Nowall and I are very far apart ideologically. But he's missing, or at least sidestepping, my real point, which has nothing to do with affirmative action and everything to do with the quality of published science fiction. Sure, Mr. Nowall, women have *as much right* as men to be foul and violent and amoral. If a woman wanted to set herself up in business as the next Hitler, the next Attila, the next Jack the Ripper, who are we to tell her that such roles are reserved only for members of our sex? Are we to keep our women barefoot and pregnant, peeling potatoes in the kitchen, while we alone go out to lie, cheat, maim, plunder, and destroy?

But—granting the right of women to equal-opportunity evil—I need to point out that most fiction about space pirates, interstellar drug smugglers, black-hearted slave traders, and other deplorable types tends to be pretty dumb junk. When we're kids, we all have a certain innocent love of dumb junk, which is why comic books maintain their popularity generation after generation. There used to be a science fiction magazine called *Planet Stories* when I was a boy, that deliberately set itself up to be a kind of comic book in prose, and its pages were full of gorgeously silly stories about snarling villains and bug-eyed monsters. Isaac Asimov and Ray Bradbury and Poul Anderson wrote some of those stories (the better ones, I ought to add) and I would have written some too, if the magazine hadn't happened to go out of business just about the time I was getting ready to sell my first stories, thirty-odd years ago. We all loved *Planet Stories*. We all still do, those of us who grew up on it; we're likely to say to one

[*Amazing Stories*, September 1985]

another, "That there's a real *Planet Stories* yarn," and we'll know exactly what we mean.

But there's more to life—or literature, or even science fiction—than being twelve years old forever. A lot of us who loved *Planet Stories* worked long and hard during the 1950s and 1960s to create a kind of science fiction that might be of interest to grownups. In the 1970s we saw the flowering of that movement, and a lot of fine mature science fiction being written by the likes of Ursula K. Le Guin, Gene Wolfe, James Tiptree, Kate Wilhelm, J.G. Ballard, Brian Aldiss, and a host of others. But here in the 1980s we are starting to see the whole revolution of literacy within science fiction being undone. A horde of new readers, lured by *Star Trek* and *Star Wars*, have been rushing in, looking for paperbacks that give them that good old *Planet Stories* pizazz, and the stuff is selling and selling and selling. That's no surprise. Junk always sells well. But it's sad to see so many of the bright female writers who came into the field in the 1970s turning out the junk too, and thinking that because their villains are female they're making some sort of feminist statement, when in fact all they're doing is writing the same old junk with one little modification. That, Mr. Nowall, was my real point.

A kind of Gresham's law obtains in fiction as well as in coinage. Bad fiction drives out good. A publisher can put out only so many titles a month, and there's only so much room in the bookshops to display them. It's getting hard for some of the outstanding s-f writers of the 1970s to keep their books in print more than a few weeks, and some of the most demanding and individual of them can't even get published at all in the United States. (It's a different story in Britain and France.)

A process is going on here that has become known in academic circles as "dumbing down." A generation of readers has emerged that has no real notion of history, of grammar, of art, or, it seems, of anything much else except the current pop music and hit movies and perhaps the latest in interactive computer games. They aren't stupid; they're simply empty. The kind of intellectual training they've had at home and in the elementary schools has given them a line-of-least-resistance mentality that makes it difficult for them to learn. To quote Charles Muscatine, a professor of English at the University of California/Berkeley, "They can't read the same books as in the past, their attention spans are shorter, and their vocabulary is smaller. Their capacity to deal with abstract ideas is about two years behind what it was."

Realistic teachers and textbook writers, seeing that the situation is hopeless, are therefore hard at work "dumbing down"—making the courses easier, simplifying the textbooks, and in many other ways caving in to the catastrophe. If your students aren't up to Joyce and Faulkner, give 'em a course in science fiction; and if they can't handle Le Guin or Ballard either, why, give 'em *Planet Stories* stuff. Which sets in motion a self-propelling downward slide in education that will have even more horrendous consequences a generation from now when today's kids are the parents and the teachers themselves.

I object to the female villains in the new pulp s-f not because they're female, but because they're villains—simple blackhearted incarnations of evil, stereotyped and boring, depressing revivals of dumb old cliches. All fiction needs conflict, sure. But conflict can take many forms, and the conflict of villains and heroes is the simplest, least subtle, and (I think) least interesting of them, especially in science fiction, where the interplay of challenging concepts is, or was, a primary aim. Evil in literature can be interesting and revealing—I need only cite Iago and Richard III—but most of the time a reliance on the presence of all-out evil to motivate a plot results in fiction mainly of interest to relatively undemanding children looking for a good wild roaring story.

It was useful to have *Planet Stories* around to lure twelve-year-olds into reading science fiction, and for those of us who were more than twelve it was a cute magazine, a kind of campy thing, that no one took seriously but everybody enjoyed. But that was thirty-five years ago. Now, with the "dumbing down" process going on on our campuses and science fiction reverting to adolescent triviality as it becomes overwhelmingly successful commercially, I can't help getting a little upset by the return of the interstellar dope-smugglers, no matter what their sex may be.

All Those Picture-Books

Not long ago, while visiting a medium-sized western city, I paused in front of one of the largest bookstores in town to examine an impressive window display of science fiction books, complete with some toy robots and other glittery decorations. Or perhaps I should have said " 'science fiction' books," because what was actually visible in that handsome window were such titles as—

H.R. Giger's *Necronomicon*. The photo-book of the movie *Alien*. Chris Foss's *21st Century Foss*, a book of reprinted book-jackets. *The Flight of Dragons*, by Peter Dickinson. *Alien Landscapes*, edited by Robert Holdstock and Malcolm Edwards. Plus several *Battlestar Galactica* books, an array of *Star Wars* and *Star Trek* items, some collected comic strips from the magazine *Heavy Metal*, and assorted material on gnomes, fairies, monsters, and vampires. Beneath all this gaudy and flamboyant stuff, scattered offhandedly at the very bottom of the display, were a few volumes of what we term prose fiction—a novel of Anne McCaffrey's, a recent Arthur C. Clarke book, one of mine (maybe they knew I was in town for the weekend), and two of the currently fashionable bulky pseudo-Tolkien fantasy novels.

Science? Not much. Fiction? Well, at second or third remove, I guess. A beautiful book containing reproductions of science-fiction magazine and book-jacket illustrations does have some peripheral link to the stories being illustrated; and a book of comic-book-style adaptations of Roger Zelazny stories, which was also in the window, is after all based on the Zelazny stories on which it's based, right? But yet—but yet—

The whole display chilled me. Here were all these large and lovely volumes, at $8.95 and $9.95 and $17.95 and such, lavishly produced and widely distributed, displayed as "science fiction"—but they were nearly all picture-books, and most of those that required actual reading were of the simplest sort, proffering elementary soft-headed fantasies of the kind we used to dote on in the fourth grade. Sure, Clarke's austere speculations on the future of technology and my own somber novel of college students searching for immortality were in the window too, but tucked away down where they'd be noticed only by a visiting author uneasily hunting for his own works.

Is this the new illiteracy of which we were warned since television became the national kiddie pastime a quarter of a century ago? Is science fiction—real written-down science fiction, using words ar-

[*Amazing Stories*, May 1981]

ranged in grammatical structures—doomed now to become an insignificant adjunct to picture-books drawn from fifth-rate Buck Rogers movies and compilations of goblins and beasties? The science fiction on which I was raised in my pre-adolescent and adolescent days, that of Heinlein and Asimov and Kuttner and van Vogt and company, never really taxed the intellect a great deal, at least not in comparison with the books of Messrs. Joyce, Faulkner, Proust, and Mann that some of my more earthbound high-school friends were reading, but it did require the ability to comprehend simple declarative sentences. I suspect that that ability still is fairly widespread in American culture, but that science fiction, like so much else, is falling victim to line-of-least-resistance living in these days of visual culture. Just as it was considerably easier, and probably more fun, to read *The Caves of Steel* or *The Puppet Masters* a quarter of a century ago than to wrestle with the intricacies of Joyce's *Ulysses*, so nowadays it must be more appealing to flip through some elegantly lithographed picture-book than to furrow the brow over the actual *words* of John Varley or Ursula K. Le Guin. This is an uncomfortable concept for someone whose life has been devoted to manipulating verbal symbols on paper, let me tell you. In that same bookstore, glancing nervously through one of my own novels, I found myself wondering if I had pitched the level of reading comprehension too high, if I had perhaps been too demanding in my use of language. When you start making silent apologies to an imagined half-literate audience for having used semi-colons, you're in trouble.

It all worries me, and ought to worry you—you who must still be literate, since *Amazing* has only occasional pictures between all those words. People can still read, but it's a declining skill, and the seduction of those marvelously produced lithographed picture-books has probably been felt even by you. I ask you only to remember, as you leaf through *Heavy Metal* or the latest books of elves and leprechauns or one of the myriad new *Star Trek* spinoffs, that in the beginning was the word—that Homer didn't draw pictures in the sand for his listeners—that even at Lascaux, where they *did* draw some nifty pictures on those cave walls, they probably also used words to tell stories—and that all this new-fangled stuff emerges quasi-parasitically from what is in fact a verbal literature.

I have no hostility toward the visual arts. The craftsmanship of such people as Giger and Chris Foss is superb, the *Heavy Metal* artists often attain splendid levels of surreal inventiveness, and the special-effects people in Hollywood can make even the dumbest sci-fi flick seem miraculous. But what the bookstore was passing off as "science fiction" was actually secondary work, derivative work, generating its energy and power by drawing images from the minds of Fritz Leiber and Roger Zelazny and Theodore Sturgeon and Ray Bradbury and Harlan Ellison and J.R.R. Tolkien and Anne McCaffrey and Larry Niven and Brian Aldiss and A.E. van Vogt and a lot of other people whose vision was expressed in *words*, assembled in *sentences*, and published in *books*. To relegate their work to an insignificant corner, to bury it in a flood of pretty but mindless coffee-table decorations, is to do a disservice not only to the people who write books but, ultimately, to those who love to read them.

Picture-Books, Continued

A couple of columns back I lamented the intrusion into science fiction publishing of picture-books—large handsomely produced volumes made up entirely or almost entirely of lavish color plates of dragons or monsters or old magazine covers, which drain millions of dollars a year away from the purchase of the old-fashioned word-oriented fiction on which the whole fantasy-picture industry is based. I expected some angry letters from the fans of Frazetta or Wayne Barlowe or Chris Foss or the other splendid artists who do those books, but what I didn't expect was this angry message from Mark Cashman of Hartford, Connecticut:

> "The decline of science-fiction literature that Bob Silverberg discusses in his 'Opinion' column (May '81) began when science fiction, embarrassed by its own optimism and view of man as an effective being, tried to become 'literature.' It took as its model the existentialist novel where disconnected or random events take the place of plot, where details and the exposition of defeatism take the place of character, and mysticism takes the place of logic in a malevolent universe beyond man's comprehension.
>
> "The people who read science fiction want the experience of its spirit of human achievement, its view of man and his technology expanding his frontiers and his freedom.
>
> "If Bob Silverberg really wants to know why there were more picture books than novels in that bookstore window, he should look to himself as one of those responsible. Look at your story 'The Feast of St. Dionysus,' Bob. The story of a former astronaut wandering aimlessly through the desert until he joins and is sacrificed by a drunken, irrational religious cult. Or your novel 'The World Inside,' the novel of a brutal, communo-religious society, where men own nothing, not even themselves, and the penultimate act of freedom is to kill yourself. Or 'Tower of Glass,' where the climax is the act of destroying another man's achievement. You, Bob, and Delany and Russ and all of the other 'malevolent universe' literateurs, are responsible for the very condition you bemoan. You ought not complain so much."

Cashman's letter saddened me because he's obviously intelligent and literate, unlike most of the people who buy the pretty books full

[*Amazing Stories*, January 1982]

of pictures of dragon and full-breasted wenches. And yet what he wants is even dumber than what they want. They simply are after pretty pictures. No harm in that, really—I just came back from France, where I spent a few hours every day looking at pretty pictures in places like the Louvre. But what Cashman wants is to turn a literature that at its best provides penetrating insight into society, technology, science, and the human condition into a cheery, uplifting, *Readers Digest* species of pap.

I deny, of course, that much of my own work can be described as "disconnected or random events" that "take the place of plot, where details and the exposition of defeatism take the place of character." I don't recognize that as typical of my fiction. But that's beside the point. *Do* people read science fiction to get a view of "man and his technology expanding his frontiers and his freedom." Heck, they can simply walk outdoors and stare at the nearest freeway, or a passing Boeing 747, if that's what they're after.

What about such science-fiction classics as *Brave New World*, *1984*, *The Martian Chronicles*? Is Huxley's soma a virtuous use of technology? Do Orwell's torturers and brainwashers inspire a thrill at the recognition that technology expands human freedom? Do the hot-dog stands that Bradbury's voyagers set up on Mars show us the spirit of human achievement?

Are those books deplorable? Have they gone without readers? Have they driven true fans to picture-albums?

Come off it, Cashman. Science-fiction writers, like any other writers, bring their personal visions of the universe to bear in their work. If they see a malevolent universe out there, or a world where communo-religious societies somehow tend to evolve, or where astronauts discover that their values are empty, they may write about those things, and if they do it eloquently and passionately enough they may create a work of art out of their vision of something bleak and disagreeable. Certainly they aren't *responsible* for the evils out there, not are they required to provide cheery and sweet visions in the place of truth. The policemen don't cause the crimes; the finder of a counterfeit bill has no obligation to replace it with a valid one; the camera doesn't create the slum. The writer isn't making up dark stories just to be perverse and to annoy Mark Cashman.

The arguments that he puts forth are ones we heard a great deal a decade or so ago, when a horde of new writers began letting some truth about society creep into the field of science fiction, which previously had simply ignored the problem of evil. (When the villain takes a potshot at Luke Skywalker, that's not evil, it's just a nuisance. When you come out of Room 101 and you love Big Brother, you have experienced real evil.) The old s-f was strictly on the Luke Skywalker level; writers like Delany and Russ and Malzberg and Spinrad and Ellison and Laffery and Disch and Dick and Brunner and, yes, Silverberg, let a little reality in, moved everything up to the next level of intensity, and changed the whole nature of science fiction. Some of the readers didn't like that.

Those readers, if they're still around, now buy the picture-books, or buy the simply cozy fantasy novels that are the prose equivalent of picture-books, or just spend their money on *Close Encounters of the Third Kind*, and *The Empire Strikes Back*. Okay. It's their money; it's their privilege to entertain themselves as they please.

But it saddens me to see intelligent people trotting out that weary old stuff about how much they hate existentialism or nihilism or pessimism or whatever in their science fiction. What they're asking for is a kind of juvenile see-no-evil hear-no-evil speak-no-evil fiction. It is very hard for adult writers to write that kind of thing, if they take their craft at all seriously. It is very hard for non-adult readers to read what adult writers write. Maybe the problem is that the writers have grown up and the readers are still predominantly fourteen years old, at least between the ears.

"Human kind cannot bear very much reality," T.S. Eliot once wrote. Eliot is probably on Mark Cashman's hit-list too. But he spoke the truth.

Maybe it was a mistake to let so much reality into science fiction. Maybe we really ought to be turning out the kind of sweet, bland, positive-minded glop that the Cashmans of the world prefer. Huxley didn't think so, nor Orwell, nor Bradbury—but the first two weren't science-fiction writers at all, and Bradbury really wasn't, either. I am, and I have the Mark Cashmans to contend with. Go buy a picture-book, Mr. Cashman. It'll make you feel a lot happier.

Too Many Sequels

This one sounds the alarm at the outset of the avalanche of series books that by now has flattened nearly all science-fiction novels belonging to the class quaintly termed "singleton" or "stand-alone" novels. You will observe me here, writing in the autumn of 1981, saying quite emphatically that I doubted I would ever write a sequel to my own novel Lord Valentine's Castle. I was at work on one by January of 1983, for reasons that are explained in an essay to be found near the close of this book. I constantly surprise myself in little ways like that; it keeps me young.

Close students of the Hugo awards process have pointed out that of the five novels on the 1981 ballot, three—Larry Niven's *Ringworld Engineers*, John Varley's *Wizard*, and Frederik Pohl's *Beyond The Blue Event Horizon*, are sequels to successful novels, two of which were themselves award winners. A fourth nominee, Robert Silverberg's *Lord Valentine's Castle*, is in the process of acquiring a companion book, not exactly a sequel but certainly a closely related work; and now comes a report that the fifth item, Joan Vinge's *The Snow Queen*, is due for a sequel shortly also. If the Vinge story is correct, it means that all five of the Hugo nominees will turn out to be pieces of some larger saga—an unprecedented and startling situation, which says a great deal about the present state of science-fiction publishing and consumer habits in the United States.

The sequel phenomenon is nothing new in science fiction. Half a century ago E. E. Smith, Ph.D., was winding up his *Skylark* trilogy and getting ready to begin his seven-volume *Lensman* extravaganza; and all those books, which are quite spectacularly badly written but irresistibly inventive, have had a large and enthusiastic following ever since. Edgar Rice Burroughs, about the same time, was bringing forth his innumerable John Carter of Mars books, a Venus series, and of course the Tarzan items. Asimov's *Foundation* books caused much fuss in the 1940's, as did van Vogt's *Weapons Shops* and Null-A projects. The Professor Jameson stories of Neil R. Jones, Simak's *City*, de Camp's *Viagens*, Poul Anderson's Flandry and van Rijn tales, Blish's spindizzy stories—the list goes on and on. No, nothing new at all.

The popularity of the series for the writer is easy to comprehend. It allows him to serve up more of the same: to return to familiar territory, to use well-established backgrounds and characters and even, in the case of the most mechanical of series concepts, the same

[*Amazing Stories*, March 1982]

plots. Science fiction is peculiarly self-devouring in its demand on a writer's inventiveness: to dream up an entire world, down to the smallest cultural and geographical details, is no minor task, and to do it three or four times a year in a market that pays a cent a work or thereabouts is a formidable drain on even the most fertile mind. How much more comforting to go back to Barsoom, already conveniently in stock in the warehouse, or to tack on one more episode in the adventures of Captain Future, or to think up yet another twist on the slow and inevitable workings-out of Hari Seldon's far-seeing plan!

(I should add that in my own case I always found the familiarity of series material more of a drawback than a benefit. It seemed a bigger burden to go back to something I had written two or three or ten years ago and regain a mastery of the details than it was to dream up something brand new; I hated being bound by my own old ideas. And so, after writing a two-book series in collaboration with Randall Garrett more than a quarter of a century ago, I never again attempted in any serious way to launch a series, although a couple of my novels did appear in magazine form as sequences of novelets and one or two of my other books did make glancing and usually inaccurate references to events that had appeared in previous Silverberg novels. But now I too am mining my own older lode. More about that below.)

What the series gives the writer, then, is readymade acceptance and quick conceptual uptake. But what does it give the reader? Challenge, strangeness, mystery? Hardly. It provides him with the same old thing that tickled his fancy last month or last year—a reprise, a cozy return to safe territory. Sometimes a writer poses a puzzle so fascinating—who built the Riverworld? Where is the Second Foundation?—that readers will go along happily from book to book to book, waiting to learn the answer. But most series simply provide one more run-though of the original production: Captain Future meets another dire peril, Dominic Flandry thwarts more bad guys, John Carter wins another apocalyptic battle. That's okay, sure, but such books offer little in the way of revelation, illumination, transformation.

And the irony is that science fiction is supposed to be a literature of the strange, the luminously unfamiliar. The theory I always held was that a science-fiction story puts the reader down in some truly unfathomable situation that he could never had conceived himself—in the future society of S. Fowler Wright's *World Below*, let's say, or Huxley's *Brave New World*—and leads him to an understanding of its nature and an internalization of its wondrous alienness. To ask of science fiction that it give you more of the same is to defeat one of its great central virtues.

And though I too have made my way pleasantly through many a series, enjoying renewed contact with character or ideas or scenery that gave me pleasure before, I think that the novels that rewarded me most intensely were always one-of-a-kind items—Bester's *Stars My Destination*, Clarke's *Childhood's End*, Sturgeon's *More Than Human*, David Lindsay's *A Voyage to Arcturus*, and half a dozen more. Much of the power of those books comes from the sudden shock of strangeness that a sequel, virtually by definition, is incapable of delivering: not "I have been here before" but "I have never even DREAMED of this before."

The worrisome thing about all those sequels and prequels on this year's Hugo list is that it shows the fans voting overwhelmingly for more of the same, for the tried and true, for the cozily familiar. Publishers take note of such things. Already there is what I think to be an excessive demand for multiple works: I sometimes suspect it's easier to sell a trilogy these days than a single novel. And the more vociferous the demand for sequels becomes, the harder it will be for that single unique piercing vision, that never-to-be-recaptured idea that positively needs no reprises, to win an audience. Present-day readers seem almost *afraid* of works that stand by themselves. Frank Herbert's *Dune* had only modest success in its early days of publication; but the fourth go-round of the same idea has done astonishingly well, and after months on the best-seller list *God-Emperor of Dune* may turn out to be the most profitable novel in science-fiction history. Nice going for Frank Herbert and his publishers; a little troublesome for those of us who look at long-term trends.

What about Silverberg, now at work on *Majipoor Chronicles*? It is not, I insist mildly, a sequel to *Lord Valentine's Castle*, since it involves a host of other characters and takes place at earlier periods of Majipoor's history. But it is quite definitely more of the same. I would be very much surprised to find myself writing a true sequel to *Lord Valentine's Castle*—and the idea dismays and depresses me—and even though you might point out that I also found myself surprised to be writing LVC in the first place, I'm fairly confident that it won't happen. I can't bear the notion of trundling out Carabella and Deliamber and Valentine and the rest of that crowd for another set of adventures. They had their moment on the stage; I'm done with them forever. But the two books are definitely akin.

Then why *Majipoor Chronicles*?

Because I felt like it. Because I see which way the commercial winds are blowing, and writing is my livelihood. And because I thought I had left some things unexplored in the original book.

All the same, when every book on the Hugo list is only a fragment of a greater work, something in the artistic integrity of the concept of the science fiction novel is being undermined. We are all merrily collaborating in a development whose sequel is likely to be trouble.

The Way the Future Looks:
Blade Runner and THX-1138

We are in Los Angeles, but it is not the familiar city of palm trees and perpetual bright sunshine. Above us loom colossal sloping high-rise buildings of intricate and alien design, patterned perhaps, after Aztec temples or Babylonian ziggurats, that turn the narrow congested streets into claustrophobic canyons and hide the dark pollution-fouled sky. A cold, bleak, maddening rainstorm goes on interminably. Great searchlights, intended, possibly, to substitute for the absent sun, send intrusive beams slicing across vast distances from sources mounted somewhere far overhead.

Down here on surface level we move warily through a densely packed district, largely Oriental in population and in architecture, a crazy hyped-up version of Hong Kong or Tokyo, where a dizzying multitude of flashing electronic signs seeks insistently to draw our attention to games parlors, massage houses, noodle counters, drug-vending shops, and a thousand thousand other commercial establishments. Dull-eyed coolies, bending under immense burdens, jostle us aside without apology. Myriads of spaced-out fanatics in fantastic costumes dance along beside us down the street, each lost in some private bubble of self-absorption. High above us, helicopters moving with reckless velocity buzz like crazed dragonflies between the skyscrapers: police, most likely, searching for the deadly fugitive androids that are said to be loose in the city. At any moment, we think, one of those helicopters may descend from the sky in lunatic spirals and land in the middle of the next block, disgorging policemen who set about making arrests with Kafkaesque implacability.

The mood is oppressive and scary. We are trapped in one of the ultimate urban nightmares: a city of a hundred million people, every one of them hostile to everyone else. The look of the place—dark, menacing, congested, dominated by those immense ponderous towers that crouch like monsters upon the land—is unique and uniquely horrifying. Everything manages to glisten with futuristic pizzazz and nevertheless reveal itself simultaneously to be tinged with rot and decay: new and old, light and dark, airy and ineluctably heavy, both at the same time. The year is 2019, and this is the world of Ridley Scott's 1982 motion picture, *Blade Runner*.

Try another world? Well—

We are indoors. Perhaps within some giant building, perhaps

[From *Screen Flights/Screen Fantasies*, edited by Danny Peary, 1984] deep underground in a labyrinth of tunnels—it makes little difference. The essential point is that there are no windows and no doors to the outside, that the sun and the sky and the stars are no part of this place, and we inhabit a realm of sterile corridors, bright lights, white walls, a megalopolis with a hospital's grim aseptic dazzle. Here there is neither clutter not squalor: the prevailing esthetic here is that of the surgical operating chamber, not of the crowded Oriental marketplace. Though the population density is high, perhaps as high as in the world of *Blade Runner*, there is no sense of overcrowding because there is no random motion. A bland lobotomized-looking populace, clad in standardized costumes rather like prison garb, makes its journeys from place to place in obedient tidy files, while guards with impassive inhuman faces step in quickly to see to it that no one gets out of line or deviates in any other significant way from the flow of traffic. From gleaming grilles in the walls comes a constant low incomprehensible electronic static, an aural wallpaper of blurps and bleeps and soft crackles, interrupted at frequent intervals by cryptic instructions that are instantly accepted and followed by those to whom they apply. Flickering television screens provide two-way monitoring; computer eyes scan and count and record; Big Brother's minions, unseen but omnipresent, oversee the flow of data. The color scheme is a blinding white-on-white: there is not room for untidiness here, no space what- ever for irregularity. The mood, once again, is oppressive and scary. We are trapped, once again, in an ultimate urban nightmare, though of a kind quite different from the last one. The year is something like 2200 A.D., and this is the world of George Lucas' first film, *THX 1138*, released in 1971.

These two movies, *Blade Runner and THX 1138*, strike me as two of the most valuable science-fiction movies ever made. To me they embody the highest virtue the science-fiction film can offer: they show the way the future looks, and they show it with such conviction, such richness of detail, such density of texture, that the visions of tomorrow that they offer will remain embedded forever in my im- agination. They have provided a kind of time-travel experience, in a sense, and they have done it so well that I am willing to ignore entirely the manifest failure of both these movies in most other aspects of the art of science fiction.

If *Blade Runner* and *THX 1138* were novels, they would be undis- tinguished ones. *Blade Runner* is indeed based on a science fiction novel, and an outstanding one: *Do Androids Dream of Electric Sheep*, by the late Philip K. Dick. But—although Dick reported himself pleased with the screenplay that David Fancher drew from his novel, and would, I think, have been please by the finished film itself had he lived to see it—*Blade Runner* bears only the most skeletal resemblance to the book on which it was based, taking from it nothing but the essential plot-idea of hunting down a group of escaped androids. As for *THX 1138*, it began life not as a novel but as a film treatment, produced by the very young George Lucas while he was still a student at U.C.L.A. After Lucas and Walter Murch had expanded it into the full-length script for the final version of the movie, that script was indeed "novelized" for paperback release by the experienced science-fiction writer Ben Bova, but not even Bova's professionalism could lift the story beyond the level of the perfunctory. Science fiction is, among other things, a literature of ideas; and the problem that each of these movies has *as science fiction literature* is its pervasive mediocrity on the level of idea.

Blade Runner is simply silly. We are asked to believe that humanity, just a few decades from now, has colonized not merely the Solar System but the stars; that we have populated those stars with "replicants," synthetic human beings that are superior in most ways to ourselves, although they are designed to live only four years; and that a handful of these replicants, having rebelled at being assigned to slavery in the star-colonies, have found their way back to Earth and are running amok in Los Angeles. Out of this cluster of manifest implausibilities is generated a perfunctory plot in which the androids, hoping to find a way to have their lifespans extended, seek to enlist the aid of their designer, while a police officer follows their trail, taking desperate measures to destroy them—at the risk of his own life, even though the androids have only a few weeks left to live anyway. Since none of these concepts makes much sense, either taken by itself or in conjunction with any of the others, it is hard to find much useful speculative thought of a science-fictional nature in *Blade Runner*: it tells us nothing much that is useful about the human-android relationship, the colonization of the stars, the use of genetic engineering to produce superbeings, or anything else that might seem to be contained in the main premises of the story. If we filter out the self-cancelling absurdities of the plot, we are left with only two concepts that a demanding reader of science fiction might find nourishing. One is the depiction of the female android Pris, a mysterious acrobatic creature in whom the life-force rages so powerfully that when she dies it is with an astonishing display of superhuman fury, the outraged death of an extraordinary though limited being; the other is the question of how to distinguish readily between humans and androids, which was at the core of Dick's novel and which here is crowded into convenient corners of the script, only occasionally to be confronted directly. The rest is straight private-eye stuff, dogged pursuit culminating in a terrifying but conceptually empty rooftop chase.

The ideas around which the story of *THX 1138* are built are not at all foolish—merely hopelessly stale. They go back at least as far as H.G. Wells' *When The Sleeper Wakes* of 1899 and E.M. Forster's *The Machine Stops* of 1909, with touches borrowed from such later but hardly recent works as Zamyatin's *We*, Huxley's *Brave New World*, and Orwell's *1984*. That is, we are ushered once more into the complete totalitarian state, where computers make all decisions and the populace is drugged into complaisance. Uniformity of thought, costume, and behavior is imposed by law and enforced by automaton-like humanoid police; unseen monitors keep watch on everything and everyone; any sign of individuality is relentlessly suppressed. The protagonists are those familiar characters, the rebels against the conformity of it all: THX 1138 and his female roommate, LUH 3417, who surreptitiously cut down on the dosage of the drug they are compelled to take to reduce their sexual impulses, and, after restoring their libido, set about conceiving a child, which is forbidden by the regulatory powers. They are apprehended; LUH 3147 is destroyed, but THX 1138 manages to escape the hive-like city into an outer realm where other rebels and nonconformists have taken lodging. A pair of implacable robots pursue him; and the film, which until this point has been pure if overfamiliar science fiction, devolves in its final third into a mere chase story, an endless sequence of frantic zoomings through subterranean tunnels, until THX 1138 at last eludes the police and escapes into the open-air world beyond.

But—even though one of these films is cobbled together from nonsensical premises and the other is manufactured from cliches—it is, I think, beside the point to pay much attention to those failings. These are *not* novels, with a novel's scope for explication and analysis. They are movies, that is, visual events, pictorial compositions extended along a narrative axis by complex technological means. It is possible to wish that *Blade Runner* had relied more on the intricacies of Philip K. Dick's novel and less on the formulas of detective fiction, or that *THX 1138* had given us more of a look at the assumptions on which its totalitarian society was founded and less of a mad chase in those tunnels, but to express such wishes is to ignore an ugly reality, the Catch-22 of science-fiction movie-making: science-fiction films require special effects, special effects are costly, costly films need to pull in big audiences in order to break even, and big audiences are snared only by reliance on familiar plot-mechanisms. (As it is, *Blade Runner*, which cost something like $30,000,000 to produce, was a commercial failure. *THX 1138* was the relatively inexpensive work of a novice film-maker, and in its way was an uncompromising and diffi-cult movie, revealing its plot in an oblique and demanding way, but without its harrowing if meaningless chase finale it might have drawn no audience at all, with consequent difficulties for George Lucas' further career.) It is precisely in those special effects that the merits of the two movies lie; indeed, *Blade Runner* and *THX 1138* provide startling evidence that an important science fiction movie can be assembled out of unimportant science fiction material. If their failings as fiction had not been as great, they would have been finer movies yet; but perhaps that is asking too much.

They are visionary movies in the most literal sense of that word. They show us futures, and they do it, not as a novelist might, with a few deftly chosen adjectives cunningly disposed on the page, but with nuts-and-bolts reality. In *Do Androids Dream of Electric Sheep?* Philip K. Dick created his atmosphere of gritty, dismaying urban decay with quick little touches ("the tattered gray wall-to-wall carpeting....The broken and semi-broken appliances in the kitchen, the dead ma-chines....Tufts of dried-out bonelike weeds poking slantedly into a dim and sunless sky.") Ridley Scott, at an expenditure of millions of real dollars, builds an entire gigantic city of enormous pseudo-Aztec temples and flashing pseudo-neon signs, fills it with weird little shops where commodities as yet uninvented are sold, and whisks his camera swiftly through it, giving us tantalizingly elliptical glances at a future world that he has in fact realized in immense detail. I have seen it argued that it is somehow a higher achievement for a novelist to create the texture of a world by quick descriptive touches than it is for a movie producer to turn loose a battalion of carpenters and electri-cians, but—despite my own novelist's bias—I'm not so sure of that; the effects that Scott creates by building sets and letting us have mere glimpses of them are at least as elegant and cunning as any instance of the science-fiction writer's descriptive art. The Los Angeles of *Blade Runner* is a unique invention, actually owing relatively little to the Dick novel; however preposterous the adventure of Rick Deckard may be as he stalks his way through that somber, ominous city in search of the crazed replicant Roy Batty, the city itself remains the essential imaginative achievement, and it does the essential science-fictional thing of displaying and illuminating a landscape not otherwise accessible to the eye. It mattered very little to me whether Deckard pushed Batty over the edge of the roof or Batty pushed Deckard over; what did matter, and a great deal, was the hypnotic power of Scott's camera as it panned down the face of one of those overwhelming buildings, and showed me the architecture of an era yet to come.

So too with *THX 1138*. "Imagine, if you can, a small room, hexagonal in shape, like the cell of a bee," wrote E.M. Forster in 1909. "It is lighted neither by window nor by lamp, yet it is filled with a soft radiance. There are no apertures for ventilation, yet the air is fresh." And we are launched into the stiflingly circumscribed world of *The Machine Stops*. Or we turn to Zamyatin's *We*, on which, I suspect, *THX 1138* was founded, and we read, "As always, the Music Plant played the 'March of the One State' with all its trumpets. The numbers walked in even ranks, four abreast, ecstatically stepping in time to the music— hundreds, thousands of numbers, in pale blue unifs, with golden badges on their breasts, bearing the State Number of each man and woman." But Lucas makes us *see* it. He makes us *hear* it. The faces, the eyes, the shaven scalps, the white-on white corridors, the electronic buzzes and murmurs, the flow of computerized commands so baffling to the twentieth-century eavesdropper—the movie is an astonishing experience, an all-out immersion in a world of the future, without explanation, without apology. If Lucas is using other writer's material, he is making it altogether his own by the vivid way he realizes it and by the sheer uncompromising strangeness of the place into which he thrusts the viewer. (Scott does that too. Though he uses a crude voice-over technique to explain details of the plot, he offers the startling urban landscape largely as a given, without footnotes or commentary, thereby greatly enhancing the power of its strangeness.)

The task of the science-fiction novelist, ideally stated, is to discover a unique speculative concept, develop its implications through a rigorous intellectual process, and make it accessible as fiction through an appropriate choice of characters, plot, and narrative style. Since science fiction usually involves the depiction of an unfamiliar landscape, the novelist's craft requires the mastery of descriptive techniques that will convey that landscape to the reader with maximum visual impact (a craft which entails more than a little collaboration on the part of the reader, but is a collaboration which the skilled novelist knows how to elicit.) The task of the science-fiction movie-maker, ideally stated, should be the same, and perhaps some day it will be, although, as I have suggested, commercial considerations at present seem to demand certain oversimplifications of concept and plot and character, and, in any case, even the most uncompromising of films are necessarily unable to achieve some of the things a novel can manage.

So far, most and perhaps all of the science-fiction movies that have been made have failed the highest tests of science-fiction excellence, I suppose; but in the domain of depiction of an unfamiliar landscape, that is, in the domain of special effects, there have been notable successes: *Alien, 2001, Star Wars, Forbidden Planet*, and many more. I think it is no trivial achievement to make futuristic visions concrete in that way; as I have said, I am not among those who would claim that building a movie set is somehow a less worthy artistic accomplishment than composing a paragraph of vivid descriptive prose. What those films managed in the way of putting the look of the future on the screen was far from trivial. But I can think of no others in which the special effects are dedicated so powerfully to the creation of a coherent imagined environment that wholly enfolds and houses the story that is set within it. That the story is foolish in one case and stereotyped in the other is regrettable but fundamentally unimportant. What Ridley Scott accomplished in *Blade Runner* and George Lucas did in *THX 1138* is notable despite all peripheral failings: to create a landscape of the mind, vivid and compelling and complete, that for one breathless moment of suspension of disbelief seems to be the real thing, the authentic future, which we can in no other way experience than through the medium of lens and light and screen.

Science Fiction and the Future

There are moments when I have the feeling I am literally living in the future—not so much because I earn my living writing science fiction as because I've been reading it for more than thirty years. When I was a boy, "the future" was the gaudy place I read about in gaudy-looking magazines with names like *Astounding Science Fiction* and *Amazing Stories*; and amazing and astounding it was, too, a world of glistening gadgetry and sleek convenience far different from the drab, wartime era I lived in. Now I live deep in that future of my childhood's science fiction, and these are some of the wonders I encounter in a single not atypical day:

My digital solid-state radio clock awakens me at half past seven in my home near San Francisco. I leave my electrically-heated waterbed and breakfast on orange juice, bacon, and English muffins, all purchased months ago and stored in my home freezer until yesterday. I give myself a quick once-over with my electric shaver. Then I make a few telephone calls, tapping the numbers out swiftly on the electronic pushbuttons; without the help of an operator I reach a friend in Los Angeles and an editor in New York. Now I get into my rotary-engine car, which transports me silently and almost without vibration down a maze of soaring freeways to the airport. The transistorized car radio, coming to life instantly at my touch, brings me news of the Skylab astronauts at work in their orbital space station far above the Earth. More immediately overhead I perceive a noisy whirlybird, the helicopter that a local radio station uses to monitor rush-hour traffic. At the airport I board the hourly shuttle to Los Angeles; because the hop downstate takes only 45 minutes, the plane is relatively small, a three-engine 120-passenger jet. As it sweeps down the runway I see a giant wide-bodied plane with 350 people on board getting into takeoff position for its nine-hour non-stop flight to Tahiti. By mid-morning I am in Los Angeles International Airport, where I present my credit card at the car-rental desk, sign the computer-printed rental agreement, and drive off in a two-tone sedan with automatic transmission. Via freeway I head for the fifty-story curtain-wall high rise tower where I have a business conference; the conversation is recorded not by a stenographer but by a tape machine and we pause after an hour while a new cassette is inserted in the deck. Then I have lunch—just a quick snack at a drive-in—and browse at a paperback book store and at a record store in a nearby shopping center. I buy a new stereo recording of

[*Horizon*, Summer 1974]

Wagner's *Die Walküre* on four disks. Then I return to the airport, drop off my rented car, and board my home-bound flight. I sit next to two engineers who are helping to design a new nuclear power plant upstate; they spread papers all over their laps and work intently, using pocket-sized integrated-circuit calculators. By dinnertime I'm home, and later that evening I settle in front of the color television set to watch a concert by the Leningrad Philharmonic, broadcast live by way of an orbiting communications relay satellite.

Scarcely any aspect of that busy day existed in the real world of 1945. There were no commuter jets, huge freeway interchanges, space stations, or nuclear power plants—not even shopping centers or frozen orange juice. But virtually all these things were standard furniture in the future world that science fiction conjured for me then. Not all: you will look in vain in the old magazines for the rotary-engine car, the water bed, and the transistorized radio. But all the rest, down to the credit card and the computers, was there. Like everybody else I take these things for granted most of the time; but now and then I look around and blink and feel a bit of a shiver as I realize that this is the year 1975, which sounded so impossibly far away in the stories I read as a boy, and that the fantastic future has erupted all about me right on schedule, that I come in contact, a hundred times a day, with yesterday's science fiction.

Does that mean that science-fiction writers are such clear-eyed prophets that we can turn confidently to today's science fiction for an accurate depiction of the world of 2005? Hardly. For one thing, many science-fiction writers—myself included—do not see themselves primarily as prophets, and are apt to create in one story a set of projections completely contradicting those of the one before. For another, even those science-fictionists who go at the business of prophecy seriously are infinitely better at foreseeing general patterns than at discerning particular details. It is not really difficult to extend broad technological or social trends into the future, but making sharp and specific predictions is more a matter of luck than genius, even for the best of science-fiction writers.

Consider an example from the work of a writer certainly among the very best: Robert A. Heinlein, author of *Stranger in a Strange Land* and many other widely-read novels. Heinlein, an Annapolis graduate with a strong grounding in the sciences, takes an engineer's approach to the future: everything he writes is developed rigorously out of a broad and deep knowledge of our own world, forming a coherent and internally consistent vision of times to come.

In 1949 a Hollywood producer asked Heinlein to do the screen-play of a documentary-style movie about the first voyage to the moon, and to serve as the film's technical adviser. The result was *Destination Moon* (1950). It was thoughtfully done down to the smallest touches. Cunning special effects provided authentic representations of a rocket launching, of the gravitational effects of acceleration, of a spacewalk, of the lunar surface. *Destination Moon* was a sincere and intelligent attempt to depict man's initial flight into space as it was probably going to happen.

It was a fine film. But, we now know, it got practically every major detail wrong.

Heinlein's lunar ship was an atomic-powered single-stage rocket designed and built by three men on behalf of a small syndicate of private investors. When the government refuses to let the inventors test their engine at its California construction site, they hastily decide to blast off before anyone can stop them—and launch their expedition in less than 24 hours, with an untested engine and themselves as the improvised crew. A Federal court order is issued to block the takeoff, but the intrepid astronauts escape by advancing their departure time by several hours. Once in space they recalculate their orbit—using a slide rule, an almanac, and an office calculator—to correct their course. Off they go to Luna, where they manage a hazardous manual landing, don their spacesuits, and step forth to claim the moon in the name of the United States.

In 1950, the story seemed perhaps too melodramatic but other-wise plausible and technologically convincing; today it seems merely quaint, if not absurd. Neither Heinlein nor anyone else in science fiction foresaw that it would take a decade of work and twenty billion dollars to get men to the moon; no one realized that the job would have to be a colossal cooperative enterprise by scores of the nation's largest corporations; no one imagined the immense network of track-ing stations and the gigantic computer installation required to guide the mission. The complex Apollo scheme—a multi-stage liquid-fueled rocket, separate orbital and moon-landing modules, abandonment of most of the vehicle along the way, homecoming by parachute drop into the ocean—went altogether unanticipated. Nor did science fic-tion predict the most astounding aspect of the entire venture: that the astronauts, at the moment they opened their hatch, would unveil a television camera and transmit to Earth a *live* video view of man's first footsteps on the moon.

What remains, then, of Heinlein's carefully devised movie? Only some clever special effects and the fundamental notion that mankind would reach the moon in the middle decades of the twentieth century. Tim has turned virtually everything else into fantasy.

So it has gone with most attempts at nuts-and-bolts prophecy. As Arthur C. Clarke, another of science fiction's most highly respected seers, has pointed out, "The real future is not *logically* foreseeable." Looking through the science fiction of earlier generations, we find a few remarkably good guesses embedded in an enormous mass of error and shortsightedness. Many 19th-century writers anticipated the airplane, but no one, apparently, foresaw the internal combustion engine, the radio, or motion pictures. Lt. A. M. Fuller's *A.D. 2000* (1890) told of an era that had underground railways much like the New York subway system, electric clocks not too different from ours, and a national newspaper published simultaneously in many places by a sort of teletype network called a "sympathetic telegraph"—but air traffic was conducted in dirigibles, and surface transport still made use of horse-drawn buggies. Rudyard Kipling's "With the Night Mail" (1909) also saw gas-filled airships rather than planes, though Kipling's vision of aerial traffic control was a perceptive one.

Social predictions were almost always wide of the mark; 19th-century science fiction dresses 20th-century Americans in Victorian garb and Victorian ideals, modified only slightly, and nowhere can we find a realistic augury of today's informal dress, casual nudity, and sexual permissiveness. Political predictions were generally no better. The decline of Great Britain as an international power went unanticipated. The rise of Japan and the United States was obvious enough for most writers to see, but in the often-predicted Japanese-American war it was usually assumed that Hawaii's Japanese-Americans would defect to the side of their ancestors, whereas in World War II they fought loyally for the Allies.

On the other hand, some surprisingly keen predictions have been made. Edward Everett Hale's short novel *The Brick Moon*, published in *The Atlantic Monthly* in 1869, described the construction and launching of a hollow space satellite sent into orbit 4000 miles above the Earth as an aid to navigation. H. G. Wells, in *The Land Ironclads* (1903), virtually invented the military tank. Wells' *The War in the Air* (1908) portrayed aerial warfare much as it would be conducted in Europe less than a decade later; and his *The World Set Free* (1914) told of the tapping of the atomic energy of uranium in 1953 and of the devastation of the world by atomic bombs, called by that name, which Wells imagined would be dropped by hand from airplanes.

In 1941 *Astounding Science Fiction* published a story called *Solution Unsatisfactory* by Anson MacDonald—a pseudonym, as it turned out, for Robert A. Heinlein. This, too, forecasts atomic warfare as a consequence of unlocking nuclear energy. Heinlein envisioned not bombs but a radioactive dust capable of rendering large areas uninhabitable. In his story use of the dust knocks Germany out of World War II within a week—and then Heinlein goes on to examine the problems of a post-war world in which the United States alone possesses the superweapon while Soviet physicists struggle to duplicate it, a stunning glance forward into the Cold War realities of 1945-50.

That story caused no great fuss when it appeared, but another that the same magazine ran early in 1944 stirred considerable official anguish: *Deadline*, by Cleve Cartmill. This routine tale of cloak-and-dagger operations on another planet included such phrases as:

"U^{235} has been separated in quantity sufficient for preliminary atomic-power research....It was extracted from uranium ores by new atomic isotope separation methods....The explosion of a pound of U^{235}...releases as much energy as a hundred million pounds of TNT...."

The story went on to describe a plausible atomic bomb—just as Manhattan Project scientists were nearing the climax of their work. Military intelligence agents hurriedly called on *Astounding's* editor, John W. Campbell, to trace the source of this security leak. Campbell calmly pointed out that everything in Cartmill's story was based on technical reports openly published as far back as 1939—and, when asked to stop publishing stories about atomic energy for the duration, the editor observed that a sudden disappearance of such themes from his magazine might arouse the very suspicions the government was eager to suppress.

The Cartmill incident illustrates how limited the prophetic powers of science-fiction writers actually are. When they predict a specific technological development, as Heinlein and Cartmill did, it is usually done by keeping close watch over current scientific research and projecting consequences of some known datum forward in time, a process known as *extrapolation*. Well's 1914 vision of atomic bombs, conceived at a time when nuclear fission and chain reactions were still unknown, was simply a more remarkable leap from existing facts to ultimate possibility; Wells did know about radioactivity, and saw the rest. Prediction, in science fiction, very often consists of putting into story form concepts that scientists have already discovered and examined; a knack for combing the scientific literature for story ideas is the main secret of the science-fictionist's apparent prescience.

Most contemporary science fiction writers prefer not to think of themselves as being in the business of prophecy at all. They are concerned with possibilities rather than probabilities; they begin with a premise about the future that has a certain logical plausibility and extend it to its farthest consequences, primarily to see what the consequences of such a premise would be. They do not necessarily need to believe that their premise *will* come to pass—only that it *might*. An example from my own work is the novel *The World Inside* (1971), set in the 24th century. In it I propose one outcome of continued population growth: the confinement of Earth's 75 billion people in giant towers, a thousand stories high, each housing close to a million people and surrounded by huge uninhabited agricultural zones. I doubt very much that a world consisting exclusively of such "urban monads" will ever come to pass, but there is no basic reason why it couldn't; and my purpose in writing the book was chiefly to examine the technological aspects of designing such gigantic residential towers and the social consequences of spending one's entire life inside one.

Similarly, Fritz Leiber's short story *Coming Attraction* (1950) extrapolates the violence and sadism of modern American life into a horrifying but not inevitable tomorrow; Wyman Guin's *Beyond Bedlam* (1951) gives us an unlikely but fascinating society in which schizophrenia is the accepted social norm; Philip K. Dick's *The Man in the High Castle* (1962) defies history to plunge us into an alternate universe in which the Axis won World War II and the United States has been partitioned into Japanese and German protectorates. These stories, and hundreds like them, are only incidentally predictive; their main intent is to create a logical, internally consistent imaginative construct, self-contained and exhaustive, showing all the ramifications of a single possible future situation. It is a kind of intellectual game, and when played fairly and well it can be a marvelously stimulating one for writer and reader.

The exhaustive investigations of a single fantastic premise's potential consequences is a hallmark of the best science fiction. Heinlein's *Solution Unsatisfactory* does not merely predict the development of atomic weapons—which anybody who was keeping up with nuclear physics in 1940 could have seen—but goes on to delineate the new kinds of political crises that the existence of such superweapons will create. *The World Inside* does not only invent ultra-high-rise apartment houses but attempts to show what sort of society might evolve within them. Any mediocre popular novelist of 1875, with the example of the railroad before him, could have imagined a horseless carriage—but only a true science-fictionist would, having dreamed up the automobile, have gone on to hypothesize freeways, parking lots, speed limits, traffic jams, a nationwide network of gas stations, and all the rest that the existence of automobiles implies.

Science fiction, then, is not extraordinarily successful at predicting the unpredictable. Its writers show us not one future but many. By so doing, and making us aware that small changes usually have big effects, they serve the valuable purpose of conditioning us against "future shock"—Alfred Toffler's useful phrase for the psychological impact of ever-accelerating technological change. As the celebrated science-fiction writer Isaac Asimov pointed out more than twenty years ago, "Its authors, as a matter of course, present their readers with new societies, with possible futures and consequences. It is a social experimentation on paper; social guesses plucked out of air. And this is the great service of science fiction. To accustom the reader to the possibility of change, to have him think along various lines— perhaps very daring lines."

Science fiction accomplishes this not only by quasi-realistic portrayals of future gadgetry but, often, by taking a metaphorical and symbolic approach to the future that opens the sympathetic reader to an infinite range of possibility. Asimov's own far-flung galactic empires have no immediate predictive value, but they turn one's eyes to the stars with a new receptivity. Ray Bradbury's sensitive, poetic *The Martian Chronicles* (1950) does not even make a pretense at scientific accuracy, yet it arouses awe and respect for what is alien and fragile, and prepares us to meet the ample strangeness of our own complex world. Arthur C. Clarke's *Childhood's End* (1953) is so far from being literal prediction that its flyleaf carries the extraordinary disclaimer, "The opinions expressed in this book are not those of its author"—and it provides an unforgettably stirring vision of mankind's ultimate transformation into a single communal cosmic entity. These books do not presume to tell us what events lie in the future; they want us only to contemplate that future, to face it with heightened awareness and joyous acceptance of the universe's unfathomable plan.

The point is perhaps best made in the greatest of all visionary novels of the future, Olaf Stapledon's *Last and First Men* (1930). In a calm historical reverie Stapledon's narrator traces the evolution of humanity though the next two billion years—a period in which the Earth itself is destroyed and mankind must take refuge first on Venus, then on Neptune. Several times the human race is reduced to a few dozen individuals; always they begin again, reconstructing civilization and reshaping even their own physical forms. Species succeeds species; the Fourth Men are giant brains, the Fifth Men superb titanic creatures, the Seventh amiable bird-like beings. Stapledon does not mean us to take these fanciful inventions literally; what he is saying is that the future will bring unimaginable change, incredible change, yet he thinks the human spirit will endure all transformations, even unto the time of the Eighteenth Men, who are demigods, with a life span of a quarter of a million years. It is Stapledon's Eighteenth Men who must submit to the final catastrophe, a cosmic explosion that will destroy all life in their part of the galaxy, and from which there is no escape. It is a painful irony that these men, the summit of human evolution, must be wiped out by an irrelevant event, but they accept it, and one of the Eighteenth Men pronounces this epitaph for humanity—the noblest and most moving passage, I think, in all that literature about the future we call science fiction:

> "Man himself, at the very least, is music, a brave theme that makes music also of its vast accompaniment, its matrix of storms and stars. Man himself in his degree is eternally a beauty in the eternal form of things. It is very good to have been man. And so we may go forward together with laughter in our hearts, and peace, thankful for the past, and for our own courage. For we shall make after all a fair conclusion to this brief music that is man."

Boomers and the Science Fiction Boom

In the previous essay and elsewhere in this book I speak about the difficulty of accurately predicting the future. A glance at the final paragraph of this next one, and at the one following (which I wrote a dozen years later) will show that it sometimes can be done, though.

During the fall and winter of 1982-83, somewhere between half and three-quarters of the books on the hardcover best-seller list in the United States were science fiction.

The impact of that sentence on anyone who, like me, has been closely associated with science fiction for a generation or more, is almost impossible to communicate to an outsider. I grew up in a world where science-fiction magazines were sleazy-looking magazines that you wouldn't want your friends to see you buying; where it was possible to keep a complete collection of science-fiction paperbacks in one shoebox; where libraries, if they bought the few s-f hardcover books that were published, stashed them next to the westerns and listed them in the card catalog as "pseudoscientific literature." That was the state of the art, circa 1949. Things changed greatly, of course, after science fiction became an important part of mass-market paperback publishing in the 1950's, after the hardcover publishers began doing serious s-f programs in the late 1960's, and after the success of *Star Trek* on television and *2001: A Space Odyssey* in the movies demonstrated that non-dumb s-f could have vast commercial appeal beyond the established hard-core audience. But still—

Here we have James Michener's *Space* sitting on the top of the list for months. It's not exactly science fiction of the Heinlein/Asimov/Clarke breed, but it's not that far removed, and the only thing that makes us hesitate to claim it as true s-f is that it reads more like historical fiction, albeit historical fiction of the very near future. Right behind it is Clark's *2010*—the genuine item, no doubt of it—and then Asimov's *Foundation's Edge*, equally simon-pure s-f. Elsewhere on the list we find Jean Auel's *Valley Of Horses*, a tale of Neanderthals and Cro-Magnons that certainly qualifies for our field, and William Kotzwinkle's *E.T. Storybook*, and the latest in Douglas Adams' *Hitchhiker's Guide To The Galaxy* Series. There's also Stephen King's *Different Seasons*, which isn't science fiction at all, but King operates in a closely related field and is no stranger to the science-fictional way of thinking. Counting his book, that's seven out of ten—barely leaving

[*Amazing Stories*, July 1983]

room for the latest Judith Krantz or Sidney Sheldon to squeeze onto the list, and pushing a lot of best-seller perennials like Robert Ludlum, Len Deighton, and Kurt Vonnegut into the lower reaches.

What's going on?

Why is science-fiction suddenly the dominant factor in the publishing industry—not merely a big item, but the hottest thing around?

Each of those best-sellers can be provided with a special explanation to account for its success. *The E.T. Storybook*, of course, is riding along in the wake of a vastly successful motion picture. To some degree, so is *2010*. *Space* bears the Michener name, and he is so formidably popular a writer that he would probably have reached the top of the list even if he had chosen to offer a book of sonnets. Ditto King. Asimov, though he has no Hollywood push behind him and has not previously been in bestseller territory, is a familiar public figure, the basic s-f household name. Jean Auel's prehistoric book, sequel to an earlier bestseller of similar nature, combines genuine s-f thinking with the apparatus of the woman's saga novel in an irresistibly commercial way. And Douglas Adams' book is a spoof, a lark; that sort of stuff, done as well as this, has always enjoyed big sales regardless of the subject being spoofed.

And yet, and yet—Heinlein's *Friday* was on the best-seller list last year. The last two segments of Frank Herbert's *Dune* series have had astonishing sales. Stephen Donaldson's Thomas Covenant books, likewise. Anne McCaffrey has had her unicorn books on the list. There have been some others. In all those cases, the traditional techniques of book promotion were employed to build and sustain sales, but it's impossible to credit the success of those titles to Hollywood associations, tv appearances, or other peripheral advantages. They were true science-fiction books of the sort that might have been serialized in the s-f magazines of my boyhood and then might have gone on to sell ninety thousand copies, or so, in paperback, at 35 cents apiece; and instead, priced as $15 hardcovers, they reached hundreds of thousands or readers, and millions more in paperback.

The explanation, I think, grows out of the great social upheaval that we conveniently label "the Sixties," though the peak of it actually fell between 1967 and 1972. In that time, basic political structures in the United States and other western industrial nations began coming apart; new styles of music, sexual behavior, dress, and physical appearance were adopted; the use of mind-altering drugs other than alcohol became commonplace; there was intense interest in mysticism, Oriental religion, and other intellectual disciplines not previously pursued here. *And science fiction became intensely popular.* Such books as *Dune* and *Stranger In A Strange Land* and Vonnegut's *Cat's Cradle* became virtual handbooks of behavioral guidance for the millions who, in that dark and unstable time, found themselves venturing into all that unfamiliar territory. The torrent of s-f paperbacks that still washes through our bookstores began to flow at that time.

Paperbacks, because most of the social astronauts of the Sixties were 17 to 25 years old. Not only did they necessarily live on paperback-sized budgets, but they came to regard hardcover books, I think, as symbols of the repressive, stuffy, and obsolete older generation against whom they were in rebellion. Because there were so many in that age group—millions upon millions, the celebrated Baby Boom kids of the postwar era—they came to exert an immense demographic impact on all forms of popular consumption.

And now it is fifteen years or so later. Once again we are in a time of troubles—economic chaos, primarily, much of it the result, ironically, of the very solutions we applied to the problems of that earlier troubled era. The Baby Boom people are still around—but now they are 30, 35, 38 years old. Science fiction still speaks to them; it offers, as ever, insight or at least the illusion of insight into what may lie beyond this immediate moment of pain and confusion. But they are no longer a paperback generation. They can afford hardcover books; having waited this long to find out where Asimov's Foundation was heading, they are unwilling to wait another year for the paperback, when $14.95 gives the answer this afternoon. Instant gratification was always important to the people of the Sixties. I think there are a great many reasons why dislocated times send people to read science fiction; but to explain the topheavy presence of s-f on the hardcover bestsellers list, I invite you to consider once more the power of the Baby Boom as it makes its steamroller way through our society. When they manifest their tastes, as they often do, en masse, entire industries pay heed. But I wonder: are we heading for an era, a decade or two hence, when science fiction, our soaring and mind-expanding literature, is a musty and ritualized entertainment consumed only by elderly Baby Boomers, hearkening back nostalgically to the good old days of their twenties, while the illiterate young 'uns divert themselves with the electronic hardware that science fiction predicted?

The Audience Grows Older

Our esteemed colleagues over at *The Magazine of Fantasy & Science Fiction* ran a survey of their readership a couple of years ago to gather demographic information for potential advertisers. Editor Kristine Kathryn Rusch, reporting on the results in last February's *F&SF*, found the news "disturbing." The readership of her magazine, she said, is getting older:

> "The bulk of the readers," she said, "fall in the 26-55 year age group. Only two percent of our readers are under the age of 18. Only five percent are between the ages of 18 and 25....Fifty-five percent of our readers are over 35." A similar survey in the s-f trade journal *Locus* produced similar data. Doubtless the survey mavens in the advertising department of *Asimov's Science Fiction* have turned up the same information. "The fact that s-f is losing its young readers is a problem for the genre," Kris Rusch wrote. "It is also curious, given the rise in popularity of s-f films, games, and video games."

Even if the *F&SF* survey's findings are somewhat skewed because only the older readers bothered to reply to it—something that I suspect from the fact that 48% of the respondents said they had been reading the magazine eleven years or longer, leading me to think that a lot of newer and perhaps less dedicated readers ignored the survey— there seems no doubt that the audience for the kind of science fiction that magazines like *Asimov's* and *F&SF* publish is failing to replace itself, and the same is true of the audience for the books that once were regarded as the defining center of the field—the straightforward non-media-connected books that are our classics, the novels by such people as Heinlein, Asimov, Sturgeon, Blish, Simak, Herbert, Bester, Dick, etc., etc. Sales of these writers' books have begun distinctly to slide now that their authors are no longer producing new work, and in many cases they have vanished from print altogether.

I have seen the aging-audience effect myself, most vividly, whenever I do a book signing at a science-fiction convention. I get a gratifyingly long line of people who want my autograph, yes—but most of them are in the 35-45-year-old range, readers who were hooked on my stuff fifteen or twenty years ago and now want me to sign their aging copies of *Dying Inside* or *Tower of Glass*. The younger members of the line, who seem to be in the 25-30-year age-group,

[*Asimov's Science Fiction*, October 1995]

generally ask me to sign *Lord Valentine's Castle* or other books in my popular Majipoor series. And hardly anybody younger than 25 seems to be on the line at all, except those helping their fathers or mothers carry a stack of cherished old books for me to sign. My one-man demographic survey has me convinced that the Robert Silverberg audience is aging at a rate of one year per year, just like Silverberg himself. I'm keeping my loyal fans as they turn gray and weary, but I'm not getting a lot of new readers down at the younger end of the scale. And neither, as far as I can tell, is anybody else who works in the traditional modes of s-f.

Kris Rusch puzzles over the fact that the readership for traditional s-f isn't growing, "given the rise in popularity of s-f films, games, and video games." But I think that that is *precisely* the explanation for what's going on. The kids I see at the conventions crowd eagerly around the video games and the dealers who sell them *Star Trek* memorabilia and role-playing cards; Robert A. Heinlein himself could walk through their midst and they wouldn't have a clue to who was among them. What had been the periphery of the field is now its center, and *we* are at the periphery, an aging bunch of cultists full of nostalgia for the good old days of *Dune* and *Stranger in a Strange Land*. When the youngsters get tired of playing *Magic: The Gathering* or watching *Star Trek: Voyager*, they may buy a *Magic: The Gathering* anthology or a *Voyager* novelization, but it won't occur to them to pick up a magazine full of stories by people they've never heard of (Connie Willis, Kim Stanley Robinson, John Varley, Ursula K. Le Guin) telling stories dealing with situations *with whom they are not already familiar.*

It's that element of *a priori* familiarity, the sense of returning to a place they already know, that modern s-f magazines are lacking. As Gregory Benford trenchantly put it, commenting on the *F&SF* findings, "S-f became a huge media phenom through *shared experiences* of the future: *Star Trek*, then the continuing family-like adventures...of *Star Wars*. This taught a generation to seek the 'sci-fi' experience in this associative way, which isn't the root experience of reading books or magazines. So the media parade missed the written medium. The hoped-for transference of *Star Trek* book readers to mainline s-f didn't happen....

"It suggests that the way to reach this enormous audience is to find a shared, quasi-communal vehicle. I wonder if this is even possible in magazines, though it might be in books."

But I remember—and Greg Benford probably does too—a time when the s-f magazines provided younger readers with just that sort of quasi-communal reading experience and built-in ongoing familiarity. There was, in the 1940s, a pulp magazine called *Captain Future*, a kind of comic book in prose, featuring the lively adventures of a band of gallant spacegoers clearly ancestral to the heroes of *Star Trek* and *Star Wars*. The central figure was Curt Newton, "the red-haired young wizard of science known to all men as Captain Future," a "thinker and dreamer" of great dash and glamour who roared around the Solar System righting wrongs and thwarting bad guys. His entourage included Simon Wright, the Brain, "a living human brain housed in a square, transparent case whose circulating serums kept him alive;" Grag, the robot, whose "mighty metal figure, bulbous metal head and gleaming photo-electric eyes made him an awe-inspiring figure;" and Otho, the android, whose "body was quite human in shape but was of rubbery white synthetic flesh."

Edmond Hamilton, the grand old pulpster who created the *Captain Future* epics, churned out 50,000 words of prose like this in every issue:

> " 'The conclusion is inescapable that Ul Quorn has some secret base at which he plans to build a giant spaceship. In that ship, fueled with radite, Quorn and his band will go into the co-existing universe in search of the mysterious treasure Haines told about.' "
>
> " 'Good reasoning, lad,' approved the Brain. 'I believe now we're getting somewhere.' "

The kids loved it. In the back of each issue, meanwhile, there was room for a few non-Captain Future short stories. These—by such writers as Ray Bradbury, Henry Kuttner, and Jack Williamson—were generally of somewhat higher literary quality, so that more sophisticated readers might be tempted to pick up the book as well.

Then there were *Startling Stories* and *Thrilling Wonder Stories*, two garish-looking pulp magazines that in fact ran excellent s-f by many of the best writers of the era. What provided the month-by-month cornball continuity was a letter column presided over by a character named Sergeant Saturn, who would introduce ten pages of letters from faithful readers with stuff like this:

> "If it's red meat you want, and alive and on the hoof, then the old space dog is your mutton. If you'll just wait until I square off and have a go at knocking you junior astrogators into shape for the ensuing cruise. Take your stations now and look alive while we seal the exit ports and prepare to blast

off. Okay. The all-clear signal is blinking. So we'll start spacing this voyage with a brief snort of the starboard rocket bank from a spot south of the Border."

Which was the lead-in to a letter from Harry Tawil of Mexico City in the August, 1943 *Thrilling Wonder*.

Puerile? Sure. Silly? Beyond a doubt. But the formula worked, just as it worked for another grand old pulp magazine, *Planet Stories*, the contents page of which was bedecked with stories with titles like "Lorelei of the Red Mist," "Prisoner of the Brain-Mistress," and "Captives of the Weir-Wind." You knew exactly what you were going to get when you put your twenty cents down for a copy of *Planet Stories*—rip-roaring space adventure—and the fact that the stories were by people like Ray Bradbury, Poul Anderson, Theodore Sturgeon, and (on one famous occasion) Isaac Asimov was no drawback to your innocent enjoyment of them, however hifalutin' those writers might get when they wrote for other magazines.

And that is the point. At age thirteen or so, you were drawn in by *Captain Future Magazine* or the antics of Sarge Saturn or the comic-book-like gaudiness of *Planet Stories*; but if you stuck around a couple of years, you noticed that the same writers were appearing in the more austere magazines aimed for older readers, and you tried one of those out of curiosity and perhaps moved along to become a regular reader of them.

Nobody's publishing magazines for entry-level s-f readers nowadays, and perhaps that's the problem. It's a big leap from the media-oriented stuff to the sort of fiction found in *Asimov's* and its contemporaries. That may be a big mistake. Maybe if there had been a magazine all along that ran a Han Solo/Luke Skywalker novella up front, or Kirk-Spock-McCoy stuff, and had stories by Bruce Sterling, Gregory Benford, Orson Scott Card, and Pat Cadigan in the back pages, just to provide new readers with a hint of the fact that there's more to science fiction than what they've already discovered, the demographic picture would look a lot brighter for today's adult-oriented s-f magazines.

Is it too late? Can we catch that huge media-oriented readership young, and teach them the habit of getting their science fiction in the magazine format? Or will magazines like this one and *Fantasy & Science Fiction* continue to serve an ever-older, ever-smaller audience until the doddering Kris Rusch and the age-withered Gardner Dozois are carted off to the home for superannuated editors? I'd like to see someone make another stab at an entry-level s-f magazine, heavily but not totally media-oriented, before we give up entirely on the concept of magazines as a viable medium for stimulating and challenging science fiction.

Gresham's Law and Science Fiction

Gresham's law is at work in science fiction, and bad books are driving out good ones. The prospect is that the process will continue and grow even more harmful with time.

A little economic history first. Sir Thomas Gresham (1519-1579) was an English banker who lived during the reign of Queen Elizabeth I. Gresham's great contribution to economics was the idea of forming an equalization fund to support the exchange rate of his country's currency—an idea that the Queen rejected, apparently because the royal treasury didn't have enough cash on hand to make the concept work, but which is common practice everywhere today.

One concept for which Gresham was *not* responsible was Gresham's Law. The economist Henry D. MacLeod, propounding it in 1857, attributed it erroneously to Gresham. In fact, the mathematician and astronomer Nicolaus Copernicus, he who overthrew the concept of the geocentric universe, stated the principle in a book on coinage a generation before Gresham was born. And in Gresham's own time the concept was put forth by one Humphrey Holt, who in 1551 observed that the debasement of English currency late in the reign of Henry VIII was causing coins of pure silver to disappear from circulation, leaving only the base coins in use and bringing about severe inflation, "to the decay of all things."

Regardless of who deserves the credit for putting Gresham's Law into words, the basic idea has been understood by merchants and moneychangers since coinage first began. It works this way:

Bad money drives out good.

One example of this occurred in the Roman Empire in the third century A.D. For everyday circulation the Romans had long used a small silver coin, the denarius, and a heavy bronze coin, the sestertius. The purchasing power of one denarius equalled that of four sestertii, and the two coins were interchangeable at that ratio for centuries. But about 220 A.D. Rome fell on hard economic times, and the emperors began to debase their silver coinage. At first this was barely apparent, to the great profit of the government, but the debasement went on and on until the supposed "silver" denarius consisted mostly of bronze, with a light wash of silver on its surface to make it look legitimate.

The first thing that happened was that the old pure-silver coins vanished from circulation. They were worth more as silver bullion than they were as denarii, and so they were melted down and used for

[*Asimov's Science Fiction*, February 1995]

jewelry, or recycled into the new base-metal coinage. Then the bronze coins began disappearing too, because the old four-to-one ratio was now out of whack: there was a lot of useful bronze in a big, heavy sestertius, whereas the new "silver" coins had hardly any intrinsic value at all. So the Roman people melted down their sestertii and turned them into things like nails and swords and plumbing fixtures, or else hoarded the coins against some future time when the old currency ratios would return.

Something similar happened in the United States about thirty years ago. Our coinage used to be made of silver, valued at a dollar an ounce. That is, the old silver dollar weighed just about one ounce, the half dollar contained half as much silver, and so on. But during the 1960s the market price of silver rose far out of parity with the official coinage rate. The ounce of silver in a silver dollar was now worth three or four dollars as melted-down bullion. Obviously this made no economic sense; and so our silver currency was abolished and re-placed with dollars, half dollars, quarters, and dimes struck from a copper-nickel alloy that had only token value as metal.

That completed the process of driving our good silver money out of circulation. The remaining silver coins immediately disappeared, most of them melted for their metal, the rest hoarded by collectors or speculators. When I was a boy, I would not infrequently find coins 60 or 70 years old in my pocket change; but today you will never be given a dime or a quarter older than 1965, when the alloyed coinage was introduced. Gresham's Law has seen to it that all of our silver coinage of earlier years has gone out of circulation.

What does all this have to do with science fiction?

Simply this: since about 1975, when books based on popular s-f movies and television shows began to be published and enjoy huge sales, a gradual debasement of the stuff we like to read has taken place. Once upon a time—when science fiction was exclusively the province of a few low-circulation magazines—s-f editors and readers put a premium on thoughtful, serious ideas and crisp, literate writing. That was the heyday of John W. Campbell's superb *Astounding Science Fiction* (now *Analog*) and, a little later, Horace Gold's *Galaxy* and the *Fantasy & Science Fiction* of Anthony Boucher and J. Francis McComas. That was the heyday, too, of the great writers who gave modern science fiction its character: Asimov, Heinlein, Sturgeon, De Camp, Simak, Kuttner, and the rest of Campbell's team in the 1940s, and Leiber, Kornbluth, Pohl, Clarke, Bradbury, Bester, Vance, Ander-son, Blish, Dick, and many others a little later on.

Since the readers knew what they liked and magazine circulations varied very little from month to month, editors were motivated to publish the most challenging and vigorous stories they could find. They didn't have to worry about driving readers away by publishing excessively challenging and unusual fiction: the audience was steady, issue after issue, so long as the general quality level remained consistent. For young and unsophisticated readers, there were such action-oriented magazines as *Planet Stories* and *Amazing Stories*; when they were a little older, they would usually graduate to *Astounding* or one of its handful of adult-oriented competitors.

The coming of paperback publishing changed all that. Each book now was a unique item, with its own highly visible sales figures; but each of those unique books fell into a larger class of fiction according to type—the old Campbellian cerebral s-f, the wild-and-woolly *Planet Stories* type, the fantasy-tinged sword-and-sorcery type, and so forth. Unsurprisingly, books of the more simpleminded sorts sold better—sometimes a great deal better. In a free-market economy there will always be more cash customers for Schwarzeneggeresque tales of violent conflict than there are for sober Campbellian examinations of the social consequences of technological developments.

Paperback publishers are not charitable institutions. They are in the business of what is accurately called "mass-market" publishing. The sales figures were unanswerable; and, gradually, over a period of ten or fifteen years, the older kind of science fiction, the kind that we who first discovered it forty or fifty years ago thought of as "good" science fiction, began to disappear just as completely as Roman sestertii and American silver dollars had.

You aren't likely to find many of the wonderful novels of Theodore Sturgeon, Fritz Leiber, or Alfred Bester in your neighborhood bookstore. Simak is a rarity; Blish is forgotten except (ironically) for his *Star Trek* novelizations; Kornbluth and Kuttner are utterly unknown. Much great work of Vance, Dick, even Bradbury, Clarke, and Heinlein, has been shoved to the back rows in favor of the latest adventure of Princess Leia, the fourteenth volume in some popular robot-warrior series, and the ninth installment of a cops-and-robbers-in-the-asteroid belt epic. I confess that I'm having trouble keeping some of my own best books in print these days. It isn't that these books of twenty and thirty and fifty years ago are creaky and obsolete. They aren't. It's that they can't hold their own competitively in the stores with the flashy new media-oriented kind of s-f and the interminable sequels to the mediocre books of a few years ago. Aside from the occasional brilliant Zeitgeist-shaping novel like *Neuromancer* or *Snow Crash*, just about the only s-f books that do well commercially nowadays are series books and Hollywood spinoffs.

This is sad on two accounts. One is that the books I'm talking about have a lot of great reading to offer. (Where are Sturgeon's *More than Human*, Ward Moore's *Bring the Jubilee*, Hal Clement's *Mission of Gravity* these days? In and out of print in the wink of an eye whenever some courageous publisher reissues them.)

Worse—far worse, I think—is the loss of these classics as exemplars of the type. Young science fiction writers traditionally take the work of their great predecessors as models for their own early books and stories. I grew up reading the classic s-f of what is still called the Golden Age, a period that began in 1939 and ran, by my estimate, to the early 1950s. When I began writing, my goal was to equal the attainments of those writers who had filled my head with their wondrous visions years before. I still keep that goal in mind with every word I write.

But what of the young writer of today, who has no access to those classics, and who may very well come to regard the crudely written and crudely conceived formula-ridden mass-market stuff of today's paperback racks as the proper ideal to follow? What they read is what they will write. Junk begets junk. So the newer writers will give us imitations of works that themselves would probably not have been able to see publication a generation ago.

That's what I mean by bad science fiction driving out the good. As our classics go out of print, we are losing touch with our ideals, our Platonic forms of the finest s-f. Superb work is still being done by some writers, of course. Indeed, some of the best science fiction ever written has appeared in the last decade. But most of that high-quality work struggles in the marketplace and has a sadly short shelf life, driven out of sight by the vast tide of you-know-what, often causing its writers to wonder why they had bothered. Thus does Gresham's Law operate on our field, "to the decay of all things." I wish I saw a remedy for it.

Gresham's Law, Continued

I spoke last month of the operation of a kind of literary Gresham's Law whereby the flood of hackneyed mass-media-derived science fiction and endless rehashes of a few well-known series novels is driving out of print the kind of work that we used to cherish. In place of the thoughtful, provocative, powerful books that writers like Isaac Asimov, Fritz Leiber, Theodore Sturgeon, and other luminaries of the Golden Age gave us, we are inundated now by a sorry tide of third-rate stuff, a kind of print-media version of shabby "sci-fi" movies and television shows, that is leaving no room on publishers' lists for anything more seriously conceived.

I've been wrestling with this problem for twenty years, now, ever since the immense popularity of George Lucas' *Star Wars* brought hundreds of thousands of new s-f readers into the fold and forever changed the demographics of our field. So please forgive me if I give the subject some further mastication here.

I am not, by the way, arguing that *Star Wars* was a terrible movie (I liked it quite a lot) or that the needs of the people who like to read novels set in the *Star Wars* and *Star Trek* universes should go unmet. There has always been a place in our field for well-done action-adventure science fiction. I remember fondly the glorious space epics of Leigh Brackett and Poul Anderson and even Ted Sturgeon in the lively magazine *Planet Stories* of the 1940s; and I wrote plenty of stuff in the *Planet Stories* vein myself, later on. That kind of fast-moving, colorful, melodramatic fiction has a great deal to offer, especially to younger readers who might later go on to read, well, *Isaac Asimov's Science Fiction Magazine.*

What I am saying is that modern-day publishing's emphasis on the bottom line seems to be killing science fiction as a genre that appeals to adult readers. I loved *Planet Stories*, sure, but I doubt that I would have stuck with s-f past the age of 15 or so if I hadn't been able to move on to John Campbell's *Astounding Science Fiction* and Horace Gold's *Galaxy*, with their great array of stimulating stories by Asimov and Heinlein and Blish and Sturgeon and Kornbluth and Clement and so many other wonderful writers. We are heading to a point now, at least in book publishing, where the slam-bang kind of fiction is not only dominant but has driven our classics from print and is hurting the distribution and sales of new science fiction intended for an intelligent readership.

[*Asimov's Science Fiction*, March 1995]

As I said last time, I don't like it. As I also said last time, I see no remedy. In a free-market economy, the bottom line rules. (In the Soviet Union, state-controlled publishing houses served up a steady diet of classic Russian novels, poetry, and the collected works of Lenin to a huge audience starved for books of any sort, and scarcely any popular fiction was printed. In today's anything-goes Russia, Dostoyevsky and Chekhov are taking a back seat to pulp fiction of the tawdriest sort. The readers are voting with their rubles, and the publishers have to pay attention, or else.)

So I am playing the part, I guess, of that stuffiest of old bores, the *laudator temporis acti*—he who praises the glories of the past at the expense of the present. (As W.S. Gilbert put it, "The idiot who praises, with enthusiastic tone/All centuries but this, and every country but his own.") I can't help it. I've spent much of my life reading and writing science fiction. I love it for its visionary potential; I hate to see it turned into something hackneyed and cheap.

(Yes, I know, plenty of worthy s-f of the classic kind is still being published. Just in the past few years we've seen Kim Stanley Robinson's Mars books and Connie Willis's *Doomsday Book* and Vernor Vinge's *A Fire Upon the Deep* and a dozen others equally worthy of taking their place beside the great books of the past. And I have no doubt that *Asimov's Science Fiction* has been for most of its existence a magazine that ranks with the *Astounding* of Campbell and the *Galaxy* of Horace Gold. But more and more, it seems to me, science fiction of this kind is being crammed into a corner of the field, published purely for reasons of prestige by houses who are making their real money churning out the formula books.)

The vanishing from print of most of the great science fiction of previous years, and its replacement by miles and miles of the less-than-mediocre stuff that we are offered today, has a number of unhappy consequences. I spoke last time of the disappearance of the classics as an influence on new writers. When young writers no longer have access to a broad historical overview of science fiction— when they are unable to absorb and digest and transmute, as we did, such books as Heinlein's *Beyond This Horizon* and van Vogt's *The World of Null-A* and Sturgeon's *More Than Human* and Bester's *The Demolished Man*, then a whole world of creative possibilities is lost to them: either they merely strive to replicate the simple, badly written books that they think of as the best of s-f, or else they expend their creative energies reinventing wheels that were better designed by the writers of a generation ago.

The vast oversupply of science fiction today exacerbates this problem. Publishers fighting for display space on the racks pour out eight, ten, twelve science-fiction books a month, hundreds a year all told. This keeps a lot of writers eating regularly, yes, but it also means that a lot of s-f is published that never should have seen print. There are only so many writers at any one time who are capable of doing the sort of memorable work we crave. Just as expanding the major leagues to fifty or sixty baseball teams from the original eight will not bring forth a phalanx of new Babe Ruths and Ty Cobbs, so too will publishing a thousand s-f novels a year instead of the dozen or so of years gone by will not of itself unleash a horde of new Heinleins and Sturgeons. All that this overproduction of s-f books has accomplished has been to make it impossible for anyone to read more than a fraction of what appears, thus depriving us of the invaluable sense of community we once had—that universe of shared references and concepts held in common, to be elaborated and embellished by all, that evolved when all of us were able to read just about all the science-fiction that was being published. No one now has much of an inkling of the totality of what's going on in the field; there may be no overlap at all between one person's annual reading and another's.

The torrent of bad s-f has the additional drawback of driving away mature readers just beginning to be curious about modern science fiction. Perhaps they read some Bradbury or Asimov long ago, and now they want to sample some of the current product; or it may be that they've never tried s-f at all, and somehow have decided to sample it now. So they wander into the bookstore, stare with glazing eyes at the garish covers in the science-fiction section, finally pick up *Vengeance of the Galaxy Eaters* or the ninth volume of the *Glibabibion* Saga or the novelization of *Vampires of the Void*, riffle through it in growing dismay, put it back, and cross the aisle to the mystery-novel section, where the interests of adult readers are currently being well attended to. And are lost to us forever.

It isn't the publishers' fault. They're simply delivering what the audience wants, as they always do. If an audience for Sturgeon or Blish or Bester is no longer there, and if the work of modern writers of similar skill and ambition sells poorly also, they'll simply crank out the next *Glibabibion* volume, the one in which the Wand of Total Power is recaptured by the Lord of Utter Evil. What choice do they have?

Writers of s-f can't operate in a vacuum. Without an eager, demanding audience for first-rate material, it isn't possible to sustain for very long a career built on writing that kind of material. Seeing a book that you've spent a year writing go out of print in six minutes is a disheartening thing. Eventually the best and brightest among us find some other way to make a living, perhaps in Hollywood, perhaps in some other field of fiction, perhaps by turning out their own versions of the Wand of Total Power stuff.

Readers not only get the kind of books they want, they get the kind of books they deserve. I don't begrudge the manufacturers of the interchangeable cotton-candy trilogies the audience they have won. I just wish there were some way for the work of writers who ask more of themselves and of their readers to stay in print.

TWO

ABOUT SCIENCE AND SOCIETY

Genetic Hysteria

Like most people who spend their professional lives staring futureward, I don't find advances in technology particularly scary. I can see negative sides to such devices as television, the telephone, the computer, and even penicillin, and surely life in the second half of the twentieth century would have been a little less edgy for us all if the atomic bomb had never been invented; but in general I think most of the technological developments of the last few thousand years have been useful things, and I have (just enough) faith in the good sense of human beings to believe that if we were smart enough to invent all those things, we'll probably be smart enough to use them in ways that won't destroy us.

Many of my essays, then, have been aimed at the uneasiness and downright paranoia with which many recent technical achievements have been greeted. The dread that gene-splicing research seems to elicit is something that I've dealt with at length over the years, as the following group of pieces demonstrates.

Nearly a hundred years ago, H.G. Wells—the first and, I think, the greatest of modern science-fiction authors—wrote a powerful short novel called *The Island of Dr. Moreau*, in which a brilliant scientist surgically reshapes apes, cattle, pigs, and other animals into human-oid creatures. Though Wells can hardly be accused of being hostile to science in general—he held a heartily optimistic view of the benefits that technology could bring—his primary aim in *Moreau* was to write a terrifying tale of horror, and in that he succeeded splendidly. His Dr. Moreau is the maddest of mad scientists, and the beast-people, though some are sympathetically depicted, are bestial indeed, reverting quickly to the feral state once their creator has been slain: "As I approached the monster lifted its glaring eyes to mine, its lips went trembling back from its red-stained teeth, and it growled menacingly...."

Wells wanted his readers to react with shock and dismay to his account of the achievements of Dr. Moreau, but later science-fiction writers have approached the theme of metamorphosis more positively. James Blish, in his impressively inventive novel *The Seedling Stars* (1957), told of the human race undergoing extensive adaptation so that it would be capable of colonizing alien worlds. Blish wrote of "the application to the germ cells of an elaborate constellation of techniques—selective mitotic poisoning, pinpoint X-irradiation, tectogenetic microsurgery, competitive metabolic inhibition, and perhaps

[*Amazing Stories*, May 1985]

fifty more....which collectively had been christened 'pantropy.' The word, freely retranslated, meant 'changing everything'—and it fitted." A few years later, Cordwainer Smith brilliantly portrayed the lives of genetically transformed humanoid dogs and bulls and cats in such dazzling stories as "The Ballad of Lost C'Mell" and "The Dead Lady of Clown Town." And in the work of such recent writers as John Varley and Greg Bear the notion of genetic modification of all sorts of creatures, human and otherwise, is a routine part of story back-grounds. As well it should be, for we find ourselves living at a time when the concept of genetic engineering has moved from science fiction to industry. Dozens of corporations are at work right now finding ways to create new life-forms. The U.S. Patent and Trademark Office has 26 patent examiners working in the area of biotechnology, twelve of them specializing in genetic engineering, and just now they have a backlog of 2600 patent applications undergoing processing in the area of biotechnology—so busy a schedule that it takes an average of 28 months for an application in the field of genetic engineering to be acted upon.

But it's not likely that any significant marvels of genetic engineer-ing will emerge soon from these busy laboratories. At a meeting of the Industrial Biotechnology Association in San Francisco in the summer of 1984, speaker after speaker warned that anti-technology activists are already at work arousing fear and trembling in the general popu-lace in the hope of blocking genetic-engineering research through legal action. The same people who created the hysteria that has paralyzed or perhaps destroyed the nuclear-power industry are mov-ing on toward their next triumph over technology.

"It would not surprise me one bit," said Harold Green of George Washington University, counsel to Genex Corporation, "to see some of the anti-nuclear negativists extend their negativism to genetic engineering." Lawsuits are already being filed under provisions of the National Environmental Policy Act to tie up genetic research in the courts. NEPA, enacted in 1968, requires federal agencies to make a thorough study of environmental issues before approving any action that could significantly affect the environment. "The litigation could be endless and enormous in cost," Green pointed out, drawing a parallel with the legal strife that has kept nuclear power plants out of service for a decade or a more after completion, at a cost of billions to power companies and electricity users.

Opposition to genetic research is founded, apparently, on the fear that the gene labs are staffed with amoral scientists who will, intentionally or through sheer negligence, flood the world with terrifying new organisms. Once the Pandora's box of genetic engineering is allowed to open, it is argued, a host of nightmarish foes will spring forth: plague-bearing microorganisms meant for use in germ warfare, say, which will get loose instead among innocent civilians. Or horrifying science-fictional monsters that will rampage through quiet suburban streets. Or mutated bacteria which, although intended for benevolent functions, turn out to have some hideous capability, unforeseen and uncontrollable. Worst of all, say the anti-genetic crusaders, *human beings themselves* may one day be modified, in some super-Nazi campaign to create a perfect world. The children of the wealthy may be turned into superbeings, they say; the children of the poor will be altered in the womb to make them sturdy and docile, the better to perform menial tasks. And so forth.

These insecurities have already had some real-world results. The city of Berkeley, California—always in the forefront of social concern—made it illegal, in 1977, for the dreaded genetic research to take place within its city limits. Since the University of California at Berkeley is one of the world's great scientific centers, gene-research corporations wishing to use the university's facilities have found it necessary to set up headquarters in nearby Emeryville, an otherwise insignificant Bay Area town that thus by an accident of politics may become the capital city of genetic engineering. When one of the Emeryville companies produced a modified bacterium that was capable of helping farm crops resist frost, anti-biotechnology activists successfully kept it from being tested at a University of California agricultural facility. No less a judge than John Sirica of Watergate fame issued an injunction keeping the new organism bottled up until all possible environmental consequences of releasing it, even under controlled conditions, had been checked out, a process likely to take some years.

Nobody wants a horde of mutated amoebas getting into our water system and blotting out all life on earth. Nobody, I think, wants to see human embryos turned into scientifically-engineered street-sweepers and dishwashers. Some government regulation of the genetic-engineering industry is not only inevitable but desirable, say the genesplicers themselves.

But what is beginning to happen sounds dishearteningly familiar: the old humanist loathing of technological advancement coming to the fore once more. The Luddites who smashed textile-factory machinery in 1811 for fear that their jobs would be lost, those who thought that vaccination was a dangerous invention of the devil, the diehards who opposed the chlorination (let alone the fluoridation!) of drinking water, those who just a few years ago argued that the space program was a monstrous waste of effort and that computers were inimical to all human values, have their counterparts in the modern-day activists who see a new Hiroshima in every nuclear power plant and a new Dr. Moreau in every genetic-engineering researcher. If they have their way, it will be a long, long time before the pantropically modified space explorers that James Blish envisioned begin their journeys toward the distant worlds of space.

More Genetic Hysteria

L ast issue I took up the question of the environmental-activist campaign against genetic engineering—a movement which threatens to stir up a wave of anti-technological hysteria as vehement as the one that has effectively destroyed the nuclear power industry in the United States. Herewith some further details on the subject:

About a decade ago, botanists discovered that certain commonly found bacteria known as *Pseudomonas syringae* tend to act as catalysts for the formation of ice crystals on the leaves of plants. A plant that might otherwise go unharmed by frost down to a temperature of 23 degrees Fahrenheit or so will freeze and die at 31 degrees if substantial colonies of *Pseudomonas syringae* exist on it.

In 1982, two University of California plant pathologists, Nicholas Panopoulous and Steven Lindow, found that a single gene—out of the 4000 making up each strand of *Pseudomonas syringae* DNA—was responsible for the ice-promoting characteristics of these bacteria. Working in conjunction with Advanced Genetic Sciences, Inc., of Oakland, California, a small genetic-engineering company, they developed a technique for snipping out the troublesome gene, thereby producing a strain of *Pseudomonas* identical in nearly all respects to the natural kind but lacking the capacity to induce the formation of ice. They nicknamed the artificially rejiggered bacterium "Ice Minus" and the natural form "Ice Plus."

The genetic engineers reasoned that if "Ice Minus" were to be sprayed on fields of crops in areas of frost risk, it could displace the "Ice Plus" form and reduce the risks of agricultural loss. "There's no question that these efforts could hold great promise for farmers," declared the California Farm Bureau Federation. "Millions of dollars worth of damage are done each year to crops by frost." That figure applies just to the United States. Worldwide, the annual losses run to many billions.

First, of course, some field testing was necessary. The scientists applied to the National Institutes of Health's Recombinant DNA Advisory Committee for permission to conduct tests during the 1983 frost season, and in due time they were given the go-ahead for spraying a few gallons of a concentrated "microbe soup" on a quarter-acre plot in Siskiyou County, California, near the Oregon border.

Enter the environmental activists—specifically, one Jeremy Rifkin, who has been campaigning against genetic engineering since

1977 with such books as *Who Should Play God?* and *Algeny*. Lining up the support of such groups as the Foundation on Economic Trends, Friends of the Earth, and the Wilderness Society, Rifkin took the National Institutes of Health to court, calling the proposed experiment "ecological roulette." Rifkin asserted that *Pseudomonas syringae*, which in its normal form is widespread in the atmosphere, might conceivably play an essential role in the earth's climate through its ice-forming capacity. Who could say, Rifkin asked, what climatic effects there might be if "Ice Plus" were replaced by the artificially created "Ice Minus" variety? For all anyone knew, world-wide droughts might result—or other, stranger consequences beyond our fathoming.

Rifkin's onslaught startled Lindow and Panopolous, who had spent three months preparing their NIH application and believed that all they meant to do was carry out a carefully controlled small-scale experiment with a notably unthreatening microorganism. The way Rifkin made it sound, they said, it would seem that they intended to spray "the entire North American continent with bacteria."

But the doughty Federal Judge John J. Sirica, the Watergate man, was impressed by Rifkin's arguments and handed down an injunction against NIH and the University of California prohibiting the experiment. There would be no release of genetically engineered organisms into the environment, said Judge Sirica, until a full-scale study of ecological consequences had been carried out. The *Los Angeles Times* hailed the decision as "a stunning victory for environmental activists," and a television news commentator described the experiment on the day of the injunction as making use of "new life-forms with potentially catastrophic effects." And so the dreaded bacterium was not let loose. Catastrophe was averted; the Earth's climate will not be changed by the genetic engineers this month.

The "Ice Minus" form of *Pseudonomas syringae*, nevertheless, is about to have its field test in California. Perhaps the silliest aspect of this whole controversy came to light in mid-November of 1984 when Advanced Genetic Sciences let it be known that it would soon begin outdoor testing of a *naturally occurring* mutant variety of the bacterium that also has the ice-inhibiting gene. Its existence has been known for some time, and in fact Lindow has already tested its frost-proofing abilities on a potato patch in Northern California. He did not think it was particularly dangerous to life on Earth, since it has existed naturally for millions of years without any evident negative effects. Since it was not produced by the dreaded genetic engineering technique, it seems to be legal to give it a try. It is gene-splicing alone that stirs primordial fears, apparently.

If "Ice Minus" was available all along in a natural mutant strain, why did the scientists go to the trouble of duplicating it in the genetics lab? Because, says Advanced Genetic Sciences, the genetically engineered bugs can be produced in greater quantities and seem to be more stable when applied to plants in the field. It is, therefore, a better idea commercially. Developing it also allows the gene-splicers to extend their reach and perfect their skills.

Toward what end, though? Will scientists ultimately succeed in setting horrifying organisms loose upon the world despite the best efforts of the Jeremy Rifkins?

I think not. I think genetic engineering is a science that will prevail over the obstructionists now crowding the courts. It offers so much that we cannot afford to let it be swept away by panic and ignorance. Only a day after Advanced Genetic Sciences announced its "Ice Minus" plans, another California gene-splicing form, Genentech, Inc., told the American Heart Association about a genetically engineered blood-clot dissolver called TPA that it had recently tested on 49 patients who were in the throes of coronary attacks. In 35 of them, the blood clots causing the attacks disappeared within 45 minutes after treatment. This promising drug is produced by splicing the human gene that controls the secretion of TPA into bacteria. No doubt some energetic activist, horrified by this unnatural and diabolical alliance of man and microbe, is at work at this moment on a legal brief that he hopes will save us from this latest menace. But I suspect that it is too late; large-scale clinical trials are underway from Japan to Europe, and the early reports from hospitals across the world are enthusiastic. It will be hard to keep such a drug out of use through paranoia alone, if indeed it can spare millions from the threat of coronary blockage.

Certainly some regulation of genetic engineering is necessary and desirable. (And five government agencies are competing with one another right now for jurisdiction in the field of recombinant DNA.) But I think the time of automatic opposition to any and all artificial life-form creation will soon be at its end. Once the manifest benefits of this startling new science are widely perceived, the purveyors of prophesies of doom will literally be laughed out of court.

Those Sinister Antifreeze Bacteria Again

Dreadful mutant bacteria are loose among us. I hope the world lasts long enough for this to see print.

The sinister bugs are laboratory products, the results of artificially induced mutation via gene-spicing. They were developed by Advanced Genetic Sciences, Inc., a biotechnology company based in Oakland, California—the same placid pastoral community where I live myself. After a legal struggle that lasted for four years, Advanced Genetic Sciences finally received permission to let its new bacteria loose on an experimental plot in the town of Brentwood, California, a farming community of 5800 people located 60 miles east of San Francisco.

The new microorganism bears the trade name of Frostban. It was designed to help plants resist frost, and if it works as intended it may help farmers avert billions of dollars of losses each year and greatly expand the world's food-producing capacity. At first glance that sounds like an entirely meritorious project to which no one could possibly have objections. Why the four-year legal battle, then? Ah, never underestimate the ability of the American public—aided and encouraged by eager "public-interest advocates" and assorted lawyers—to drive itself into a frenzy of hysterical terror when some new scientific development with a scary name appears on the horizon.

Advanced Genetic Sciences began with a bacterium called *Pseudomonas syringae*, which has the capability of inducing water molecules to form ice crystals at low temperatures. By deleting a single gene from its makeup, the scientists produced a form of the bacterium that lacked this ice-inducing capability. Their hope was that Frostban bacteria, released in a field of plants, would displace the less vigorous natural form of *Pseudomonas syringae* and inhibit frost damage on the plants it occupied. Since the original bacterium has no harmful qualities whatever, other than its ability to intensify frost, and the new form differed from its predecessor only to the extent of a single gene, there seemed relatively little risk in releasing Frostban on an experimental test plot to see if it really could ward off injury to plants.

But the moment the plans for tests were announced, the guardians if genetic purity closed in. Jeremy Rifkin, who heads an antibiotechnology group called the Foundation on Economic Trends, filed suit in September, 1983, to block all testing of Frostban, claiming

[*Amazing Stories*, November 1987]

that the altered microbes might multiply uncontrollably beyond the test area with unspecified dangerous consequences. In May, 1984 a Federal District Court ruled in Rifkin's favor, leading to a two-year delay while the Environmental Protection Agency came up with a set of regulations designed to guard against such calamities. Advanced Genetic Sciences persevered through all the legal challenges and finally received permission in February, 1987, to test its critter outside the laboratory. The tests themselves were held, after a flurry of last-minute lawsuits, late in April, 1987.

The precautions that were taken were worthy of some truly Frankensteinian experiment. In the midst of a 200-by-200 test plot were 2300 month-old strawberry plants, surrounded by a wide dirt buffer to keep the microbes from straying. Around the site were 16 generator-powered vacuum machines that the California Department of Food and Agriculture would use to monitor the air around the site. For further scrutiny of possible bacteria migration the state had set up 38 white trays in which barley was growing. Seven steel towers equipped with additional sophisticated devices rose on the borders of the plot. State officials stood ready to spray chemical pesticides into adjoining fields if any Frostban bacteria should escape. The technicians who would spray the bacteria on the plants were enclosed in head-to-toe protective gear very much like space-suits, complete with goggles and respirators.

Despite all this, terror ran high. One 27-year-old Brentwood housewife, four months pregnant, left her home four miles from the test site and moved into a hotel in another town, saying she planned to remain there "until my money runs out. If I was rich I would have moved." Other local people expressed misgivings also, though not so dramatically. And Andy Caffrey of Earth First, a radical environmentalist group opposing the test, declared, "There are too many vested interests involved in regulating and evaluating this technology. How can we be sure that these bugs are receiving objective evaluations and are safe?"

The night before the experiment, environmental-minded vandals cut through the chain-link fence surrounding the text plot and uprooted four-fifths of the small plants that were to be used. "I'm thrilled," Caffrey said the next morning. "I'm sorry they didn't do a better job." The plants, though damaged, were put back in the ground and the experiment proceeded as planned—covered by television crews from as far away as Japan. Since frost does not occur in California in late April, the plants bearing the altered bacterium will now be transported to a laboratory where they will undergo simulated winter conditions. Apparently there was no escape of Frostban bacteria into the surrounding countryside.

"I'm elated," said Dr. John Bedbrook, one of the scientists involved in the project. "It's good for the company and it's good for the industry. The judicial system has evaluated and recognized the thoroughness of the regulatory process for this industry." Elgin Martin, whose 110-acre pear farm is located right next door to the test site, was equally pleased. "This is the wave of the future, I think, in dealing with our bug problems, our frost problems," he said. "Hopefully, it'll really take off." But from Jack Doyle of the Environmental Policy Institute in Washington came the warning, "The people of California should really carefully weigh the high-tech fever that seems to be sweeping the nation," and other leaders in the campaign against genetic manipulation called for intensified legal opposition to such research.

Did the release of Frostban in Brentwood, California bring an end to life on Earth as we know it? As I write this, a few weeks later, it's much too early to tell—but you may already be feeling the dire impact by the time this issue reaches you in the autumn. Or perhaps not. It seems to me that legitimate concern over uncontrolled scientific experimentation became fused with a peculiarly anachronistic fear of science in this case—as though perhaps the specter of atomic holocaust now rises so high above the world of the late twentieth century that *all* scientific research has come to seem equally threatening, and an easily manipulated populace sees new devastating horrors lurking in every laboratory. Even Frostban's opponents privately admitted that the altered bacterium was almost certainly harmless. But they saw a way of launching a test case that might choke off gene-splicing research before it could lead to more dangerous things.

I am not, of course, advocating letting the folks in the white coats do whatever they want. Scientists, as a class, are just as prone to misjudgment as anyone else, and the time to monitor their activities is *before* the carnivorous amoebas are accidentally let loose in the water supply. But the dialog between the genetic sciences and the guardians of the status quo must not be turned into a shrill demand for suppression of all research.

Nor will it be. Frostban has been tested, finally, and gene-splicing work of many another kind goes forward elsewhere. At the University of California at Davis, a laboratory run by Dr. Donald Durzan has inserted the gene responsible for a firefly's glow into cells of fir and pine trees. The project is one of pure research; but Dr. Durzan says playfully that it might some day have significant commercial results. Christmas trees in the next century, he quips, might come with their own built-in lights.

The Case Against the Antifreeze Bacteria

Some further words on genetic engineering—
Regular readers of this column will be aware that I've devoted considerable space to an examination of the widespread public uneasiness over all manner of gene-splicing experiments, including some that even the dedicated enemies of such research privately admit are harmless. (Which doesn't stop them from going into court to block tests of them, nor from encouraging vandalism of experimental sites.) I have argued that genetic research of this kind, while of course holding the potential for danger if misapplied or improperly conducted, is perhaps our best available route for dealing with such problems as famine, disease, and hereditary physical defects; and that much of the opposition to it comes from those who have allowed themselves to be stampeded into a panic response to *all* scientific research, be it designed to produce spaceships, cures for cancer, or bigger nuclear bombs.

From reader Leslie Fish of El Cerrito, California—a town near San Francisco, where much of this campaigning against science originates—comes a lengthy letter discussing my column on the "Frostban" bacterium that apparently enables agricultural crops to put up greater resistance to killing frosts. This microorganism finally was allowed a field test in 1987, after several years of legal delays, and no harmful results have yet been detected from its exposure in the Northern California atmosphere.

Ms. Fish notes that the recent tests, despite elaborate security precautions, still failed to come up to her ideal safety standards:

> "Sure, the field was enclosed by berms and ditches and air-monitoring towers—but it was still open to air. *Pseudomonas* [the frost-fighting bacterium] has been known to hitch rides on dust-motes and travel a good long way on a favorable wind. What use would those air-monitors be in such a case, except to note that the beastie was, indeed, escaping?
>
> "Second, even supposedly-harmless bacteria and viri [sic] have been known to mutate into dangerous forms, and there's good reasons to believe that gene-splicing tends, by weakening intergenetic bonds, to encourage further mutation. Besides, not all members of the *pseudomonas* family are harmless; some of them cause nasty infections in human beings. It isn't wise to give *pseudomonas syringae* any encouragement to imitate the black sheep of the family.

[*Amazing Stories*, May 1988]

"Third, the whole program was wastefully unnecessary. Its basic premise (The Screwfly Solution!) of having the non-iceforming bacteria replace the natural iceforming variety is a gamble at best. Why *should* the laboratory-bred beastie displace its wild cousin? The wild *pseudo. s.*, having evolved in the natural environment, is thoroughly adapted to survival therein; the laboratory-bred *pseudo.* may very well not be. If the lab-bred beastie is, in fact, 'more vigorous' than its wild cousin, then there's reason to worry about its future spread, mutation, adaptability, and possible danger. You can't have it both ways. Besides, there already exists several topical *pseudo*-cides on the market; it wasn't necessary to create a new bug to push out the old one. The risks and the costs of this little experiment totally outweigh the possible benefits."

These are not foolish arguments, nor are they foolishly set forth. Even so, what they come down to, it seems to me, is a combination of reactionary attitudes toward progress and out-and-out panic over scientific research. Ms. Fish fears mutant bacteria more than she fears a killing frost. (Farmers might take the opposing position.) True enough, not all agricultural aids have been ultimately beneficial: consider the havoc that the insecticide DDT worked in the environment before it was suppressed. But must we shut down the gene labs because there is the *chance* that a harmless bacterium will mutate into a dangerous one? Must we get along with current frost-protection techniques (smudgepots, etc.) because there's the *risk* that this new one may develop into some lethal menace? How big a risk is there, anyway? And what is the risk of never taking risks?

Ms. Fish's underlying position is revealed a little later in her letter:

"But beyond the Frostban caper itself, why should you assume that all opposition to any new scientific development is no more than superstitious hysteria? God knows, modern science has given us several hellish inventions to fear! I'm not just talking about The Bomb, or even other vicious weapons that tunnel-visioned scientists have duly created and obediently handed over to assorted generals. Consider also the unlovely developments in germ warfare, spy-devices, privacy-invading electronics techniques, new methods of torture and mind-control, exotic new poisons, the joys of toxic waste, iatrogenic diseases and high-tech crime."

Against the *reductio ad absurdum* the gods themselves contend in vain. Yes, Ms. Fish, science has given us all those dreadful things. But also we have been provided with the polio and smallpox vaccines, safe and easy travel to other continents (and other planets!), open-heart surgery, flashlights, anesthesia, oxygen tents for premature babies, and several other such things which all but the most confirmed anti-modernist is likely to agree have improved the quality of life. "So long as scientists continue to whore for governments and big business (two groups notorious for valuing money and power far more than the well-being of citizens) they will be feared and hated along with their masters," Ms. Fish declares. It's a familiar argument, even a stale one: to me it sounds like radical rhetoric out of the 1930's.

Fortunately for our future, most people disagree with the sort of arguments Ms. Fish presents. A nationwide poll taken in the fall of 1986 by Lou Harris & Associates found that "as in other areas of science and technology, people favor the continued development and application of biotechnology and genetic engineering. Obstruction of technological development is not a popular cause in the United States in the mid-1980's." The survey showed that two thirds of those questioned believed that genetic engineering would improve the quality of life, and would approve testing genetically engineered organisms in their own communities. 58% favored widescale use of genetically-altered microbes. 80% said it was not morally wrong to change the genetic makeup of human cells to cure hereditary diseases. (But more than half disapproved of using genetic engineering for cosmetic changes such as altering eye or skin color, or to improve human intelligence.)

All the same, I think such critics of gene-splicing research as Leslie Fish and Jeremy Rifkin are valuable and even necessary. Optimistic though I am about the future of this work, I'm not so naive as to be unaware of the risks. (Nor are the people polled by Lou Harris: a majority felt that it was likely that genetically engineered products would someday cause serious danger to people or the environment. Nevertheless, they are willing to take the risk for the sake of the benefits that may be gained.) We are venturing into unknown territory, and the debate over aims and methods is a useful dialectical process that will curb excess, reduce risk, and hold in check just the sort of scientific arrogance that Ms. Fish perhaps too keenly fears (but which certainly exists.) Nothing will halt genetic research now: the genie, Ms. Fish, is out of the jar to stay. But people like you, much as I disagree with you, are helping to see to it that we keep our wits about us as we ask that potent but unpredictable genie to work his miracles on our behalf.

Killer Tomatoes from Outer Space

On the one hand, we have denial. ("The bad things that I read about in the newspaper can only happen to other people.") On the other hand, there's credulity. ("I understand that the sky is due to fall next Tuesday and NASA has suppressed a scientific report about it.") Most people these days seem to veer from one extreme to the other, rarely pausing to spend much time in the moderate middle, which some of us (me, Socrates, you) find a calmer place to inhabit. And so it goes, the world getting sillier as things get more complex. The latest example of sky-is-falling credulity is the great Killer Tomatoes from Outer Space uproar that enlivened our lives for a few days in the spring of 1990.

Since by the time this piece appears, the world and the media that bring the world to us will have moved on to five other scary subjects, perhaps I'd better refresh everybody's memory about this one:

The space shuttle *Challenger*, during the course of a voyage it made in 1984, launched into orbit an eleven-ton satellite that contained various experiments designed to provide information about the long-term effects of space exposure on living cells. Among other things, the satellite was carrying some 12,500,000 tomato seeds.

The satellite spent six years orbiting the Earth. Then it was recovered, in January of 1990, by the space shuttle *Columbia*. NASA packed the tomato seeds into little envelopes marked SPACE EXPOSED SEED and sent 120,000 of the packets to teachers all over the country, on every educational level from elementary school to college. The idea was that the students would plant the seeds and report back to NASA on their viability after having spent six years being bombarded by cosmic radiation.

Perhaps it was a dumb idea to use schoolchildren to carry out this experiment. Whatever research on irradiated seeds needed to be done could probably have been performed just as easily, with none of the attendant bad publicity, in some government research facility in Louisiana or Kentucky. The seeds would have been planted, a dozen government botanists would tend them for six months, the tomatoes would ripen and would be taken home for dinner by the botanists. And a couple of years later, at a cost of $145,000,000, a report would have appeared to the effect that it appears to be quite feasible to grow normal tomato plants from seed that has spent six years in space.

[*Amazing Stories*, November 1990]

But no: NASA wants to involve the schoolchildren of the nation in the noble work of space exploration. What simpler way to do it than to hand out tomato seeds and let them plant little Space Gardens in 120,000 classrooms?

NASA should have remembered that those seeds were carried into space in the first place by the shuttle *Challenger*. And, a couple of years later, it was that very shuttle, then attempting to involve schoolchildren in the space effort by carrying an actual teacher into space, which met such a tragic end in the skies over Florida. Perhaps there was a curse on the thing—one specifically designed to blight all of NASA's high-minded efforts to link space exploration and classroom life.

Here's what happened with those space-going tomato seeds:

The Los Angeles *Times* somehow discovered that a NASA contractor had written a memorandum speculating that "radiation-caused mutations could cause the plants to produce toxic fruit." The fear was that a toxic substance frequently found in tomato foliage might penetrate the fruit of tomatoes that had undergone space-induced mutations. The memo—which wasn't supposed to be circulated outside NASA—went on to say that the research director at Park Seed Company, from which NASA had obtained the seeds, "seemed to favor against" consumption of the tomatoes.

NASA officials had looked at the memo and had treated it as the nonsense it was. They filed and forgot it—but then it fell into the hands of the crusading journalists of the Los Angeles *Times*.

Oh, my! The schoolchildren of the nation exposed to lethal mutated tomatoes from space!

A normal level-headed reaction on the part of the public might have been to say that anyone who uses phrases like "seemed to favor against" must be a life-form of very low-grade intelligence indeed, and dismiss the whole absurd notion just as NASA itself had done. But this is the late twentieth century, when people get frightened very, very easily, especially when terms such as "radiation" and "mutation" are used. So there was, of course, a tremendous if short-lived flap over the risky tomatoes. Parents demanded explanations. Teachers feared lawsuits if they dared let their precious little charges so much as handle the deadly seeds. Newspapers all around the country had a field day.

NASA, seeing its experiment going down the drain, sent a one-page statement to all the teachers who had received the seed packets, telling them that there was nothing to fear. A NASA public-relations man declared, "We have absolutely no evidence to suggest that there is any safety risk associated with these plants above and beyond that of growing tomatoes or other plants in any normal setting....I would certainly hope that on the basis of the press reports or whatever that schools would not make a decision to withdraw from the program." When asked whether NASA should have included a warning with the tomato seeds that they might have the potential for producing monstrous progeny, he replied, "We are not at all uncomfortable with how we handled it. In fact, we are very comfortable. We feel we did a very responsible job."

From Alvin Young, a science adviser to the Department of Agriculture who had helped organized the experiment, came corroboration: "I've never heard of a killer tomato, and I don't think we've got a killer tomato planted here either." Young admitted that there was a slight chance that such a mutation might occur, but regarded the possibility as "very, very remote." He noted that "we can't say with 100 per cent certainty. There is always a small risk with every research experiment. But that is why it is research. That is the fun part."

These words of reassurance probably had the opposite effect on the most timorous of the teachers. Alvin Young's admission that there might actually be some risk—a chance in a million, say—probably led some of them to get rid of the seeds immediately. This is, after all, a society that has come to abhor all risks, even one-in-a-million ones.

More to the point, maybe, was the statement from Jim Alston, director of research at Park Seed Company in South Carolina, where the dreaded seeds originated. The space seeds, Alston said, had been exposed to far less radiation during their six years overhead than seeds used in "normal breeding programs" on Earth, in which X-rays and gamma rays are regularly used. Such a statement might induce people of a certain way of thinking to give up eating tomatoes altogether, but it does indicate that there's nothing unusual to fear from the seeds from space.

At any rate, some of the seeds were prudently discarded, and some were planted despite all fear, and we'll soon know the answer. As I write this, the dear little yellow flowers are sprouting all over the nation's classrooms, and shortly afterward the first sweet little red fruits will be appearing. By the time you come to be reading these words, some of the tomatoes, at least, will be ripe, and some will have been eaten by reckless sixth-graders, who may be the only people in the United States who haven't yet become afraid of their shadows. If your little boy has begun glowing green, you might want to have your lawyer get in touch with NASA, the Department of Agriculture, and Park Seed Company of South Carolina. (Jim Alston is the man to give the summons to there.) But I suggest you wait and let your sixth-grader grow up, and see what *his* kids are like. Your ultimate damage claim can be a lot higher if your grandchildren turn out to have extra heads or nasty extrasensory powers.

Genetic Luddites Yet Again

Against stupidity," Isaac Asimov would say, quoting Schiller, "the gods themselves contend in vain."

The gods have been losing a lot of battles lately. The latest buzzword marking mankind's continued descent into mindlessness is *Frankenfood*—the nifty instant cliche coined by one Paul Lewis of Newton Center, Massachusetts, to describe agricultural products that have been created by genetic engineering.

What products does he mean? Chy-max, for instance, a coagulant currently used in making cheese. Since nature's own coagulants tend to be a little unpredictable, gene-splicing technology was employed to devise Chy-max, which makes completely consistent cheese.

Or the Flavr-Savr, a rot-resistant tomato that is going to be placed on sale in 1993. Unlike conventional tomatoes, which are picked when still green and tasteless and then artificially reddened so that they will *look* (though not taste) ripe when they finally reach the market a few weeks later, Flavr-Savrs (from which the gene responsible for making ripe fruit soften has been excised) will be harvested when they're nearly ripe, since they won't turn soggy during the time it takes them to go on sale. They should not, however, be confused with the as yet unnamed tomato, now in the gene-engineering stage, which would be frost resistant thanks to the addition of a fish gene that has antifreeze properties—thus significantly reducing crop losses.

Coffee plants that produce natural decaf? Wheat with built-in growth stimulants, making environmentally risky chemical fertilization unnecessary? Chickens in which a DNA fragment has been added to make them resistant to salmonella? All of it accomplished by genetic manipulation—employing enzymes to move genes from one organism into another, or to suppress or eliminate certain genes altogether. O brave new world, that has such biotechnical wonders available for its farmers!

But, of course, the know-nothings are lining up in opposition already. "Frankenfood," they call it. Or, with equal verbal vulgarity, "Sci-Fi food." Once again we see the great American consuming public being literally scared silly by the merchants of fear, with inevitable harmful consequences for everybody.

"The public is scared of the word genetic," says Dr. Jean-Marc

[*Asimov's Science Fiction*, November 1992]

Pernet, a biotechnologist for the Rouquette Corporation, which is doing genetic research on carbohydrates in Gurnee, Illinois. "We are working on a number of products, but we know very well that developing the technology will be easier than marketing the technology." To which Dr. Susan K. Harlander, a professor of food science and nutrition at the University of Minnesota, adds, "There's a distrust of technology, distrust of corporate profits, distrust of Government regulatory agencies, and general fears about the safety of the food supply." But genetic technology, she says, should not casually be lumped in with the Chernobyl power-plant catastrophe and the environmental damage caused by DDT and other insecticides. Its techniques are simply a high-tech extension of techniques that farmers have been using for centuries. "If the public understood the technology, they would understand that part of their emotional reaction is irrational," says Dr. Harlander.

What has touched off the current uproar over genetic enhancement of agriculture is the Federal Government's announcement, early in June of 1992, that it would not require specific testing or labeling for an assortment of genetically engineered food products due to come on the market over the following eighteen months. Advance testing will be done, we were told, only if products are altered in such a way that safety issues are raised—for example, if genes from peanuts, to which some people are lethally allergic, should be added to grains.

There was an immediate barrage of protest from a variety of self-styled "advocacy groups" already noted for their anti-science attitudes—led, naturally, by Jeremy Rifkin, the arch-enemy of genetic engineering, who warned of dire consequences arising from the mixing of genes and called for boycotts of the new products by farmers and food distributors.

Can it be that there are certain foods that mankind was not meant to eat?

So say the chefs of some of the country's upscale restaurants, who—always quick to detect trends among their well-heeled customers—banded together in July of 1992 to denounce the new foods and to announce that they would not be allowed into their kitchens. "I am not willing to offer my patrons, my family, or myself as a testing ground for a new generation of bioengineered foods," said Rick Moonen, chef at New York's Water Club restaurant. "I know what Mother Nature intended with regard to food, and I trust in that. I have not yet been convinced [that] bioengineered foods deserve that same trust." And from Nathan Peterson, chef at Oakland's top-ranked Bay

Wolf, came the comment, "Who needs it? And what is going to come along next, tomatoes grown in Antarctica? It makes no sense and it upsets me, especially when I start wondering who is profiting from all this."

Which brought a retort from the other side: Jeffrey Needleman, a spokesman for the Grocery Manufacturers of America: "Efforts to cast genetically engineered foods as unsafe are based on Chicken Little science and are being led by nutritional neurotics. Consumer safety is our first priority." As for the boycott by the top chefs, cynical onlookers have noted that the restaurants where they work would not have been very likely to use the new products in any case, and that the chefs are merely posturing to reassure their finicky, easily alarmed customers. As Catherine Brandel, the chef at Berkeley's famed Chez Panisse, observed, "This type of food has nothing to do with us. Why would we want shelf-life and season extenders, when we can buy fresh produce and meats from local growers every day?"

Not everyone, though, can eat at Chez Panisse every day. Nathan Peterson wonders who will be profiting from the new food products. Here's a brief list:

—Gene-splicing scientists, naturally.
—Farmers. (Including the dreaded Large Agricultural Corporations.)
—Food distributors and marketers. (Some of them Very Large also.)
—People who shop for food and cook and eat it at home.

Note that the list of the beneficiaries of gene-splicing technology begins with the sinister Dr. Frankensteins of the food laboratories, descends through the vile profiteers of agribusiness, and ends with, basically, you. You will be buying and eating riper, fresher, more flavorful food, and the chances are that you will be paying less for it than you do now, because crop productivity is likely to be enhanced and many current-day spoilage problems that cause waste between growing fields and supermarkets will be solved with artful placement of DNA. Grumbling about "Frankenfood," it seems to me, is pretty much like complaining about refrigeration, which wasn't available to the decent farmers and shippers of the nineteenth century and is probably corrupting our present-day foodstuffs with who knows what strange emanations.

I don't mean to say that technology is omniscient and all-benevolent, or that there aren't problems in the new science that need to be addressed. Would the use of peanut genes in wheat, say, affect that fraction of the population that reacts catastrophically to peanuts? Nobody knows yet, and it's important to find out. And the issue of those who observe food taboos has been raised: Moslems and Orthodox Jews, for instance. Suppose genes from pigs were inserted in cucumbers. Eating pork is forbidden by the teachings of Moses and Mohammed: but do those teachings apply to a bit of pig DNA in a vegetable? That would be one for the theologians to decide; but should the orthodox not at least be warned of the animal content of their groceries?

These are real issues—at least, if you happen to be allergic to peanuts, or reluctant to eat pork in whatever form. But I'm certain that they'll be dealt with in a responsible manner. What I'm concerned with is the fundamental anti-scientific character of the opposition to gene-splicing: the know-nothing hysteria of it, the frantic and fearful knee-jerk hatred of the new. "The public is always critical and afraid of change," says Jerry Caulfield, who heads the biotech company Mycogen. "We need to evaluate risk by separating the probable from the possible." And Roger Salquist of Calgene, which has developed the Flavr-Savr tomato, adds, "The idea that we are interested in producing science-fiction creations is nonsense. We're doing meat-and-potatoes type work to develop food and food production systems that are user friendly, that consumers say they want. It's very expensive to develop products; we're looking for things that will sell."

What will happen, I suspect, is that technology will ultimately prevail, as usual—a hungry world needs every food-producing improvement it can develop—but with a political and economic cost. The know-nothings will succeed in getting all manner of complex labeling rules imposed on food producers, after which the new products will appear, but at a higher price. (If we ban gene-splicing here, which I don't see as likely, improved foods will be shipped to us from other countries that lack our finely developed sense of technological phobia.) In ten years the controversy will be forgotten and the products will be established—complete with the mystifying and costly set of restrictions designed to protect us against mad scientists—and the Jeremy Rifkins of the day will be tilting at a different set of windmills. Too bad. Against stupidity, the man said, the gods themselves contend in vain.

The Last of the Codfish

The kids are illiterate and toting semiautomatic weapons, all the nice soft jobs are being restructured out of existence, the ozone layer is giving out, frogs seem to be going the way of the dodo and the passenger pigeon, and now our fishing fleets are coming home with empty nets because the sea is running out of fish.

That's the bad news, folks. The good news is that all these twenty-first century horrors that are descending on us simultaneously in such terrible haste may simply be part of a normal cycle. In the natural course of events, the scientists are telling us, things tend to get bad for a while, and then they get better. Apparently it's been going on like this for millions of years. If we can only stay out of the line of fire long enough, that is, we may very well survive into a world where the little no-neck horrors all around us aren't pushing AK-47s into our faces.

Let's take a look at the fish problem first. Then we can try to soothe ourselves with the hope of rescue through inevitable cyclical upturn.

The news from the seas is definitely bad. More than half of the animal protein we consume comes in the form of seafood. The U.N. Food and Agriculture Office has broken down the seventy percent of this planet that is covered by ocean into seventeen main fisheries. Of these, four are now officially classified as "commercially depleted" and nine are described as being in "serious decline."

What this means, in more concrete terms, is that the Pacific Northwest fishermen whose livelihood depends on salmon may have to take the entire year off, because the salmon aren't there any longer in quantities worth going after.

In New England, where vast harvests of cod, haddock, and flounder have been reaped since the seventeenth century, the number of fish has dropped to such a low level that the Government has put in force a plan restricting fishing days, so as to allow the remaining fish to rebuild their populations, and has banned fishing altogether along the Georges Bank, east of Cape Cod, where once-plentiful stocks of fish have been virtually exhausted. On the Grand Banks of Newfoundland, cod fishing has also been banned—the cod has been designated "commercially extinct"—and 30,000 people have lost their jobs.

The Chesapeake Bay oyster industry is largely a thing of the past. The grouper and red snapper that were taken in such great numbers

[*Asimov's Science Fiction*, January 1995]

in the Gulf of Mexico are pretty much history. In California, Monterey's Cannery Row is now a street lined with art galleries and restaurants and T-shirt shops, because the sardines that kept the canneries busy all during the first half of this century no longer are found in Monterey Bay.

What's going on? Are we facing a future in which the bagels will have no lox, the Caesar salads will lack anchovies, and shrimp cocktails will be available only on the third Tuesday of the month? Probably not, as a matter of fact. But the era of hunting seafood in the wild may very well be coming to an end.

Pollution and other environmental abuse—as in the case of the Pacific salmon, whose freshwater spawning grounds have been fouled or blocked by dams—is part of the problem. But it's a surprisingly small part. The draining of wetlands and the dumping of toxic substances into estuaries and the breakup of huge oil tankers on the high seas have all had sorry consequences, of course; but the world's oceans are vast beyond even our capacity to fill them up with junk. The real villain seems to be something a lot more elementary: too many fishermen chasing a finite quantity of fish.

Gone are the days when little bands of plucky men went down to the sea in ships to wrest precarious livelihoods from the turbulent waves. They have been replaced, largely, by giant corporate trawlers, equipped with sonar and other sophisticated devices and employing satellite communications to track their prey, that swoop up whole marine populations in enormous gulps. The inhabitants of the sea, immense though their numbers may be, can tolerate only so much swooping before the rate of consumption begins to exceed that of reproduction. And the effects of a decade of steady overfishing are now being felt worldwide.

To some degree the seafood shortfall is being made up by farm-raised fish, grown in pens off the coast of Scandinavia and South America. (The easy availability of certain types of fish from these sources has, paradoxically, accelerated the destruction of the conventional fisheries; faced with the competition of cheap pen-grown fish, fishermen who harvest the seas have been making ever deeper inroads into the available fish schools in order to earn a living.)

And in places where conservation measures have ensured some degree of population balance, the fisheries are actually on the upturn. Salmon are far from extinct in Alaska, where a record 200 million fish were caught in 1993. The size of the Alaskan salmon catch is carefully regulated, though, to allow a surplus of spawning over harvesting. In

New England, the lobster industry is still doing well, and sea bass and mackerel are returning along the East Coast now that some degree of protection has been imposed. These are promising signs, and they may signal a trend. Even diehard libertarians—and I incline in that direction myself—find themselves applauding government intervention where reckless and uncontrolled harvesting of the marine crop has begun to triumph even over the economic self-interest of the harvesters.

And then, from another quarter, comes the suggestion—of considerable philosophical interest, and possibly of economic value too— that large-scale fluctuations in animal populations may in fact be random events, the product of inherent instability in the natural world. It may, in fact, be quite normal for any animal species to undergo wild and unpredictable population swings over long periods of time, whether or not the trawlers have sonar.

This is not to say that the extinction of the dodo, say, was the result of a mere stochastic blip. The dodo was a slow-moving, defenseless bird, incapable of flight, that happened to live on a small and isolated island where it had no natural enemies, human or otherwise. Dutch explorers showed up there in 1598. They found dodo meat good to eat; their pet dogs developed a fondness for gobbling dodo chicks; and the rats that slipped ashore from the Dutch ships went after the dodo eggs in the unprotected nests. In less than a century there were no dodos left. That was no statistical event, though: it was simple genocide.

But larger animal populations, according to a study done at the University of California at Davis and published in *Science* some months back, appear to experience startling fluctuations in their numbers for reasons that seem to be wholly unconnected with the onslaughts of predators, environmental changes, climatic shifts, or any other apparent external cause.

Computer analysis of the life cycle of the Dungeness crab, extended over tens of thousands of generations, showed chaotic patterns of population size to be the norm. Environmental conditions were left entirely out of the model; the only factors for change in population that went into the equation were internal ones such as competition for food or living space. One might expect that in any one zone inhabited by crabs, the size of the crab population would fluctuate in direct homeostatic response to these two factors—a population explosion in times of easy food availability, followed by a population decline when the number of crabs along that coast increased to a point where food became scarce. Instead, the Davis researchers found that total population numbers might remain steady for thousand of generations, and then suddenly undergo a startling quantitative change—an immense boom, or an equally emphatic crash that seemingly is without rational explanation.

All of which is very disturbing to the pure Darwinian thinker. It introduces an unwelcome note of chaos into our understanding of how the natural world functions. As Dr. Simon Levin, the director of the Princeton Environmental Institute, puts it, "The recognition that systems are not at or very close to equilibrium certainly complicates the world view of some people who are trying to manage systems." Yet there are ample real-world examples of such volatility. History records any number of sudden pestiferous plagues of locusts or mice. Huge increases in bat populations are not uncommon; frogs, as we are seeing, now seem to be in worldwide decline; the sardines stopped coming to Monterey in 1947; the lobster population off Maine is some 50% higher now than it was a decade ago, a change that can't be accounted for simply by improved conservation policies.

Perhaps we can evoke chaos theory to console ourselves for more than one contemporary problem. The development of excessively efficient fish-harvesting technology, let us say, has coincided fortuitously but unfortunately (note the distinction!) with a random downward fluctuation in certain marine populations. What must be done now, therefore, is to cut back on commercial oceanic fishing, as much as is possible consonant with the nutritional needs of the world's human population, until the next random twitch of the reproductive cycle restocks our oceans. And all our current societal problems are, likewise, just a random disequilibrium event that will sooner or later undergo compensatory damping and go away.

It would be nice to think so, anyway.

Extinct Again

Shed a tear for the ungainly old coelacanth. Very likely it's about to become extinct for the second—and, alas—final time.

The coelacanth (pronounced SEE-la-kanth), which is not the prettiest fish in the ocean but is surely one of the most interesting, belongs to that select group of life-forms that we call "living fossils": life-forms which for one fluky reason or another have resisted the pressures of time and evolution and have survived down through millions or even hundreds of millions of years, virtually unchanged from their primeval forms. Cockroaches, silverfishes, centipedes, and horseshoe crabs all belong to this group. Their fossil histories go back to the Mesozoic, or even earlier. The large flightless birds of the Southern Hemisphere—the ostrich, the rhea, the emu, the cassowary— also qualify as survivors from a remote time. The penguin is another; so is the little kiwi of New Zealand, and the curious aquatic South American bird known as the hoatzin. The whole marsupial fauna of Australia falls into the living-fossil class—kangaroos, wallabies, ko- alas, bandicoots, and wombats—and so does, of course, the strangest Australian animal of all, the duck-billed platypus.

Charles Darwin was the first to propose a reason to explain the survival of these creatures across the epochs. Darwin, who coined the phrase *living fossil* when he wrote *Origin of Species*, wrote, "They have endured to the present day from having inhabited a confined area, and from having been exposed to less varied, and therefore less severe, competition."

That accounts for such animals as the marsupials, living in grand isolation in remote Australia, cut off by great expanses of ocean from the other continents and thus untroubled for millions of years by the need to compete against the later-evolving placental mammals that are so much more efficient in so many ways. Other creatures are naturally long-lived, and have many offspring, so they are difficult to wipe out. Some are so tough and durable that they can withstand almost any change in their living conditions. And some are so per- fectly adapted to their niche in the biological scheme of things that there doesn't seem to be any pressing need for them to evolve any further. The cockroach is a perfect example of all these traits. The fossil record shows that its form has undergone no essential structural change over the past two or three hundred million years, and very likely it will go marching on virtually unchanged into the unimagin-

[*Asimov's Science Fiction*, April 1996]

able future, despite the best efforts of Johnny-come-lately species like our own to interfere with its way of life.

The coelacanth first turned up in fossil form in England in 1840. It was an odd-looking fish indeed, heavy-bodied and notably un-streamlined, with thick, fleshy fins shaped like small paddles with soft fringes at one end, set on odd stumpy stalks that must have looked almost like the beginnings of legs. Other discoveries of similar primitive-looking fossil fishes followed, in strata ranging from 60 million to 350 million years ago, and they were all grouped as *coelacanths,* meaning "hollow-spined fishes." One spectacular find was made in New Jersey when Princeton University was building a new university. The excavations revealed hundreds of 180-million-year-old coelacanth fossils packed a dozen to the square foot in the rock.

What no one expected was the discovery of a *live* coelacanth, But just such a thing made its appearance three days before Christmas, 1938, when a fishing trawler pulled into port at East London, South Africa, bearing a huge, weird-looking blue fish that had been caught in the warm waters along Africa's southeastern coast. It was four and a half feet long, weighed more than a hundred pounds, and had an enormous mouth, oversized scales, and fins set on thick meaty stalks. The captain, aware that he had pulled in something unusual, notified the East London Museum, which called in a local chemistry instructor, Dr. J.L.B. Smith, the leading authority on the fishes of South Africa.

By the time Dr. Smith—who was away on Christmas holiday—reached East London, the fish had died and begun to decay; the museum people were forced to discard its flesh and inner organs, but were able to mount its skin and bones. Dr. Smith's first sight of the stuffed fish, he wrote later, "hit me like a white-hot blast and made me feel shaky and queer; my body tingled. I stood as if stricken to stone. Yes, there was not the shadow of a doubt, scale by scale, bone by bone, fin by fin, it was a true coelacanth."

The discovery touched off an enormous scientific uproar. The coelacanth, so far as anyone knew, had been extinct as long as the dinosaurs—and now, suddenly, one had come forth into our own time like an ambassador from the Late Cretaceous. Were there more of them skulking in those deep African waters? Dr. Smith distributed thousands of leaflets along the coast in English, Portuguese, and French, offering cash rewards for other coelacanths.

Fourteen years passed before the next one was found, taken by a native fisherman from the Comoro Islands, which lie between Madagascar and the African mainland. The big fish had put up such a fight that the fisherman had to hit it with a stick to kill it; then he took it to the market to sell for food, but another man recognized it as the fish for which the reward had been offered, and brought it to a local English skipper, who quickly preserved it in formaldehyde. Dr. Smith, dissecting it soon afterward, was astonished by the archaic structure of the fish's internal organs. Beyond doubt it belonged to the ancient group of fishes known as *crossopterygians*, from the Greek words from "fringe" and "fin"—the only species of crossopterygian that has survived to the present day.

September, 1953 saw the discovery of a third coelacanth; three more were taken in January, 1954, and another ten months later. All came from the waters around the Comoro Islands; all were dead when brought to shore. In November, 1954 an eighth coelacanth was found, and this time it was captured alive; but despite all efforts to care for it, it died within a few hours.

Four decades of extensive scientific research have demonstrated the presence of an extensive colony of coelacanths, numbering many hundreds or even thousands, dwelling in a narrow zone of the Indian Ocean near the Comoros. Some 200 have been caught and brought ashore for examination; and scientists using submersible vehicles have studied and photographed living coelacanths in their own habitat. They make their homes close to shore, in submarine caves that lie about 650 feet deep, from which they emerge at night to cruise even deeper waters in search of the bottom-dwelling fish that are their prey. They are, of course, protected by law: the Federal Islamic Republic of Comoros has made it illegal to catch them.

The problem is, though, that the coelacanths are only too catchable. Fishing is a major source of livelihood for the Comoro Islanders, and the big, bizarre-looking coelacanths readily take hooks that are meant for more ordinary fishes. The island fishermen would be happy to unhook them and toss them back, but that isn't so simple: coelacanths are powerful fighters, equipped with dagger-sharp teeth, and in order to retrieve their valuable hooks the fishermen generally have to kill them. Even those that are released alive usually die from the damage done by pressure changes during their journey up from the depths.

The ironic result is that the coelacanth, having eluded scientific discovery until our own era, may soon actually be as extinct as it once was thought to be. Studies made between 1991 and 1994 along one five-mile stretch of the coastline of the largest of the Comoro Islands show that the once extensive population of coelacanths in the caves there has fallen in just three years from an average of 20.5 fish per cave to 6.5. There may be only 200 of the primeval fish still alive in the region of the Comoros—not enough, really, to ensure the species' survival very much longer.

Nor can much be done to halt the coelacanth's plunge toward final extinction. Capturing some and putting them in aquariums to breed is apparently impossible: no captured coelacanth has ever lasted more than a few hours. Banning all fishing in the waters where they live is equally impossible: it would destroy the economy of the Comoro Islands.

So it appears that the Comoro fishermen will go on catching the occasional coelacanth, and bashing it on the head and throwing it back after retrieving their fishhooks, and one by one these last of the crossopterygians will perish. "The coelacanth," says Dr. Hans Fricke of the Max Planck Institute for Behavioural Physiology, which makes an annual census of the Comoro coelacanth population, "is something special....A remarkable fish, a window into the distant past and a treasure of nature. If we let him die out it will be a tragedy." But this tragedy, like that of Oedipus Rex and most other true tragedies, appears to be unavoidable, a matter of immutable destiny. The coelacanth has had a good long run, hundreds of millions of years. But there are too many of us and too few of it, and its time is just about over. Which I regret very much. Still, the coelacanth did pretty well for itself, as the lifetime of a species goes. As Isaac Asimov might have said, we should only live so long.

A Species Saved Is a Species Earned

Environmentalists and people who wear "Save the Planet" T-shirts and those who worry about what they call "the ecology" can rejoice. Another precious and endangered species of life on our planet has been rescued from the brink of extinction, at least for a while.

The great auk? The quagga? The moa? No, sorry—they're all irretrievably gone. I'm talking about the smallpox virus. What once was a vital, passionate part of the Earth's immense population of living things had been reduced to a tiny semblance of its former self, a few hapless captives sealed in laboratory flasks; and even those last remaining valiant survivors were about to be handed over to the executioners. But no! A reprieve has been ordered! These tiny, frail organisms will not be wiped out after all—not immediately, anyway.

Does all this sound crazy to you? Do you think I'm whipping up some sort of black-humor spoof? Actually, I'm not. This is a true story. And it leads us into consideration of some very tricky philosophical issues.

Smallpox is, of course, a nasty disease. Over the course of human history (and prehistory) the barely visible smallpox virus condemned millions of people to death or, at best, to horrible disfigurement. It altered the destiny of nations and undermined entire civilizations. Humanity fought back, though, containing and then destroying the disease in most Western nations over a period of two hundred years by means of vaccination. The climax of the war against smallpox got under way in 1966 when a team of World Health Organization medics equipped with smallpox vaccine and special jet injectors set out through the remaining smallpox-infested territories of the Third World to find and immunize all those still at risk of infection. Hundreds of millions of people in South America, Asia, Indonesia, and Africa were vaccinated, essentially ridding the world of the disease. There has not been a naturally occurring case of smallpox on this planet since October, 1977, when one was detected in Somalia. Very likely there will never be one again anywhere.

The disease was officially proclaimed eradicated by the World Health Organization in 1980; but the smallpox virus itself still survives, in deep-freeze storage vials kept under tight security at the Center for Disease Control in Atlanta and at the Research Institute for Viral Preparation in Moscow. These samples were set aside so that their molecular structure could be mapped and studied, a job that

[*Asimov's Science Fiction*, December 1995]

was completed a few years ago. Then, according to the W.H.O.'s plan, the last smallpox viruses were to be ritually destroyed in formal ceremonies in Russia and the United States at midnight on December 31, 1993, by heating the flasks to a temperature of 248 degrees Fahrenheit for 45 minutes.

All well and good, except, perhaps, for diehard Sierra Club members and Friends of the Earth who find the extinction of any species—even this one—abhorrent. But during the course of the genetic mapping of the virus, scientists stumbled on a less sentimental reason for keeping the smallpox bugs alive. The mappers discovered startling links between the smallpox virus and certain natural substances that permit the virus to bypass the human body's defenses. Such lofty scientific figures as Dr. Bernard Fields of Harvard and Dr. Joshua Lederberg of Rockefeller University argued that it might be possible to learn a great deal about the human immune system from studying the smallpox virus, knowledge that could be put to use in dealing with more esoteric diseases now beginning to ravage Third World nations. The possibility even existed that data derived from research done with smallpox could be applied to the treatment of cancer and AIDS. Furthermore, new anti-viral drugs are being developed all the time, but it would be impossible to test their efficacy against smallpox without the availability of live viruses on which they could be tried under laboratory conditions.

And so Drs. Fields and Lederberg, and others, spoke out against the scheduled ceremonial immolation of the last stocks of smallpox virus. Extinction, after all, is forever: they called for further research before the axe was allowed to fall. The W.H.O. responded with a one-year reprieve; then, in September, 1994, it postponed the execution date again, to June 30, 1995; and a few months later, as further clemency appeals came in, the governing board of the W.H.O. cancelled that date as well, remanding the entire issue to indefinite consideration and discussion. The debate may go on for several more years: the virus is safe for now.

But why, if these carefully secured samples of this deadly killer hold the promise of great value in scientific research, are advocates of destroying them still pressing the case for total extinction? There's nothing to lose, and possibly a great deal to gain, in keeping these last few flasks of viruses alive, right?

Wrong, says Otar Andzhaparidze, the director of the Moscow lab where half the virus supply is stored. "Kill it," he says. He raises the spectre that the viruses may be stolen by terrorists or blackmailers or lunatics. His institute keeps the virus in ordinary kitchen freezers behind glass doors equipped with alarms that will ring in a nearby police station if someone attempts a break-in. But what if the police don't come? he asks. What if they come too late? The night of the October 1993 rebellion against the Yeltsin government, Andzhaparidze had to hire private security guards to watch over the lab.

"The atmosphere was alarming," he told a New York *Times* reporter. "But everything worked out. We've been keeping the virus for about thirty years and so far God has spared us." Best to get rid of the stuff altogether, this scientist believes. "No one has asked the populations of the world whether they want the sword of Damocles held over their head."

Scientists on the other side maintain that terrorists would have a hard time turning the frozen viruses into an effective biological weapon, and in any case that lab security could always be beefed up. One solution might be simply to get the virus flasks out of unstable Russia; the ones in Atlanta are kept in sealed vaults and gaining access to them is very difficult indeed. Still, strange things do happen even where security is supposedly air-tight, as can be amply documented through the long history of espionage. The possibility of an accidental infection has also been raised. It's hard to see how viruses kept locked in a sealed freezer can infect anybody, but the viruses won't necessarily *stay* in those freezers if they are to be studied, and then the situation would be quite different. You will note that I spoke of the 1977 Somalian smallpox case as the last "naturally occurring" one. There was, in fact, one later outbreak—in 1978, at a laboratory in Birmingham, England, where smallpox research was going on. Although precautions supposedly were being taken to contain the viruses properly, a medical photographer named Janet Parker, who was working one floor above the lab, somehow came down with the disease and died of it—the world's last known smallpox victim. (The director of the laboratory committed suicide.)

What to do, what to do?

Destroy the remaining stocks of smallpox viruses and provide the world with an absolute guarantee that this dread disease will never return, or keep the bugs alive, under close guard, for the use of medical researchers?

I find myself on the side of the plucky little virus, here. Let the Russians boil their flasks, maybe, if they aren't confident of their own security arrangements; but our own stocks should be kept alive—guarded in the most careful way—so that their secrets can be explored. We don't know what information this diabolical germ can yield to the researchers of today or tomorrow or the day after tomorrow, but it's absolutely certain that nothing at all will be learned from it if it doesn't exist any more. As for the risk of an accidental escape of the virus, or even of some hellish exploitation of it in biological warfare, I say that that's a risk worth taking. We did, remember, wipe out smallpox once already. We can surely do it again if we have to.

As for my remark in the first paragraph about "those who worry about what they call 'the ecology,'" it has to do with my annoyance as a linguistic purist over the recent corruption of that word to make it synonymous with "the planetary environment." My dictionary defines ecology as "a branch of science concerned with the interrelationship of organisms and their environments." It isn't the place where we live; it's the *study* of that place, and especially of the web of life that binds all creatures together.

The smallpox virus is part of that web. For better or for worse, it has played a role in the growth of the human population—serving as a regulator, if you will. Now it is at the edge of extinction; its fate is in our hands.

It's a legitimate part of the ecological web, no question about that. But does it deserve to continue to live? Or should we finish the job of wiping it out, as we have done with so many other life-forms that we find inconvenient? What do you think, you partisans of "the ecology?"

Vote early, vote often.

Ovary Transplants?

Once again the scientists are way out ahead of the science-fiction writers. And once again the lay public is several light-years behind both groups, muttering that There Are Some Things That Mankind Was Not Meant To Achieve.

I'm talking about the latest startling new development in reproductive technology: specifically, the controversial proposal to transplant ovaries from aborted fetuses into infertile human women, ovaries containing fertile eggs that could develop into normal babies. So far as I know, none of our most ingenious science-fictional thinkers ever came up with that one—neither Robert Heinlein nor John Varley nor Greg Bear, to name three writers whose books and stories are particularly rich in speculations located along the interface between society and technology.

But Dr. Roger Gosden, a scientist at Edinburgh University, has already performed fetus-to-adult ovary transplants on mice and brought forth living mice from the fertilized fetal eggs. He says that within three years he expects to be able to do the same thing with human fetal ovaries. The ovaries of a 10-week-old human female fetus, Dr. Gosden points out, contain six or seven million eggs. If one of these ovaries were to be transplanted to an adult woman, it would need about a year to grow to mature size, after which it would begin producing fertile eggs. He has asked the ethics committee of the British Medical Association to offer an opinion on whether he should proceed with his research.

The British ethics committee's report will not be released for some time to come. But already intense reactions to Dr. Godsden's work are emerging.

"The idea is so grotesque as to be unbelievable," said George Annas, a lawyer and "ethicist" (a new philosophical specialty, apparently) at Boston University.

"It seems to me that it would be devastating to grow up knowing you were the product of a situation in which your mother was aborted," declared Dr. Arthur Caplan, a University of Minnesota ethicist. "There are many difficult things a child may have to deal with in life, but I just think we don't have any scale yet for someone to find out that they exist but their mother did not come into personhood."

And syndicated newspaper columnist Ellen Goodman weighed in with: "We need some ethical stop signs. One stop sign goes up at the

[*Asimov's Science Fiction*, August 1994]

idea of using fetal eggs at all....Even if this technology does produce a picture-perfect baby for some couples, it's fair to ask how much we should sacrifice in moral and scientific terms for that portrait."

The immediate popular consensus was that the use of fetal ovary transplants to allow infertile women to become pregnant was bizarre, unnatural, weird, disturbing, frightening, and repellent. And we are only just at the beginning of the debate.

Let me offer an analogous situation.

A terrible contagious plague is ravaging the world. It spreads so easily that it strikes whole communities, killing many of its victims and leaving those who survive so hideously disfigured that they are often unwilling to let their faces be seen. No cure is known. But an obscure country doctor announces that he has found a method for injecting infectious fluid from lesions of a similar but much milder disease common among cows into the bodies of those who have not yet caught the plague—young children, for example. This practice, he says, will immunize those who receive it against the more virulent disease that everyone dreads.

What? Inject infectious material into the bodies of healthy babies? What a bizarre, unnatural, weird, disturbing, frightening, and repellent thing to do! The process is condemned by journalists and medical experts alike; dire fears are expressed; cartoonists draw sketches of people sprouting cowhorns and talking in moos after they have been treated. But experiments continue all the same; and, behold, the dreaded plague is utterly wiped out.

That dreaded plague was smallpox; the country physician was Edward Jenner of Gloucestershire; the process he devised is called *vaccination* (from the Latin *vacca*, "cow"), and it has been close to two hundred years since anyone has seen anything grotesque or scary about injecting young children with cowpox virus to defend them against the related but far deadlier smallpox. What seemed like the wildest madness in the 1790s is routine medical practice throughout the world today.

But vaccination is one thing, you may say, and the artificial creation of human beings is something else entirely. We are talking, after all, about the sacred area of reproduction. Terms like "golem" and "android" and "Frankenstein's monster" quickly enter the discussion. And then comes the clincher: "It's—unnatural."

Sure. So is vaccination. So are eyeglasses. So is chemotherapy. So are heart transplants. None of those existed naturally in the world before we invented them. Adam and Eve had to make do without any of them. They are widely used and accepted all the same. Our definition of what is "unnatural," and therefore forbidden, keeps changing all the time.

In the field of reproductive technology, *in vitro* fertilization—an unnatural process if ever there was one—arrived in 1979, when Louise Brown was born. She was engendered by the meeting of her father's sperm and her mother's egg, yes, but the meeting took place not in her mother's womb but in a petri dish, after which the fertilized embryo of what would become Baby Louise was surgically implanted in her mother's uterus.

By now *in vitro* fertilization has become an established procedure when special conditions prevent a couple from having a child by conventional means. And in recent years we've also seen the impregnation of women past menopause—one was 59, one was 62—with eggs fertilized by their own husbands but taken from the bodies of other women. We've seen women implanted with fertilized eggs from their own daughters and carrying them to term, thus giving birth to their own grandchildren. We've heard of cloning techniques that could soon enable parents to have identical twins or triplets born several years apart. Unnatural, every one. But, step by step, these outlandish science-fictional techniques are working their way into normal medical usage.

The fetal-ovary proposal stirs strange new emotional responses, though. Columnist Ellen Goodman wonders, "Will brain-dead or dying females become egg donors the way they are now kidney and liver donors?" Why not? I reply. If their eggs can be of as much use to some other person as their kidneys or livers, why waste them?

Ethicist George Annas asks, "Should we be creating children whose mother is a dead fetus? What do you tell a child? Your mother had to die so you could exist?" But that problem disappears if we distinguish between the genetic mother and the gestational mother. The child's maternal genes were contributed by someone who may herself never have existed in the usual sense of that word, yes; but that child then spent nine months within the real womb of a real mother, who would provide motherly nurture for years to come.

That child will have had a living mother, though half its genetic complement will have come from another source. This seems no more unnatural to me than the process of artificial insemination, long accepted in our society. It is possible now for a woman to conceive a child using the sperm of a man who died years ago, or of one who is homosexual and has never had sexual intercourse. (The woman may never have had sexual intercourse either. I speak of lesbian mothers—not an unknown phenomenon today.) Unnatural? Certainly. Fulfilling the real human needs of the real human beings involved? I have no doubt of that. Unfair to the child thus brought into the world? George Annas thinks so; but would the eagerly wanted child born through a fetal-ovary transplant prefer not to have been born at all?

We are at the threshold of the twenty-first century. One era's bizarre and unnatural technological development becomes the next one's standard practice. There are millions of people who desperately desire to have children and for one physiological reason or another are unable to bring them into the world in the natural way. Fetal-ovary transplants and post-menopausal pregnancies certainly seem strange and visionary even to me, and I have been a professional creator of strange visionary ideas for forty years. But I see a direct logical line leading from artificial insemination through in vitro fertilization to post-menopausal pregnancies and fetal-ovary transplants—and on beyond them to immensely more astonishing developments in this area in the centuries ahead.

There will be great outcry and anguish over the new reproductive technologies, yes, much discussion of ethics and principles, and, maybe, even some hasty legislative action. But if the technical skills exist and the demand for their use is strong, and the real benefits of the new processes clearly outweigh the supposed ethical drawbacks, this entire debate will seem as quaint a couple of generations from now as the debate over smallpox vaccination was in 1796.

As for my own interest in all this: well, I am not by nature a parenting kind of guy, and I have no personal stake in seeing that fetal-ovary transplant technology is allowed to develop. But whenever I hear that line about Some Things That Mankind Was Not Meant To Achieve, I find myself asking, "Why?" and "By whom?" That was the line they gave Vesalius when he began dissecting corpses to find out what human anatomy was all about, and Galileo when he pointed his little telescope at the moons of Jupiter. It makes me uncomfortable to hear the old cliche trotted out once more, this time for Dr. Roger Gosden and his fellow explorers on the genetic frontier.

The Gay Gene: One

What may be a startling discovery indicating that male sexual behavior is at least in part determined by genetic imperatives was announced late last summer. The immediate reaction to the announcement indicates how complex the politicization of American culture has become in the late twentieth century.

The controversial study—done by Dr. Simon LeVay of the Salk Institute of Biological Studies in La Jolla, California—reports preliminary findings showing that the hypothalamic nucleus, a small but important structure in the brain, is much smaller in homosexual men than in heterosexual ones. This structure is normally twice as big in men as it is in women, but there had been no reason to suspect that there were notable differences in its size among men.

It was already known that male rats and monkeys who have suffered damage to their hypothalamus lose interest in the sexual pursuit of females, while continuing to express sexual vigor through such acts as masturbation. So there was reason to think that a relationship might exist between the hypothalamus and sexual orientation, specifically involving attraction to the opposite sex.

Dr. LeVay, using autopsied brain samples from 19 gay men, 16 men believed to have been heterosexual, and six heterosexual women—no tissue samples from homosexual women were available—discovered that the hypothalamic nucleus in the gay men and in all of the women was only a quarter to a half the size of the same structure in the heterosexual men. All the brain samples came from subjects who had died at about the same age—about 40—and so aging itself could not have been a factor in the disparity in hypothalamus size. All of the gay men whose the tissue samples had been used had died of AIDS; but six of the presumable heterosexuals had also died of AIDS, contracted as a result of intravenous drug usage, which would tend to rule out AIDS as a significant factor in the difference in the size of the hypothalamus.

It is, of course, a very small statistical sampling. But the consistency of the results even in so limited a group is impressive. Dr. LeVay, who is himself homosexual, has drawn no conclusions thus far from his study except to say that he feels he has detected something worth further investigation, which he intends to carry out. That is an appropriate scientific position to take, at this stage of the research. Those of us who look at the findings from the outside, though, can readily see good reason now to suspect that male homosexuality may in fact be a biological rather than behavioristic phenomenon: that one becomes homosexual not primarily because of one's family background or out of cultural preferences but because one's brain itself *is organically designed to make one respond sexually only to members of one's own sex.* As Dr. LeVay himself has pointed out, suddenly the study of homosexuality and its causes moves beyond the province of the psychologist and the psychoanalyst into that of the biologist.

A host of questions instantly arises. Is the hypothalamic size difference genetic, or is it the result of hormonal fluctuations in the womb or other external factors during fetal development? We have no data on that yet. Since relatively few homosexuals have children, though, how could such a trait, if it is genetic, manage to persevere in our species for so long? One would think that the failure of homosexuals to reproduce would have bred it out long ago. Or what if the small size of the hypothalamic nucleus in male homosexuals is a *consequence*, rather than a cause, of homosexual behavior? (The monkey experiments would seem to argue otherwise, but again the information on hand at this time is too skimpy to support any firm position.) Where, also, do bisexuals fit into the scheme of things? If there's biological programming that governs one's sense of who is sexually attractive and who is not, they seem to be able to override it. And what about lesbians: they too feel sexual attraction toward members of their own sex, but does their hypothalamic nucleus differ in size from that of heterosexual women? Perhaps it does. Perhaps it is as large in them as it is in heterosexual men. Dr. LeVay plans to investigate that and many other points in follow-up studies.

Early reactions to the LeVay findings have been varied and sometimes surprising. No one has any doubts about Dr. LeVay's scientific qualifications. "Simon LeVay is a top-notch, world-class neuroanatomist," said Dr. Thomas R. Insel of the National Institute of Mental Health, "and this is a very provocative paper." Dr. Sandra F. Witelson, a behavioral neuroscientist at McMaster University in Canada, commented, "I think this work is very interesting and very important." But she went on to say, "It doesn't mean that other anatomical differences aren't also present. I'm sure additional biological factors, perhaps related to hormones, will also be found." And Dr. Richard Nakamura, chief of the cognitive and behavioral neuroscience branch at the National Institute of Mental Health, offered, "Biology is not destiny, and this shouldn't be taken to mean that you're automatically homosexual if you have a structure of one size versus a structure of another size."

All very reasonable, very properly cautious, very scientific.

From the gay community—and probably I should insert here, by way of defining my own biases and perceptions in this matter, that I am not a member of that community and have never claimed to have much understanding of why people are homosexual—have come some very different responses.

The one that seems most comprehensible to me is that of gay rights activist Andrew J. Humm, a member of New York City's Human Rights Commission. "The fact that the report talks about homosexual behavior as something innate is good, because that's what most of us experience. Homosexuality used to be seen as a character or a moral defect, so if you want to look at it as hypothalamic in nature, that's probably a step toward looking at it for what it is." That makes sense to me. If homosexuality is seen by the heterosexual majority as some sort of dark and unnatural behavior that is willingly *chosen* by a depraved minority, what real hope is there for any sort of acceptance by that majority of the deviants within their group? But if it is, rather, something that is hard-wired into the genetic mix—the way skin color is, or height, or physical agility—then surely it would be reprehensible to condemn people for behaving the way they were designed by nature to behave.

From the highly political San Francisco gay community, though—and San Francisco is near the city where I live—have come some vehement negative reactions. John Paul De Cecco, a professor of psychology at San Francisco State University and the editor of the Journal of Homosexuality, called the LeVay study "preposterous," saying, "What determines preferences is very complicated. Are we born to like hamburgers or American football or big-breasted women? I think a lot of people are very uncomfortable with the fact that they're homosexual, and one way of handling that discomfort is to claim that you have no choice." Dr. De Cecco warned against attributing homo-sexuality to a "malformation" of the brain—his term, not Dr. DeVay's—and said that "the idea that you can describe a person by looking at the brain is a dreadful 19th-century invention." Others—betraying that fear of science which is so prevalent in the United States today—were quick to say that if LeVay's findings turn out to be correct, it might lead to attempts by parents to test for hypothalamic size while their children are still in the womb, and to abort those that showed the potential to turn out to be homosexual, or to use some kind of genetic surgery to "correct" the condition while there still was time. And Carole Migden, a member of the San Francisco City Board of Supervisors who is also a lesbian, said, "There are many reasons why people are gay and lesbian. It would be far more useful if scientists turned their microscopes to discovering the cause of homophobia and whether there's some biological deficiency that causes such virulent hatred of lesbians and gays."

I see what Ms. Migden is driving at, but I think she's heading in the wrong direction—unless playing to her local political constituency is her only purpose. We don't need a lot of scientific research to determine why many heterosexuals are uneasy about gays or downright hostile toward them. Heterosexuality is the biological norm—not just for humans but for most animals—and the continuation of the species depends on it, at least so far. An ongoing society consisting only of women has been depicted in science fiction many times, most recently and brilliantly in James Tiptree's classic story, "Houston, Houston, Do You Read?," but we are not yet ready or able to carry on the race by purely parthenogenetic means. The "virulent hatred of lesbians and gays" that Ms. Migden rightly says is felt by many heterosexuals is caused not by any biological deficiency that needs to be discovered in the laboratory, but by a biological *normality* that motivates all too many human beings to despise those who don't happen to share it.

And so there have been attacks on LeVay from the hard right, too. The Rev. Louis Sheldon of Southern California's Traditional Values Coalition, which takes anti-gay positions, rejects the hypothetical conclusions of LeVay's work and still insists that "homosexuals choose their lifestyle by virtue of their actions." He would assert, I suppose, that those who refuse to be "cured" through therapy should be suppressed or persecuted in other ways. If I were gay, I think I'd rather listen to such voices as that of the aide to Los Angeles Assemblyman Terry Friedman, the sponsor of a state gay-rights bill, who said, "The new study is one more from a respected scientist that indicates that sexual orientation may not be a conscious decision. I would expect now that some people may think with a little more openness about the possibility that people are being discriminated against for reasons that are beyond their control." The discomfort that many gays in New York and San Francisco have voiced to the new theories leaves me puzzled, therefore. If I were gay, I think I'd be more comfortable having the straight majority believe that my sexual behavior was a matter of innate and immutable biological destiny rather than one of blatant flouting of societal norms. But of course I'm not gay. There's another side to this discussion, evidently, that I'm not able to see—perhaps because of my own innate and immutable biological destiny.

The Gay Gene: Two

A few months back, the authoritative research journal *Science* carried a report of the discovery of an apparent link between one portion of a human chromosome and a predisposition to male homosexuality. The powerful and conflicting responses to the announcement of the existence of what is already being called "the gay gene" shows just how complexly interwoven science and morality have become as the twenty-first century peers over the horizon at us.

The "gay gene" label is, of course, premature and simplistic. What has been disclosed so far is this:

A research group at the National Cancer Institute in Bethesda, Maryland studied the family histories of more than a hundred men who identified themselves as homosexuals. The scientists were surprised to discover that a great many of these men had close relatives who also were gay—to a degree far out of proportion to the generally accepted heterosexual/homosexual numerical relationship in our society. Current estimates hold that between two and four percent of American men are homosexual. But 13.5% of the men studied had brothers who were gay; 7.7% had gay cousins who were the sons of their mother's sisters; 7.3% had gay maternal uncles.

Homosexual links on the male side of the family were very much less pronounced. Not one of the 114 reported having a gay father; just 1.7% of the paternal uncles were gay; and 5.4% had gay cousins on their father's side. The number of gay cousins on the mother's side who were the children of male uncles was notably lower, at 3.9%, than the gay sons of the maternal aunts.

The apparent conclusion that emerges from this welter of statistics is that if there is any kind of genetic predisposition toward homosexuality, it is more readily transmitted through the maternal line than through the paternal. The researchers' next step was to look closely at the large group of gay men with gay brothers in their sample, since their maternal genetic link would necessarily be closer than in cousin-cousin or uncle-nephew pairs.

This part of the investigation centered on the X chromosome, which men inherit only from their mothers. (There are 23 pairs of chromosomes in the human genetic makeup. Each chromosome in every pair is identical to its partner except in the 23rd pair, which determines the sex of the child. In women that pair consists of two so-called X chromosomes, and in men of one X chromosome received from the mother and one Y chromosome received from the father.)

Of a woman's two X chromosomes, one is inherited from her father and one from her mother, and either of these can be passed on to her sons. In any pair of brothers, then, there is a 50-50 chance that both have inherited the X chromosome that has descended in the maternal line. The Bethesda scientists took blood samples from 40 pairs of homosexual brothers and tested the DNA content of the blood cells to see how many of the sets of brothers had the same X chromosomes. The arithmetical probability was that 20 of them would; but in fact 33 of the 40 pairs of brothers were carrying identical X chromosomes. That is a strong indication that mothers can transmit to their sons, via their X chromosomes, a gene that seems to cause an inclination toward homosexual behavior.

There is nothing new about the idea that there may be a genetic predisposition toward homosexuality. As far back as 1952, a study of homosexual twin brothers by R.J. Kallman in the *American Journal of Human Genetics* pointed toward just such a conclusion. Edward O. Wilson, in his extraordinary book, *Sociobiology* (1975), considered the possibility that homosexuality might actually be a valuable genetic trait in primitive societies, arguing that homosexual members of such societies, "freed from the special obligations of parental duties, could have operated with special efficiency in assisting close relatives. Genes favoring homosexuality could then be sustained at a high equilibrium level by kin selection alone." And many other studies in recent years have purported to show a biological basis for sexual orientation. But scientists consider the Bethesda research a significant step forward in this area.

We are still a long way from pinpointing a "gay gene," though. The Bethesda hypothesis has targeted a small section of the X chromosome known as Xq28—but that section alone contains several hundreds of genes, and even if one of them actually does govern sexual orientation, it will take a great deal of further research to discover which one, if any, it is. The Bethesda scientists themselves take a skeptical view. "Sexual orientation is too complex to be determined by a single gene," says Dr. Dean H. Hamer, the primary author of the National Cancer Institute report. "The main value of this work is that it opens a window into understanding how genes, the brain, and the environment interact to mold human behavior." Edward O. Wilson made much the same point in 1975: "If such genes really exist they are almost certainly incomplete in penetrance and variable in expressivity," meaning that which bearers of the genes develop the behavioral trait and to what degree depend on the presence or absence of modifier genes and the influence of the environment. And from geneticist Paul Billings of the Stanford Medical School comes the observation, that the supposed "gay gene" may merely be "associated" with homosexuality rater than a "cause" of it.

Furthermore, the whole study may turn out to be just a statistical anomaly. A sampling of 114 men, a few dozen of whom have gay brothers or cousins, is far from being representative of the population as a whole; and though those 33 brother-pairs with identical X chromosomes seem strongly to support the concept of genetic homosexuality, it too may turn out to be only a statistical fluke when submerged in a population of 1000 or 10,000 pairs of gay brothers, where the 50-50 chromosomal distribution may in fact prove to be the norm. So the whole notion, at this point, must be regarded merely as an interesting speculation awaiting more extensive research.

An essential aspect of science fiction, though, is to develop extrapolative conclusions from speculative hypotheses. It's a good measure of the science-fictionization of our society to observe how quickly an array of extrapolative conclusions has leaped forth here.

Those who believe that homosexuality is an innate and inescapable trait, rather than an arbitrarily chosen "preference," see confirmation of their ideas, and have been quick to seize on the political implications. If homosexuality is inborn, then to discriminate against people because of their sexual orientation is as unfair and unacceptable as to discriminate against them because of the color of their skins. So, then, Gregory J. King, a spokesman for the Human Rights Campaign Fund in Washington, largest of the gay and lesbian lobbying groups: "We think this study is very important. Fundamentally it increases our understanding of the origins of sexual orientation, and at the same time we believe it will help increase public support for lesbian and gay rights." And Lyle Julius of San Francisco, who is gay, had a similarly favorable reaction to the idea that homosexuality is "natural," saying, "This is allowing Americans, especially middle America, to know we're all people. I have a favorite phrase, 'God works in mysterious ways, why could He have not created the homosexual?' "

But even genetic determinism is no justification for homosexuality, say those who find such behavior abhorrent. "If it's discovered that one person has a set of urges to a greater degree than another in a specific area of behavior, that does not mean the person has to yield to that behavior," said Lon T. Mabon, chairman of an Oregon anti-gay group. "Some people have said there's a genetic link to alcoholism, but that does not excuse the drunk."

And some members of the gay community, far from being pleased to hear that homosexuality may be innate, take a dark view of the Bethesda findings, as do non-gay scientists and sociologists. Darrell Yates Rist of the Gay and Lesbian Alliance Against Defamation sees the possibility of attempts "to identify those people who have it [the homosexual gene] and then open them up to all sorts of experimentation to change them." Laura Duggan of the San Francisco organization Lesbian Avengers takes the same view: "It can lead to testing for gay babies, testing children as youngsters and trying to alter who they are." Such genetic testing, says New York University sociologist Dorothy Nelkin, co-author of a book called *Dangerous Diagnostics*, "could be used to abort perfectly healthy people, and it could be used by the military and by employers to discriminate" against carriers of the gene. Dr. Billings of Stanford Medical School makes the same point: "The military wouldn't have to ask people if they were homosexual; they could just do a blood test."

The ramifications are endless. Insurance companies, worried about the potential for AIDS infections, might demand genetic examination before issuing new policies. Parents unwilling to bring a homosexual child into the world might abort a fetus carrying the troublesome gene, or else employ technology already entering medical use to alter the gene while the child is still in the womb. Even children already born might be subjected to genetic surgery to give them a different chromosomal pattern, just as if homosexuality were simply a birth defect. And so on and on, as we shamble forward into the ever more intricate future.

I tend to a more cautious outlook, myself. The "gay gene," if there is such a thing, is a long way from being found; and if it can be located, it will be very hard indeed to demonstrate an inexorable and inescapable link between its presence and homosexual behavior. On the other hand, I think it's likely that if the Bethesda work is confirmed in whole or even in part a certain amount of prenatal genetic surgery may be practiced in the centuries ahead on behalf of parents determined to keep their children on the straight and narrow path. And the possibility that some people will choose to abort fetuses bearing genes indicating homosexuality—a kind of prenatal genocide—is a very real one.

But the whole area of prenatal genetic tinkering is so laden with explosive complications, and human society is subject to such unpredictable changes from one century to another, that it's rash to come to any conclusions this early about the nature of the moral, ethical, and legal ramifications that it's going to bring. Anti-homosexual feelings today are far less pronounced in our society than they were only twenty years ago. For all we know, homosexuality may be a *desirable* condition in tomorrow's overcrowded world, a mark of elite status, and some parents may tell the genetic engineers that they *want* their children to be born gay. The only thing certain, I think, is that our attitudes, our fears, and our speculations on this and many other subjects are going to seem terribly quaint to the people of 2093 A.D.

Warning: Radiation Zone

When governmental bureaucracies start turning out reports that read like something out of a novel by Poul Anderson or L. Sprague de Camp, how can we doubt that science fiction has inextricably established itself as a major problem-solving tool of the late twentieth century?

I'm referring to a group of studies commissioned by the U.S. Department of Energy to deal with the question of keeping the people of future generations from stumbling unawares into hazardous nuclear waste dumps left behind by their remote ancestors. It is currently thought that the sites chosen for dumping of nuclear junk from civilian and military power plants and weapons will remain dangerously hot for the next 10,000 years. How can we be sure that the warning messages we erect will be comprehensible to our descendants of thousands of years hence? How well will we be able to communicate with the citizens of Earth 300 generations from now? To help it in grappling with this problem, the Department of Energy hired the Battelle Memorial Institute, an Ohio research organization, to create what it called a Human Interference Task Force, made up of sociologists, communications experts, lawyers, and specialists in the difficult field of nuclear waste disposal. The first reports of this task force are now being made public, and they are fascinating indeed.

I think it's surprising—and highly commendable—that the Department of Energy should see a problem here at all. My own first response to the issue was to argue that there's really not a lot to worry about. We ourselves have done quite a good job deciphering and decoding ancient languages, after all. Nineteenth-century scholars operating without benefit of computers managed to crack the secret of 5000-year-old Egyptian hieroglyphic script without much difficulty, thanks to the convenient discovery of the Rosetta stone, which provided Greek equivalents for hieroglyphics. Then came the decipherment of the long-forgotten Assyrian and Babylonian cuneiform scripts. Again, that was made possible by studying multilingual texts; for the cuneiform technique of writing had also been used in ancient times by the Persians, whose language had never been lost, and Assyrian and Babylonian were Semitic tongues closely related to ancient Hebrew, which likewise has remained part of the fund of human knowledge for thousands of years. Once Assyrian and Babylonian cuneiform had been deciphered, it became possible to

[*Amazing Stories*, November 1988]

penetrate the mysteries of the oldest known human language of all, Sumerian, which goes back at least 6000 years into Mesopotamian prehistory. Sumerian is not related to any other language, so far as we know, but the discovery of dictionaries providing Assyrian equivalents for Sumerian words opened the way to its decoding.

Even though there still are some ancient scripts and languages that remain total mysteries to us—the Indus Valley hieroglyphics, for example, or the Etruscan language—our record of decipherment is outstanding. Since we have cracked Sumerian and Linear B and Hittite and so many other thoroughly dead scripts, why, I wondered, did the Department of Energy think that our remote descendants, who would have the benefit of a technological society's superior information-processing techniques, would have any difficulty making sense out of a sign that said WARNING: DANGEROUS RADIATION ZONE? But then I realized that for once the bureaucrats were way ahead of the science-fiction writer. I was falling into the old trap of extrapolating from the past. The cryptographers who had solved the puzzles of hieroglyphics and cuneiform had been lucky enough to have Rosetta Stones and other multilingual texts to work from; and they had had a working knowledge of Greek or Hebrew or Persian to help them find entry to the lost languages. But what if some cataclysm (not necessarily nuclear; a worldwide famine or change of climate could do it) creates a total discontinuity between twentieth-century languages and the languages of our remote descendants? All the computer-power in the world is not likely to make sense out of mere symbols without any available cognate referents. And why do we think that the people of 10,000 A.D. will be our descendants at all? What if we have vanished without a trace, leaving only our radioactive waste dumps behind, and Earth comes to be inhabited by non-human successors who don't have a clue to our languages?

Good thinking, Department of Energy. And good thinking too—first-rate science-fictional speculation—is to be found in the first of the task force reports, the work of Dr. Thomas A. Sebeok of the University of Indiana. Dr. Sebeok, an expert in the arcane branch of communications theory known as *semiotics*, proposed the use of various non-verbal warning systems to keep the people of the future away from the toxic dumps:

—A "modern Stonehenge" ringing the dumps with gigantic stone monoliths, bearing symbols that might be understood as keep-away warnings.

—Making nuclear waste so "repulsively malodorous" that no one in centuries hence would be able to go near it.

—Setting up stylized cartoon-like inscriptions on stone that would depict in simple and unambiguous pictures the perils of nuclear material.

—Coding a warning into the human gene structure by "micro-surgical intervention with the human molecular blueprint" that the waste dumps are not to be approached. (Dr. Sebeok notes that "this form of temporal communication is far from available as yet.")

—Creating an "atomic priesthood" that will spread a "ritual and legend" to warn future generations against the dumps?

It seems to me that that last idea, which has been proposed in science fiction stories many times over the past forty years, holds the most promise. Building some Stonehenge-like thing is more apt to attract the attention of future archaeologists to the dumps than to keep them away; the stylized cartoons are likely to seem quaintly primitive, not threatening, to our distant descendants; stenches aren't going to work if those who try to explore the sites are robots or aliens; the genetic reprogramming idea carries with it all manner of political and technological problems. But exploiting the apparently ineradicable human susceptibility to superstition might just do it.

Dr. Sebeok proposes that "information be launched and artificially passed on into the short-term and long-term future with the supplementary aid of folkloristic devices, in particular....an artificially created and nurtured ritual and legend," to produce "accumulated superstition to shun a certain area permanently." To spread the myth, he says, the government should create "an atomic priest-hood."

If ever there was an argument in favor of more and better mumbo-jumbo, this may be it. (But what will happen when some future Age of Enlightenment spawns skeptics who boldly venture into the hot sites to prove that the priesthood is full of beans?) In any event, this is a fascinating area for speculation and discussion—and the most fascinating part of it, for me, is the fact that our government, no less, is seriously pondering ideas of this sort, which just a generation ago were limited to the pulpy pages of *Astounding Science Fiction* and *Amazing Stories.*

Embalm Your Spouse

In these splendid years of the late twentieth century, the newspapers bring us every day the sort of technocultural thrills and chills that we used to get, long ago, only in the pages of science fiction magazines.

I offer today for your consideration the remarkable achievement of the giant Washington State timber company, Weyerhauser, which is about to put embalmed houseplants on the market.

Embalmed. That's right.

Weyerhauser, which has a nursery-products subsidiary that does about $280 million a year in business, has noticed that many of its customers experience grief, depression, frustration, irritation, and other negative emotions when the houseplants they purchase come to untimely ends. So the Weyerhauser Specialty Plants Division of Auburn, Washington, has perfected a process developed a few years ago in Sweden that will allow it to sell immortal plants, guaranteed not to wilt, wither, drop leaves, turn yellow, or do anything else of a disturbingly metabolic nature.

These are, in fact, dead plants. But the eager consumer will never notice. Or care.

Weyerhauser used preservative chemicals which are allowed to seep into actual living plants by way of their roots. When the plant has absorbed a sufficiency of the stuff, it attains a condition of permanent resistance to decay. It looks absolutely lifelike, or even better than lifelike—Weyerhauser also uses dyes to simulate a plant's natural coloring or even to improve on it—but it will need no watering, fertilizing, pruning, repotting, or any of those other annoying little housekeeping jobs that old-fashioned plants demand.

All they will need, says Stephen Barger of Weyerhauser, is "an occasional light cleaning."

The illusion of a lifelike state, Mr. Barger declares, is total. "Holy moly," he told an interviewer, "these things look real!"

Indeed, the Weyerhauser spokesman asserts, marketing studies have shown that the average consumer is unable to distinguish the embalmed plants from live ones. (They do not, of course, flower or grow, but neither do a lot of people's living indoor plants.) Nor do they deteriorate. Plants preserved eight years ago during the pioneering work in Sweden continue to "look and feel fresh," says Weyerhauser's Mr. Barger.

[*Amazing Stories*, July 1987]

The first embalmed Weyerhauser plants to hit the market will be small bonsai conifers. Experienced horticulturists know that bonsai, which are miniature trees carefully held to dwarf size by a painstaking process of trimming and root-pruning, are expensive and difficult to keep alive. Their tiny root systems are prone to drying out quickly, often with fatal consequences. This will no longer be a problem with the Weyerhauser products, thus reducing the risk of impairment of your bonsai investments. Weyerhauser will kill your bonsai *before* you buy them, and then will fix them up so they'll look healthy forever.

In Japan, bonsai several centuries old are handed down in families from generation to generation. This can now become a cherished American custom too, even though Americans in general have tended to be more negligent about plant care than Japanese. Negligence won't be an issue any more.

After the bonsai we're likely to see all sorts of preserved plants going on the market. Weyerhauser claims to have worked its magic successfully on oak trees as tall as sixteen feet, and also on such trees an eucalyptus and beech, which thus far have proven hard to grow indoors.

The price for an eight-foot specimen, Mr. Barger suggests, will probably be $250 to $300. That's two or three times as much as an equivalent live tree would cost you, but when you figure in the aggregate cost of water, fertilizer, and labor over the lifetime of a tree, you can easily see that the Weyerhauser specimens will prove to be bargains in the long run.

One can only admire this stunning technological coup, which at one stroke will spare us from the sadness of losing beloved houseplants and from the blight of plastic imitation shrubs and trees in our shopping malls, restaurants, and hospitals. We can also expect to see a far greater botanical range of plants than the average temperate-zone hotel lobby or parking lot can afford at present: Weyerhauser doubtless will make available the full range of exotic marvels, which currently can be seen only in tropical nations or in California or Florida.

The preserved plants, Mr. Barger tell us, "will be a boon for people who love plants but who for whatever reasons, can't seem to keep them alive."

And there's no reason to stop with embalmed plants. What about those people who, for whatever reason, can't seem to keep pets alive? Embalmed cats and dogs for them! Lifelike! Impossible to tell from the real thing—but no annoying barking, no changing of litter basins, no dreary bother of opening pet-food cans!

And what about those who, for whatever reason, have trouble keeping an even keel in married life? Embalmed mates! Avoid the expense and emotional stress of divorce!

We can go even father than that. Already the Soviet Union and China have led the way in embalming political leaders: the lifelike bodies of Lenin and Mao Tse-tung are on display to hordes of Marxist faithful daily in Moscow and Peiping, respectively. But perhaps they are not lifelike *enough*. Weyerhauser's new process provides a much closer approximation of the living state. "Holy moly, these things look real," Mr. Barger of Weyerhauser has said. Imagine, for instance, a completely Weyerhauserized House of Representatives, perpetually in session, striking impressively statesmanlike poses round the clock—while never once passing a bad law or uttering a fatuous phrase. How grateful we all will be to the anonymous Swedish scientists who devised this miracle, and to the marketing experts of the Weyerhauser Company who have made it available to suffering humanity!

My information on plant embalming comes from a piece in the *Wall Street Journal*. Time was when we had to pore over gaudy magazines like *Amazing Stories* or *Astounding Science Fiction* to find such mind-stimulating concepts. But this is the late twentieth century, my friends, and science fiction invades our daily life on every side nowadays.

Creationism

Not *all* the news is bad this morning. On the very day that the American Association for the Advancement of Science is convening its vast 155th National Meeting in San Francisco, the State of California Board of Education has released a set of new guidelines that has the effect of putting the theory of evolution back into the science curriculum of the state's schools, and keeping "creationism" out.

Of course, there will now be vast legal battles all up and down the state over this. Already the first counterblast has been sounded—by the Reverend Lou Sheldon, chairman of the Southern California-based Traditional Values Coalition. His organization, which he says represents 6,000 churches, will "go throughout the state of California and make sure local districts will have that door of opportunity [to teach creationism] open." And I'm sure they'll give it a good fight.

My own bias, in case there are any doubts out there, lies on the side of Darwin. I think the theory of evolution as set forth somewhat over a hundred years ago by him, and modified to a certain degree by later thinking in the field of genetics, is a reasonable hypothesis that does much to explain the course of the organic development of living things on our planet. I think the fossil evidence we have unearthed in the past few hundred years does much to support the Darwinian hypothesis of natural selection, and that such experimentation with low-phylum organisms as has been done in our time strongly indicates that mutation and change is a rule of life.

These positions of mine were not generally considered very daring ones when I was growing up, some forty years ago. I knew about Darwin's difficulties with some nineteenth-century religious and political leaders. ("Is man an ape or an angel? I, my lord, am on the side of the angels," declared Disraeli in 1864. "I repudiate with indignation and abhorrence these newfangled theories.") But I believed the Darwinian concepts had generally triumphed over the forces of reaction by the end of the nineteenth century. And I knew about the Scopes trial of 1925, in which a Tennessee law prohibiting the teaching in public schools of theories that deny the divine creation of man as taught in the Bible was debated and openly mocked.

Although the Scopes trial actually resulted in the conviction and token punishment of the young teacher who had dared to advocate the theory of evolution in his classroom—and the constitutionality of the law prohibiting such teachings was ultimately upheld—it seemed

[*Amazing Stories*, July 1989]

to mark the last victory of the Fundamentalist Christian position. By the time I got to school a couple of decades later, the theory of evolution was being openly taught everywhere, with no footnotes required in the textbooks to indicate that students also should keep in mind, of course, the possibility that the world had been created by God in six days in the year 4004 B.C.

But time passed, and things changed in the United States. And those who believe in the literal truth of the Christian scriptures—I am not one of them, obviously—managed to bring the whole idea of teaching evolution in the schools into question all over again. Most Fundamentalists realized that it was too late to throw Darwin out of the textbooks entirely, as Tennessee had tried to do in 1925. But they argued, insistently and in some places quite successfully, that their own view of how the world came into being should be taught *as an alternative hypothesis* wherever evolution was offered to schoolchildren.

Why not, you say? Shouldn't all viewpoints be given equal opportunity for testing?

Well, actually, no. The Fundamentalist Christian view of creation rests entirely on the evidence of revelation: it is, they say, the Word of God. In other cultures God has offered other and quite contradictory revelations. The ancient Egyptians, the Sumerians, the Hopi Indians, the Chinese, the Maori, all have their own ideas of how the world came into being. To them, the argument that the Fundamentalist view is the true revelation and their own beliefs are mere noise is unacceptable. If we teach Adam and Eve and the Garden of Eden to our children in school, should we not also teach the Creation myths—pardon me, the Creation theories—of all other cultures?

Darwinism, though, is not a matter of revelation. It is a hypothesis built on an examination of evidence. It can be challenged—and has been, by many scientists—but its foundation in empirical fact is very difficult to deny. (Why was there no Brontosaurus family on Noah's ark?) (Fundamentalists will tell you, though, that when God created the Earth, He created the fossils right along with everything else—a difficult argument to refute, if you let the initial assumptions of "God" and "creation" slip under the tent.)

The last couple of decades have seen a resurgence of old mythologies and the birth of plenty of new ones. In our democratic society, the notion is abroad that any idea is as good as any other. And so along with the crystals and the Tarot decks of the New Age folks has come a triumphant rebirth of Fundamentalist Christianity, and so-called "Creation Science" has forced its way into the schools in many places where that form of Christianity is the predominant belief.

Those of us who are not Fundamentalists, or Christians of any sort, would prefer that such teachings be kept at home, in the families where they are accepted. We think it is perfectly permissible for people to tell their children—at home—that the world is flat, that blood transfusions are evil, that Satan is behind the manufacture of certain brands of detergents, and that the world was created in six days. But we don't want the vocal minority that believes such things to impose those beliefs on our own children, nor do we want our children to be prevented from learning of current non-revelatory theories of the way the world works.

It looked bad for a while. But now the biggest school system in the country has found the courage to say that it means to make explicit which subjects belong in science classes and which do not. "Religion," says a California Department of Education spokesman, "belongs in social science or language arts classes." Textbooks in the state henceforth are not to dilute evolution instruction with a mass of qualifications designed to make it sound as though evolution were mere conjecture. "As a matter of principle," the policy statement declares, "science teachers are professionally bound to limit their teaching to science and should resist pressure to do otherwise. If a student should raise a question in a natural science class that the teacher determines is outside the domain of science, the teacher should treat the question with respect. The teacher should explain why the question is outside the domain of natural science and encourage the student to discuss the question further with his or her family and clergy."

No doubt the battle will not end here. A good many of our fellow citizens believe so passionately in the revealed doctrines by which they comprehend the world that they want to impose them on everyone. The rest of us prefer that the major tenets and methods of scientific thought be made available to the young, unencumbered by declarations to the effect that those things need not be taken seriously because they are, after all, only mere conjecture. That way lies the new dark ages. We have enough trouble competing with the stubbornly unChristian nations of the world as it is, these days, without pulling the hood of mythology over our children's eyes. How brave of the California Department of Education to tell its science teachers that they are free to teach science! And how sad, in the year 1989, that such a declaration should have been necessary at all.

Feedback

"Positive feedback"—that's what we all want, right? Smiles, applause, praise—all that good stuff. Who would object to positive feedback? It's *positive*, isn't it?

Yes. But "positive" doesn't necessarily mean "good." In the case of the catchphrase "positive feedback," what we're dealing with is a scientific term that has undergone some corruption as it passed into popular speech. And the result is a distortion of what the extraordinary man who gave it to us had in mind.

Who coined the term "feedback" is a matter of some etymological dispute. But there is little doubt that we owe its popularization to the American mathematician and philosopher Norbert Wiener (1894-1964), author of *Cybernetics* and *The Human Use of Human Beings*.

Wiener, a prodigy who learned to read by the time he was three and had a Ph.D. in mathematics from Harvard at the age of 18, spent most of his life as a member of the faculty at the Massachusetts Institute of Technology. In 1940 he became interested in the development of "thinking machines"—what we call computers today—and that work led him, during World War II, to a study of control devices for anti-aircraft guns. The entire problem of automatic control would concern him, in an increasingly profound way, for the rest of his life.

His concern centered on the concept of feedback: the effect on a system caused by a return of some of its output.

The ordinary house thermostat is an example of a device which keeps itself operating correctly through the use of feedback. The thermostat is set to maintain a desired temperature in a house, and is equipped with sensors that constantly tell it whether the temperature is above or below the desired level. If the temperature in the house is too low, the thermostat sends a signal to the furnace, telling it to get the heat going. Eventually this will drive the house temperature above the desired maximum. The thermostat, detecting this consequence of its earlier order, will send a countermanding order and shut the furnace down until the temperature has dropped below the set figure once again.

Another classic feedback device is the governor of a steam engine: two balls mounted on pendulum rods and swinging on opposite sides of a rotating shaft. The speed at which the shaft turns imparts a centrifugal action: when the shaft is turning quickly, the rods will rise and the balls will swing outward. If the speed of the shaft exceeds the desired maximum, the position of the rods will close the engine's intake valves and cause the rods to drop; if the engine slows down too much and the control balls drop too far, the governor will send a signal that opens the valves and gets things moving again. Thus conditions in the system are constantly *fed back* to the control device, so that the system is able to regulate itself and maintain the correct level of operation.

What reaches the thermostat, or the steam-engine governor, or any other kind of control device, is quantitative information: the amount of departure from the desired condition. It can be expressed as a negative quantity: "The temperature is minus three degrees from optimum in this room." The appropriate response is to alter whatever the system is doing: if the room is three degrees too warm, the furnace must be shut down, and if it is three degrees too cold, the furnace must be turned on. Either way, the effect of the feedback is to oppose whatever the system may currently be doing; and so it can be termed *negative feedback*.

When Norbert Wiener went on to develop his studies of feedback into broader considerations of advanced automatic control devices and man/machine interaction, the concept of negative feedback was at the heart of his theories. Negative feedback, he wrote, is the essential stabilizing factor that allows all self-regulating devices (including the human brain) to correct undesirable situations.

And *positive* feedback?

It does the opposite, obviously. Positive feedback is an input of information that tends to increase a system's deviation from the optimum—i.e., to make a bad situation worse. It does this by supporting, rather than negating, whatever the system is already doing. In electronic terms, it is information that tends to increase the net gain of an amplifier—that is to say, to turn things up, and up, and up and up and up. The nasty squealing noise that you hear when two microphones are brought close together is a feedback effect—*positive* feedback.

So much for the scientific background. Now that the concept of feedback is loose in everyday chatter, the underlying conceptual purity is being buried under semantic distortion. Everyone knows that "positive" is good and "negative" is bad. That isn't so in physics— nobody would seriously argue that electrons, which carry a negative charge, are nastier particles than protons—but in non-technical use the words have different shadings. To most people, "positive feedback" is praise, constructive criticism, the good old hearty slap on the back. And "negative feedback" is grumbling, hostility, general obstreperousness. Given your choice, which would you rather have?

And yet—and yet—which is really more valuable?

I think that if we were to cast our loose metaphorical use of these notions aside and return to Norbert Wiener's original way of thinking, we'd see that negative feedback is still the key to effective functioning, whether employed in our thermostats, our steam engines, or our daily lives. The properly functioning human being, like the properly functioning thermostat, must constantly monitor the surrounding environment and make decisions on the basis of the information that's coming in. If we are told what we want to hear, rather than what we need to know, then our decisions are apt to lead us farther and farther away from where we need to be.

Imagine a device on the dashboard of your car, for instance, that tells you when you're driving too quickly or too close to the car in front of you. It constantly monitors the distance between you and surrounding cars, and when you come within a pre-set danger zone, a voice will tell you, "You're only four car-lengths away from the car ahead of you now. Better slow down a little." If you keep on speeding forward, the voice will warn you, "Three car lengths now. You're much too close." And if you don't respond even then, the gadget will send an electronic message to your car's engine that will slow your speed no matter how hard you want to hit your accelerator.

That's negative feedback at work.

And positive feedback? Well, imagine a different kind of device that tells you nothing but what a great driver you are. "You took that curve like a champ....You can really handle these speeds, all right....Now let's see you drive even faster....Hey, that's it! You're leaving all the traffic way behind....Wow, you showed him a thing or two, didn't you!....You ought to sign up for the Indianapolis 500!" And so on and so on, a constant stream of reassurance and encouragement, right up to the moment when the ambulance arrives.

The next time you tell someone how much you appreciate the positive feedback you're getting, pause a moment and reflect on the original meaning of the phrase, and how it has become garbled in popular use. Like the hedgehogs that the inhabitants of Wonderland were trying to use as croquet balls, words and concepts have a way of getting up and moving around as they please, and there's not much we can do about it. But I think we are all the losers when they do.

Alternative Energy Sources

There has been much talk, in this era of energy crises and heightened sensitivity to environmental problems, of the development of renewable-energy resources as an alternative to the use of fossil fuels. But a report released in the closing days of 1982 will surely create some somber second thoughts among the supporters of these energy alternatives. Among its conclusions were these:

Biomass energy production—the burning of wood and animal wastes—could, if improperly managed, bring about air pollution, deforestation, soil erosion, and the disruption of wildlife habitats.

The large-scale development of geothermal energy sources might release toxic gases, cause earthquakes, and create water shortages.

Further damming of rivers for hydroelectric power removes valuable land from cultivation, fosters silt buildups, and causes soil erosion and stagnation of streams.

Large-scale use of windmills for power generation may cause noise pollution and could interfere with transmission of radio, television, and microwave signals.

Oceanic thermal energy conversion—the exploitation of temperature differentials between ocean surfaces and deep water to produce electricity—might disrupt marine life cycles and cause weather changes by altering ocean currents.

The manufacture of solar photovoltaic cells will create troublesome shortages of such substances as cadmium and gallium, and the deployment of such cells in great quantity will consume large areas of land.

The interesting—and depressing—thing about this report is that it is *not* the privately sponsored product of some large oil company or any of the other corporations generally regarded as villains in popular energy-crisis mythology. No, this litany of sobering observations was released by the National Science Foundation, and the organization that conducted the study was one of our major environmental groups, the Audubon Society. I suspect that not even in the farthest-out fringes of the alternative-energy movement is there anyone who thinks that the Audubon Society is in the pay of Mobil Oil or the sinister nuclear-energy tycoons.

Of course, the renewable-energy technologies that the National Science Foundation's report urges us to regard with such caution are currently on the back burner anyway. Several virtually simultaneous and interrelated developments have recently created a notable over-supply of oil and natural gas. OPEC, by imposing huge price increases on those fuels in the past decade and largely making them stick, so enhanced the profitability of finding and producing oil and gas that enormous new supplies came on the market; but the same price increases sent the economies of the industrialized nations into such prolonged slumps that consumption of oil and gas has fallen precipitously—which is now starting to bring down the price, but not to anything like the pre-OPEC levels.

With such things going on, the motivation for developing new energy technologies is weakening. Shell Oil, which had been working on cadmium sulfide solar cells, now says that its "revised time frame" for mass production of the cells "is apt to be longer than expected." RCA finds itself unable to locate outside financing for its unique "thin film" photovoltaic device. An entrepreneur who hoped to build giant "wind farms" of windmills in California and Hawaii is having similar financial troubles. And so on.

But economic slumps don't last forever, and underconsumption caused by overpricing is eventually corrected by price reductions: which is why it's folly to think that the present glut of fossil fuels is anything but a short-term phenomenon. The supply of those fuels is just as finite as ever, and mankind's need for energy, plotted on a curve extending—one hopes—through millions of years, is infinite. Sooner or later, we're going to need those alternative energy sources.

What, though, of the Audubon Society's warning? Dare we build all those windmills, if they're going to foul up Channel Nine? Can we risk tapping geothermal energy if it's going to unleash the San Andreas Fault?

The answer, of course, is that we'll need to move cautiously and think through the consequences of whatever steps we take. But the real significance of the National Science Foundation's energy study, I think, lies deeper than mere consideration of this or that specific energy-generation problem. The underlying truth arising from that report is this:

ALL forms of energy production have an environmental price.

Or, as Robert A. Heinlein put it, There Ain't Any Such Thing as a Free Lunch.

The opponents of nuclear-energy power generation—I am not one, incidentally—have so effectively blocked all nuclear power plants in the United States that there has been a resurgence of coal-burning generation, previously deemed obsolete. Coal, unlike oil and gas, will be plentiful in the United States for centuries; the trouble is that we seem to be having a bothersome increase in the acid-rain phenomenon as a consequence of burning all that coal. Acid rain is harmful stuff. It may actually turn out to be more harmful, in the long run, than anything those nuclear power plants might have done to us. I suspect that before long, as awareness of the acid-rain menace grows, the same citizens who brought down the nuclear power industry will be out there demonstrating against the coal-burning plants, and calling for solar technology, biomass conversion, and all those other science-fiction things that—oh, my—the National Science Foundation is suddenly warning us about.

The lesson is clear enough to me. Not even the starriest-eyed Sierra Club member is apt to propose that we roll back our civilization to the level that obtained before Thomas Edison and Henry Ford. (Where would we stable all the horses? What about the problem of manure disposal? How could today's reduced whale population keep all our lamps burning, and what would Greenpeace say about that, anyway?) We *do* need electrical energy, lots of it, and we *do* have to keep those internal-combustion engines combusting, somehow, until their replacements are at hand. And since we are going to continue to produce energy, we must do it in clean and economical ways. But it is absolute folly to think that we can run an industrial society of billions of people without paying some sort of environmental price for our energy. And it is unwise to let ourselves be so blinded by emotion—by the fear and hysteria, for example, that have throttled the nuclear-power industry in this country—that we fail to understand that there is no free lunch, that risk confronts us *wherever* we turn for our energy.

Even windmills.

Getting Rid of Acid Rain

The deadly menace of acid rain—precipitation tinged with vegeta-tion-killing oxides of sulfur and nitrogen—is the target of a bill now working its way through Congress. Acid rain, which is swiftly ruining forests and lakes across much of the northern hemisphere, seems primarily to be caused by the release of pollutants through the burning of coal in power plants. The proposed legislation would curb acid rain primarily by compelling public utilities in 31 eastern and midwestern states to reduce the quantity of sulfur dioxide that they emit in the course of power generation from 22 million tons a year to about 12 million tons. This can be done in one of two ways: by installing scrubbing devices on the smokestacks of their power plants, or by cutting back on the use of coal with a high sulfur content.

One can hardly disagree with the intentions of this bill. There is mounting evidence of the horrors caused by acid rain, horrors that can only multiply over the years ahead. But what about the costs of this legislation? As Mr. Heinlein sagely observed some years back, there ain't any such thing as a free lunch. Environmental cleanups have a way of exacting a price, somewhere along the line.

In this case, shifting to low-sulfur coal would put thousands of coal miners out of work in already depressed Appalachia, where most of our present high-sulfur-coal supply comes from. Installing scrub-bing devices would involve costs of billions of dollars that ultimately would have to be paid for by the consumers of electricity, requiring increases in electrical rates that would range, over the next five years, from 18 percent in Illinois to 36 percent in Ohio. But even after that, we'd have no assurance that the problem will have been satisfactorily dealt with. Burning coal to generate power is a dirty business at best. It is altogether conceivable that within a decade the acid-rain problem will be so acute that environmentalists will be calling for a total ban on coal-burning power plants.

It is not likely, though, to be accompanied by a total ban on the use of electricity. But where is the power going to be coming from, if coal is *verboten*?

We used to burn a lot of oil and natural gas to keep the boilers hot in our power plants. That began to stop in 1973 when the first OPEC oil shock made us understand that we could not go on consuming those precious hydrocarbons as if they were infinitely available. Our domestic oil supply, despite the current glut, is just about gone; natural gas will last a little longer, but not much. At a cost of billions of dollars the power companies converted their plants away from oil and gas to reduce our national dependence on imported energy sources. (They converted them to—*coal*.)

It hardly makes sense to convert all those plants back to oil, and deliver ourselves again into OPEC's hands, or to return to natural gas when our remaining supply is probably good for no more than another few decades. But the demand for electrical power is great, and growing at three or four percent a year nationally. Those shiny new computers and television sets and stereos around the house don't run on batteries, after all.

What other sources of electricity are there? Well, there's hydro-electric generation—but our available hydro sources are pretty well developed already. Solar power? It has its appeal, but its range is limited: it works fine for suburban houses in sun-belt states, but it doesn't seem really practical just yet for supplying power in any quantity to large northern cities. Burning of garbage and other exotic fuels? Again, a small-scale solution. Atomic fusion? The technology isn't in place yet, and won't be for at least twenty years. Beaming power down from L5 satellites? Ditto.

Of course, there's nuclear power....

We get something like 13 percent of our electricity from nuclear power plants right now, from 76 nuclear plants. (In Europe the figure is 25%. In Japan, which has no fossil fuels of its own, it's even higher.) Without those reactors in service, we'd either be dumping much greater quantities of coal-caused pollution into the air or we'd be buying hundreds of billions of dollars more of OPEC oil. Nuclear power plants are clean. They do virtually no environmental damage. No filthy coal-heaps, no belching smokestacks. (The dams by which "clean" hydroelectric energy is created cause immense backups of silt that eventually choke the rivers they harness.) They cost less to operate than fossil-fuel plants. (Or they used to, before government regulations strangled them.) And they are safe. There have been no meltdowns, no explosions, no significant releases of radiation from any nuclear power plant, not even during the notorious Three Mile River accident. At Three Mile River, there was much *fear* of radiation release, but not much really did get loose. Coal-burning, by the way, actually does release a certain amount of radioactivity. And mining coal kills people. On the day of the Three Mile Island event—which caused zero fatalities—half a dozen coal miners were killed in a mine accident in the same state. In the general hysteria their fates were overlooked; but they are dead nevertheless, sacrificed to our need for electricity.

Other nations, mindful of the acid-rain problem and their own shortages of oil, gas, coal, or hydro sites, are building nuclear power plants as fast as they can. Japan alone has eight coming on line between here and 1990. Western Europe will have 181 nuclear power plants in operation by then. Russia plans to complete four or five thousand-megawatt reactors a year over the next five years.

Not here. In the United States the last new order for a nuclear plant was placed in 1978. The ones under construction now are reaching completion years late, because of court challenges and retroactive changes in government regulation, and their costs have been grotesquely inflated, causing havoc for their owners and increases in power costs for their customers. Even when a plant is completed there's no assurance it will go into service; at this very time a four-billion-dollar job is sitting idle on Long Island, ready to go but kept dormant by political crossfighting.

Fear is the reason why the United States, where nuclear technology originated, is the only nation in the world that has turned away from this energy source. We are literally scared silly of it. We worry about release of radiation from the plants, we worry about China Syndrome meltdowns, we worry about where to store the spent radioactive fuel. Meanwhile the rest of the world is moving swiftly ahead of us in power generation, finding ways of building cheap, efficient, standardized, *safe* nuclear power plants. (Including one in eastern Canada that is intended solely to sell electricity to the New England states, where the Seabrook and Millstone atomic power plants remain tangled in problems while demand for power grows.) And meanwhile we burn coal to make our electricity, and the acid rain falls impartially upon the living and the dead.

The social, economic, and psychological implications of all this, I think, are worth considering carefully.

Getting Rid of Acid Rain, Continued

I spoke last time of the current paradoxical environmental problems growing out of the United States' abhorrence of nuclear power—the growing incidence of deadly acid rain that is largely caused by coal-burning power plants. Since political considerations make it impossible to build additional nuclear power plants in this country, and additional electrical capacity of some sort will be required in the next decade, power companies are turning by default to coal, the outmoded fuel of the 1920s and 1930s—with unavoidably horrendous results.

Not only is the acid fallout from coal-burning plants trashing forests and lakes all across the land right at this moment, but the burning of fossil fuels to generate electricity is liberating carbon dioxide that is heating up our atmosphere through the "greenhouse effect." At the rate the CO^2 buildup is proceeding, global temperatures may increase as much as 9 degrees Fahrenheit by the year 2100—turning northern lands into torrid tropical jungles, flooding coastal regions, disrupting patterns of food production, and probably creating vast upheavals in every aspect of human life. That process is already under way. Meanwhile, terrified of *potential* dangers from nuclear power plants, the citizens of the United States have turned their backs on what seems to be our only hope for a cheap and reasonably safe power supply over the next two or three decades.

The rest of the world doesn't share our horror of nuclear energy. The Japanese, who have more reason than anyone to dread the forces locked up in the atom, are building nuclear power plants at a swift clip. So are the French, the Russians, the British. The Chinese have asked us to help them master nuclear-power technology. (They already have the bomb; now they want the power plants.) At home we fret about radiation discharges, the chances of catastrophic meltdowns, the problems of waste disposal, and all manner of other stark contingencies, while bringing a complete halt to new construction of nuclear power plants and forcing to the edge of bankruptcy those companies who find themselves in the middle of building one. Are all these nations blindly plunging ahead with insane programs, while we alone maintain our sanity? Or has some sort of quasi-medieval panic fear spread among us like an epidemic of unreasoning foolishness?

Certainly we look odd to our neighbors. Up in Canada, where thirteen commercial reactors are in use and nine more are under

[*Amazing Stories*, March 1985]

construction, nuclear power is an uncontroversial issue. The Canadians, who use a heavy-water reactor of their own design that is apparently the most efficient in the world, are preparing to take advantage of our chaos by selling some of their surplus nuclear-generated energy to us. Already, a nuclear plant in the province of New Brunswick ships a third of its power to the New England states. Since New England is a center of anti-nuclear phobia here but desperately needs new sources of energy, the obliging Canadians are getting ready to build another nuclear plant to supply us. Under a long-term contract, we will spend billions to buy electricity from Canada through the 1990s—paying for the plant several times over in power purchases alone, a nice deal for Canada and a very dumb one for us.

Our turning away from nuclear power is, so it seems to me, part of a general abdication from technological leadership that is likely to have ghastly consequences for the United States in the century to come. Except in the area of computer technology—where, for the moment, we are leading the way—we have become a nation of mere consumers, blandly importing the superior products of other nations. The Japanese make our television sets and tape recorders, and most of our cars (except for the deluxe ones, which come from Germany.) Our cameras, our phonograph records, our precision instruments, all come mainly from overseas. Americans invented the television set, the automobile, the phonograph. Other people have improved on our pioneering designs. We invented the nuclear power plant, too. (And the atomic bomb, for that matter.) If a time ever comes when we overcome our fear of nuclear reactors and try to re-establish a nuclear industry here, we will probably have to hire Japanese or French technicians to build the plants for us. "We've certainly fallen behind in the front end," says Harvey Brooks of Harvard, chairman of the Commitee on Nuclear and Alternative Energy Sources. "New design, thinking about the future has practically disappeared." From George Keyworth 2nd, President Reagan's science advisor, comes this warning: "We're going to find our nation's capacity for industrial growth choked—and choked at a time when our foreign competitors, who don't face the kinds of hurdles in developing nuclear energy that we do, will be more than happy to pick up the slack." Dr. Alvin Weinberg of the Oak Ridge National Laboratory in Tennessee puts it more succinctly: "Giving up on nuclear energy is insane."

Insane? What about the China Syndrome? What about the radiation leaks? What about waste disposal? What about the theft of fissionable nuclear materials by terrorists?

Real problems, sure—but some have been preposterously exaggerated by those whose profession it is to terrify the public. (Nuclear power plants have been around for a generation. How much plutonium have terrorists stolen so far, and when will they announce their demands?) The rest surely have real solutions. Such accidents as have taken place in nuclear power plants have been caused by incompetent personnel or by faulty safety-mechanism design, not by anything inherent in the concept of nuclear power generation. Those errors are correctable and by now have been corrected; overseas, where standardized reactor design is the rule, they have not been a problem. Meanwhile the need for electricity continues to rise: 35% of the energy used in this country today is in the form of electricity, up from 18% in 1968. The various utopian schemes for "soft" energy production—solar power and the like—still offer no large-scale solutions. Coal is the only alternative source we have at the moment, and the problems it creates are real and current, not merely potential. Disposing of spent nuclear fuel may be a problem, but so is acid rain. So is the greenhouse effect. So is the economic burden of burning fossil fuels. (And the cost in lives. Mining coal requires the real deaths of real people: cave-ins, black lung disease, emphysema. How many deaths have nuclear power plants caused?)

A new proposal—the thorium reactor—holds promise for getting around the hysteria and ignorance blocking nuclear power generation in the United States. Thorium is much more plentiful than uranium; when used in a reactor it would create only a fiftieth as much plutonium as a standard reactor, and that plutonium would be an isotope unsuitable for nuclear detonation. Thus thorium reactors could be built in politically unstable third-world countries without fear of what they might do with dangerous fissionable byproducts. Meltdown possibilities also would be greatly reduced. Thorium reactors would be simple to build and safe and cheap to operate; and the cost of converting present-day reactors to thorium would be relatively small.

The developer of the thorium reactor is Dr. Alvin Radkowsky, who was chief scientist of the U.S. Naval Propulsion Program from 1948 to 1972. He thinks it would take less than a decade to bring his concept into use, with a very modest development cost. Unfortunately, no one in the United States seems to be thinking much about thorium reactors these days. Dr. Radkowsky is currently professor of nuclear engineering at Tel Aviv University.

The Green Flash

So there I was at sunset, sitting on the terrace of my hotel room outside the medieval town of Siena in Tuscany with a drink in my hand on a lovely May night, waiting to see the green flash, as I have done here and there around the world for the past thirty years.

I'm not talking about a comic-book superhero. (*Was* there ever a Green Flash? My days of comic-book reading are far behind me. But if there wasn't, there should have been.) No, the green flash of which I speak is a little-known solar phenomenon. I've searched for it over the Grand Canyon, and on the isles of Greece, and looking westward across the Nile at Luxor, and in all manner of other exotic and wonderful places. But never have I had a glimmer of green to reward my quest.

Certainly everything was propitious there in Siena. Our hotel room faced west, looking out on the green Tuscan hills, dark with the spiky columns of cypresses. The air was clear and still. The setting sun hovered in a reddening sky. The drink in my hand was grappa of the finest quality.

"Here it comes," I said to Karen. "Any moment now."

"Call me if you see it," she said.

"But it'll last only a fraction of a second. There won't be time for you to get out here."

"Call me *quickly*," she said.

I love her for her skepticism.

The sun moved slowly downward behind the lovely hills. The red of the sky deepened. The yellow disk touched the topmost spire of the hills, and slipped lower until it was half hidden, and then more than half. I was convinced that the flash I had sought so assiduously would surely come at the final moment of visibility, just as the sun went entirely behind the hills: a sudden burst of brilliant emerald, the culmination of my decades-long search.

Another moment—another—

"Here it comes," I said.

The sun, yellow to the end, disappeared behind the hills. The sunset colors—the usual gorgeous reds and purples—intensified against the darkening sky.

"Well?" Karen called.

"Nothing," I said. "Just the standard terrific sunset."

"What time would you like to go for dinner?" she asked.

[*Amazing Stories*, September 1992]

I first heard of the green flash in the waning days of 1959. The January, 1960 issue of *Scientific American* had an article about it, richly illustrated with color photographs: the cover of that issue showed a swollen, almost extraterrestrial sun, mainly orange-hued with a band of yellow across its upper limb, generating an eerie burst of green at its very summit.

"Some clear evening as the sun is sinking below the horizon," the article began, "you may, if you are fortunate, witness one of nature's most unusual and beautiful displays. Just as the last of the solar disk is about to disappear, it may momentarily turn a brilliant green."

The author of the piece—D.J.K. O'Connell, S.J., director of the Vatican Observatory at Castel Gandolfo—had me hooked. I read on in fascination, learning that the green flash is not easy to see from most places, and that some people, having looked for it in vain for years, tend to dismiss it as a fantasy. Even those who have seen it—astronomers and physicists included, Father O'Connell said—often have spoken of it as a mere optical illusion. But here, indeed, were pages and pages of photographs: a series of black-and-white photos first (Father O'Connell understands the ways of faith better than I do) that showed a green flash in several stages of development, and then, for the benefit of skeptics, two stunning color photographs to go with the one on the cover. So much for the astronomers and physicists who thought it was an optical illusion: their eyes might be capable of being fooled, but not the camera's!

The green flash very likely was known to the ancient Egyptians, since it is a common phenomenon in the clear dry air of their country. A Fifth Dynasty pillar 4500 years old shows the sun as a semi-circle colored blue above and green below. And apparently there was an Egyptian belief that the sun turns green during its journey beneath the earth every night.

But I was amused to learn that the first published reference to the green flash seems to be in a science-fiction novel: Jules Verne's *Le Rayon Vert*, published in 1882, which describes an elaborate search for the enigmatic "ray" of the title. (A French movie of the same name, about ten years ago, told a tale of two young lovers who have read Verne's book and go on a similar quest.) How Verne heard about the "ray," which astronomers now refer to as the "flash," is anybody's guess. Perhaps he saw it himself. Or he may have encountered it in some traveler's memoirs, though no one has located the source.

What modern observers describe is a thin green band that is visible for a flickering instant at or just above the top edge of the sun as it drops below the horizon. Usually it covers about ten seconds of arc—the same apparent width as a one-inch ribbon seen at a distance of 1500 feet—and, Father O'Connell noted, it is not necessarily always green. "Sometimes it is blue, or turns from green to blue," he wrote. "Sometimes it is even violet. On rare occasion it appears while the whole disk of the sun is still above the horizon, and then there may be a red flash at the bottom of the disk as well as a green or blue one at the top." The flash may be seen at sunrise, too, usually green, occasionally blue or violet.

The sunrise flash was described in the authoritative journal *Nature* as far back as 1899 by none other than the great physicist Lord Kelvin, discoverer of the second law of thermodynamics. Kelvin had seen the green sunset flash about 1893, and over the next five or six years often searched for its counterpart of the dawn, finding it finally on a trip to the Alps. "I....resolved to watch an hour till sunrise," he reported, "and was amply rewarded by all the splendors I saw....In an instant I saw a blue light against the sky on the southern profile of Mont Blanc; which, in less than the one twentieth of a second became dazzlingly white."

Despite Kelvin's impressive testimony, many scientists continued to regard the flash as apocryphal folklore, or else as some trick of the eyes. The difficulties photographers had for decades in capturing it on color film added to the general skepticism. ("The real trouble," Father O'Connell tells us, "is simply that the focal length of their camera lens is too short to form a visible image of the narrow band of color. For example, in a 35-millimeter camera with a lens five centimeters in focal length the image of a normal green flash would be only .005 millimeter wide, much too narrow to be recorded on the film.") But with the aid of the Kodak Research Laboratories and a 16-inch Zeiss the scientists at the Vatican Observatory were able to make satisfactory photographs of the green flash in the late 1950s, and thereafter its existence could no longer be doubted.

It is caused by the refracting or bending of the sun's light as it enters the atmosphere. The amount of refraction depends on the wavelength of the light, shorter waves being bent more than longer ones. This produces a spectrum, with the red wavelengths at one end and the violet ones at the other. The lower the sun, the greater the thickness of air through which its light must pass on the way to our eyes, and so the refraction effect is greatest at sunrise and sunset.

If we had exceedingly precise vision, we would be able to see the colors of the spectrum disappearing in an orderly progression as the sun sets, the red rays going first, then the orange, yellow, green, and so on. In fact too much mingling and scattering of light is going on in the atmosphere at sunset to allow us such a sight. But sometimes, evidently, under perfect viewing conditions, we are given just the quickest glimpse of the green component of the solar spectrum as the sun sinks, green being the color least affected by the atmospheric refraction. In high altitudes, and when the air is very still, even shorter waves may come through in that last moment, and a blue or violet flash is the result.

It must be a remarkable effect, and certainly I long to see it. But, as you know, I've had no luck, despite diligent searching in some of the world's most picturesque places. Egypt, I thought for sure, would provide me with a flash or two—but it didn't.

Perhaps my unfortunate dislike of chilly weather is one problem. The farther you go from the Equator, the more readily visible the flash is. At a place in Norway at latitude 79 degrees north the flash in midsummer may last up to 14 minutes: seven at sunset and seven at the sunrise that follows immediately. And Admiral Byrd, in Antarctica in 1929, reported seeing a green flash at 78 degrees south that endured on and off for 35 minutes.

No trips to McMurdo Sound are on my present travel schedule, nor am I planning to head into the remote Arctic in the immediate future. But I'll keep on looking for the green flash in more temperate places. And if I ever see it, you'll be the first to know.

Gods Almighty

I am not the confirmed and outspoken atheist that Isaac Asimov was; but, like him, I have never managed to affiliate myself with any organized religious group, and for most of my life I've been looking with bemusement and incomprehension (and some occasional cynicism) at the whole phenomenon of religious faith.

Isaac simply had no use for religion. He regarded religious belief as superstition, and organized religions as instruments of ignorance and repression. "I have never, in all my life, not for one moment, been tempted toward religion of any kind," he wrote in his final biographical work, *I, Asimov*, which was published shortly after his death in 1992. "The fact is that I feel no spiritual void. I have my philosophy of life, which does not include any aspect of the supernatural and which I find totally satisfying. I am, in short, a rationalist and believe only that which reason tells me is so."

My own upbringing and educational path followed Isaac's in ways that were astonishingly similar, as we occasionally liked to point out to each other—we were both Jewish boys from Brooklyn, wise guys a lot too smart for our own good, who went off to college at eerily young ages (both of us to Columbia, fifteen years apart) and became successful science fiction writers with equal precocity. (Isaac had published his classic story "Nightfall" by the time he was 21; at the same age I had already won my first Hugo.) Neither of us had managed to find any spiritual or emotional comfort in the religion into which we were born—Judaism—and neither of us had ever been tempted to enroll in any Christian sect or anything more esoteric.

Isaac did, however, spend a great deal of time *studying* the phenomenon of religion, since religion is, of course, an important factor in human history and anything that was important in history was of interest to Isaac. He didn't believe, but he wanted to understand. And so he wrote no less than six book on the Bible, including the magisterial *Asimov's Guide to the Bible*; he produced an annotated edition of Milton's *Paradise Lost* that reflected his considerable knowledge of Christian theology; and he was well versed also in the Greek and Norse myths, which are, of course, religious in nature. (It was, in fact, childhood readings of just those myths that led both Isaac and me away from the religion of our families: we both became convinced, he in the 1920s and me in the early 1940s, that the miraculous tales of the Bible were made-up myths just like the tales of Odin and Zeus, every bit as entertaining and every bit as fictional.)

And, like Isaac, I too have studied many religions deeply—always as an outsider, in my case partly out of a love of scholarship and partly in an attempt to understand why religion has no hold on my soul. This curiosity and this bewilderment both have played central roles in my fiction. Again and again, the characters of my novels have gone on quests for some sort of understanding of the supernatural, of the transcendental. Sometimes they plunge eagerly into what they find; sometimes they turn in horror away from it. I made my most explicit statement of these problems, I suppose, in two novels written back to back (*The Face of the Waters*, 1991, and *Kingdoms of the Wall*, 1993), in which my protagonists come to diametrically opposed conclusions: the hero of *Face of the Waters* ultimately surrenders himself to metaphysical engulfment, whereas the narrator of *Kingdoms of the Wall* goes in search of his gods, finds them in the most literal way, and is not pleased by what he discovers.

In the course of pondering these matters and writing these books, I've amassed a considerable library of works on religious subjects. Which leads me to the book I want to discuss today—a book I didn't even remember that I owned, until I stumbled on it inadvertently while looking for something else entirely. It's an obscure and very probably now hard to find work that provides, in a charming way, an example of what both Isaac and I found so fascinating and so personally off-putting about the phenomenon of religious belief.

I speak of Manfred Lurker's *Dictionary of Gods and Goddesses, Devils and Demons*, a book published originally in Germany in 1984, and in English in 1987 by the firm of Routledge & Kegan Paul. It is precisely what its title says it to be: 394 pages of alphabetical listings of the gods and demons that mankind has managed to imagine for itself (or to discover, let us concede, through divine revelation), beginning with Aatxe and ending with Zu. This is followed by an appendix listing the various gods by their functions and spheres of competence (divine messengers, mother goddesses, gods of death, etc.) and a second appendix arranging them by their physical attributes (panther-gods, pig-gods, snail-gods) and other defining characteristics of appearance.

For the would-be fantasy or science-fiction writer, it's a wonderful compendium of imaginative imagery and wild philosophical conceptualization. For the unbeliever, the Isaac Asimov or the Robert Silverberg, it's also a profoundly sobering reminder of what we see as human gullibility, human credulousness, human folly. It's also a great deal of fun. A few examples:

Here's Egres, a fertility god worshipped by the ancient Finns. His particular area of responsibility was turnips. The Finnish turnip farmer, hoping for a bountiful crop, paid homage to Egres in ways that we hardly dare guess; but the turnip-god's congregation has, I suspect, relatively few members today.

And here is Kis, a god once venerated in the Egyptian town of Kusae. His name means "the tamer," and he is portrayed as a man who holds two creatures—giraffes, or sometimes snakes—by their long necks as a way of pacifying them. Any god who can quiet a snake by holding its neck, or who could, perhaps, hold a giraffe's neck in one hand and a snake's in the other, would come in handy in today's world of difficult political tasks. Could Kis, I wonder, persuade our squabbling Democrats and Republicans to come up with a balanced budget?

Then we have Sarkany, a weather-demon of the early Hungarians. This Magyar marvel had seven or nine heads, carried a saber, and came forth on horseback, waving the planet Venus around as he went about his work of bringing storms and turning people into stones. I try to stay indoors when Sarkany is making his rounds; it's one of the benefits of the free-lance life that you can work at home, and I take full advantage of it.

A particularly pretty one is Vanth, a female demon of the Etruscan underworld, one of the messengers of death. She's got a large eye on the underside of each wing—a reminder that Vanth is everywhere at once, keeping an eye on everything. Vanth is a watch-demon watching you.

She's not nearly as spooky, though, as the Aztec goddess Coatlicue, whose gigantic stone statue once brought gasps of amazement from me in the great archaeological museum in Mexico City. Coatlicue as I saw her in Mexico was a nightmarish figure ten feet high, six feet wide and thick, with terrible clawed feet, a skirt of writhing serpents, a necklace made of human hands and hearts, and an appalling Lovecraftian face of plainly extraterrestrial origin that I won't even attempt to describe. The role of this monster in Aztec life? Why, she was the goddess of birth, the beloved mother of the culture-hero Quetzalcoatl.

And so it goes, as I've said, from Aatxe to Zu. (Aatxe, let me tell you without further ado, is Basque, an evil spirit in the form of a bull, who comes forth on stormy nights disguised as a human and makes trouble for the unwary. As for Zu, down at the far end of the alphabetical pantheon, he is, strangely enough, an evil demon also, a Mesopotamian storm-bird who steals the tablets of fate in order to make himself the master of the gods, but is put in his place by the warlike Ninurta (who, when he isn't vanquishing unruly demons, causes herds of cattle to flourish and fields to be fertile and productive.)

The catalog is endlessly fascinating. And it must represent only a fraction of the total divine population this planet has managed to spawn. The gods of the Cro-Magnons and Neanderthals are not represented here, nor will they, I suppose, ever be. Nor will we find the thousands of divinities whose worship came and went in pre-literate or non-literate societies without any record of their might and power being left behind.

But there's plenty in this book to engage the thoughtful and wondering mind. Who or what were the formidable Jabru, Jagaubis, Janguli, Jarovit, Julunggul, Jurojin, and Jyotiska? You'll find them all here, with the more familiar Janus, Jehovah, Juno, and Jupiter interspersed among them. Zababa, Zalmoxis, Zaltys, and Zam? They're on the page before Zeus, who precedes Zocho, Zotz, and our old friend Zu. And, yes, Amenominakanushi and Ameretat and Amm, Bangputys and Bebellahamon and Boldogasszony, Caturmaharajas and Cernunnos and Culsu: each one gets his or her or its paragraph in this astonishing collection of deities.

What a tribute to foolishness and credulity, as Isaac might have said! Or, as one might hear from someone less hostile to the religious impulse as he was, what a record of the human yearning for the answers to ultimate questions of destiny and purpose! Either way, Lurker's *Dictionary of Gods and Goddesses* is an instructive and awesome compilation that illustrates the richness of the human imagination. Track it down somewhere: it's worth the hunt.

The Voyager Photos

I've been looking back over the results of the epic journey of the Voyager spaceships through the Solar System lately, and I've been reading a little science fiction, and the juxtaposition doesn't give me a good feeling about the reach and sweep of the science-fictional imagination.

What I see, on the one hand, is the sheer *strangeness* of the information about the moons and planets of our astronomical neighbors that the two Voyagers sent back during that phenomenal decade-long cruise to Jupiter, Saturn, Uranus, and Neptune. And what I see on the other hand is the downright *ordinariness* of the planets that science-fiction writers tend to concoct.

It's pretty dismaying to look at the Voyager pictures, and then to pick up a novel by my esteemed colleague X or Y or Z. What Voyager told us is that the Solar System is a damned weird place. What X and Y and Z seem to be telling us is that someday we'll be traveling to other planets of other stars which will be just about as dissimilar to our Earth as Chicago is to Brooklyn, no more, no less. Their characters get off the interstellar spaceliner—which is like a Boeing 747, only a little bigger—and step out into a spaceport much like O'Hare Airport or Los Angeles International or John F. Kennedy—and then they hop into a taxi and onto a freeway and off they go to town. Where they check into the galactic equivalent of the Hilton and take a nice refreshing shower before setting out in search of their next dazzling adventure.

Whereas the Solar System, as reported to us by Voyager—

Just *consider* this stuff a moment.

Even before Voyager 1's 1979 visit, we knew how weird Jupiter is: a ferocious maelstrom of whirling gases, with an eerie red spot bigger than Earth on its flank and lightning crackling perpetually around it. Poul Anderson brought Jupiter vividly to life for us a generation ago in his classic story "Call Me Joe."

But who ever imagined that the moons of Jupiter would be anything like what they turned out to be?

Voyager showed us the surface of Io: not the expected pockmarking of craters, but a relatively smooth land of brilliant white patches alternating with mottled areas of red and yellow and orange. A Voyager scientist, seeing the first close-up pictures, said that Io looked like a pizza. The red areas were found to be sulfur dust. To everyone's

[*Amazing Stories*, September 1991]

amazement, volcanoes were active on this "dead, frozen" moon. There were lakes of what seemed to be lava-like sulfur, and sulfur geysers rising with tremendous force. Huge plumes of sulfur descended from them. Sulfur, it appeared, was the water of Io—great seas of it frozen on top but molten beneath, and bordered by white strips of sulfur-dioxide frost.

Then came Ganymede, which had craters aplenty, one next to another, but also areas of strange parallel grooved valleys, twenty or thirty miles long, as though it had been worked over with a giant rake. Callisto too had craters; one immense impact region had ripples reaching out for two thousand miles, signifying an ancient collision with some inconceivably huge meteorite. And startling Europa, photographed in amazing detail by Voyager 2: almost entirely smooth, a billiard ball in space, all its craters eradicated by, it is supposed, great heat coming from beneath its icy surface.

The two Voyagers flew past Saturn in November 1980 and August 1981, and new wonders emerged. We learned about Saturn's spooky rings, marked by unsuspected spokes and whorls, and held together by "shepherd" moonlets invisible to our best telescopes. We found that what we thought were gaps in the rings were occupied by more rings, little ones, intertwined and sometimes kinky or helical. Voyager showed us a moon of Saturn—Tethys—with a trench forty miles wide running nearly from one end to the other, as if the little moon had cracked from within. Its neighbor Enceladus was crater-free, so smooth and white that it reflected light like a mirror. Mimas had a crater 100 miles across, the scar of a collision four billion years ago that must have nearly blown the moon apart.

Onward then to Uranus, in 1986—new moons discovered, old ones offering new perplexities. Uranus turned out to have rings, similar to Saturn's but with significant differences. The off-center magnetic field of Uranus provided mysteries also. The larger moons of Uranus showed signs of fierce volcanic activity, odd chevron-like grooves, unanticipated fracture patterns. Umbriel was covered by a paint-like coating of some currently inexplicable smooth substance. Miranda, a place of improbably tormented terrain, appeared to have been shattered again and again and reassembled by gravitational force. Voyager 2 saw ice cliffs on Miranda higher than the walls of Arizona's Grand Canyon.

And, finally, Neptune in 1989: it turned out to have a ring too, but no shepherd moons, and violent weather with winds of 1500 miles an hour. Its moon Triton was colder than expected, the coldest body in the solar system at -391° Fahrenheit. Triton was sealed in ice as hard as stone, but volcanic activity was going on somewhere within, for signs of eruption could be seen—volcanoes hurling geysers of ice five miles high!

I was at Pasadena's Jet Propulsion Labs, along with many other science-fiction writers, for most of the Voyager excitement. Hours would pass without event: then some new picture of an alien moon would appear on the screen, and we would stare at it in confusion and wonder, and after a while would come word that the scientists in the back rooms at JPL were just as puzzled as we were. It was an experience to be repeated again and again: mystery upon mystery, startlement upon startlement.

How different it all is in the science-fiction novels. We talk glibly of "Earth-type" planets, so that we and our readers can enjoy the convenience of running around on "alien" worlds without any of the awkwardness of life-support gear. But all these "Earth-type" worlds are no more than little exotic pieces of Earth generalized up to planetary size. Arabia becomes a desert world; the Amazon basin becomes a steaming tropical world; Antarctica becomes an ice-world; New York or Los Angeles or New Orleans become the models for "alien" cities. True invention—true strangeness—is a rare commodity indeed.

The Voyager photographs told us that our own little solar system is a place of amazing oddity. The many moons of the outer planets proved to be very little like our own moon and not at all as they were expected to be. In inventing alien planets, should we not try to be at least as resourceful? Think of Hal Clement's famous novel, *Mission of Gravity*—how many of our invented worlds show the fantastic ingenuity of that one, where gravity itself varied in intensity with latitude?

But perhaps it's not possible, not if we want anyone to read our books. A little alienness goes a long way, it seems: make the landscape too strange and it steals the show from plot and character. And plot and character—especially plot—are the items that hold reader attention, however much we of the s-f world like to think they come to our work for the intellectual stimulation of confronting the unfamiliar. So the novels pour forth, set on galactic equivalents of Texas or California or New York. All the same, looking at the marvelous Voyager scenes, I feel a need to work harder at creating plausible strangeness. An alien landscape should be *alien*.

Of course, there's one built-in limitation that even the best of us has to struggle under. We're mere mortals, with finite powers of creation. All we can do is reassemble familiar patterns into somewhat less familiar ones, whereas the Universe, in bringing forth its wonders, suffers from no such restriction. I think it was the famous British astronomer Sir James Jeans who once said that the Universe is not only stranger than we imagine, it is stranger than we *can* imagine. If that's true—and I'm afraid that it is—then even the supreme inventive achievements of science fiction are doomed to seem prosaic and mundane when compared with the real wonders waiting for us out there.

Six Trillion Miles High

I'm looking at the most awesome photograph I've ever seen—or
expect to see. It may well be the most extraordinary picture in the
entire history of photography.

It's a dazzling color photo (in the San Francisco *Chronicle*; at any
rate; the more conservative New York *Times*, which I, as an expatriate
New Yorker, continue to read out here in California, ran it in prosaic
black and white.) The picture shows three craggy-looking pillar-
shaped objects of differing sizes. The left-hand one, which is the
tallest, reminds me of the upright growths I used to see occasionally
while snorkeling around coral reefs in the West Indies, or perhaps of
a stalagmite sprouting from a cavern floor. The middle object, smaller
and simpler in form, is somewhat phallic. The small one on the right
has an irregular, nondescript two-pronged shape. They are shown
against a background of blue sky (at least in the San Francisco paper)
with some twinkling stars in view behind them. Fluffy masses of
bright light can be seen around the tops of all three of the vertical
objects.

The three pillars, although they look like gnarly outcroppings of
rock, are in fact dark clouds of gas out of which three new stars, eight
or ten times as massive as our own sun, have just formed. The swirls
of fluffy brightness looking like so much cotton candy that we see at
the tips of those three pillar-shaped objects are actually the emanations of the newly born stars, which are in the Eagle Nebula, M16 in
the constellation known as Serpens, 7,000 light-years distant from
Earth.

Those three craggy upright objects in the photograph are each
about *six trillion miles high*. If one end of the smallest of them were to
be attached to our sun, the other end would jut out into space well
beyond the orbit of Pluto. Yet there are all three of them in a single
snapshot, covering perhaps fifty square inches of the front page of my
daily newspaper. That one lovely image provides us a privileged look
at the act of stellar birth.

Now do you see why I think it's the most awesome photograph
ever taken?

The orbiting Hubble Space Telescope snapped it in April, 1995.
NASA released it about six months later, along with others showing
some fifty new stars in varying stages of development. I don't know
which aspect of the picture I find most astonishing: that the pretty

[*Asimov's Science Fiction*, January, 1997]

swirls of bright fluffiness at the ends of the long columnar structures are in reality gigantic stars seen in the moment of their coming into being, or that we are peering back seven thousand years in time to watch those stars being born, or that the three columns themselves, hardly longer than my fingers in the photograph, are colossi of unimaginable size. (What does "six trillion miles" mean to us, really, except "very very big?")

I suppose it's the compression of six-trillion-mile long objects into a single photograph that stirred the most immediate surge of wonderment in me when I opened the newspaper that morning. But on some reflection I realized that what astonished me most was that the picture had been taken at all—done at the behest of ordinary mortals right here on Earth in the year 1995. That's only some 160 years since Michael Faraday discovered the principles of the electric dynamo, 101 years since Guglielmo Marconi managed to send radio signals across a distance as great as a mile and a half, 92 years since Orville and Wilbur Wright made their first wobbly little airplane flight at Kitty Hawk. And just 38 years since human beings succeeded in launching the first artificial space satellite—the Soviet Union's tiny Sputnik I. Whatever its other flaws may be, a species that can manage to traverse a course in less than two centuries that carries it from its first uncertain generation of electricity and its earliest crude experiments with flight to the taking of pictures (from a camera parked in space) of the birth process of stars seven thousand light-years away has to be regarded as a non-trivial kind of species. We make a lot of messes on this planet, but we are an intelligent life-form even so.

The particular life-form who brought these flabbergasting photos into being was Dr. Jeff Hester, an astronomer at Arizona State University, who worked in association with Paul Scowen, a postdoctoral fellow there. At the time of the pictures' release Dr. Hester explained that what we are looking at in them is a group of immense and relatively dense clouds of hydrogen gas. (In the photographs they seem like solid rock outcroppings, or perhaps like great thunderheads against the sky, but in actuality they are dense only in comparison with the virtual vacuum about them; their thickest portions, according to Dr. Hester, are less than a trillionth as dense as the atmosphere of Earth.) These clouds are undergoing bombardment by intense ultraviolet radiation coming from big stars in their vicinity. This radiation is causing the gas that makes up the huge pillars to boil away, a process that exposes even denser masses of gas within the column.

It is within these inner masses that the genesis of stars takes place. Dr. Hester likens the erosive effect of the ultraviolet radiation to that caused by high winds scouring across a desert, sweeping away sand and laying bare the boulders that had been buried within it. The hidden globules of dense gaseous matter have already begun to collapse of their own weight, setting into operation the process of star formation. As these globules begin to stand out as a result of the impact of the ultraviolet radiation, and then themselves start to evaporate, the nascent stars inside them are gradually revealed.

"In some ways it seems more like archaeology than astronomy," Dr. Hester says. "The ultraviolet light from nearby stars does the digging for us, and we study what is unearthed." Hester, who can be dazzlingly quick to shift metaphors, tells us that the globule at the stage when the newborn star first becomes visible "looks something like an ice cream cone, with a newly uncovered star playing the role of the cherry on top."

After a time, the dense globules are connected to the mother cloud by nothing more than thin bridges of gas, and the young stars can be seen at the ends of stalks protruding from the cloud masses that spawned them. As the evaporative process continues, the new stars eventually become completely isolated from the surrounding gas clouds, and the clouds themselves ultimately evaporate altogether. (Hester could not resist giving the star-generating cloud globules the name of EGGs, "evaporating gas globules.")

This is not the only process by which stars are born, nor the only one that the orbiting Hubble telescope has photographed since its launching in 1990. The evaporative effect caused by the ultra-violet output of the neighboring stars is hastening the emergence of the Eagle Nebula stars from their cloud matrix, so that it is unlikely that planets will form around them. Elsewhere, where the ultraviolet factor is not present, newborn stars remain in their formative cloud masses a much longer time, continuing to grow until their own radiation and other dynamic processes frees them from the surrounding gas.

The 94-inch Hubble, which began its career in space under something of a cloud itself (after having been put in orbit, it needed a tweaking by shuttle-borne astronauts to correct a focusing problem) promises to inundate us with wonders in the remaining ten or twenty years of its probable time in orbit. A few months after the flabbergasting Serpens photographs came the even more flabbergasting announcement at the American Astronomical Association convention in San Antonio, Texas, that the Hubble, when aimed over a twelve-day period in December, 1995 at a remote part of space that through ground-based telescopes appears to be almost devoid of stars, had discovered no less than 1,500 young galaxies out there. Not stars, but galaxies. (Millions of stars, that is....possibly a whole slew of planets. The whole starry panorama that you see in the skies at night represents just one galaxy, the local one that we call the Milky Way, and not all of it at that.) The conclusion was that if this supposedly empty corner of space is crammed with previously unknown galaxies, then the universe must be far more crowded than we have until now believed it to be.

So crowded, in fact, that instead of there being a mere ten billion galaxies in the universe, astronomers now think that there may be *fifty* billion. One click of the Hubble's cute little shutter and forty billion galaxies, with Isaac only knows how many stars and planets in them (and—dare we say it?—planets bearing intelligent life), have been added to our cosmos overnight.

Forty billion previously unsuspected galaxies....

Clouds of dust six trillion miles high....

Photographs of clouds of dust six trillion miles high in the newspaper....

Things aren't perfect on our little planet these days. We have a vanishing ozone layer, nasty little wars happening in too many places, people going hungry, et cetera, et cetera. There's lots of room for improvement. But it's an age of wonders, all the same. Never let anybody tell you otherwise. We are flawed entities, yes; but we are not all that contemptible a species if we can manage to poke our little cameras into the cradles of the stars and at galaxies fifteen billion light-years away.

THREE

THE PROFESSION OF WRITING

The Making of a Science-Fiction Writer

This lengthy essay served as the introduction for an anthology I did called Robert Silverberg's Worlds of Wonder: Exploring the Craft of Science Fiction, *first published in 1987. The book was intended, among other things, as a textbook for beginning science-fiction writers; it contained thirteen classic stories that had deeply influenced me when I was beginning my own career, along with my technical commentary on each of the stories. It's tempting to reprint all thirteen of the essays here, since they summarize most of what I know about the craft of writing short science fiction; but that really would also require me to include the stories to which they refer, and that would give us a complete reprint of* Worlds of Wonder *interpolated within this collection, which probably isn't a feasible idea. Instead I've used my foreword here, which has plenty of my notions about the craft of writing also, and a goodly helping of autobiography besides.*

I must have been a peculiar little boy. Most people who grow up to be professional science-fiction writers were peculiar little boys, except for those who were peculiar little girls. (Most, not all. I doubt that Robert A. Heinlein was peculiar, for somehow he is our Great Exception in almost everything, and I suspect that Ray Bradbury may have *appeared* normal at a casual glance. But I know that Isaac Asimov seemed like an oddball to his classmates; surely young Jack Williamson felt shy and gangling and utterly out of place; and the mind boggles at the thought of John W. Campbell, Jr., going out to play stickball with the gang after school.) We are not, by and large, a clan who found it easy to get along with other people when we were young. (Imagine Harlan Ellison as a fifth grader and you'll see what I mean.) Which is probably why we became dreamers in the first place, retreating into private worlds of extraordinary vividness; and which may be why, now that we have learned to turn those dreams into dollars and live successfully in the world of mundane folk, we still prefer the company of our own kind to that of those others.

Perhaps we were maladjusted little brats, but we were smart ones. Certainly, I was. I walked early, I was a precocious talker, I learned to read when I was three. By the time I was five I was in the first grade; after a year I skipped to the third grade, where I founded and edited a school newspaper, most of which I wrote myself. (I was six.) I collected bugs and stamps and coins and anything else I could think of, became something of an expert on botany, learned all there was to

[*Robert Silverberg's Worlds of Wonder*, 1987]

know about dinosaurs, fooled around with a microscope, and knew the names of all the kings of England in order. (I think I still remember them.) Somewhere around that time I began writing short stories too. I was small, untidy, and very free with my opinions. I must have been an enormous pain in the neck. (The world will never know how many potential science-fiction writers were strangled or pushed off the tops of tall buildings in childhood by irate classmates or enraged siblings. But I was quick enough and agile enough to elude my classmates, and I didn't have to worry about siblings, thank God, which is why I survived and was able to bring you all those wonderful books and stories.)

The one thing I didn't do when I was busy being a child prodigy was read science fiction. That came later, when I was 10 or 11. Instead, I read things like Henrik Van Loon's *The Story of Mankind* and Charles and Mary Lamb's *Tales from Shakespeare*, and A. Hyatt Verrill's *Great Conquerors of South and Central America*. For my fiction I tended at first toward books like *Huckleberry Finn* and *Penrod* and *Tom Sawyer*.

But I also had an insatiable appetite for stranger things. I virtually committed *Alice in Wonderland* and *Through the Looking Glass* to memory. I read *Gulliver's Travels*, not for political satire but for the exotic civilizations it depicted. I read *The Hobbit*, a decade before *Lord of the Rings* was published. The Dr. Doolittle books, the tales of George MacDonald, Jules Verne's *20,000 Leagues Under the Sea*, and such escapist stuff—I couldn't get enough of it. I was eight, nine, ten years old. (My copy of the Modern Library Lewis Carroll, 1,293 pages long and many times to be read end to end, bears an inscription from my father dated two months before my eighth birthday: "This reminds me of you—a little jabber-*wacky*." I had just entered the fourth grade.) I read fairy tales galore. I gobbled books of mythology, mainly retellings of the Greek and Norse myths, but such esoterica as the Persian *Book of Kings* as well, and the *Thousand and One Nights* in a translation—Sir Richard Burton's—far less expurgated than my parents could have suspected.

Oddly, it never occurred to me, avidly reading and rereading the adventures of Theseus or Thor or Kaikhosro and searching for more of the same, that what I was looking for was fantasy. Not ordinarily boyish fantasy ("Let's build a raft and go down the Mississippi") but something spectacular and flamboyant, with frost-giants in it and Scylla and Charybdis and Valhalla and the Nibelungen and dragons and heroes. I didn't then know, or didn't care that all those things could be categorized as fantasy. But I knew what I wanted, and I found it with singleminded zeal, hauling books home from the library every Saturday and finishing every one before next week's trip.

And though I read such books as *20,000 Leagues Under the Sea* or H.G. Wells' *The Time Machine* or Mark Twain's *Connecticut Yankee at King Arthur's Court*, I certainly had no idea that those books belonged to that branch of fantasy known as science fiction. In fact, that was the sort of fantasy I preferred—the kind that might almost have been real, except that it was built around a fantastic premise. Since I was definitely science-oriented, trying to decide whether I'd be a botanist or a paleontologist when I grew up, but also had a distinct taste for imaginative fantasies, the chances are good that I'd have jumped at the science-fiction magazines of the wartime era if I had only known they existed. Something called "*science* fiction" (and I would have put the accent on *science* then) unquestionably would have appealed to me right away.

But the term wasn't all that commonly used, back then in the 1940's. The New York Public Library classified science-fiction books under the uninviting and vaguely disreputable-sounding heading, "Pseudoscientific Literature." There were eight or nine science-fiction magazines in those days, but with one exception they were flashy-looking, trashy-looking pulp magazines with names like *Startling Stories* and *Thrilling Wonder Stories*. A serious little boy like me wasn't likely to seek out magazines with names like that, nor did anyone happen to leave them where I might find them accidentally. (The only magazine with "science-fiction" in its title was also the only one that didn't look like a garish pulp magazine: John Campbell's austere, dignified *Astounding Science Fiction*. Perhaps I would have wrinkled up my nose at that *astounding* in the title, or perhaps I would have tried an issue and found the stories too abstruse for my 10-year-old mind. But I simply didn't run across any copies.)

Then I did stumble upon science fiction that was plainly labeled as science fiction. I think I was eleven, maybe twelve; and after that everything was permanently changed for me.

Since one of the purposes of this book is to reprint the stories that helped shape me into the writer I was to become, I wish I could include in it the entire contents of the first five or six s-f books I discovered. Their impact on me was overwhelming. I can still taste and feel the extraordinary sensations they awakened in me: it was a physiological thing, a distinct excitement, a certain metabolic quickening at the mere thought of handling them, let alone reading them.

It must be like that for every new reader—apocalyptic thunderbolts and eerie unfamiliar music accompanying you as you lurch and stagger, awed and shaken, into a bewildering new world of images and ideas, which is exactly the place you've been hoping to find all your life. A different set of stories, of course, provides that moment of apocalypse for each neophyte. The ones that struck my spirit with such stunning force at that first moment of revelation might seem hopelessly old hat to today's readers, which is one reason why I am not filling this book with them. But this I do know, that every day of the week someone who has never read science fiction comes upon an odd-looking book—one of mine, perhaps, or one of Asimov's, or one by some cluck of a writer whom any knowledgeable reader would scorn—and opens it not knowing what to expect, and reads, and reads on, and reads through the night, and is forever transformed.

For me it was Donald A. Wollheim's *Pocket Book of Science Fiction* that did the trick—the first of all paperback s-f anthologies, published in 1943 and discovered by me in the public library three or four years later. In it I found Theodore Sturgeon's "Microcosmic God" and Stribling's "Green Splotches" and Heinlein's "—And He Built a Crooked House" and above all Weinbaum's "A Martian Odyssey," and H.G. Wells was there too, and Don A. Stuart, and John Collier.

From there it was on to Wollheim's *Portable Novels of Science*, which I remember buying at Macy's when I was twelve. This was even a deeper, stronger dose: an incurable infection, in fact. For here was John Taine's *Before the Dawn*, which spoke to my boyhood passion for dinosaurs, and here was Wells' quaint and charming *First Men in the Moon*, and here too was H.P. Lovecraft's powerful *The Shadow out of Time*, which I will remember always for a single chapter, the fourth, in which Lovecraft showed me giant alien beings moving about in a weird library full of "horrible annals of other worlds and other universes, and of stirrings of formless life outside of all universes. There were records of strange orders of beings which had peopled the world in forgotten pasts, and frightful chronicles of grotesque-bodied intelligences which would people it millions of years after the death of the last human being."

I wanted desperately to explore that library myself. I knew I could not; I would know no more of the furry prehuman Hyperborean worshippers of Tsathoggua and the wholly abominable Tcho-Tchos than Lovecraft chose to tell me, nor would I talk with the mind of

Yiang-Li, the philosopher from the cruel empire of Tsan-Chan, which is to come in A.D. 5000, nor with the mind of the king of Lomar who ruled that terrible polar land one hundred thousand years before the squat, yellow Inutos came from the west to engulf it. But I read that page of Lovecraft ten thousand times—it is page 429 of Wollheim's anthology—and even now, scanning it this morning, it stirs me with the hunger to find and absorb all the science fiction in the world, every word of it, so that I might begin to know the mysteries of these lost imaginary kingdoms of time past and time future.

There was another novel in the Wollheim collection that stirred me even more profoundly than Lovecraft's, though. It was Olaf Stapledon's *Odd John*, the quintessential peculiar-little-boy book, a haunting and tragic tale of a child prodigy—one far beyond my own attainments, but with whom, nonetheless, I was easily able to identify. You are not alone, Stapledon was saying to me. You will find others of your sort; and if you are lucky you and your peers will withdraw to a safe island far from the cruel and clumsy bullies who clutter your classroom, and do your work in peace, whatever it may be. Even though it all ends badly for John and his friends, *Odd John* must be a powerfully comforting work for any bright, unhappy child. Certainly, it was for me. I was unhappy because of my brightness; through Stapledon I saw a mode, fantastic though it might be, of escaping all of that into a more secure life. If it is a novel that also feeds paranoia, arrogance, and elitist fantasy, so be it. It made me feel better. I think I am not the only one who used it that way.

The book department at Macy's now became my gateway to other worlds. Some time late in 1947 or early in 1948 I brought home the astonishing collection *Adventures in Time and Space*, edited by Raymond J. Healy and J. Francis McComas (which gave me Hasse's "He Who Shrank," Robert Heinlein's "By His Bootstraps," A.E. van Vogt's "The Weapons Shop," Asimov's "Nightfall," and thirty-one others) and the only slightly less dazzling *Treasury of Science Fiction* (C.L. Moore's "No Woman Born" and "Vintage Season," Jack Williamson's "With Folded Hands," Arthur Clarke's "Rescue Party," and many more) that Groff Conklin had assembled. It was an easy leap from there to the science-fiction magazines of the day, gaudy though they might have been. The full commitment was made. I came home each afternoon with *Weird Tales* or *Amazing Stories* or *Super-Science Stories* under my jacket.

Of course I would try to write my own science-fiction stories, then. Of course.

I have the manuscript of my first attempt on my desk beside me. God knows how it has survived all these years. "The Last Days of Saturn" is its name; I was no more than 12 when I wrote it, in collaboration with Saul Diskin, a boyhood friend. We worked on it in class, I recall, whispering details of the plot to each other despite our teacher's scowls. How much of it was my work and how much his I have no way now of telling. I'd like to believe now that most of it was Saul's, but I suspect the truth is that I'm the main guilty party. All but one of the eight pages seem to be in my handwriting, and I have no doubt that I was the one who wrote jubilantly on the final page, "1,948 words. FINIS, THE END, COMPLETED, ALL DONE." This is how it opens:

> The following report is an extract from the records of the Western Hemisphere Council of War against the Eastern Hemisphere, Anno Scienti 3012 [in the Year of Science—ed.] (5013 A.D.):
>
> "The chair recognizes Dr. Neil, the Delegate from the Northern Sector."
>
> "Mr. Chairman, I have received a message through the Magnemit Machine [a machine that hurls messages through space by means of gross atomic magnetism of silverite, a substance known only to the Council] from the Council's expedition to Saturn, to seek room for our excess population. I shall read it.
>
> " 'Saturn is slowly but surely being destroyed. A series of meteors have disrupted the gravitational pulls of the tiny particles which make up Saturn's ring. Hence, each is pulling in a separate direction, and chasms of indescribable size are being formed. Three axial rotations ago we saw our abandoned projectile disappear into a huge Saturnian fissure. Our living quarters have already been destroyed....The days of the planet are decidedly numbered....The Saturnians are panic-stricken....' "

No need to continue, is there? The opening two hundred words plainly demonstrate the gifts that would carry me on to a career of scores of published books, hundreds of anthology appearances, and a long shelf of Nebula and Hugo awards. (What? You can't see even a *shred* of ability there? Look again. Look more closely. You see all that dazzling scientific extrapolation ["gross atomic magnetism of silverite, a substance known only to the Council"]? You see the quick and deft establishment of a crisis ["Saturn is slowly but surely being destroyed"]? You see—well, never mind. I was only a little kid. You think Heinlein did any better when *he* was 12?)

Looking at "The Last Days of Saturn" now, I see that one of the real problems with it was that my antiquarian urges had led me to use the wrong models. I hadn't read much contemporary science fiction— indeed, not much contemporary fiction at all. H.G. Wells' *First Men in the Moon*, which surely provided me with the inspiration for silverite, dated from 1901. Wells was a splendid storyteller, but the fictional conventions of 1901 allowed a writer to halt a story at any point for lengthy expository passages. Neither Lovecraft, Taine, nor Stapledon, the other authors in *Portable Novels of Science*, minded expository passages either. They weren't writing for pulp magazines. Neither was I. So I wrote a story that was virtually *all* expository passages. There were about ten lines of dialog, and even they were basically expository. (" 'Dr. Neil—he's just collapsed.' 'No wonder. His brother was up there in that crumbling hell.' ") The rest is stolid, cheerfully stodgy narrative. ("I was impressed with a will to live longer than they did, even for a primitive feeling of satisfaction. We devised a clever scheme for beating them in hand-to-hand combat: we put on hobnailed boots. Since they were balloon-like, filled with that greenish fluid, a puncture would kill them....")

If I had taken a closer look at the stories I was reading in the issues of *Amazing* and *Super-Science Stories* that I had lately begun buying, or those in such anthologies as *Adventures in Time and Space*, I might have noticed that contemporary s-f writers tended to open their stories with a dramatic situation, which they went on to develop through action, dialog, and (to some degree) the interplay of character, until the story reached a climax and a resolution. Maybe I did notice that, and simply decided it was too hard to do. But I was also rooting around in dusty secondhand shops and acquiring antique, even antediluvian s-f magazines, such as *Science Wonder Stories* from 1929 and *Amazing Stories* from 1932. Those magazines were *full* of fiction cast in the form of Reports of this or that futuristic Council and set in the Year of Science 3012, or its equivalent. The primitive technique of many of the authors didn't include such frills as the ability to create character or write dialog.

I didn't notice, I guess, that that school of fiction was obsolete. No one told me that the editors of the early science-fiction magazines had found it necessary to rely for their material largely on hobbyists with humpty-dumpty narrative skills; the true storytellers were off writing for the other pulp magazines, knocking out westerns or adventure tales with half the effort for twice the pay. So my early attempts at science fiction were imitative of something that hadn't had much craftsmanship or vitality behind it in the first place. No wonder they were so awful.

That didn't stop me from sending them to the s-f magazines of the day. I don't know if I actually submitted "The Last Days of Saturn" anywhere—I hope not—but within a year or so I certainly was sending some stories out, because I have the rejection slips to prove it. On July 18, 1949, for example, kindly Sam Merwin of *Startling* and *Thrilling Wonder* let me know that "Beneath the Ashes"—my sequel to "Last Days of Saturn"—had been "found not quite suitable for any of our science-fiction magazines." He was holding the manuscript for my pickup. (I didn't even have enough sense to include return postage.) About the same month I got a printed form from Street & Smith Publications, which put out *Astounding*, thanking me for the opportunity of examining the enclosed material, and regretting that they could not make use of it at this time.

Probably rejection slips of that sort are still in use by magazines today. I still get stories turned down by editors occasionally, you know, and so does every other well-known science-fiction writer I can think of—if God were a science-fiction writer, *He*'d get rejected once in a while too, editors being what they are—but of course I get tactful, apologetic letters now, not impersonal notes or printed forms. That's only to be expected, a courtesy extended to a veteran professional writer. The heartening thing about my early career, though, was that I stopped getting the printed forms, and began getting encouraging little letters, by the time I was seventeen or so. I still wasn't ready for professional publication. But I was learning fast, and the editors could see the speed of my progress. However it may seem to a beginner, most editors really want to help new writers get started. All they ask of them is that they learn how to produce something that's better than "The Last Days of Saturn." Which I did, way back when, and quickly. I have always been a quick learner.

At the time of "The Last Days of Saturn" I still had no notion of making my livelihood by writing. Such vocational ambitions as I had, age 12, were directed vaguely toward the sciences. Somehow my parents had detected the truth even before I knew it, though, and communicated it to one of my teachers. One day in an eighth-grade class we had a vocational-guidance session, during the course of which that teacher said to me, "I understand from your parents that you're thinking of becoming a writer."

That was complete news to me. I stood there stunned, examining and reexamining the thought. A writer? Well, of course, I was writing all sorts of stories, always had, and I was the editor of the school paper, because I was always the editor of the school paper wherever I went to school, and I plainly had a way with words, and won spelling bees—but a *writer*? Someone who wrote for his living? That had never crossed my mind. Honestly. I was going to be a paleontologist, I thought, and spend my days out in Wyoming digging up dinosaurs. Or do something in botany, maybe. A *writer*? Did that make any sense? Well...maybe...

I think the damage was done, right then and there that afternoon in the eighth grade. If it seemed obvious to everybody but me that I was going to be a writer, why, maybe I should give the idea a little thought. By such glancing blows are our fates determined.

I thought about the idea and the more I thought, the more I liked it. I imagined what it would feel like if one of the manuscripts I was sending to *Startling* and *Astounding* were to bring me not a printed rejection slip but an actual check, say as much as fifteen or twenty dollars. I thought of taking a copy of *Thrilling Wonder Stories* to school for show-and-tell and pointing out the magical line on the contents page, "By Robert Silverberg." Yes, that would be fine. But if I really intended to be a writer, I knew I was going to have to learn a little more about how it was done. I could see already that nobody was likely to publish the crude little stories I was writing.

I didn't see anything seriously wrong with my basic material—the dumb implausible ideas, the crude cardboard characters. So far as content went, my stories seemed as good as some of the junk then being published, and maybe they were. The problem, I thought, lay in the *way* I was writing them. You couldn't use the 1929 modes of narrative, I realized, and hope to get your stories published in the advanced, sophisticated s-f magazines of 1949. Technique, that's the problem.

Technique. A word that would obsess me for years.

I know exactly when I became aware that such a concept as technique—narrative technique—existed. It was in the autumn of 1949, and the man who told me about it was a 30-year-old American expatriate living in Tecate, Mexico. His name was Clif Bennett, and I know very little more about him than that, though my sense of him now is that he must have been a restless young Greenwich Village intellectual wandering around the warmer parts of the continent with a little library of Kafka, Kierkegaard, and D.H. Lawrence, supporting himself by making sandals or playing the guitar in coffeeshops or whatever. The last contact I had with him was in 1950, and I have no idea what became of him after that.

He was, in 1949, publishing a neatly mimeographed avant-garde magazine called *Catalyst* in association with another American whom he had met in Mexico. Somehow it was mentioned in a column in *Amazing Stories* and I sent for it. What I got was far beyond my barely adolescent level of comprehension, a magazine that quoted St. Augustine and Lewis Mumford, ran essays on Spengler and Toynbee, and published poems, some of which didn't rhyme. It also included a fantasy story by Clif Bennett. I responded with a letter of comment— I'd love to know what I said—and with great chutzpah sent along some of my own stories.

Clif Bennett's reply has vanished somewhere in the archives, and I don't expect to see it again. But the operative sentence that survives in my memory from our brief correspondence went something like this, and I think my recollection of it must be 95 percent accurate:

"Thanks for your stories. You plots are excellent, but somewhat underfurnished. I recommend you read Thomas Uzzell's *Narrative Technique*."

My plots were excellent! Look, Clif Bennett said so! But "somewhat underfurnished." What did that mean? Short of dialog? Short on action? What *is* a plot, anyway? Is that the same thing as a story? How can I find out? Why, by reading this Thomas Uzzell book, *Narrative Technique*. Of course! Technique! That's what I need to know: the way it's done. The secret of writing fiction. The mysterious secret that makes stories by Heinlein or Lewis Padgett or A.E. van Vogt so wonderfully engrossing. The secret that obviously I don't know, which is why my stories get sent back by the magazines, with printed rejection forms.

I ran off to the public library and behold! There was Thomas Uzzell's *Narrative Technique*, which I checked out and brought home and read in a feverish frenzy of rising bewilderment.

I don't have a copy of it today. I couldn't have afforded to buy my own in 1949 and by the time I could, it would have had purely sentimental value for me. Probably it went out of print long ago. So my recollection of what I found in it is pretty hazy; but what I do recall is the terror that it inspired in me. Writing stories was far more complicated than I ever suspected. It wasn't just a matter of thinking up some far-out idea ("Meteors are pulling the rings of Saturn apart, and the whole planet is breaking up") and describing its effect on a little group of people. No, there was the whole problem of plot, which Uzzell (I'm sure) distinguished from story.

Story, he must have said, was the total construct: situation, characters, style, everything. Including plot. Plot was just one ingredient of story, one that could be summarized in a sentence or two; and plot, I believe Thomas Uzzell probably said, was *the working out of a conflict*. That was what fiction was, basically: the record of a conflict, its development and its resolution. ("Agamemnon wants Achilles to come out of his tent and get over to the battlefield and fight the Trojans. But Achilles is annoyed because Agamemnon grabbed his favorite slave-girl, and refuses to stop sulking. So Agamemnon tells Achilles...")

Reading Uzzell on plot shook me up plenty. I saw now that a little piece about the unusual nature of life on Mars, or about what it's like to travel six million years in time, is not a story, because it has no plot, meaning that there's no conflict in it. At best it's an incident or an anecdote. It might be nothing more than a simple speculation. Let the Martians invade Earth, or let the time traveler fall in love with one of the Eloi who inhabit the far future, and you've got the makings of a plot. Most of my "stories" were failing because they didn't have plots.

That was news to me. Honestly. And it annoyed me. I didn't like conflict much. (Still don't.) I wanted to read, and to write, visions of strange places and times. Did that mean I had to put in villains, and chase scenes, and violent showdowns, if I hoped to get my stories published? Well, yes, I did. Not in such literal terms, but I began to recognize—age 13, 14, thereabout—that *a story has to be built around a pattern of oppositions*. If you want anyone else to read it, that is. At first it seemed tremendously limiting to me, an arbitrary and irrelevant rule that had little or no connection with what I had been writing or, I thought, with much of what I was reading.)

And then I realized that every story I had ever read, myths and fairy tales included, was built on conflict. Perhaps the protagonist is in conflict with the forces of nature, perhaps with villainous human beings, perhaps with his own inner feelings; but some sort of struggle is always present. Theseus is in the Minotaur's maze; he has to find his way out if he wants to win the princess and go home to Athens. Odysseus has to outwit the enchantresses and elude the monsters if he's ever going to see Ithaca again. King Lear has surrendered all his power to his daughters and now they're being nasty to him. The Martians have landed and they're destroying our cities. Don Quixote lives in a world where romance is dead, and he hates that, so he goes out trying to stir up a little, and attacks windmills that he thinks are evil giants. Conflict. Strife. Opposition of needs. If it isn't there, there's no story. Homer knew that almost three thousand years ago. Shakespeare knew it. Robert A. Heinlein knows it.

Uzzell told me much more than that—more, really, than I could absorb or handle. Character, for example, has to be integrated with plot. People get into conflict because they are the sort of people they are; they deal with conflicts in a way that illustrates their individual characters, and they resolve them in a way unique to their own character traits. Hamlet, who had a murder mystery to solve and a kingdom to inherit, was an indecisive man; Odysseus was wily; Lear was impulsive and rash. So was poor Oedipus, who got himself into a terrible mess because he struck first and stopped to think afterward. They weren't anonymous, interchangeable beings like my explorers of Saturn. Put Hamlet in King Lear's position and you'd get a very different story indeed. Odysseus, faced with Oedipus' problems, would certainly have found a more effective way to deal with them. (Hmmm. "Hamlet and His Daughters," by Robert Silverberg. "Odysseus and Jocasta." Might be worth fooling around with. Let's see..."Othello in Capetown.")

Uzzell's strictures on the role of character development in fiction plunged me into gloom. It wasn't enough to put a professor, a brave newspaper reporter, and the professor's beautiful daughter together in the time machine, the way they used to do it in 1931. Somehow I would have to give my characters individual traits—make them seem like real people, that is—and make the outcome of my story depend on the nature of those traits. That is so much a part of my method now—of any writer's method—that I've scarcely thought about it consciously in decades. But to me in 1949 it seemed like an impossible juggling-trick.

Then there was stuff about the proportions of dialog to exposition, about finding the right starting-point for a story, about building suspense, about point of view—well, I don't know. There was a lot of it, and it was all intimidating. I don't recall it in detail, but I know what had to have been there, even though it's close to forty years since I last looked at Uzzell's book. A three-hundred-page book on narrative technique had to be full of matters bound to be bewildering to a fledgling writer like me, no matter how clever.

And then there was the homework. I'm pretty sure that each chapter ended with a long list of exercises I was supposed to do, writing little character descriptions and making up story situations and working out an unfinished plot outline. I'm utterly certain that I put the book aside with a sinking feeling in my stomach. The art of fiction seemed as complicated and difficult to master as the art of brain surgery, and plainly, you had to learn all the rules before editors would let you through the door. Violate even one of Uzzell's commandments and it would be immediately apparent to any editor that the manuscript before him was the work of an incompetent. This was how I proposed to earn my living? I felt I could no more manage to write a proper story than I could walk on water.

There obviously were people who *could* write proper stories—Heinlein, Asimov, Henry Kuttner, Jack Williamson, and dozens more in the science-fiction world alone. They, so it seemed to me, were the elect. They were the ones who had been admitted to the sanctuary, while I stood on the outside glumly peering in. Why? I had thought it was because they knew some special secret, some fundamental trick of the trade, that was unavailable to me. But no, that wasn't it: here were all the secrets laid out in Thomas Uzzell's book for anyone to see. What you needed, I realized, was the ability to make use of the secrets. Anybody could tell you the secret of hitting a home run in Yankee Stadium: you wait until the precise moment when the ball is approaching the plate, and you step into it and whip your wrists around and hit it as hard as you can. Fine. But Joe DiMaggio could do it and I couldn't, and no matter how many books on batting technique I studied I wasn't ever going to hit the ball out of Yankee Stadium, because I didn't have the right muscles, the right reflexes, the right timing. You had to be born with those things, I supposed. You couldn't be a DiMaggio, or a Caruso, or a Picasso, or a Shakespeare, just by wanting to be, or by taking courses in technique. You had to be born with something extra, something special. The people whose stories I loved in the magazines and anthologies had been born knowing the secrets of storytelling already—the Secret, as I thought of it. Obviously, I hadn't been. If I had, I wouldn't find all of Uzzell's stuff about plot and point of view and characterization so intimidating. I'd *know*. Homer hadn't read any books on narrative technique.

(In fact I was both right and wrong. Any special skill requires certain innate abilities *and* the mastery of some degree of technique, but that doesn't mean that it can be practiced only by those whom the gods favor. All it takes to hit a baseball is reasonably good physical coordination and the willingness to learn how to swing a bat. Becoming a major-league player requires a considerably higher level of innate physical ability plus a considerably more intense study of the technique of the game; but there have been plenty of players with mediocre physical skills who overcame that drawback by dedicated work and study. The same is true in painting, in singing, in writing, or anything else. Some people are born with special advantages—keen vision, or perfect pitch, or an unusually retentive memory—and they have head starts as a result, in certain fields; but those who lack such advantages can nevertheless achieve noteworthy things, unless some outright insuperable handicap interferes. There are those who find reading difficult or boring, and they are not likely to be successful as writers; but anyone with normal verbal skills who is willing to study the craft of fiction ought to be able to write an acceptable story. To reach the level of Shakespeare—or Caruso, or Picasso, of DiMaggio— is a different matter. They really *must* have been born with something extra. But achievement of their kind is very rare. Good as they were, the science-fiction writers who were my boyhood heroes were all of sub-Shakespearean caliber, nor had they emerged from their cradles fully equipped to write memorable fiction. What I didn't let myself see, in that moment of adolescence despair, was that hard work rather than superior genetic endowment is the basic component of most writers' success. Maybe that was something I didn't want to see, just then.)

I gave up the fantasy of becoming a professional writer. I guess I was fourteen or fifteen when I decided that it was a hopeless dream. All my stories were being rejected by the editors and now I had managed to convince myself that successful writers were born, not made. Either you had the right stuff or you didn't, and plainly, I didn't.

Still, if I could only sell *one* story, what a glorious thing that would be! How they would admire me at school when word got around that there was a story by me in the latest issue of some gaudy pulp magazine! It wouldn't be a great story—only the favorites of the gods had the knack of writing those, I now believed—but it would at least have been a publishable one. My best shot might just meet the minimal requirements. It wouldn't match Kuttner. It wouldn't equal Heinlein. I was pretty certain that I never could achieve that, and certainly not at the age of fifteen. But once the first spell of despair was past, I resolved to go on trying, at least until I had managed to sell one humble little piece of fiction. It seemed overwhelmingly difficult but not fundamentally impossible. If I kept on swinging the bat, I told myself, I might eventually hit the ball as far as the front row of seats, maybe. Maybe.

Instead of reading dismaying books like Uzzell, I tried to puzzle out the Secret for myself. That seemed a better way to learn; Uzzell was only confusing and frightening me with his hundreds of pages of how-to-do-it manual. Besides, I hated the idea of doing all those end-of-chapter exercises. So I began to study the stories in the current issues of the s-f magazines with passionate intensity. I concentrated on the lesser magazines, the ones that ran simple stories by not-so-famous writers, and I took those stories apart and stared at the pieces, thinking, This is an opening paragraph, This is how dialog works, This is as much exposition as you can get away with before the reader gets bored. And by 1950, just about the time I needed my first shave, I was producing stories that opened this way:

> A beam of red light glinted on the rocks of the cavern. Stretching out for untold miles, a rippling river flowed, strange blind fish playing in its bottomless, inky depths. The torch flickered once, twice in Mara's hand, casting an eery glow in the dark cavern. A serpent rose up, questioningly, to pass before Mara and slither back to its watery home. Struggling though the dim light, he walked on.
>
> He strode forward into the darkness, standing on the mold-encrusted banks of rock bordering the river. Al'p-he, the Sacred River, the great underground mystery of Venus. Mara battled forward.

Not Hugo-quality stuff. But there's struggle, if not exactly conflict. There's scenery. A mystery is hinted at. I sent it off to Jerome Bixby, the editor of *Planet Stories*, who returned it on April 25, 1950, but said, "Great Ghu, keep it up....You're bound to connect sooner or later. Probably later, though, when your collection [of rejection slips] has grown some."

Bound to connect! Sooner or later! Could he mean it?

I kept on studying stories and writing my own. Conflict, they wanted. Hard choices, decisions, resolution. This is the second page of "Vanguard of Tomorrow," later in 1950:

> When he saw the four men materialize out of an unoccupied floor space, he took it calmly, in stride, almost as if he had expected it.
>
> Inwardly, he gulped.
>
> He stared at them in mild surprise.
>
> "What in hell are you doing here?" he growled.
>
> He looked directly at the one who seemed to be the

eldest. He was totally bald. Bill noted idly that he had no eyebrows, either.

Bill noted with a shock his clothes.

They were strange clothes. Short—knee-length tights, with a healthy bronzed calf below. They were bright-colored, made of some soft and shimmering cloth. Or was it cloth? Bill blinked his eyes.

Hanging at the man's side was a sword.

"What in hell are you doing here?" Bill softly repeated.

The four men silently shifted around, uncomfortably, looking nearly as surprised as Bill himself. Finally the eldest one licked his lips and spoke, in soft, oddly slurred accents. The words gave Bill a jolt.

He said, "We've come to prevent your marriage."

The plot was vaguely adapted from Heinlein's classic "By His Bootstraps," one of my favorites. The bald guys from the future were something I had picked up from Clifford D. Simak's "Time Quarry," which was currently running as a serial in the new magazine *Galaxy*. The editor of *Galaxy*, H.L. Gold, had described Simak's novel as "a powerful story of suspense, mystery, and ideas," and I decided that its power was in the punchiness. I can still remember thinking, as I sat there knocking out "Vanguard to Tomorrow" on my old portable typewriter one humid evening in the late summer of 1950, "This is powerful writing."

It was, at least, commercial-looking writing. As I look through the manuscript now, it seems to me not a whole lot worse than some things that were getting published in 1950. But Morton Klass, the associate editor of *Super-Science Stories*, returned it on February 6, 1951, with the observation that "most of the trouble lies with the plot, which—as you probably know yourself—is one of the oldest in science fiction. Well, you say, why can't somebody give an old plot a new twist? Heinlein took this plot and did it. Trouble is, we're not all Heinleins—at least not every day." Klass suggested I write something I knew from personal experience, like going to high school. "What would high school be like on Mars? Procyon? Another time-stream? Hit 'em with the stories no one is writing, and see what happens. We'd be happy to see more of your work."

Not a bad idea, high school in another time-stream. I wish I had tried it for him. But I suppose I would have messed it up. I was coming close now to figuring out the right mix of storytelling ingredients—a novel background, an interesting character, a tough problem, an ingenious solution. And I was learning, not by studying Thomas Uzzell's book but by writing fiction after school all the time, how to move my story along through dialog and action. But I was still a little pisher, remember. I knew zilch about life and only minimally more than that about the art and craft of fiction. What editor was going to push Ray Bradbury off his pages to make room for my klutzy imitation pulp-magazine stories?

Keep trying, kid, I told myself, nevertheless. Just sell *one* story, and then you can relax and forget this obsession with writing science fiction and go on to do whatever it is you're going to do for the rest of your life.

Strangely, the next thing that happened to me was that I sold one story. I think I was 16. I may have been 15. Certainly I was still in high school. The story was "The Sacred River," which is the one I quoted a little way back about Mara struggling through the cavern on Venus. Lilith Lorraine, the editor of a magazine for amateur poets called *Different*, paid me five dollars for it. (By the time she used it, in 1952, *Different* had gone out of business and it appeared in something called *The Avalonian*.)

Selling a story to *Different*, which was available only by subscription and had an audience of—who knows, eight hundred readers?— was not quite the same as selling one to *Startling* or *Astounding*. None of my classmates would ever see the story unless I went out of my way to show it to them, and even then they weren't likely to be impressed, since *Different* (and the later *Avalonian*) looked a lot like high-school poetry magazines. But someone had been willing to pay—even if it was only five dollars—for the privilege of publishing my fiction, all the same. That was the important thing. Instead of letting me off the hook, that trifling first sale inspired me to keep on plugging forward. If it had happened once, it might happen again, and the next time it might be a real magazine that sent me the check.

I went on writing, went on studying the craft. I picked up the tips out of thin air. Some book reviewer, discussing I know not what novel, said of its author that "he writes the sort of dialog that doesn't merely fill space but actually advances the plot. Which of course is the only sort of dialog any story should contain." Or words to that effect.

It was a revelation to me. *Everything* was a revelation to me then. Oh, I said. The dialog is there to move the plot along. Dialog is actually a form of exposition. You can't just chatter about the weather or the fact that your shoes hurt, the way people do in real life: whatever the characters say should help to unfold the story. Of course, a lot of dialog reveals character, and revealing character is part of building the unfolding story. But the dialog must be seen as an essential structural unit, not a decoration. The best writers handle dialog in such a way that it simultaneously illuminates character, provides needed information, and advances the plot, with not a word going to waste. You can, naturally, waste plenty of words and still get published. A science-fiction novel I recall from the early 1980's was absolutely bubbling with needless dialog ("Thank you, Doctor. You've told us what we need to know. I'm sorry we took so much of your time. I'm sure you're doing your best.") and not only got published but won the Hugo and Nebula awards. It was a book of many worthy aspects, which is why it won awards, but effective dialog was not one of them. Still, patterning your work after horrible examples is no way to master a craft. I still think that the role of dialog is to move the story along, and not just to vary the typography of the page by sprinkling it with quotation marks.

Actually, I see by looking through my primitive early stories that I had already figured that much out, at least unconsciously. But I didn't *know* that I had figured it out, which is why it came as such a surprise to me when I saw someone else state it explicitly. A lot of narrative technique is actually something that you figure out unconsciously as you absorb other people's narratives; later you may consciously codify a set of rules, and later on you internalize them again so that they operate without your having to stop to think about them. At that point you're a professional writer.

Though I had made that lone five-dollar sale, I certainly didn't think of myself as a professional writer in 1951. My stories now had begun to look much more like the ones I saw in the magazines, but I didn't even come close to selling one, and the idea that I would someday break through into the ranks of the published was once again beginning to seem unrealistic to me. And now there were more immediate challenges to deal with, such as getting used to my new almost-adult body, and girls, and applying for college. For the next year, perhaps a year and a half, I did little or no writing. But on some level I refused to give up; and all during 1952—my first year of college—I continued to study the science-fiction magazines with crazy intensity, still hoping to discover the Secret.

That was a golden age for the science-fiction short story. The day of the cheap and sleazy pulp magazine was just about over. A flood of new s-f magazines had come into being, and most of them were small, compact, slick-looking publications with serious-sounding names

(*Galaxy, Other Worlds, Worlds Beyond, Fantasy & Science Fiction.*) Whereas just a few years before only John Campbell's *Astounding Science Fiction* and then to some degree Sam Merwin's *Startling* and *Thrilling Wonder* had made a point of publishing stories that might be of interest to a reasonably intelligent adult reader, now virtually all the new magazines were looking for material that was clever, original, and well written. Their editors were men who had been outstanding writers themselves—Anthony Boucher, Horace Gold, Damon Knight, Frederik Pohl, Lester del Rey. Many of them had been associated during the formative days of their own writing careers with the brilliant and demanding editor John W. Campbell, and they were determined to live up to Campbell's high standards of performance or even surpass them.

These sparkling new magazines paid relatively high fees for their material, usually two or three cents a word at a time when the going rate had been a cent or a cent and a half. (Fred Pohl's *Star Science Fiction*, a magazine in paperback form, opened up in 1951 by offering *nine* cents a word, which is more than many science-fiction magazines pay even in today's inflated market.) The lively, sophisticated new editors let it be known that they would not be catering to the action-pulp readers. They would be receptive to writing at the highest level of skill; indeed they would publish nothing less than that. And the little community of professional science-fiction writers, overflowing with story ideas and eager to experiment with fresh and startling ways of handling them, responded with astonishing fervor.

Some of the writers who flocked to the new magazines were veterans, five or in some cases ten years into their careers: Theodore Sturgeon, James Blish, Jack Vance, Fritz Leiber, Alfred Bester, C.M. Kornbluth, Poul Anderson, Isaac Asimov, Arthur C. Clarke, Philip Klass ("William Tenn"), Henry Kuttner, and Kuttner's wife, C.L. Moore. They had little interest in writing conventional pulp fiction and most of them had come to have less and less liking for dealing with the increasingly dogmatic and difficult John Campbell. Gold's *Galaxy* and Boucher's *Fantasy & Science Fiction* and Pohl's *Star* paid them well and gave them creative freedom they had never known before. The results were extraordinary.

But there was also a rush of gifted newcomers—writers in their twenties or early thirties, mainly, who had read and loved science fiction for years and who found a ready welcome for their first stories in the suddenly expanded market of 1952 and 1953: Philip K. Dick, Robert Sheckley, Philip José Farmer, Algis Budrys, Chad Oliver, Kris

Neville, Jerome Bixby, Walter M. Miller, Jr., Mack Reynolds, Gordon R. Dickson, J.T. McIntosh, Michael Shaara, Katherine Maclean, James Gunn, and many more. Some passed through and went on their way. Others remained for long and splendid careers.

And I? Where was I while all this was going on?

I was up at Morningside Heights, a freshman at Columbia, reading Dante and Aeschylus with one eye and *Galaxy* and *Fantasy & Science Fiction* with the other, and still desperately trying to figure out the Secret. How I envied all those new writers, just five or ten years older than I was, who were rampaging through the pages of the new magazines! How I stared at the tables of contents, imagining my own name there! It's impossible even now for me to look at one of those magazines without feeling a renewed surge of that old envy and yearning. Nor can I ever shake the belief that the stories in those issues were written by demigods and that their quality will be forever beyond my hope of equalling.

Technique. It's all a matter of technique, I told myself. I can come up with ideas for stories that are just as good as these. But I must learn to match their dazzling technique. I looked at Bester or Sheckley: how quick and supple the prose, how sparkling the dialog, how agile the leaps and pirouettes of the plot! I looked at Blish and Asimov and Clarke: how intricate the conceptual underpinning, how fascinating the ideas! I looked at Sturgeon and Farmer: how rich the emotional tone, how full and strange the vision of life! Dick was clever, Budrys seemed to know how everything worked, Vance brought to life a galaxy of colors and textures, Kuttner and Moore produced stories that functioned like beautifully designed machines. I wanted to be able to do everything that any of them could do, and do all of it in the same story, and more. (I still feel that way.) Chutzpah? Hybris? Maybe so. I had big ambitions. How to fulfill them? Technique was the answer. Learn the tricks of the trade. And finish growing up, too. Read everything you can. Travel widely. Talk. Listen. Poke into strange dark corners. Eat strange things. Hear strange music. If you mean to tell stories, you must have stories inside you that are worth telling. And you must master the craft of telling them, so that when you say to a reader, "Listen to what I have to relate," he will stand still and listen.

In my pursuit of technique, four names stand out: Blish, Knight, Kitto, Gold. Blish and Knight were outstanding science-fiction writers who, on the side, wrote criticism of the most merciless kind. Kitto was professor of Greek at Bristol University in England. Gold was the infuriating, opinionated editor of *Galaxy*. Much of what I learned about writing fiction I learned from them—not so much in the form of explicit rules, but in what I took from them in an indirect way, through my own process of observation and internalization.

Blish, who died in 1975, was a cool, precise, somewhat waspish man devoted to the music of Richard Wagner and Richard Strauss, the poetry of Ezra Pound, the fiction of James Joyce, and the philosophy of Oswald Spengler. He also wrote science fiction of a cool and precise and intellectual kind, much of which impressed me to the point of awe. Strangely, he won his widest fame, if that is what it can be called, by turning *Star Trek* teleplays by other writers into short stories that were published in a series of hugely successful paperbacks. I met him first when I was about 16, and—based on nothing more than a ten-minute conversation—he seemed to think I had potential, and said so to a mutual friend. A couple of years later I made myself his disciple, without ever telling him so. Later—when I was a successful professional writer—we became close friends, a friendship that endured (with a few bumpy moments) to the end of his life.

Blish took the business of literacy technique very, very seriously, and set forth his beliefs on the subject with firmness and ferocity. Listening to him hold forth about the art of fiction, or reading the formidable essays that were collected in 1964 in a volume called *The Issue at Hand*, I had a sense of him as the high priest of an arcane cult in which I was the merest novice. If Thomas Uzzell had intimidated me in 1950 by letting me see how much there was to learn about writing fiction, Blish positively terrified me a few years later by making it seem as though Uzzell had just skimmed the surface of the topic. Through much of my career, I imagined Blish reading my stories as they appeared and shaking his head sadly as he tossed them aside. I don't think he actually did, but the image provided a useful goad to me, driving me ever onward to meet my notion of his standards. At first that seemed an impossible goal. Yet he and I both lived long enough so that in 1973 he could write of one of my books that it was "so unobtrusively, flawlessly written that even at its most puzzling it comes as perilously close to poetic beauty as any contemporary s-f novel I've ever read." If I had a time machine handy, I would have rushed back twenty years to show that astounding review to my younger self. Who would probably have just shrugged and smiled, the arrogant little bastard, and told me that he knew all along that he'd be capable of writing a book someday that Jim Blish would find flawless. But he would have been lying through his teeth.

In truth I didn't feel arrogant at all, that day in late 1952 when I read the first essay in what eventually would become Blish's *The Issue at Hand*. I felt frightened and overwhelmed.

> "We know," he said, "that there is a huge body of available technique in fiction writing, and that the competence of a writer—entirely aside from the degree of his talent—is deter- mined by how much of this body of technique he can use.
>
> "We know (from study, from our own practice, or from both) the essential features of good narrative practice; we expect writers and editors to know no less than we do.
>
> "We also know that at least half of the science fiction writers being published today are, from the point of view of technical competence, taking up our time unnecessarily...."

My God! If half the s-f being published in the golden year of 1952 was technically inept and worthless, what hope was there for me, still an amateur, still collecting rejection slips? In panic I read and reread Blish's essays as they appeared, looking for clues to this mystery of technique. I knew by then that stories were built around conflict, that they had beginnings, middles, and ends, that they needed dialog and exposition in some reasonable mix, that they had to show appealing or at least interesting characters engaged in coping with obstacles and either succeeding or else failing in some way that was revelatory of character. But what else was there? What were the inner secrets that the true writers had learned? What was that "huge body of available technique" that Blish knew, and Sturgeon, and Bester, and the other masters?

Some of the answers were in Blish's essays, which appeared quarterly all through the early 1950s in a mimeographed, "little" magazine called *Skyhook*, and which I studied as though they were scripture. In each issue he reviewed the current crop of s-f magazines, praised a few stories he found praiseworthy, and shredded the rest without mercy. ("This may seem to be heavy artillery to bring to bear upon a story which can be little over a thousand words long, but I can't see why a story should be excused for being bad because it is short." "For this story, with its cuddly animals with the telepathic ears, nausea is not enough. I can only suggest that both authors—not their story, but the authors themselves—be piled in the middle of the floor and set fire to." "The story is one of the worst stinkers ever to have been printed in the field. To begin on the most elementary level, Mr.—'s prose includes more downright bad grammar than any single *Astounding* piece since...")

Of course, there was much more to Blish than hatchet-swinging and vitriol-flinging. His praise was intelligent and searching. Discussing Damon Knight's "Four in One," he pointed out that "the major idea in this story is not only as old as Homer, but has been handled before by science fiction writers of stature: the Proteus, the creature which can assume any shape. Knight makes no attempt to surprise anybody with this notion; even had he himself never encountered the idea before outside his own head, he is too good a craftsman to assume that an idea alone is enough. The contrasting idea is that of escape from a totalitarian society, again a piece of common coin. The result is 'Four in One,' which is compelling not because it contains a single new notion but because nobody but Knight ever before showed these two old notions in such an individual light, and because, in addition, the light is individual throughout—the story contains hardly a single stock reaction."

That one paragraph was worth a year of courses in "How to Write" for me. From it I drew an immensely valuable method for constructing science-fiction stories—not simply stories, but *science-fiction stories*—that would go beyond minimal mediocre attainment. (There is a general art of writing fiction, which I had struggled all through my adolescence to learn, and there is a special art of writing science fiction; the second art requires mastery of the first, but has some unusual requirements of its own.)

It was no news to me, of course, that science-fiction stories had to be based on a speculative idea, a what-if hypothesis. ("Suppose the Martians invaded Earth." "Suppose it was possible to travel through time." "Suppose someone invented artificial servants that would do all our work for us.") The problem is that most of the obvious speculations, being obvious, were proposed long ago. H.G. Wells took care of the Martian invasion and the trip through time—and a great many other themes besides—back in the 1890s; the Czech Karel Capek thoroughly explored the artificial-servant theme in his 1921 play, *R.U.R.*, which gave the world the word *robot*. The ideas that were not obvious and had not been handled before ("Suppose explorers get to the moon and find it made not of green cheese but of bleached salami") had, I suspected, gone unused because they were too dumb to use. What was a young science-fiction writer to do? Helplessly recycle the standard themes of his forebears?

Blish, using Knight's "Four in One" as an example, gave me the clue. Nobody could found a science-fiction career on coming up with dazzling new ideas all the time. You might manage the trick once or twice in a career, if you were lucky; but to pay the rent you needed to produce salable copy day in and day out. At that point in my life I would have been happy to produce something that was merely salable; but I knew that if I intended to make a career out of writing science fiction I would need to get beyond that minimal level and attain some degree of real excellence. It wouldn't be enough just to write the millionth the-Martians-are-landing or someday-we-will-have-robots story. One way of getting there, I saw now, was to yoke a couple of familiar themes together so that they illuminated one another and provided new insights. Knight had done that in "Four in One." Jack Williamson's superb "With Folded Hands" had done that for the robot theme by asking whether robots designed to free us from the boredom of menial labor might turn out to be *too* effective in sparing us from toil. John W. Campbell's scary "Who Goes There" had linked the alien-invader theme with the old medieval shape-changer idea. And so on.

Not only did Blish discuss current stories that he thought were unusually fine or unusually awful examples of science fiction, and substantiate his opinions with close analysis of text, but he also scattered little technical tips throughout his essays. It is a good idea, he said, to give your major characters names, and to describe them physically, early in a story. It is a bad idea, he said, to use metaphors of the concrete-is-abstract form ("She was love....She was ache and anguish and doubt....") because such metaphors create wooliness and vagueness where clarity is desired. It is unwise, said Blish, to use synonyms for "said" in writing dialog ("He shouted....He repeated....He instructed....He grunted....He half-whispered....He lipped thinly....") because such tags are redundant at best—the content of the sentence ought to tell the reader right away that something is being shouted or repeated—and at worst they became preposterous. It was permissible sometimes to give a clue—"He whispered," for instance—but all too often the amateur writer, Blish noted, would go on beyond using tags that represent a manner of speaking and substitute ones that represent facial expressions ("He sneered") or adjectives ("He flustered") or verbs ("He pointed"). Worst of all, said Blish, was the complete sentence dropped in between two chunks of dialog as a substitute for "He said," in this manner:

> " 'You will never get me to sign that document,' Stanley flung the sheet of paper from him, 'so long as it contains the loathsome Clause Seventeen.' "

To Blish such stuff read "like a freshman translation from the German."

These were only working rules, of course—not absolute commandments. They could be broken from time to time, and some writers could get away with breaking them *all* the time. (One best-selling science-fiction novelist of the 1970s and 1980s scatters dozens of "said" substitutes over every page; but readers love her books anyway, and stand in long lines to buy the new ones when they come out. When another well-known writer used a complete sentence as a "said" substitute and I objected, he showed me where Hemingway had once done the same thing. Well, I said, even if Hemingway did it, it's still a dumb thing to do. Besides, you're not Hemingway.) But though it might be possible to violate such ad-hoc rules and get away with it, Blish made me see that they did have intrinsic underlying value. The idea, after all, is not so much to get away with things as to know what tends to work best—and what does not—in building the bond between the writer and reader that makes him keep on reading with pleasure.

Filling your page of dialog with strings of "She asserted hotly" and "He protested vehemently" and "She cudgelled" and "He parried thoughtfully" may seem to you a good way of enlivening a passage of conversation. But it might well induce a reader with a keen sense of style to begin skipping down the page looking for the next silly substitute for "said" instead of paying attention to the dialog itself. Failing to describe characters' physical appearances is likewise not a criminal offense, and in certain cases may actually be necessary for the strategy of your plot; but as a rule, readers are drawn into stories more quickly if they have some idea of what the people they're reading about look like. A little landscape painting doesn't hurt either. (Too much description will have the opposite effect, though.) The point is to draw the reader in, not to push him away. Distracting your reader from the narrative material of the story by cluttering the page with extraneous stuff is rarely a useful tactic, unless your story itself is so thin that it's best to hide its failings under a welter of mannerisms.

It was easy enough for me to accept these stylistic dictates. My ear was acute and I had already come to be able to distinguish good writing—that is, direct, effective communication—from bad. I was, remember, a college boy who, when he was not reading *Galaxy* and *Star Science Fiction*, was busy taking courses in Joyce and Faulkner and Shakespeare. But what Blish also showed me was that a story could be well written—*beautifully* written, even—and still be bad science fiction.

For instance, good science fiction ought to be built around some idea (or cluster of ideas) that stimulates thought. A story about little furry long-eared animals called smeerps that go hippity-hop and eat lettuce does not become science fiction because you have called your rabbits smeerps. Telling us that the smeerps live on Mars doesn't change anything if your Mars looks just like Illinois. There are ways to turn such stories into science fiction (the smeerps may have interestingly nefarious reasons for masquerading as rabbits; Mars may look like Illinois because the Martians are playing a trick on the visiting spacemen from Earth) but the would-be writer needs to be aware that what is needed is ingenious speculative thinking, not just a bunch of funny names.

A science-fiction story ought to make sense. An idea that contradicts itself within five pages illuminates nothing and irritates the intelligent reader. Blish cites a Ray Bradbury story that proposes that the Messiah is traveling through the universe one world at a time. Having brought His message to Earth, He is now moving on to Mars. Blish found the idea "a numerical absurdity," pointing out that it would take forever for Jesus to spread the word through the entire galaxy, and that surely an omnipotent God could find some more efficient way of bringing about the Advent in the universe than by "turning His Son into the Wandering Salesman." Similarly, a story that depends for its plot complications on a character's failure to notice some screamingly obvious fact is going to annoy rather than entertain readers, and one with a plot that functions only because everyone acts like a total nincompoop will not arouse much sympathy for, or interest in, the events that stem from all the nuncompoopery.

Blish thought that science-fiction writers should know something about science and make use of it in their stories. This notion was beginning to seem old-fashioned thirty years ago and must strike many writers of today as downright odd. What he was saying, though, was not that it is the writer's job to include a wiring diagram for every gadget in his stories or to provide lengthy footnotes describing the underlying astronomical assumptions he is using. It was simply that a science-fiction story ought to be based on some speculative departure from real-world conditions, and in order to do a good job of framing his speculation, the writer first needs to know something about how the real world is put together, or at a bare minimum "that anything one wishes to call a science-fiction story should contain some vestige of some knowledge of some science."

This was another way of saying that a story has to make sense.

It will not do to have your hero get from Mars to Venus in a rowboat, or rebuild a flashlight so that a deadly radioactive beam issues from it, or turn a mushroom into a gorilla by applying powerful magnetic forces. A really clever s-f pro probably could make any of those three notions plausible if he put his mind to it, but the fact is that in the ordinary sense of things we know that all three are impossible and pretty silly besides. A story that blithely violates the present body of scientific knowledge—by telling us, say, that ferns have lovely flowers or that table salt is made up of equal parts of carbon and potassium or that a squid has a skeleton—may in fact get published, if the editor is as ignorant as the writer, but it's going to bother a lot of readers. *Falsus in uno, falsus in omnibus*, as the lawyers say: "False in one thing, false in all." A reader who sees that you believe ferns have nice blossoms is going to suspect the rest of your story of being nonsense too: characters, background, plot, resolution. A knowledge of science not only gives the s-f writer something to work with in coming up with story ideas, but also helps in avoiding blunders of fact in a field where such blunders are more than usually fatal to a writer's aspiration.

So I studied Blish with care, and polished my stories to avoid the infelicities of style and construction that he so acidly deplored in others, and checked the logic of my ideas for hidden nonsense, and pored over *Scientific American* and textbooks of astronomy and physics to fill in the gaps of my education. And went on writing. And sold a few stories, finally, and then some more. They were pretty mediocre, sure. Some of them were less than mediocre. But to my great relief, Jim Blish never found any of them bad in a way that was interesting enough to discuss in his column in *Skyhook*. By the time he did get around to writing about my work a few years later, I was an established pro, doing work that was not wonderful but competent and in no danger of being held up to public scorn. (From other corners, as you will see, would come private scorn— because I seemed willing to settle for being merely competent. Precocious as ever, I had learned my lessons well enough so that no one was likely to poke fun at my stories; but in my youthful zeal to attain technical competence I had forgotten about attaining excellence. I'll get to that in a little while.)

The second of my teenage mentors was Damon Knight—writer, editor, ferocious critic. In person Knight was not much like the dry, astringent Blish; he was and is a gentle man of much charm and playful, oddly goofy wit. But when he turned his hand to the critical analysis of science fiction he proved to be an even more effective demolisher of all that was foolish, technically inadequate, or lazily conceived. Here are a few samples from his remarkable volume of collected essays, *In Search of Wonder* (1956, second edition 1967):

On Robert Sheckley:

> Most of the stories in Robert Sheckley's *Citizen in Space*...are brief, brightly inventive, and logically unstable. Sheckley's faceless characters chirp, twitter, whirl with captivating grace around the idea, but seldom settle down long enough to exercise ordinary intelligence upon it....Sheckley's heroes weigh in at an I.Q. of about 90, just sufficient to get aboard their shiny machines, but not enough to push all the right levers....Once in a while, when Sheckley bothers to put something under his slick surfaces, his work comes brilliantly and even movingly to life....Like it or not, what Sheckley does is art. But he could use a little less art, and a little more craftsmanship.

On A.E. van Vogt:

> John W. Campbell has said editorially more than once that *The World of Null-A* is "one of those once-in-a-decade classics of science fiction." I offer the alternate judgment that, far from being a "classic" by any reasonable standard, *The World of Null-A* is one of the worst allegedly-adult science fiction stories ever published.
>
> I'll try to prove that assertion by an analysis of the story on four levels: Plot, Characterization, Background, and Style....
>
> *The World of Null-A* abounds in contradictions, misleading clues, and irrelevant action....Van Vogt has not bothered to integrate the gadgets into the technological background of his story; and...he has no clear idea of their nature....Examples of bad writing could be multiplied endlessly. It is my personal opinion that the whole of it is written badly, with only minor exceptions; but this is a purely subjective judgment and is not susceptible of proof....By means of his writing style, which is discursive and hard to follow, van Vogt also obscures his plot to such an extent that when it falls to pieces at the end, as it frequently does, the event passes without remark....

On John Wyndham's novel *Re-Birth*:

These first few chapters have the genuine autobiographical sense—that Wellsian retrospective clarity, the torment of writers who can't do it themselves. More's the pity that Wyndham, for once, failed to realize how good a thing he had. The sixth toe was immensely believable, and sufficient: but Wyndham has dragged in a telepathic mutation on top of it; had made David himself one of the nine child telepaths, and hauled the whole plot away from his carefully built background, into just one more damned chase with a rousing cliché at the end of it.

Wyndham's unflaggingly expert writing, all the way through, only proves that there are no exceptions: this error is fatal.

Knight's vigorous, detailed, and total destruction of van Vogt's famous novel was great fun to read for everyone except, I imagine, van Vogt, but it struck me then and now as largely unfair, a mixture of justified criticism and a studied misreading of van Vogt's intentions. Knight's pieces on Sheckley and Wyndham, though—and indeed the bulk of his criticism—began from a position of respect for the writer, and singled out disturbing flaws *within a context of appreciation*. That seemed admirable to me and immensely instructive. And where Knight found nothing at all to criticize, but offered only warm praise (" 'The Census Takers' is a beautifully compact exercise in indirection. Entirely successful on its own terms, it plays one speculative idea...against another without wasting a word or a motion," or "When it's all done, the story means something. Harness' theme is the triumph of spirit over flesh....This is the rock under all Harness' hypnotic cat's-cradles of invention—faith in the spirit, the denial of pain, the affirmation of eternal life," or "Jack Vance's *Big Planet*...shows this brilliant writer at the top of his form. Big Planet, where most of the action takes place, is as vividly compelling as the dream-world of Eddison's *The Worm Ouroboros*: and that's the highest praise I know"), off I would go like a shot to the story under discussion, and I would read and reread it, trying to locate the qualities that had elicited such praise from Knight so that I could come up with my own equivalents of them in the work I was doing. You will find some of the stories that Knight singled out for such praise in this collection.

Of course it was impossible for me, now age 18 or 19 or so, to match the achievements of other writers that brought forth Knight's warmest encomiums. But by studying them, as also I studied the works praised by Blish, I could at least attain an Idea of the Good as defined by a man whose experience as a reader and a writer went far beyond my own and who had himself written notable fiction. (I don't believe that a good critic of fiction necessarily has to be capable of writing good fiction himself; but for me there is a certain unanswerable plausibility in an analysis of a story's flaws done by someone who has himself demonstrated clear excellence in the form.) The only problem I had with Knight's essays was their occasional tendency to rekindle in me the old Uzzell hopelessness, that sense that the task of constructing a worthwhile work of fiction required arcane skills that would forever be beyond the attainment of a poor mortal like me. Here, for example, is Knight discussing a story by James Blish:

> There is a really fantastic body of technique in this short novel [*Beanstalk*], but unless you are looking at it you will never notice it; it's submerged, where it belongs....Not merely embedded in *Beanstalk*, but inseparably united to make one coherent and symmetrical narrative, are whole exemplars or recognizable fragments of the following: a sports story; a love story; a Western story—plus, for good measure, a couple of panels from "Buck Rogers"....Wildly incompatible as the above-listed elements are, not one has been dragged in by the hair; every one has been almost unrecognizably altered by the author's inventiveness; every one is essential. The sports fragment is a jet-powered, gimmicked-up Titan football game, necessary to pave the way for the Buck Rogers element, which is itself (a) indispensable and (b) brilliantly rationalized, down to the last silly flange on the flying-belt-borne superman's helmet.

I don't think such a technical stunt would be beyond my skill now; it had better not be, thirty-odd years of practice behind me. But reading that paragraph in 1953, when it appeared in Knight's review column in *Future Science Fiction*, I felt myself close to tears of helplessness and bitter self-reproach. How, I wondered, for perhaps the thousandth time, could I ever attain such technical proficiency? As Knight himself had said, you couldn't even *see* what Blish was doing in that story: he had submerged it all beyond the notice of anyone but one who was already among the adept.

And then I thought: All right, dummy. Make yourself one of the adept.

H.D.F. Kitto helped me toward that goal, though I don't think he ever intended his studies of Aeschylus, Sophocles, and Euripides to serve as instruction to an ambitious young science-fiction writer. I bought a copy of Kitto's *Greek Tragedy* in 1954, as collateral reading for a course in Greek plays that I was taking during my junior year at Columbia. But 1954 was also the year when I was making the most determined assault of my life on the goal of becoming a professional science-fiction writer. Late in 1953 I had submitted a proposal for a novel for young readers, *Revolt of Alpha C*, to the old-line publishing firm of Thomas Y. Crowell, and on the first day of the new year had come a call from the legendary Crowell juvenile-books editor, Elizabeth M. Riley, telling me that she was offering me a contract for my book, though she would want extensive revisions. Later in January, 1954, "Gorgon Planet," a short story I had sent to the Scottish s-f magazine *Nebula*, was accepted and brought me a check for $12.60. A little while later I finally sold a story to a professional American magazine: my little vignette "The Silent Colony" yielded $13.50 from *Future Science Fiction*. Plainly, I had solved enough of the technical mysteries of story writing to qualify for an entry-level position. Now was the moment to build on the new confidence that these early sales had provided, and produce some ambitious work that would establish me in the ranks of the professionals.

The unwitting Kitto became my most valuable teacher. By his close examination of the works of the great Greek playwrights, he provided me with a deep understanding of the nature of drama, without which it is impossible to construct an effective plot.

I had already come to see Greek tragedy as a public ritual in which a dramatic situation—that is, a conflict unavoidable by the nature of events—is proposed, displayed, and resolved. The resolution, by demonstrating a return to the natural harmony of the universe, sends the audience home cleansed and calm—purged, as Aristotle said, of pity and fear. To this day I have continued to believe that all fiction, even the sleaziest, is a ritual healing art fundamentally akin to Greek tragedy in its purpose: that by showing the tension of opposite forces (plot, drama, conflict) and by resolving that tension (climax and ending) fiction performs a function of psychic cleansing. It seems to me that there can be no other reason for the universality of the narrative mode: patterns of story development are surprisingly similar everywhere, in cultures as far apart as those of Japan and West Africa, of ancient Sumer and modern America.

Kitto began with the premise that each Greek tragedy was built around a significant dramatic situation designed to create the kind of tension that would provide the desired release for the audience when the tension was resolved. In his *Poetics* Aristotle asserted that that was what Greek tragedy was all about: catharsis, the purging of pity and fear. Aristotle had used as his prime technical example *Oedipus Rex* by Sophocles. But Kitto observed that many other surviving Greek plays failed to follow the technical rules that Aristotle, working from *Oedipus Rex*, had laid down as the fundamental requirements for a Greek tragedy. Did that mean that other Greek playwrights (and sometimes even Sophocles himself) had done a lot of incompetent work?

No, Kitto said. We know that the plays that have come down to us were warmly hailed in their time and evidently had fulfilled the requirements of their audience. Their authors must be regarded as masters of their art, in full technical command. If sometimes their plays seem poorly constructed to us, static and undramatic, it must be because we are failing to find the true dramatic center of them. Instead of dismissing those plays as badly made, Kitto argued, we need to reexamine our own assumptions about their structure.

He begins with Aeschylus, the earliest playwright whose work has survived. "Although Aeschylus was a young man when he wrote the *Supplices*," says Kitto, "he was already Aeschylus, and we may suppose that he built the play as he felt it. Technical difficulties we may allow him, but we will not readily suppose that he got his proportions and his emphasis all wrong....We must be sure that we have made allowance before we call a play undramatic."

He analyzes the *Supplices* scene by scene. It is the story of the flight of the fifty daughters of Danaus from Egypt to Argos to avoid the unwanted suitors who wish to marry them—a difficult play, for it was the first part of a trilogy of which the other two parts are lost, and we do not know where Aeschylus meant the story to go; what remains to us seems at first reading short on action and tension. The maidens and their aged father arrive in Argos; Pelasgus, the king of Argos, is uneasy about granting them sanctuary, because it might bring war to his land if the Egyptian suitors pursue; the people of Argos vote to grant sanctuary anyway, out of fear of the wrath of Zeus if they refuse; and then Egyptian ships arrive. A herald threatens war if the maidens are not returned; Pelasgus angrily refuses to be bullied; old Danaus tells his daughters to be modest and brave and offer prayers to the gods; and the play ends with a hopeful chorus.

"What is it all about?" asks Kitto. "What was Aeschylus thinking at the age of 30? We are not certain how the trilogy went, but at least we can hold fast to what we have.

"The trilogy was not simply a stage-version of the renowned story of the Danaids. What arrests and detains the attention most in the *Supplices* is the tragic dilemma of Pelasgus; this is where Aeschylus was most engaged—not in the running about of Danaus." The center of the play lies elsewhere than in the troubles of Danaus and his daughters; Danaus is offstage most of the time and his daughters are simply a faceless chorus. The plight of the innocent Pelasgus, whose peaceful land is threatened by war over a dispute that has nothing to do with him, is more central. Pelasgus is the real tragic hero, caught inextricably in a situation not of his own making, and we know from the myth on which Aeschylus based his play that he will die in the warfare that engulfs his kingdom. But even this, Kitto demonstrates, is not the true center.

What is? "Through no deficiency of sense, intellect or morality has [Pelasgus] fallen into this awful dilemma. A disharmony in the makeup of things, and a perfectly innocent man is broken. Here, in the earliest of Greek tragedies, we find one of the most purely tragic situations; the Flaw in the Universe, which the philosophers will have none of, is plain enough to Aeschylus." And Kitto shows us—reconstructing, where necessary, the missing two plays of the trilogy—how everything in the play works toward dramatizing the harshness of Zeus' law and the necessity for humans to conform to the workings of a universe beyond comprehension. "If we suppose...there must be some middle way out, one which will not involve the innocent, we deceive ourselves. Once the moral balance of things is disturbed in this way there is no telling how far calamity will not spread....The Supplicants, unable to accept injury, involve innocent Argos. They destroy their persecutors—and it serves *them* right—but the disturbance is not at an end until they are made to bring themselves into harmony with Zeus' law. It may be hard, but Aeschylus never pretended that life was easy, or that Zeus was simple, or that only the guilty are tortured."

I was much impressed by Kitto's demonstration that the seemingly undramatic *Supplices* was in fact a carefully constructed examination of the rigors of cosmic law. There is much more to plotting a story, I saw, than pitting a hero against a villain and letting them go at it. Kitto went on, play by play, showing how seeming flaws in dramaturgy were simply flaws in our perception of the play's meaning; and I read on and on in wonder.

When he came to Sophocles, that paragon of playwrights, Kitto faced the problem of dealing with a couple of plays that do not seem at all Sophoclean in their construction: *Ajax* and *The Trachinian Women*. But once in, starting from the assumption that Sophocles was a great artist and must have known what he was doing, Kitto provided stunning illumination.

Ajax, Sophocles' earliest known play, is set during the Trojan War. The great soldier Ajax, having been defeated by Odysseus in the contest for dead Achilles' armor, goes mad with shame and chagrin and commits horrid and outrageous deeds; when he recovers his sanity long enough to see what he has done, he chooses to take his own life rather than endure disgrace. That much might make a satisfactory tragedy, but the problem is that the death of Ajax occurs at line 865 and the play goes on for another 550 lines, mostly devoted to a bitter dispute among the Greek heroes over his burial. This long wrangle, which can make the play seem like a disquisition on Greek funeral customs, has led some critics to speak of the "sense of diminished tragic feeling" or "a disastrous lowering of tone" in the closing scene. No, says Kitto. What we see as an imperfection was to Sophocles and his audience the whole point of *Ajax*. Kitto argues that the play is not really about Ajax or the burial of Ajax at all: it is about the conflict between Ajax and Odysseus and the resolution of that conflict.

The play, Kitto points out, begins and ends not with Ajax, but with wise Odysseus, Ajax' rival and enemy. At the opening Odysseus speaks in horror of Ajax' crimes of madness; in the end he prevails over King Agamemnon and his brother Menelaus and obtains a hero's burial for the dead warrior. "The unifying theme," writes Kitto, "is the antagonism of Ajax and Odysseus, of physical, and we may admit, of spiritual daring against intellectual greatness; an antagonism the more dramatic in that Ajax never understands Odysseus whereas Odysseus always understands Ajax. Ajax, lacking 'wisdom,' brings himself to ruin: Odysseus, rich in wisdom, not only is successful...but also attains moral grandeur....In [Agamemnon and Menelaus] there is no resolution of the antagonism; that comes only when the greatness of Odysseus recognizes the greatness of the defeated Ajax and above all the greatness of the fact of Death. The end is rather the triumph of Odysseus than the rehabilitation of Ajax. In the prologue he triumphs over Athena's suggestions of crude force and resentment; by the vote of the army [to give him rather than Ajax the armor of Achilles] his intellectual greatness has already overcome Ajax' soldierly greatness, now he brings the drama to a harmonious close by overcoming the moral violence [of Agamemnon and Menelaus]."

Kitto's controversial interpretations of Greek drama may or may not be "right." But, in the course of showing that if we have trouble finding the dramatic center of a Greek play, it may be because its dramatic center is actually located someplace other than where we are looking for it, he taught me what a dramatic situation really is: a zone of inevitable opposition of powerful forces that emits ever-widening reverberations until it is neutralized somehow in a way that creates understanding, insight, and harmony. Knowing that, I could work backward from my perception of my story's central issue to generate its plot. What created this conflict? What can possibly resolve it? Who is being hurt by it, and why? Those are the questions I learned to ask myself: and out of them came *Thorns, To Live Again, Tower of Glass, Dying Inside, Lord Valentine's Castle*, and all the rest.

But not right away. Though I had read my Kitto, I was not quite as good as Sophocles, yet. Though I had studied Blish and Knight and the stories they found praiseworthy, my own work continued to fall some distance short of their precepts. In fact, I was barely competent at my chosen trade, no longer a novice but only a minimally adept journeyman. But at least I had figured out, with their help, how to construct salable fiction. My basic notions of technique were now in place: find a situation of dissonance growing out of a striking idea or some combination of striking ideas, find the characters affected by that dissonance, write clearly and directly using dialog that moves each scene along and avoiding any clumsiness of style and awkward shifts of viewpoint, and bring matters in the end to a point where the harmony of the universe is restored and Zeus is satisfied.

Having learned and internalized all that, I spent my final year in college writing science fiction as fast as I could, and I sold practically everything I wrote. It was a heady feeling: too heady, perhaps. By the time I took my degree in June of 1956 my name was on the cover of a dozen magazines at once and I was earning a respectable living as a free-lance writer. A few months later the World Science Fiction Convention provided the final blessing by awarding me a Hugo as the most promising new author of the year. And so I lived happily ever after, more or less.

Except that in the course of turning myself from a trembling beginner into a smartass pro I had overlooked the biggest lesson, which is that selling everything you write doesn't mean that you know it all, or even that you know very much. The stuff I was writing, with

a few honorable exceptions, was generic boilerplate material designed
to help harried editors fill their back pages, not anything likely to live
down the ages. Once I had decided that I was missing whatever gene
it was that carries literary greatness, I chose to settle merely for
learning how to write things that someone, anyone, would publish,
and now I had accomplished that.

I had hit on a formula for turning story ideas into cash, and it
worked just fine. But the same formula can be applied in many ways,
as can be verified by comparing the bouquet and flavor of Château
Mouton-Rothschild with that of a bottle of $3.98 Basic Wino Bur-
gundy. Somehow I had failed to realize that my fiercely intense studies
of narrative technique during the years of my late adolescence had
given me the equipment I needed to construct the very best stories I
had within me, and so perhaps in time to equal the work of the writers
I idolized. Instead, still telling myself that I was inherently incapable
of matching such lofty achievements, I was content to use my hard-
won skills for nothing more than supplying a hungry market with
routine potboilers by the dozen.

Enter the final and harshest mentor: H.L. Gold, the brooding,
irascible, brilliant editor of *Galaxy Science Fiction*. I had begun sending stories to him in 1953. The first one came back with an amiable
note: "Aside from a tendency to be overexplicit in spots and repeat in
dialog something already stated in narrative, you've told your story
well. [He was right. It's a fault I still sometimes slip into.] Trouble is
that you don't have an ending. Not, at any rate, one that fantasy
readers would be happy with. Anyone who buys a fantasy magazine
naturally expects a fantasy payoff, and is understandably put out
when he fails to get one...."

That was before I began selling. Later on, after I did, I got to know
Gold and eventually sold him some stories. But he rejected as many
as he accepted, and the rejection notes were horrendous. Here's one,
from early 1956:

> If I had to pick your one biggest fault, I'd say it was your
> not thinking beneath the surface of your stories. It leads to
> almost appalling glibness. But the writing style has grown a
> great deal. Now upgrade the thinking and plotting to the level
> of style and you will be far beyond this buttery little item.

And this, a couple of months later:

> You're selling more than you're learning. The fact that you
> sell is tricking you into believing that your technique is

adequate. It is—for now. But project your career twenty years into the future and see where you'll stand if you don't sweat over improving your style, handling of character and conflict, resourcefulness in story development. You'll simply be more facile at what you're doing right now, more glib, more skilled at invariably taking the easiest way out.

If I didn't see a talent there—a potential one, a good way from being fully realized—I wouldn't take the time to point out the greased skidway you're standing on. I wouldn't give a damn. But I'm risking your professional friendship for the sake of a better one.

And this, early in 1957:

The opening is fine. How you flattened out the balance into its present featurelessness is hard to figure, but I suppose persistence can do it—in this case, being its own reward.

There's one thing that stands between our doing business: You by God will *not* squeeze the most juice—juice, not wordage—from a setup. That, because I need material, is the selfish view. The unselfish view is that I'm a writer as well as editor, and in both capacities I'm appalled and outraged that a talent should be *encouraged* to stay small, so that the least effort and maximum glibness will sell the most literary yard goods...and the hell with whether you grow as a writer. I know I'd have less trouble and fewer enemies if I bought in the same way, but I've seen too many aged hacks, Bob, and damned if I want to help even one person join that pathetic ragged crowd. The time has come for you to do some real work to learn your craft. If not now, *when?*

Gold's letters upset me, of course. But they also angered me. Hadn't I won a Hugo, the youngest writer ever to do so? (Still true, thirty years later.) Hadn't I sold stories by the dozen to X and Y and Z? (I promptly sold all the stories Gold rejected, too.) What was he saying, time to learn my craft? I *knew* my craft!

Gradually, though, what he was saying sank in—especially when I heard much the same things, in a more oblique and gentler way, from a couple of other old pros who had become close friends of mine, Frederik Pohl and Lester del Rey. They—along with everyone else in science fiction—were looking at me by this time as some sort of bizarre phenomenon, a kid who could write two short stories a day and a novel in two weeks and sell everything he wrote. They envied me that; but they also knew that my crazy facility and my growing glibness were traps, as deadly as they were profitable, and I shudder to think what they were all saying behind my back. To my face, though, they said plenty, Gold and Blish and Knight, Pohl and del Rey, Algis Budrys and Cyril Kornbluth and Judy Merril and Ted Sturgeon. I got the message. I'm grateful to them all for letting me in on the truth. Which was: You have talent, kid. God knows you have ambition. You have energy beyond belief. Now it's time you start doing something with all those gifts besides showing us how fast you can turn out minimally acceptable stuff that editors can use to fill the back pages of their magazines. Learn your craft, kid.

But I *have* learned my craft, I replied silently.

And indeed I had. Some of it, anyway. But one aspect of a writer's craft is knowing how to put the things you have learned to their best possible use, rather than doing no more than you have to, to get by. Another is realizing how much more there still is to learn—always.

So they just smiled, and waited for time to pass. Which it did; and I changed; and so, thank God, did my work, once I came to understand that a writer who is satisfied just by getting some editor to say yes is a writer who isn't really doing anything that's worth doing at all.

What I wasn't willing to see when I was 21 is that selling stories proves only that you know how to sell stories. That isn't trivial, but it isn't enough. I had been too easy on myself, circa age 15, with the circular argument that the stories I was writing were poor because I hadn't been born with the innate gift of writing good ones. If such a gift exists, very likely I *was* born with it; it certainly seems that way to me now. But what I wouldn't let myself see, back then, is that it takes more than being born with a knack for words to write something worth reading. Those stories I wrote in my teens were poor because I didn't know enough about the craft I wanted to follow and because at that age I didn't know enough about anything to have any worthwhile stories to tell. No point complaining to the gods that they hadn't given me the natural writing skills of Shakespeare, or Dickens, or Heinlein: what I needed to do was what anyone setting out to accomplish anything needs to do, which is to do the best you can with whatever gifts you may have, constantly striving with all your soul to enhance your mastery of your chosen craft. That very well may be how all those great writers whose natural endowments I once envied had had to achieve their greatness: by constant study, practice, and sweaty hard work. Shakespeare's first plays may have been better than anyone else's first plays, but even he didn't turn out *Lear* and *Othello* during his apprentice days.

Mastery of craft is a matter of process, not of a single blinding moment of attainment: you go on working toward it all your life. If you go about things the right way, you get better and better all the time, and that means you may get very good indeed. But the diabolical thing is that you never quite get good enough, ever, so you have to go on learning. Even when you're good enough to please Damon Knight or James Blish or whatever other external authority you've set up for yourself, you still won't be good enough to please yourself—not unless you've established goals for yourself that are contemptibly easy to fulfill.

Of course, there's much more to writing than mastery of technique. Technique is merely a means to an end, and in this case the end is to convey understanding in the guise of entertainment. The storytelling art evolved as a way of interpreting the world—as a way of creating order out of the chaos that the cruel or merely absentminded gods handed us long ago. To perform that task effectively, the writer must peer into the heart of the chaos; the writer must know something about the world. Even if what you want to write about is a planet a million light-years away, you must have some understanding of this one, or the inhabitants of this world will have little interest in what you have to say.

You are compelled, then, to go on seeking knowledge endlessly, knowledge of your craft and of the world—an eternal apprentice in your own eyes, however you may appear to others. I once believed that there was a single Secret of Writing that all the true writers had managed to learn: an ultimate revelation of the deepest mysteries of the art. I believed that the writers whose books and stories I admired had attained that Secret, and that everything became magically easy for them at that point. Now I'm not so sure. I suspect that that dazzling moment of ultimate revelation never does come. The secret of the Secret is that it doesn't exist. There are many things that you must master if you hope to practice the art and the craft of writing, but they are far from secret, nor do they add up to one single great Secret. You just go on, doing your best, living and reading and thinking and studying and working and searching for answers, using everything that you've learned along the way and hoping that each new story is deeper and richer than the one before.

There you have it: the truth at last, the real Secret. It took me a long time to figure out, because I had to work it out all by myself, regardless of the things that helpful teachers and editors and fellow writers tried to tell me. The process of becoming a writer involves discovering how to use the accumulated wisdom of our guild, all those tricks of the storytelling trade that have evolved around the campfire over the past five or ten or fifty thousand years. Others can show you what those tricks are. But only you can make a writer out of yourself, by reading, by studying what you have read, and above all by writing.

The Long Despair of Doing Nothing Well

An essay by Graham Greene tells of the time the great novelist encouraged his friend Tom Laughton, who had just retired after many years of running a great hotel, to write his autobiography. Laughton, Greene felt, knew the inner life of the hotel world as few others did; he brimmed with lively anecdotes; on the theory that "everyone has one book inside him," Greene urged him to set down his recollections. Laughton had never written before. But—perhaps to Greene's surprise—he promptly got to work on the book.

Before long the great novelist received a first draft from the hotelkeeper for an appraisal. It started well, Greene thought—especially for the work of an amateur—but then began to lose focus. Tactfully Greene offered a few mild criticisms. Possibly he never expected to hear any more of the project. But then came a revised draft—and then another.

"When after two years had passed," Greene writes, "I read the first draft of the book, I began to realize I was not dealing with an amateur but a professional. To an amateur his words are Holy Writ— the professional knows how far they will always fall short of what he wants to say. I became used to the letters from Yorkshire written to the signature tune, 'I think I see what's wrong. I have started again.' To what an inferno, I thought, has my unthinking encouragement condemned him. Why should a man who loves good painting, good wine, and good food, living in a happy and well-deserved retirement, suffer in the evening of life what all writers must suffer—in Masefield's phrase 'The long despair of doing nothing well?' "

Two passages in that piece struck me with special force: *To an amateur his words are Holy Writ— the professional knows how far they will always fall short of what he wants to say* and the phrase from Masefield, *The long despair of doing nothing well.*

Like Graham Greene, I have spent my entire adult life as a professional writer. I've been successful at it. I've been writing close to forty years now—and during that time I've sold virtually everything I've ever written. I've won a shelf full of awards and been showered with all sorts of honors. I've done well financially. And yet—and yet—

I don't think I've ever felt, *in the moment of writing it*, that anything I've written lived up to my own standards of excellence. I underline *in the moment of writing it* because I do actually think I've written some worthwhile stories over the years. But all my self-approbation comes

[*Amazing Stories*, December 1991]

after the fact, in some cases years after the fact. I never—NEVER—feel that way about anything I'm writing while I'm writing it. Sentence by sentence, it all seems clumsy, lame, obtuse—too sketchy or too dense, too skimpy or too wordy, something missing all the time: the words ever falling short of what I want to say, and the work-day ending always with the long despair of doing nothing well.

I'm not the only writer who feels that way. I've known dozens, over the years, who have been so critical of their own work that eventually they've become unable to write at all, for periods of months or years or, in a few tragic instances, forever. Their attitude toward their work is what Frederik Pohl once called, many years ago, "a goulash of shame and pride"—and when the shame starts to over-power the pride, silence is the inevitable result. The more ambitious the writer, the more intense this self-flagellation will be. The hack sails serenely on, moving his fingers, covering paper with words, collecting his checks. The writer who sees himself—however self-de-ludingly—as a serious creative artist will, sooner or later, come up against the fact that what he's writing seems neither serious nor creative nor art. And then follows the paralysis known as writers' block. The fact that his newest work actually may be on a par with, or even superior to, the stories with which he made his name is irrele-vant. They don't seem that way to him. And in time his critical appraisal of the work in progress becomes so harsh that he can't go on.

I said above that I do eventually develop a healthy appreciation of my own work, or at least some of it, after the fact. Some writers never get even that much solace. But the knowledge of past achieve-ment is small consolation during the agonies of writing the newest story. When in a difficult moment I'm foolish enough look back with pride at something I once wrote that actually has come to satisfy me— as I look back, say, on "Born With the Dead" or *Downward to the Earth* or *Dying Inside*—the effect is usually catastrophic. That was then; this is now; the more admiration I feel for the old stories, the more clearly I see that the new one is plainly a stinker. (Ah, but is it? I wrote one a couple of years ago called "Enter A Soldier. Later: Enter Another" that seemed to me to be at best a journeyman bit of professionalism; I thought so little of it that I nearly didn't bother to submit it to a magazine for publication. Eventually I did, though; and when it was published I re-read it and wondered why I had been so harsh on it. And it went on to win a Hugo and nearly won a Nebula too.)

Cold comfort, then, to look back on past glories. That only invites you to compete with yourself of years gone by; and the new one somehow never measures up against the ones that are safely in print, applauded and anthologized and mysteriously made acceptable even to their creator.

Even worse than competing against yourself, though, is the torment of forcing yourself to compete against *other* writers' triumphs— of trying to match, in a single prose work, everything and anything that anyone has ever written. Of all the pathological afflictions to which writers are prone, that's the most maddening. You launch into a novel and suddenly you realize that it doesn't have the epic sweep of *Dune*, the intricate mystery-story plot of *Caves of Steel*, the brilliant prose surface of *The Stars My Destination*, the warmth and compassion of *The Left Hand of Darkness*, the high-tech pizzazz of *Neuromancer*, or the visionary poetry of *Perelandra*. Worse yet, you reach outside the science-fiction field, and start comparing your pitiful six pages with *The Sun Also Rises*, *The Magic Mountain*, *The Sound and the Fury*, *Crime and Punishment*, and *The Adventures of Augie March*. Not just with one of them, but with all of them at once: you want to embody the salient qualities of every worthwhile piece of fiction since *The Iliad* in your new book. But you can't, because it can't be done. And you sit there glumly staring at the screen, telling yourself that you and your book both are worthless.

The thing to do when that happens is to remind yourself that *Caves of Steel* doesn't have the epic sweep of *Dune* either, and that *Neuromancer* written with the warmth and compassion of *Left Hand of Darkness* would be just plain silly, and Hemingway's books aren't much like Faulkner's and neither one of them had much in common with Thomas Mann. Besides which, nothing in any of those books has any bearing on what you're writing now—so knock off the foolishness, fellow, and just tell your story, one sentence at a time, in your own tone of voice. There's time to worry later, when the work is done, about whether you've surpassed Hemingway and Bester and Faulkner and Le Guin.

Usually that works. Which is why, despite the self-inflicted torments I devise for myself, I do manage to keep on writing. And so do all the other writers you read, most of whom stagger under self-imposed burdens of similar kinds.

The problem, really, is that in order to write well, the writer has to be a fierce critic of his own work: to review it sentence by sentence in the moment of creation (or soon afterward) and to prune away everything false, awkward, inept, or muddled. He needs, in

Hemingway's classic phrase, a good bullshit detector. And all too often the critic inside the writer gets too critical. Then nothing escapes the built-in bullshit detector; then every line is discarded as fast as it gets on screen; and then the writer finishes his day with "the long despair of doing nothing well."

This is not a plea for sympathy. Graham Greene has been well rewarded for his trouble, and so have I, and John Masefield, for all his despair, went on to become poet laureate of England. If writing is a depressing business, and it certainly is, it's because it necessarily requires a high degree of self-criticism and tends to attract people who are prone to depression in any case. We invent our own problems for ourselves, and sometimes the going gets very tough as a result. But we keep on going, all the same—most of us—and it's not a terrible life, just a complex one.

As for Tom Laughton and his struggle to do a proper job of writing that book on hotelkeeping: after many drafts it finally was finished and published in 1977, under the title of *Pavilions by the Sea*. In his essay on it, Graham Greene speaks approvingly of its "proud, confident, professional ring." But I don't think its author ever wrote a second one. There are mornings when I don't blame him.

Falsus In Uno, Falsus In Omnibus

Publishers send me a lot of science-fiction books I can't read them all, or even a significant fraction of the ones I get, but I do try to glance at the new ones, at least. A few months back, one of the ones I glanced at was a Berkley paperback called *The Pleasure Tube*, by a writer new to me, Robert Onopa.

This isn't a book review. I haven't read *The Pleasure Tube* and I suspect that I probably never will, although—on the basis of a quick thumb-flip—it looks like a lively and inventive novel. The reason I mention it here is that on the same quick thumb-flip I encountered a character names "Werhner" and another named "Collette."

Notice where the "h" is in "Werhner." It's not quite where Wernher von Braun wore it. It has wandered over one place, which isn't very far, but just far enough to create a combination of consonants—*rhn* that looks almost right except to somebody who knows how the German word "Wernher" is spelled. If the author had transposed letters in the other direction, to make the name "Wehrner," that might at least have sounded plausibly Teutonic. "Werhner" just sounds ignorant—the way "Smitth" or "Joanes" would in a novel by a German.

As for "Collette," that's a nice French-sounding female name, and for all I know it's a legitimate one. But all the Colettes I can think of spelled their names with a single "l"—from St. Colette of the fourteenth century on down to the twentieth-century French novelists, who was, I suspect, the person in Robert Onopa's mind when he chose his character's name.

Okay, you say, I'm being picky. What does it matter whether "Collette" is spelled with one "l" or two, anyway? And "Wernher" sounds exactly like "Werhner" to the American ear, so where's the harm? What counts is the *story*, right? Who gives a damn how the author chooses to spell his own characters' names? For all we know, "Collette" and "Werhner" may very well be spelled just that way before long.

I yield on the last point. Words are becoming separated from their underlying roots so rapidly that spelling seems purely arbitrary to most people, and in a world where spelling is arbitrary, anything goes. But words—and names are words—are spelled arbitrarily only in the decadence of a language, when communication is breaking down. The reason we insist fastidiously on correct spelling is that, for those of us who understand the language of words, words contain signals explaining their own meanings and leading to other meanings. Once you've forgotten that the word *millennium* contains the Latin *annus*, you don't have any reason not to spell it "millenium," and might get indignant at being corrected. But by knowing the root, I have a way of knowing that "millennium" literally means "a thousand years," and that leads me to all sorts of useful associations—knowing, for example, why the people of A.D. 999 got so tense as the "millennium" approached.

So it won't do to shrug and say that in the coming illiterate age we can forget about spelling accurately. "Wernher" may turn into "Werhner," but in that process we're going to lose a lot of valuable data. And Robert Onopa wrote his book in our own time—when the names he used still had fixed structures.

There's a legal phrase, *Falsus in uno, falsus in omnibus*, that every writer ought to keep in mind. It means, "False in one thing, false in everything." A harsh position, but writing is a harsh business. When I see a writer bungling the spelling of a name, I wonder inevitably whether he's bungled his geography too, his chemistry and physics, his history, and everything else. I don't think Robert Onopa did that—his book looks intelligent and informed, and he may merely be a lousy speller who writes well in all other respects. (Cf. Samuel R. Delany, who is notorious among editors for his foul spelling, and who immortalized that trait by misspelling the ancient and honorable name of "Dahlgren" in his own best-known novel.)

But *Falsus in uno, falsus in omnibus*: the fumbled detail, no matter how petty, generates mistrust among readers. Where was the copy-editor when Onopa's "Werhner" slipped through? Copy-editors are supposed to catch stuff like that—but they're too busy, I guess, changing a writer's commas to dashes and his dashes to commas to worry about real errors. And some of them, alas, figure that in a cockeyed science-fiction novel any kind of cockeyed spelling is probably okay.

Delany, again: in *Babel-17* he names a space-pirate Jebel and called his giant spaceship "Jebel Tarik," explaining that means "Jebel's Mountain" in Old Moorish. Unfortunately, Delany got things turned around. "Jebel Tarik" means "Tarik's Mountain," Tarik being an eighth-century Arab general; we have corrupted the name of the place he conquered into "Gibraltar." When Delany solemnly tells us that "Tarik" means "mountain," and brings a character named "Jebel" on stage, we can smile indulgently at a very young writer's errors; but the trouble is that *Babel-17* is a science-fiction book in which the under-lying science is linguistics, and it becomes hard to trust the rest of the text once one stumbles across such an obvious mistake. *Falsus in uno, falsus in omnibus.* Writing is hard work, and sustaining the reader's illusion that what is on the page has really happened is the hardest part of all. When I encounter characters named Werhner or moun-tains belonging to Jebel, that illusion is punctured for me just as effectively as it is by references to Queen Victoria's Italian accent or weeks of rain in Los Angeles in summer. We have to try to get it straight—down to the pettiest detail.

The Curse of Thoth

Not long ago, when doing research for a story that takes place in ancient Egypt at the time of the Eighteenth Dynasty, I found myself reading an anthology of fiction dating from that period. And at the end of one of the stories, a fantasy somewhat in the mode of the Arabian Nights called "The Tale of Two Brothers," I came upon this absolutely splendid curse directed against literary critics:

"*Whoever speaks against this book, may Thoth challenge him to single combat.*"

How marvelous! How absolutely perfect! I think I'm going to use it as the last line of all my books from now on, and I recommend to any of my fellow writers who may happen to be reading this that they do the same.

May Thoth challenge him to single combat! Way to go! The inscrutable, implacable ibis-headed god summoned from his heavenly duties to obliterate annoying book-reviewers with a single flick of his beady eyes! The final solution to the critic problem!

Not that I really have all that much animus against critics and criticism, mind you. Some of my best friends have written book reviews. I've written some myself. I even read some—the *New York Times Book Review* arrives in my house every week, and I look at the reviews in *The New Yorker*, and sometimes I even scan those in *Locus*. For the reader, reviews can be useful consumer guides, directing them toward books they'd enjoy reading and moving them away from things they probably wouldn't like.

But for the writer—

Oy, vey, what they do to the writer!

Somebody—I wish I knew who—once said, "Critics are people who come on the battlefield after the fighting is over and shoot the wounded." Beautifully put, I think. Consider this:

The writer, having succeeded in negotiating all the preliminary pitfalls of proposing a book and obtaining a satisfactory contract for it, has been out there amidst the lightning and the thunder for an interminable span of time, dancing nimbly about trying to put one coherent sentence after another while publishers, editors, friends and spouses if they've had a chance to peek at the manuscript, and sometimes even his own literary agent, all offer confusing and often contradictory advice. At last, after months or even years of *sturm und drang*, he shakily gathers up his bundle of manuscript and staggers

[*Amazing Stories*, October, 1991]

down to the post office with it. The book is finished, or at least he's decided to stop working on it.

Off it goes to New York. Back come reams of suggestions for turning everything inside out. He explains to the editor why Chapter Five belongs where it is, instead of after Chapter Sixteen. Sometimes the editor gives in. Sometimes the writer does. The title is changed. The first hundred pages are cut, at editorial suggestion, to thirty pages. Then the book goes to the copy editor, who has her own strikingly individual ideas about the use of commas. The manuscript, as edited, goes back to the writer, who spends a couple of days erasing all the copy editor's changes. It then is set in type. The typesetter, a practitioner of stochastic garbling, introduces new and highly random alterations to the text. The writer repairs the damage. The book is printed. The book is published—with a painting on the cover showing a ghastly slimy *thing*, not to be found anywhere in the text.

And then, then, then, a horde of reviewers falls upon the book like devouring locusts, and each one proceeds to explain how it *should* have been written. No two ideas are the same. Six reviewers blame the writer because the cover painting doesn't jibe with the text. Three of them mock a typographical error that was introduced into the book *after* the writer last saw the galley proofs. Four find the author's beliefs politically unacceptable, two saying he's too conservative and the other two insisting he's too liberal. One suggests that the entire novel is a thinly disguised plagiarism of a famous work by Heinlein, Proust, or Danielle Steele.

"....people who come on the battlefield after the fighting is over and shoot the wounded." Yes, indeed.

But the carnage isn't over when the horrible reviews are published. Not in the slightest. Just as the writer's battered ego is beginning to heal, the writer's mother is on the phone. She's just seen some dastardly review of her child's book, months old, in a magazine in her dentist's office. How dare they! She'll send a letter to the editor at once! She wants to know the reviewer's address too! She quotes all the offending critical phrases in the process of refuting them. It takes half an hour to calm her down, and by that time all the wounds are bleeding again.

Or perhaps the writer hasn't even *seen* the unfavorable review, because he makes a point of not looking for them. It's a good bet, in that case, that some kindly colleague of his—usually an exact contemporary with his or her own fish to fry—will come up to him at a party and say, "I just wanted to tell you how sorry I am about the absolutely foul things they said about your book in the last issue of X Magazine. It's disgraceful, the way they trashed your book. I have to tell you that I haven't read the book yet myself, incidentally, but I know it can't possibly be as awful as they said it was." Someone will do that to you at least once a year, mark my words. Assassination in the guise of sympathy—an old, old ploy. Ben Jonson probably used it on Shakespeare.

You may think from what I've written so far that I must be inordinately sensitive to criticism, indeed am afraid of it, and that I have a morbid dislike of critics. Far from it. I've received plenty of bad reviews in my time—the law of averages alone would guarantee that, considering that I've published more books than I can count over a period of nearly four decades. *But I don't pay any attention to them whatever.* Generally I ignore the media where reviews are to be found. (The science-fiction world is particularly densely infested with magazines that review books. The only ones I receive are *Locus* and *Science Fiction Chronicle*, and I skim quickly through the reviews to get to the news columns.)

I began to cultivate this indifference to reviews in 1955, when my first novel, *Revolt on Alpha C*, was published. I wrote it when I was nineteen; I thought it was a pretty good book for a beginner, and so did my publisher. This is what the *New York Times* had to say about it back then:

> "I find author Robert Silverberg's story too inept and unreal to warrant inclusion in such fast-moving company. [Heinlein and someone named Slater Brown.] Young Larry Stark, newly graduated Space Patrolman, lands with his crew on a planet of Alpha Centaurus, only to become embroiled in its rebellion against Terran control. When his best friends join the rebellion, Larry is forced into a series of old-hat adventures."

I could have let that review crush my soul, I guess. But I didn't need the *New York Times* to tell me that at nineteen I wasn't as good as Heinlein. I knew that already. I was aware of my book's flaws, but I wasn't skillful enough then to do anything about them; I hoped I'd improve; I was already at work on my next novel. Naturally I'd have preferred to have the Times say, "Heinlein, move over. Here comes Silverberg." But it didn't. So? I survived. The "inept and unreal" *Revolt on Alpha C*, by the way, remained in print, earning royalties, for the next thirty years.

To this day, if I happen to see a review of my book somewhere, I read it, shrug, and go on with what I'm doing. I have, after all, done the best job I possibly could with my book before releasing it for publication. I've planned it carefully, I've written it with thought, I've revised it over and over. If it still doesn't measure up to somebody's ideas of perfection, well, I'm sorry. But not very. Even the most searching piece of literary criticism won't help me write that book any better. The job is done; I'm already on to the next one. My faults are probably ingrained beyond eradication by outside suggestion, and my excellences, such as they are, will manifest themselves in the next book without the help of reviewers of the last one. So I don't care about the bad reviews. They slip from my mind. The favorable ones give me a nice buzz for five minutes or thereabouts; and then they slip from my mind too. David Frost once spoke of the only thing that any writer really wants from criticism: "Twelve pages of closely reasoned praise." Anything else is irrelevant.

Some writers, though, fail to achieve my detachment from criticism and suffer severe damage. Consider this case:

The June, 1954 issue of a long-vanished s-f magazine called Imagination ran a review by one Henry Bott that had this to say of a newly published book: "_____ _____ is an educated, articulate man, but he is neither a writer nor a storyteller. Heavy-handed and ponderous, _____ grinds out ream after ream of elephantine prose about his ridiculous 'Galactic Empire,' filled with endless philosophizing (on a juvenile level), obscure sociological fantasies, and massive technological monologues."

The unfortunate author of the book, learning to his dismay from Henry Bott that he was "neither a writer nor a storyteller," was so heartbroken that he gave up the profession of writing then and there. The book was called Second Foundation. The writer's name was Isaac Asimov. Who knows what fine work he might one day have managed to do, if Henry Bott's cruel review hadn't destroyed his career in its infancy?

Beginnings

Since the mid-1980s I've been one of the story judges for the Writers of the Future contest, an annual event founded by the late L. Ron Hubbard, which seeks out the work of unpublished science–fiction writers and gives lavish prizes to the best of it. My fellow judges, at the beginning, included the likes of Theodore Sturgeon, Jack Williamson, and Roger Zelazny. The first year's winners included such people as David Zindell, Karen Joy Fowler, Dean Wesley Smith, and Nina Kiriki Hoffman.

At the request of Algis Budrys, who was then the director of the contest, each of the judges wrote a short piece to accompany the first annual anthology of prizewinning stories. This is mine. (Algis Budrys is four years older than I am. When I was a new writer myself, back about 1955, he was already an established figure in the field, turning out brilliant stories at a dazzling rate and getting them published everywhere. I looked up to him as a mentor out of an earlier generation. A four-year age gap when you're twenty is very different from the same gap forty-odd years later; but yet I still regard Budrys as very much my senior, because he got into the business of writing s-f a few years before me, and still feel like something of a beginner when I'm in his company. Weird.)

We were all new writers once—even Sophocles, even Homer, even Jack Williamson. And I think we all must begin in the same way, those of us who are going to be writers. We start by being consumers of the product: in childhood we sit around the campfire listening to the storyteller, caught in his spell, lost in the fables he spins, envying and admiring him for the magical skill by which he holds us. "I wonder how he does that," we think—concerned, even then, as much with technique, the tricks of the trade, as we are with the matter of the tales being told. So we go off and wander in the woods by ourselves for a little while, thinking about the storyteller's story and how he told it, considering his opening few words and how they drew the audience in, and how he developed his narrative, and brought it to its climax, and how he managed to finish it in such a way that when he looked up, eyes glowing, and grinned at his listeners, everyone in the campfire circle knew beyond doubt that the story was over. We ponder such things, perhaps even tell ourselves a little story just to see what the process feels like, and then, perhaps the next day, we turn to a couple of our classmates and say, "I heard an interesting story last night," and so we begin.

[*Writers of the Future*, Vol I, 1985]

We begin young, most of us. That's most notably true, I suspect, in the field of science fiction, where prodigies are the rule rather than the exception. It's not hard to understand why: science fiction, like other forms of fantasy, is uniquely favored by the young reader; and the young storyteller, operating out of the imitative motives that I think are universal among new practitioners of the craft, tends to imitate the sort of thing he reads. So we see Isaac Asimov selling stories at eighteen, and writing the classic "Nightfall" at twenty-one; we have Algis Budrys on every magazine's contents page before he was twenty-two, Harlan Ellison doing the same, Bradbury famous for his weird tales at twenty-three, Theodore Sturgeon turning out "Microcosmic God" at about that age, Frederik Pohl not only a professional writer but a magazine editor at twenty-one, and so on and so on.

Of course, there are those professional writers whose first published stories appeared when they were thirty or forty or even seventy years of age. I think here of Robert A. Heinlein, starting his career at the age of thirty-two after leaving the Navy, or Gene Wolfe, who was thirty-four when he sold his first story, or Ursula K. Le Guin, first published at thirty-three, or James Tiptree, who must have been about fifty. But even late bloomers like these, I'm quite sure, were writing stories long before they ever bothered to get them published. Perhaps Heinlein was different—it's my guess that Heinlein had never written a story in his life until he sat down to turn out a completely satisfactory one on his first try one day in 1939, because that's the way I imagine Heinlein has always done things—but surely Le Guin and Wolfe and Tiptree were storytellers from childhood on, furtively scribbling curious little things and hiding them in desk drawers, or at best sharing them with a trusted playmate. Every professional writer I know—again, with the possible exception of Heinlein—began telling stories as soon as he knew what a story was.

And how does one know what a story is? By listening to them, before one can read; by reading them, insatiably, a little while later; by taking them apart, soon after that, to find their essential components; and, finally, by writing them. I remember that process in myself: the appetite for vicarious experience that could never be sated, the stacks of books carried home from the public library at age six or seven, the sheets of lined paper clumsily covered with "stories" that were really just reworkings of things I had read or heard, and, finally—by age eleven or twelve—the first stories that were something more than imitations, however crude they might be and however much they might owe to my previous reading. Out of all this came the awareness, by the time I was thirteen, that I might actually be able to create stories that other people would want to read, if only I could discover the secrets of the trade. And then, all during my adolescence, the singleminded quest to identify those secrets and penetrate to the heart of the storytelling mysteries.

I remember reading books with titles like *The Narrative Art* and *The Structure of the Novel* and even *Writing to Sell*. They taught me useful things, sure. So did a book called *Greek Tragedy*, by H.D.F. Kitto, which taught me nothing at all about science fiction but everything in the world about the relationship of plot and character. (I often recommend it to young writers, who look at me in bewilderment when I do. Generally they shrug my recommendation off, I suppose. So be it.) But I really learned about fiction by reading it. If a story held me and moved me and awed me and startled me, I read it fifty times to see how the writer had done those things to me. I looked at the opening paragraph and the closing paragraph and hunted for relationships between them; I measured the mix of dialog and expository narrative; I checked the length of paragraphs, the quantity of adjectives and adverbs, the use of punctuation, and a lot of other things. I counted the number of characters per thousand words. I studied the way complications piled up as a story unfolded.

Oh, I worked at it! I read Heinlein and Asimov and Clarke, Kuttner and Blish and Kornbluth, Leiber and Vance, Bradbury and Sturgeon. I read Conrad and Faulkner, too, and Kafka, and Thomas Mann, and Joyce and Ibsen and especially Sophocles. In particular the writers I studied closely were the ones just a few years ahead of me—Robert Sheckley, Poul Anderson, Algis Budrys, Philip K. Dick, and a few others: I figured their secrets might be easier to isolate than those of the more experienced writers. (It wasn't so.) By the time I was eighteen I had absorbed this great mass of words, I had derived from it a handful of basic principles so simple I could list them on a single page (but I've never let myself be talked into doing it), and I set out to write some stories. Since then I haven't given much thought to theoretical matters; but I don't need to, because the theory is as much a part of me as the marrow of my bones, and can be taken for granted just as readily as one's bone marrow is. I know no other way to go about the business of becoming a writer. Sit by the campfire, listen to the man telling the tale, arrive at some sense of what it is that you think he's doing, and start doing it yourself. And very shortly, if you really are a writer, you will have so deeply internalized the principles you sought so hard to find that you stop thinking about them at all; you merely tell your stories, in what you know to be your own way. And it *is* your own way: but also it's the way in which all tales have been told from Homer and Sophocles down through Kipling, Hemingway, Bradbury, Sturgeon, Zelazny, whoever. Once upon a time, you say, there lived so-and-so in such-and-such a place, and while he was minding his own business the following absolutely astonishing thing happened to him. And so you begin; and they gather close about you, for they cannot choose but hear.

To a Writer Just Starting Out

This is the essay I did for the tenth Writers of the Future anthology, a decade later. The contest director now was Dave Wolverton, who had been one of the early prizewinners and had gone on to a significant writing career.

You say you want to be a writer—specifically, a science-fiction writer. But do I believe you? Hardly a week goes by without someone telling me, "I'd really like to write some day," or "I've got a wonderful idea for a story that I'm thinking about writing next summer," or "I know I'd be a successful writer if I could only manage to get started." I'm always courteous to those people. But I don't expect them ever to do anything that I would regard as writing, and I'm always right.

Why, then, should I take you seriously when you give me the same line?

One good reason is that you've taken the trouble to pick up this book, which is made up of stories by beginning writers just a couple of years beyond your current level of accomplishment and ambition. The stories in this book are all pretty good, and a few of them are *very* good. Nevertheless, why would you buy and read a book of stories by science-fiction writers with no proven histories of achievement, when for the same six bucks (or whatever) you could have bought a volume of stories of predictable high quality by Frederik Pohl or Joe Haldeman or Isaac Asimov or—well—Robert Silverberg?

You bought this book because you want to see what other writers just graduating from the novice class are doing. You want to find out what it takes to cross that mysterious line that separates the amateur from the pro. That's reason number one why I believe you when you say you genuinely want to be a writer. *You're already doing field research. You're trying to learn the job requirements.*

What's more, you probably aren't just thinking wistfully about doing some writing "eventually," in that all-too-familiar way that non-writers have. The chances are excellent that you've *already* written some science fiction or fantasy. Perhaps you haven't let any editors see it yet, but you've been banging away at the keyboard whenever time permits, and you've written two, three, maybe five short stories, or perhaps a chunk of a novel. Now you've picked up the *Writers of the Future* anthology because you want to compare your work to that

[*Writers of the Future*, Vol X, 1994]

of some others who have crossed the boundary into publication. You want to see how far you are from making the grade yourself. *You've begun to measure your work against that of published writers.* And that's why I take your claim of wanting to be a writer seriously. You aren't just talking about writing something, someday, maybe, when the Moon is in Sagittarius and the wind is blowing from the west and Aunt Harriet has gone home to Indiana. You've actually been doing some. And now you're trying to get some perspective on the stuff you've produced. The would-bes, the wannabes, simply talk about it. You've begun to do it. You've taken the all-important first step.

What happens next? How likely is it that you'll have a story in next year's *Writers of the Future* book—and go on from there to see your name on the contents pages of the s-f magazines, and on the jackets of books, and eventually find yourself surrounded by hordes of admirers begging for your autograph?

I don't know. I'm just a science-fiction writer, myself: I don't have precognition. You've chosen a very tough path, and I have no way of knowing whether you'll get anywhere on it. (Though I might be able to judge the odds a little better after talking with you for five or ten minutes.) But what I can do is tell you what the basic characteristics of a real professional writer are, and let you rate yourself against the standard personality profile.

1) A professional writer is a self-starter. He doesn't stand around his desk waiting for a signal to start work, or for the mystic gong of inspiration to sound. Maybe his working day begins at nine in the morning, or maybe nine at night—maybe he thinks it's a good day's work if he puts in two hours at his trade, or maybe he toils from dawn to dusk—but, whatever his working methods are (and every writer has his own), he *writes*. He can't help it. There's an inevitable restlessness that sets in when he lets too much time go by without writing. He may give himself holidays—a day off, a week, a month, even more at a stretch—but always with the silent inner understanding that when holiday time is over, writing time begins again. When a published writer starts saying, "I'd really like to get some work done, but I can't seem to find time for it these days," I know I'm talking with a writer who has drifted into trouble.

2) A professional writer reads. He can't help that, either. He reads magazines and anthologies, he reads newspapers, he reads novels, he reads anything with little printed marks on it. The beginning writer will want to read the work of other beginning writers—for reassurance, for a reminder that it isn't necessary to start out on the Heinlein

level—but he'll read Heinlein too, or whoever else it may be whom he admires inordinately, just for the sake of making sure that his reach continues to exceed his grasp. He won't just read science-fiction or fantasy, either. He'll want to gobble up Faulkner and Bellow and Updike and Tolstoy and Proust and everything else that's ever been written. He can only live one life himself, at best: but all those other writers make other lives accessible to him, and he knows that he needs all the input he can get—fiction, non-fiction, the stuff on the back of cereal boxes, any data at all—in order to attain the sort of depth and breadth that good fiction needs.

3) A professional writer sticks his neck out. He is willing to accept the risk that people will say nasty things about his work. Sure, a lot of us are quiet, shy types, underneath it all, who feel uncomfortable out there in the real world amidst the swirling uncaring hordes. Even the raucous and ebullient Isaac Asimov was, so I suspect, uncertain and uneasy behind his mask of extroversion. But, even so, we put things down on paper and send them forth into the merciless world, where they can all too easily meet with blunt rejection from editors, or scorn from readers, or probing, embarrassing diagnosis by critics. We don't care, not really. None of us likes to have a story rejected, or to be the subject of scathing letters from the public, or to be lambasted in some review column. But it's happened to all of us, and we go right on to the next story.

(At a science-fiction convention about a decade ago a woman came up to me, one of those I-want-to-be-a-writer types, and told me that she had in fact written an entire novel, a detective story, but had never found the courage to send it to an editor. Nevertheless she wanted to be a published writer. I pointed out, not entirely gently, the little lapse of logic in her behavior. Pick a publishing company, I said, and send your book there, or else stop pretending that you're interested in a writing career. She promised to get the manuscript out of the desk drawer where it was languishing, right away. I figured that was the last I would ever hear of her; but no, no, just the other day I noticed a half-page ad in the New York Times Book Review for what I think was her fifth novel, quoting from ecstatic reviews of her earlier books and listing all the awards she has won. She is big stuff, these days, in the mystery field. So she was a real writer after all—with a slight underconfidence problem that I suspect she has long since outgrown.)

And so, here you are, with your six bucks invested in this anthology full of stories by writers who were just as unknown as you are, this time last year. Will you be in next year's book? And even if you are, will that small but significant triumph lead you onward to fame, fortune, a shelf of Hugo and Nebula awards, and a sense of profound satisfaction in your own accomplishments?

As I've already said, I don't have the answer to that one. You do, and nobody else. If you have the prerequisite verbal skills, the prerequisite knowledge of how the universe and its human inhabitants work, the prerequisite compulsive ache both to consume and to produce fiction, the prerequisite discipline to get serious work done—well, then, you stand a chance.

I've been browsing through some of the early volumes of this anthology series, looking at the names of the writers who were published here for the first time, just to see how many of them managed to fulfill the promise of that initial achievement. Some of the names meant nothing at all to me. Those people had passed through the contest like meteors, providing one moment of bright light and then moving onward without a trace. Like many who "want to write," they had had their moment and had gone on to other things that evidently were of greater importance to them. But then there were names like these—

Nina Kiriki Hoffman
Karen Joy Fowler
David Zindell
Dean Wesley Smith
M. Shayne Bell
Martha Soukup
Dave Wolverton
Ray Aldridge
Robert Touzalin (Robert Reed)
Howard V. Hendrix
Jamil Nasir

All of them were amateurs ten years ago, when this contest began. But you see their names regularly in print these days. Like you (and like Robert A. Heinlein, Arthur C. Clarke, Ray Bradbury, Isaac Asimov, and, yes, Robert Silverberg) they wanted very very much to be published writers, and, because they had the talent, the will, and the perseverance, they made it happen.

Will you?

Don't ask me. You're the only one who knows.

The Perils of Prosperity

These are odd and interesting times for baseball players, tax collectors, and science-fiction writers. All are pulling in a lot more revenue than they used to. The tax collectors are benefiting from inflation; as people earn more, they glide upward into bigger-biting tax brackets, with the curious result that they pay a greater proportion of their income in taxes than before, though their real purchasing power hasn't improved at all. Baseball players are cashing in on the breakdown of the traditional contract system, which used to hold them in a kind of permanent servitude; now that they have a way of making themselves free to sell themselves to the highest bidder, they're extracting quite phenomenal salaries, and mediocre athletes find themselves collecting salaries five times as great as those paid to Ted Williams or Willie Mays in their prime. And science-fiction writers? For the first time, it's possible for the professional s-f writer to earn a living, a good one indeed, writing noting but s-f.

Oh, there always were a few who did it—Heinlein, Poul Anderson, van Vogt, Dickson. Asimov, though he writes all sorts of things, has earned enough from his s-f alone to support himself comfortably over the years. At any given time there would usually be five or ten writers enjoying a decent five figure income while writing s-f primarily or exclusively. But at any given time there would usually be three or four hundred professional s-f writers.

The ones who had thriving bank accounts were generally those who by dint of long services and fertile imaginations had won large followings over many years (Heinlein, van Vogt, Asimov) or those who had in a disciplined way turned out dozens of books (Anderson, Silverberg, Pohl, Dickson) or those who had written One Big Book that established itself as a basic item (Frank Herbert, Walter Miller.) The others tended to get along just above the poverty line, and that includes some Hall of Fame stalwarts and some multiple Hugo winners. The economics of science fiction, like the economics of baseball, didn't allow for much of an income for many people. In a field where magazines sell 40,000 to 75,000 copies an issue, where paperback sales are often in the same range, where a hardcover book is doing well if it sells 6,000 copies, you don't find many millionaires.

But now—ah, but now!

Even allowing for the lessened value of the dollar, the financial returns for today's science-fiction pros are astonishing by comparison with those of just a few years ago. Advances for paperback novels were running from $1500 to about $5000 circa 1972, with the $5000 checks going to the very biggest names. Now I routinely hear of deals in the $15,000 and $20,000 range for writers who hadn't even sold their first stories in 1972. Better-known folk command two and three times as much. Of course, not everybody is cashing in with equal ease: the top pros are writing their own tickets, and so, curiously, are the best of the talented beginners, especially if they happen to be women, but a number of middle-rank veterans are looking on in confusion and mounting anger as the big money passes them by. Still, even they are able to draw $7500 to $10,000 for a novel. When you add in the increasingly lucrative foreign market ($2500 for British rights, say, $1500 in France, $500 in Italy, $1250 in Japan—it adds up!) you can see that it's possible to earn as much as a middle-management executive by writing one s-f novel a year and a handful of short stories.

There are two reasons for this, one obvious and one not. The obvious one is that s-f is vastly more popular than it used to be, and I don't just mean *Star Wars* and *Star Trek*. What was, twenty years ago, a funny little category of paperbacks tucked away down there between the westerns and the nurse novels is now out front in the bookstore, and people head for it first. The average sale of the average mass-produced s-f paperback is probably still only in the 40,000-copy range, maybe even less, but the number of books going over the 100,000-copy range is enormous and growing all the time. Bigger sales obviously mean bigger royalties for writers. The other factor is the change in the cover price of books. In 1956 s-f paperbacks, such as there were then, sold for 35¢ and sometimes 50¢. Today they're $1.75 and up. That's about a 400% increase. My own *Book of Skulls*, which happens to be at my desk as I write this, bears a 95¢ pricetag for its 1972 edition and $1.50 for the 1976 one; when it comes out again in 1979 it'll sell for $1.95, I imagine, maybe even more. That's 100% inflation in seven years. *Author's paperback earnings are a function of the cover price.* I earned about 6¢ on each of those 1972 copies of *Book of Skulls*. I'll get about 12¢ on each copy sold next year. If sales remain constant, as they have, and paperback prices inflate faster than the general rate of inflation, as they have, then the writer is way ahead of where he was a few years ago. And he is.

One effect of this is to create a large new class of *full-time* science-fiction writers. James Blish and Algis Budrys worked for public-relations firms to keep the rent paid between books. Alfie Bester was an editor at *Holiday*. Cliff Simak is a newspaperman who writes in his spare time. Writers like Fritz Leiber, Wilson Tucker, Frank Herbert, and Poul Anderson held part-time or even full-time jobs before they felt able to take the plunge into free-lance writing. The Ellison or the Silverberg who set up shop as a professional writer when he was barely old enough to vote, and made a go of it, was a rarity. Not any more. If a talented 23-year-old can earn $15,000 or more by selling a novel and a couple of short stories, what sense is there in looking for a real-world job?

I am not, I repeat *not*, in any way objecting to the sudden prosperity that has engulfed nearly all science-fiction writers, myself included. But I feel some qualms about the ease with which young writers can make themselves self-supporting these days. I know beyond doubt that I was injured as a writer by having things too easy in my twenties, and I think Ellison was some time in recovering from his own early success. Maybe the best science fiction really *is* written by part-time writers. I mean to explore that notion and some others next time, as I continue this discussion of the strange and wonderful world of the s-f professional on the threshold of the 1980's.

Starting Too Soon

I talked last time of the gaudy new income levels that science fiction writers are reaching these days—a development which, naturally, I find it difficult to deplore. But I did suggest that it is Not Entirely a Good Thing for a young writer of science fiction to be able to earn a living with his typewriter too readily, and I want to elaborate on that this time.

No sour grapes are being mashed here. I began writing s-f professionally when I was about 18, and by the time I was 20 I was earning what would still be considered a respectable income today. As a result I moved straight from college to the life of a self-employed writer, and have supported myself ever since without ever being on anyone's payroll. Which was exactly the script I had written for myself in my adolescent fantasies, and I have nothing at all to complain about. Why, then, do I wish a harsher life on those who follow after me? And why do I think the best science fiction comes from part-time writers?

Because most of what I wrote, and blithely sold with such ease, back when I was 20 and 21 and 22, was fiction without content, mere carpentry, mere yard-goods. I had, for my age, an extraordinary ability to assemble pieces of commercial fiction at all lengths, but what I was assembling was derived not from my experience of life but from my experience of reading science-fiction, because I hadn't had enough time at that point to experience life very deeply. I thought I had, but I hadn't, which is something that becomes apparent to most former adolescents only a bit after the fact.

Science fiction is unusual among the fiction genres in that most of it is written by its former readers. I doubt that that's the case with true confessions, or detective stories, or nurse novels, or gothics. But at least 75% of the people who have helped to shape science fiction are people who read it with passion and voracity first, often from an early age, and eventually decided to try writing the stuff they loved so dearly. That list includes folk like Isaac Asimov, Ray Bradbury, Frederik Pohl, Harlan Ellison, Larry Niven, Alan Dean Foster, Marion Zimmer Bradley, Arthur C. Clarke, Roger Zelazny, Richard Lupoff, Damon Knight, Lester del Rey....on and on and on. Robert Silverberg, too.

Not every writer is on the list. Some were only casual readers of s-f, turned to it more or less for a lark, and found they had a natural gift for it. I think such people as Robert Heinlein, A.E. van Vogt, Theodore Sturgeon, and Ursula K. Le Guin fit that category, though I

[*Galileo*, September 1978]

could be wrong. But most of the others were s-f addicts from the age of 12 on, started to write it when they were 14 or so, began publishing it professionally at 18 or 19, and were Big Name Writers by their mid-twenties.

You see the problem. A 20-year-old who's led a reasonably conventional life has not yet been through marriage, parenthood, divorce, mortgage negotiations, or much serious illness. He may not have traveled more than 100 miles from his native town. He thinks he know, a lot about love and sex, but his total experience of such things goes back three or four years, maybe five or six. He can probably drive a car but he hasn't had time yet to learn how more complex machinery works. He's read a lot of Asimov and Heinlein, or maybe Ellison and Silverberg, but he hasn't had a chance to get around to Faulkner, Joyce, Hemingway, or Proust. With a mind stuffed only with science fiction, he's going to write imitations of the stories that he most admires, and if he's glib enough and clever enough he'll probably find some editor desperate enough to buy them, but those imitations, however deft, aren't going to afford much nourishment to readers who didn't discover s-f last Tuesday.

The real drawback to early professional success, though is not that it fills the magazines with third-hand versions of classic stories, but that it brakes and can altogether halt a young writer's intellectual and emotional growth. "We learn everything in solitude except character," Stendhal once said. Writing is done in solitude. While most people are out in the real world, commuting and striving and winning and losing and getting roughed up, the young writer who has arranged his career nicely is sitting home typing. He can get very proficient technically that way—I know whereof I speak—but he is forfeiting that experience of people and places and things that is the true capital of the true writer.

Now we reach the crux. The beginning writer imitates Asimov or Silverberg and makes some sales if he has the knack—okay, good on him. But the developing writer, if he is cut off from the main stream of life by his own commercial success, begins to imitate himself, and what we get is imitations of imitations, the kind of pallid ninth-hand stuff that infests all our bookracks. The author earns a living, the publisher fills his slot, the reader is munching on air.

In my own case I coped with the problems of early success as a full-time writer by traveling a lot, reading a lot, getting out into the world of events and conflicts as much as I dared—and even so, I didn't produce much fiction worth reading until I was about 30, and the world of events and conflicts had to come find *me*. I also gave up the full-time writing of science fiction by the time I was 25, realizing that it simply isn't possible to save the world three times a week, twelve months a year, on a full-time basis, and hope to achieve any conviction at it.

Many of the most distinguished s-f writers of the past decade have been people who did a lot of living *before* they started writing— James Tiptree, Kate Wilhelm, Ursula Le Guin, Gene Wolfe, Joe Haldeman, R.A. Lafferty, to name half a dozen in a hurry. On the other hand, some fine stories have come from very young people, straight out of the Clarion workshops, and I won't name them because those are the ones I worry about, the ones who are gliding, as I did, into full-time writing careers before they have a very good idea of how the world works or who they really are. In the world of mainstream fiction, the classic young-writer story is the one whose first novel is autobiographical and whose second, if there is one, is worthless. In our field, the situation is one of imitative writing that never gets better because of the feedback tremors that quick success creates.

I am not, not, *not* advocating brutality to young writers. As an editor, I've been responsible for my share of first sales, and then some. But I do suggest, for your sake and for the sake of the readership, that you think twice about going into writing as a full-time career, even in these days of big advances for newcomers. To write science-fiction as it should be written, you ought to know how *everything* works, from the level of precinct politics to the level of the movements of the galaxies. Nobody in this business does, except possibly Heinlein; but that's the goal. The more time you spend pounding a typewriter before the age of, oh, 27, the less time you have to learn what a writer really needs to know. Everyone suffers that way—you most of all.

Becoming a Writer

Dear Mr. Silverberg:
"I am 16 years old [or 18, or 57] and I want to write more than anything in the world. Please tell me how to go about it. Thank you." Sometimes, but not always, the letter goes on to say, "I enclose a stamped, self-addressed envelope."

I get such letters all the time. Every reasonably well known professional writer does. Usually I don't answer them, even the ones that do enclose stamped, self-addressed envelopes, because if I did I'd have no time left over to do anything else. I sometimes think that everybody on this planet wants to write, except some of those who already are writers and wish they were almost anything else. (Cf. Robert Silverberg's Retirement Address, 1975: "I will never write for publication again," or words to that effect.) There's another reason why I rarely reply to such letters, aside from the fact that my time is finite: the sense of futility that smites me when I hear someone say, "I want to write." Silverberg's First Law of Writing holds that people who merely *want* to write aren't ever going to. Either you are a writer or you aren't; and if you are, you're doing it. Do you think the young Harlan Ellison went around telling people he *wanted* to write? Isaac Asimov? Norman Spinrad? Ray Bradury? Ursula Le Guin? Frederik Pohl? Nah. All those people, once they realized that the manipulation of words was the task for which they had been designed, immediately sat down and started writing. I began turning out stories when I was seven, and I'd be astonished if any of the others I've just named got a much later start. There may be some well-known writer who didn't begin writing for his own pleasure almost as soon as he learned how to read— Robert A. Heinlein, maybe, since he had a career in the Navy before he became a writer—but there can't be many. The corollary of Silverberg's First Law holds that anyone whom the gods designed to be a writer starts producing fiction long before anyone else in the world thinks he has the slightest bit of aptitude for the job—usually in early childhood.

That takes care of the people who "want to write" but somehow never do any writing because they're waiting around to learn the magic secret. But then there are those who say they want to be *writers*. That's different. They're already writing; now they want to know how to make a career out of it. When I encounter these people—and

[*Amazing Stories*, May 1986]

usually it's in person, not by letter—I generally offer them Silverberg's Three Rules for Literary Success:

1. Read a lot.
2. Write a lot.
3. Read a lot more, write a lot more.

That's all there is to it, folks. The true writer immerses himself in the printed words hours a day. He can't possibly satiate his appetite for words. He gobbles stories in carload lots. But he doesn't just read them; he dissects them. Analyzes the number of incidents per thousand words, measures the ratio of dialog to exposition, studies the manner of opening a story and the way of closing it. He looks at the way characters are named and the way objects are described. In the process he tends to surrender some of the innocent joy of reading for its own sake, but that's part of the price of admission to the trade.

Of course, the would-be writer doesn't just read fiction. He reads everything. He reads the newspapers, he reads *Scientific American*, he reads *Playboy*, he reads accounts of voyages to Antarctica and the Himalayas and Jersey City, he reads biographies, he reads treatises on snail-farming and city planning and medieval dentistry. There's no telling what sort of information will come in handy. Alexandre Dumas the elder, one of the most productive writers who ever lived, used the metaphor of the writer as pitcher: You fill and fill and fill yourself with everything you can, until the pitcher is full; and then you begin to pour.

I know no writers who are not also insatiable and omnivorous readers.

And having read, the beginner writes. Unceasingly. Ray Bradbury, when he was starting out, wrote a story a day. I scribbled awful little "novels" in my school copybooks when I should have been listening to the teacher. Ellison, you betcha, was doing the same thing, and so were all the rest of us. At first the fledgling writer imitates whatever has pleased him most, which is why so many ten-year-olds write their own sequels to *Huckleberry Finn* of *The Wizard of Oz* or *Star Wars* or whatever. That's all right. That's a completely legitimate way to begin. Even merely typing out someone else's published story yourself can help, as along as you don't try submitting it to a magazine; manuscripts have very different textures from printed stories, and it's useful to learn the difference at an early age. Later on will come a different phase of the imitative period, when the beginner simply borrows the style of a favorite writer and uses it in a story of his own invention—

picking up the voice of Jack Vance, let's say, or Poul Anderson, or J.G. Ballard. And then, after that, at some magical point, the voice you use becomes your own voice; and then you are a writer.

That's all there is to it. Read a lot, to fill yourself with a torrent of knowledge and to make yourself aware of the techniques by which other writers have achieved their effects; and write a lot, so that by daily practice of the craft you achieve the ability to gain and hold the attention of readers. And then do more of both, until writing becomes second nature. If the talent is there—and probably it is, if you have committed yourself to the disciplines of the art—then nothing more than immense hard work is required to turn yourself into a professional writer.

Is that all, you say? No other advice except read and write?

Well, there are a few trivial things to know, too, like typing your manuscripts on one side of the page, double spaced, using a dark ribbon. Editors tend to think that a story that *looks* drab and gray probably *is* drab and gray, and there isn't much market for drab, gray stories unless you're a genius of the order of Samuel Beckett. (And even he hasn't won any Hugos.) Stay away from dot-matrix printers, too, and enclose return postage, and don't include a letter with your manuscript that tells the editor how good it is, or what it really means, or how much your uncle, who's a professor of literature at Texas A & M, thinks of it. But everybody, even beginners, knows that list of do's and don'ts, I suspect. The key to success lies in just two things: Read until your eyes go blurry, write until your fingers ache. Every day, without fail, until you think you know what you're doing; and even when you do think you know what you're doing, don't stop learning how to do it better. Ever. The moment a writer stops growing, he starts to shrink.

One more thing you ought to know, though, before you set out to become a writer. Silverberg's Second Law:

Once a writer, always a writer. There's no escape.

It's a life sentence, folks. Writers don't retire. They may take vacations, but they don't quit. You could ask Robert A. Heinlein: he's 79, I think, and just starting a new book. You could ask Jack Williamson: he's just finished one, and he's 78. Why, you could even ask me. I retired from writing forever in 1974, with my fortieth birthday in sight. I told everyone who'd listen that I was never going to commit an act of literature again, so help me. And I've only had six novels published since then.

What a Writer Needs to Know

L ast issue this space was devoted to the questions of how to go about becoming a writer—and the advice I offered was, essentially, that what you need to do is read and read and read until you have absorbed all you can possibly hold, and then to write and write and write until the act of putting words on paper in some satisfactory pattern becomes second nature to you. A would-be writer who doesn't read is one who has cut himself off from vital sources of inspiration, information, and technical observation; a would-be writer who isn't already writing regularly, regardless of the present level of his skill or maturity, is one who's going to remain would-be for the rest of his life.

There was one aspect of Becoming a Writer that I chose not to discuss at all, last time. Implicit in what I had to say was the underlying notion that learning to write fiction is primarily a solitary task: the individual who wants to be a writer, I suggested, needs to carry out his own study of the craft of fiction as it has been practiced by his predecessors, and then, having isolated the basic principles of fiction through observation and analysis, he must teach himself how to put those principles into action. But must writing be entirely a self-taught skill? What about the multitude of writers' classes and workshops that exist across the land? Are they completely without value? What about the shelves upon shelves of books that purport to teach one how to write? Can anything be learned from them? Or—as I seemed to be saying last time—is it simply a process of hard, lonely self-education?

My own bias has probably already made itself apparent. I took no courses in "creative writing" in college: I was too busy writing. (My first novel, *Revolt on Alpha C*, was published in the summer of 1955, between my junior and senior years at Columbia.) Soon after my graduation from college in 1956 I attended the first of the famous Milford Science Fiction Writers Conferences in Pennsylvania; it was a glorious week-long party, a mini-convention for writers only, populated by the likes of Ted Sturgeon and Cyril Kornbluth and Jim Blish and Algis Budrys and Fred Pohl and Lester del Rey, and I had a grand time there as the junior member of the crowd. (There was another kid there of about my age, a fellow named Ellison, who also seemed to show promise of becoming a writer.) It was a lot of fun, and when a story of mine came up for discussion in a workshop session I got a useful suggestion for fixing it from Algis Budrys. ("Throw away the

[*Amazing Stories*, July 1986]

first ten pages," he said, and I did, and sold it a month later.) But Milford seemed a pretty cumbersome way of learning anything, and I never went back for another workshop session, although I frequently turned up on weekends for the parties.

Many years later came the Clarion Writer's Workshops, sponsored at first by Clarion State College in Pennsylvania, and later held at various campuses around the country. An awesome roster of writers has served as the faculty for these workshops: Ursula K. Le Guin, Kate Wilhelm, Harlan Ellison, Samuel R. Delany, Fritz Leiber, Frank Herbert, Theodore Sturgeon, and many more. One year I even took a turn at it myself. Among the hundreds of novice writers who enrolled at Clarion are many who have gone on to significant professional careers: Gardner Dozois, Vonda McIntyre, F.M. Busby, Octavia Butler, George Alec Effinger, John Shirley, and others. It sounds wonderful, and perhaps it is, but my feeling about Clarion is decidedly skeptical. I think that the Dozoises and Butlers and such may have learned a little there, but that basically they would have had the same sort of careers even if Clarion had never existed. I think that other writers, lesser ones, may actually have picked up new bad habits at Clarion, where the in-group reinforcement of arty tricks has been an ongoing problem. And still other writers may have gone away mortally discouraged by the criticism of their peers and given up altogether. At its best (and also at its worst) Clarion fosters a kind of solidarity among its attendees that lasts on into later life, an alumni clubbiness. But I can't escape a feeling that writing is not something best learned in a social context. Like making love, it's a private act, which one masters by repeated application of certain technical principles, and I'm not at all certain that the ideal place to learn its skills is in public.

Books about writing? Ah, that's a different matter. Though I think the best way to learn the craft of fiction is by studying published stories, I see no harm in accelerating the process by absorbing the techniques of those who have already carried out such analyses. This may seem much like attending classes or workshops, but it feels different to me: reading books on writing is a solitary preparation for what is an inescapably solitary profession. To read such a book, to argue inwardly with its author, to take part in a silent dialectic of learning—that seems ideal to me.

Three books in particular helped me learn my craft. One was *The Art of Dramatic Writing*, by Lajos Egri, a book concerned primarily with plays, but filled with invaluable suggestions for the construction of dramatically moving scenes. The second was also a book about the drama: *Greek Tragedy*, by H.D.F. Kitto. By analyzing the plays of Sophocles, Aeschylus, and Euripides, it taught me unforgettably how plot and character are related. The third was *Writing to Sell*, by my former agent Scott Meredith, which covered all sorts of issues involved in a professional writing career, including a splendid chapter or two on the basics of story construction. It was in Scott's book that I first saw formulated the basic story skeleton that underlies virtually all fiction. It goes something like this:

A sympathetic and appealing character is faced with a difficult challenge. He struggles against overwhelming odds, but everything he does lands him in ever deeper trouble, until it seems that all is lost. Then, primarily through his own efforts, he succeeds in resolving his problem, or if he fails, he fails in a way that significantly demonstrates the nature of his character.

Sounds too simple? Check it out against *The Odyssey*, or *The Epic of Gilgamesh*, or *Oedipus Rex*, or *Hamlet*. It's been around for thousands of years. No one yet has come up with an improved model for narrative. It's only a skeleton—you have to dress it up with characters, incidents, dialog, description, and such—but it's a universal skeleton. You'll find it inside last year's Hugo winner. You'll find it inside next year's Hugo winner, too.

Of course, many writers have figured out for themselves what these books on writing can teach. But I see no harm in studying such books, though it's still necessary to internalize the principles, even if someone else has codified them for you. I *do* see potential harm in traipsing around to classes and workshops, exposing one's self to input from those who don't necessarily have valid inputs to give (the blind leading the blind, all too often). Some writers have benefited from such operations; some have been harmed. On balance, I preferred to stay away. Others of a different temperament feel otherwise.

There's yet one more resource available to beginning writers: the editors of the magazines they hope to deal with. I don't mean that editors provide much in the way of instruction; but rejection notes can be invaluable guides to the way *not* to do it, if you ponder them with care instead of with resentment. (Someday I'll quote a few that I received long ago. They made me angry them, but later I saw that they had set me on the path of righteousness.) Best of all, a good editor, seeing real talent in his pile of unsolicited manuscripts, will often opt to serve as a mentor to a gifted newcomer. Not often, of course, and not in any very extensive way, usually—but there is no instruction more valuable, if you're lucky enough to find it.

Forgive me my biases, those of you who dote on workshops and other public means of learning. Go thou and sign up for next semester's session forthwith. But these are the things that worked for me, at any rate, in my own journey toward a career as a professional writer.

Short Stories vs. Novels

I was putting together a collection of some of my recent short stories—about two dozen of them, written over the period from 1983 to 1986—when it occurred to me that unlike a great many other writers I have been just about as productive as a short-story writer as I have been a novelist. That is, I've written a lot of short stories, and a *lot* of novels, without ever regarding myself as a specialist in one form or the other.

Since the beginning of my writing career, almost forty years ago, I've always written both. My first professional sale was a short story and the second was a novel, or perhaps it was the other way around. The rhythm of my writing life was established right at the beginning: a few short stories, then a novel, then some more short stories, and then another book. I never thought twice, or even once, about whether I was primarily a short-length writer or a book-writer. I was a writer, period. I've always written at whatever length seemed appropriate to the story at hand; and because I have always been a writer by trade rather than one who follows the ebb and flow of inspiration, I've also written to the needs of the marketplace. When it seemed to be novel-writing time, I wrote novels. When editors wanted short stories from me, I wrote short stories.

It isn't way that with all writers, and I'm not sure why. Some are distinctly novelists, and some aren't. Ray Bradbury has written a couple of novels, but he's basically a short-story writer: the short lengths are apparently where he's most comfortable and certainly where he's done his finest work. The same is true of Harlan Ellison and Robert Sheckley. On the other hand, John le Carre and John Fowles may have written a few short stories at some time in their lives, but I haven't seen them, if they exist at all. (Fowles has occasionally written novellas, at least.) Robert A. Heinlein wrote few, if any, short stories after the first dozen years of his career. Hemingway's lifetime output of short stories was enough to fill one good-sized volume, and very impressive stories they are, too; but he also wrote most of them in his first dozen years and rarely bothered with short pieces after about 1938.

Of course, plenty of distinguished science-fiction writers have moved easily between the short lengths and the long ones over the course of their careers. I think immediately of Isaac Asimov, Frederik Pohl, Poul Anderson, Larry Niven, Brian Aldiss, Philip K. Dick, Arthur

[*Amazing Stories*, August 1992]

C. Clarke, and J.G. Ballard; and you can probably supply as many more names in a moment.

Still, it's possible to make long lists of writers who are basically one thing or the other, but not both. On the one hand are the novelists for whom short stories, after the early years of their careers, are rare or non-existent events. In science fiction and fantasy the names of Frank Herbert, E.E. Smith, Jack Vance, Jack Chalker, Piers Anthony, Stephen Donaldson, John Taine, and Andre Norton come quickly to my mind; outside our field, those of Graham Greene, Evelyn Waugh, William Golding, John Steinbeck, Norman Mailer. And then there are the short-story writers whose ventures into longer lengths are equally uncommon or in some cases nonexistent, and whose infrequent novels are often awkward and unsatisfactory in some way: Theodore Sturgeon, Clark Ashton Smith, William Tenn, and Damon Knight; Edgar Allan Poe, John Collier, William Trevor, and Mavis Gallant.

Surely the vagaries of temperament have much to do with this. Some writers, particularly in science fiction and fantasy, feel impossibly cramped within the rigid confines of the short story: they want to create whole universes, and need hundreds of thousands of words to move around in. Others—sprinters by nature, rather than long-distance runners—see the novel as a vast and interminable journey that they would just as soon not undertake, and prefer the quick, incisive thrust of the short story. It is the same in other arts. Wagner wrote immense operas, not lieder. Schubert wrote some operas too, but they are all forgotten and his songs are immortal. Verdi once composed a string quartet, apparently to demonstrate that he knew how, but otherwise he worked on a large scale. Michelangelo specialized in sculptures and frescoes of heroic size; a miniaturist like Paul Klee, master that he was, could not have painted the Sistine Chapel; Rubens was not known for his etchings and drawings. And so on. The choice comes from within. Often enough no choice at all is involved: the artist simply follows the path that seems inevitable.

But then there are those writers who are masters of both the short and long forms and choose in the second half of their careers to work in only one of them, usually the novel, like Hemingway or Heinlein. Surely the author of "The Snows of Kilimanjaro" and "Capital of the World" still knew how to write short stories after 1940, and the author of "Requiem" and "The Green Hills of Earth" did not mysteriously lose his ability at the short lengths around 1949; but *For Whom the Bell Tolls* and *Stranger in a Strange Land* must have been matters of higher priority and the short stories ceased. Jack Vance, too, once wrote masterly short stories, but it's been many years since the last one appeared, while his splendid novels continue to appear. It's harder to cite writers who gave up novels after an early start to concentrate only on the short story: Paul Bowles, perhaps, or Truman Capote.

In today's science-fiction field, very few of the well-established writers bother much about short fiction, and even the newcomers tend to move on as quickly as they can to immense trilogies. There's a simple economic reason for this. When I was starting as a writer in the 1950s, you didn't think much about getting science-fiction novels published unless your name was Heinlein or Asimov. The field of paperback books was still a small one and the few publishers who wanted s-f used only a couple of novels a year, by the very biggest names. Magazines were where the action was—in 1953 there were close to forty of them—and they were an insatiable market for short stories. So short stories is what we all wrote; and once in a while we would dare to write a novel, hoping that some magazine would be willing to serialize it.

It is all very different now. In an average year, something like *six hundred* new novels of science fiction and fantasy are published in the United States—whereas the five or six s-f magazines and the handful of original-fiction anthologies have room for perhaps 450 stories altogether. That means that for each short science-fiction story that gets published (for which the author might receive anywhere from $150 or so up to a maximum of $5000 in a very few cases) there will be 1.3 s-f or fantasy novels (and for novels the pay begins at about $2500 and goes up into the stratosphere.) The arithmetic, for the professional writer, is unanswerable. Writing short stories doesn't make much sense financially. If you write them today you have to want to write them for their own sake. The pay is almost incidental: you do them for love, or because you don't think you can bring a full-length novel off, or because you are a very part-time writer who can't manage the investment of months that a novel requires.

Or, in my case, you write them because you really can't stop yourself.

Temperament, again, as much as economics. As I've already made quite clear, I've never concentrated on one length of fiction at the expense of the other. I've written 500-worders and I've written books 200,000 words long. But that doesn't mean I don't have a *preference*; and the preference is for writing novels.

Not simply for financial reasons. Even for the professional writer, money isn't the only decision-making factor. But I happen to find short stories a pain in the neck to write, not because I absolutely require enormous amounts of space in which to tell a story, but because I have come to take a very finicky attitude toward short stories. They have to be perfect, I feel, or they don't work at all. A novel can go completely off the tracks for three or four chapters, then recover its sense of direction and roar triumphantly on toward a grand conclusion with no real harm done; but three or four errant *paragraphs* can wreck a story completely. So writing them is full of tension and stress for me. I revise and revise and revise, and curse and mutter and curse, and dream longing dreams of the wondrous discursiveness that a novelist enjoys. (Midway through some huge and troublesome novel, of course, I begin dreaming of the miraculous brevity and conciseness of the short story. But that's another issue.) To write a 5000-word short story takes me at least three times as long as to write a 5000-word segment of a novel.

If short-story writing doesn't pay very well and is a grueling chore besides, why do I bother putting myself through the sweaty, painful task of writing them? Because of the challenge they represent, I suppose: because I don't care to exempt myself from the harsh discipline of creating something that's complete in twenty or thirty pages, even though I'd rather not do it very often. A dire internal compulsion drives me. Doing short stories is an exhausting kind of mental exercise that gets harder for me all the time. It's tremendously tempting to give it up altogether—which is exactly why I don't dare stop. Given my druthers, I suppose I'd simply be a novelist; but I continue to insist of myself that periodically I do something shorter.

And thus my oscillations between novels and short stories. It's my good fortune—and Fred Pohl's, and Poul Anderson's, and Arthur Clarke's—to be able to move from one form to the other at will. And I continue to do so, despite something of an inner preference for writing novels.

But what about a writer like Theodore Sturgeon, say, who was a wondrous short-story writer but who could manage only one or two genuine novels? Or John Taine, who wrote a dozen majestic novels in the 1920s and 1930s but apparently only one short story, and that one done as a favor? They didn't simply dislike working in the other form; for all their great skill, they apparently *couldn't*. Why? I can't say. Wagner and Schubert; Klee and Michelangelo: the mysteries of creativity, inexplicable and fascinating.

Revisions

One of the most interesting science-fiction anthologies of the season is the a book called *The Eureka Years*, edited by Annette Peltz McComas and published by Bantam Books. What I find so interesting about it is not its stories as much as its interstitial commentary; for the stories, fine jobs, though they are, by such folks as Sturgeon, Asimov, Bester, Anderson, and Bradbury, are all familiar to me from long ago. The real substance of the book—for me, and for anyone interested in the behind-the-scenes story of science-fiction publishing—is the commentary that Annette McComas has generously sprinkled throughout. *The Eureka Years* is in fact a memorial to the first five years (1949-54) of *The Magazine of Fantasy & Science Fiction*, which was founded by Anthony Boucher and J. Francis McComas; and what Mrs. McComas has given us here is a host of letters, memos, rejection slips, rewrite orders, and other backstage memorabilia that show us most vividly how two great editors set about the creation and sustenance of a great science-fiction magazine.

The rewrite orders are the most significant part, I think, and they engender some heavy brooding on my part. For example, in the summer of 1949 a young California writer sent Boucher and McComas a short story for their projected publication. McComas rejected it, with a note praising the writing but going on to say, "We feel that it isn't distinctive enough, doesn't have enough power to meet the terrifically high standard we will want to set...." Whereupon the writer, a week later, obligingly send a second story, which came closer to what Boucher and McComas wanted. But there were problems. The writer had used Ambrose Bierce, the hardbitten old fantasist, as a character; McComas wrote, "Bierce is completely incredible. Can you imagine 'Bitter' Bierce saying, 'What will happen to us? God save us?' Rather, he would chortle gleefully over the dilemma and enjoy with complete detachment the futilities of both the invaders and the exiles." Nathaniel Hawthorne was also a character in this story, and the writer, McComas felt, had been "amazingly inaccurate" about him, quoting from Benet's *Reader Encyclopedia* to show where the problems lay. And there were other minor difficulties.

To which the writer replied, "You're right about Bierce and Hawthorne. Put it down to the fact that I've never been a research man in my life, preferring to manufacture my fantasies out of whole cloth....Although you mention my bad characterization of Bierce,

Hawthorne, et cetera, you never mentioned whether the story as a whole titillated you. If you would like the story rewritten to patch up the holes, you know darn well I would enjoy correcting my own errors." McComas answered that he was pretty certain a rewrite would be acceptable; and a few weeks later, co-editor Boucher entered the discussion, proposing that when the rewrite was done another character—Henry David Thoreau—be dropped, and Charles Dickens and L. Frank Baum be substituted in his place. Boucher also had some subtle ideas about the handling of H.P. Lovecraft in the same story.

The rewrite was done; the story was accepted, and on November 27, 1949, the writer told Boucher and McComas, "Bless you both, and keep you! I really feel very fortunate in having such good and generous friends and editors."

The story was *The Exiles*. The writer was Ray Bradbury. The amount he was paid for his work was, I think, $100. Although $100 went a lot further in 1949 than it does today, it was still a relatively trifling amount for a short story—especially one that had gone through so much revision, and especially one by Bradbury, who even then was commanding $700 and more per story from such magazines as *The Saturday Evening Post* and *The New Yorker*.

Imagine the audacity of the editors! They solicit a story from Bradbury, telling him they can't possibly afford his regular wage; he sends it and they reject it (a section of *The Martian Chronicles*, no less); he obligingly sends another, and they make him reconceive two characters and replace another before they'll give him his hundred bucks. Was it worth it? Can editors really afford to be so picky over a single short story? Should Bradbury not have snatched up his manuscripts with a sneer and shipped it over to the *Post*?

Well, perhaps so. Yet the story, in its revised form, has been reprinted dozens of times, and few would deny its status as a classic of fantasy. And editors Boucher and McComas, both now alas gone from this world, are enshrined forever in the hearts of writers who, like Bradbury, were politely and patiently shown how their fine work could be made splendid.

In the same anthology we see Alfred Bester being told, "We think you've missed your real point" and asked to revise, though McComas could not give him a promise of a sale even if he did. (Bester revised and got his sale: *Of Time and Third Avenue*.) We see Manly Made Wellman being asked if the silver guitar strings of John the ballad-singer were really plausible. (Wellman quoted chapter and verse to show that they were.) We see Isaac Asimov asked for "a more subtly phrased ending" to his story *Flies*, and promptly supplying it, and then thinking the story was still not good enough after it was accepted and offering to buy it back. (The offer was turned down and the story published.) And a memo by Boucher in 1952 notes that some 50% of all stories received were returned for rewrites. It's fascinating stuff, at least to one who has been an editor and writer himself over the past quarter of a century and some.

I wonder if such finicky editing still goes on. I will tell you quite shamelessly that I regard a rewrite request on a short story as a pain in the neck; I would much rather send a piece out on Monday and get my check on Friday, without the intervention of someone else's ideas, bright or otherwise. But when the editor has a point to make, I listen; and if the editor is someone who might know what he's talking about, I do indeed condescend to take a second look at my deathless prose. Damon Knight, when he was editing *Orbit*, had me do *five* revisions, some mighty trivial, on a short story; it was *Passengers*, which won a Nebula. Alice Turner of *Playboy* had me turn a story completely inside out, which I was going to refuse to do until she astounded me by showing me how easy it would be (*Gianni*). Robert Sheckley, when he was at *Omni*, made a strong story a lot stronger with some shrewd quibbles. (*The Far Side of the Bell-Shaped Curve*.) I suppose other writers, even unto Le Guin and Herbert and Clarke, get told occasionally how to make fine work finer. But is there anyone around— Scithers? Schmidt? Ferman? Datlow? McCarthy? Who?—who consistently gets down into the innards of nearly every story to peer at the carburetor and the fan-belt, the way McComas and Boucher did a generation ago? And do the writers usually put up with it?

It's not the editor's role to impose his own personality or style on a story. The great editor simply finds the story that the writer intended to tell, and helps him bring it into higher resolution. Some editors are pests; some are geniuses. I knew all along that Boucher and McComas were geniuses—but the spectacle of such folk as Bradbury and Bester and Asimov meekly tearing stories apart for the sake of $100 sales, as demonstrated in Annette McComas' fine new book, shows me just what geniuses they really were.

Writers' Correspondence

I'm a fairly accessible man, my address is not hard to find, and I get a lot of letters. People want to tell me how wonderful or how faulty my books are, to ask me to give opinions on their unpublished short stories, to suggest to me the plot for a sequel to *Lord Valentine's Castle*, to analyze the time-travel theory of *Up The Line*, or to inveigle me into buying the magazines they publish. I answer some of these with postcards, some with full and detailed responses, and some not at all. I also write to my publishers on three or four continents, my agents, various editors, and sometimes to my mother. It's a lot of typing.

I'm not the only writer who writes a lot of letters. I know that Harlan Ellison does, Fred Pohl does, Barry Malzberg does; I suspect Algis Budrys does, and even got one from him lately that I really ought to answer. Ernest Hemingway was a big letter-writer. I know that because I'm reading his *Selected Letters* right now, and, "selected" or not, they fill 921 closely packed large octavo pages. That's a bigger volume by far than any of his novels, and he didn't write all that many novels. Might we have had another Hemingway novel if he hadn't been such a diligent correspondent? Would the long-hoped-for-Ellison novel now be on the stands if Harlan were not so passionate a writer of letters? How much vital creative time, I wonder, do we all consume in this frantic interchange of correspondent? Consider H.P. Lovecraft's five-volume set of published letters— and *read* those letters, which are rich and intricate and full of vital energy. Sure, Lovecraft as correspondent was instrumental in helping the growth of half a dozen brilliant fantasy writers who were dependent on him for opinions— but at what cost to HPL?

Hemingway is pretty explicit about it. "Any time I can write a good letter it's a sign I'm not working," he said. And writing letters was "such a swell way to keep from working and yet feel you've done something." I think he's right; and I think a writer who writes a lot of letters is generally a writer who's in trouble. (Although there are exceptions to that. I can think of at least three science-fiction writers of the generation just prior to mine who have endured writing blocks of legendary proportions through much of their career, and who don't much answer their mail, either.)

Correspondence is valuable to a writer, of course. It provides input from a wide variety of sources; and the output that that input generates yields useful opportunities for exploring and clarifying one's own ideas. It allows the writer to work stuff out of his system, too, that might interfere with the process of creativity. I choose to pick up my mail at the post office before I begin my working day, and if there's anything there that irritates or annoys me (there was one this morning!) I usually deal with it first thing, so that it's not preying on my mind while I'm trying to send my characters off to adventure in the Zorch Galaxy. There's always the danger, of course, that I'll use up vital adrenaline on the letter that might be better consumed on the story, but it's a risk I'm willing to take. Only last week, for instance, I dealt with a dumb and infuriating letter moments after coming back from the post office, working up a fine head of steam, and then, with the dispute and the disputant out of my way, I rattled off a very nifty short story in a single sitting, something that I've rarely done in the past ten or twelve years. Could it be that the outrageous Mr. X got me so energized that I worked at two or three times my normal pace? Or was I just hitting on all cylinders that morning? (I know the story's a good one. An editor just told me so and put many simoleons in my pocket to prove her point.)

Hemingway also notes the value of letter-writing as a warm-up exercise for the brain. John Steinbeck, whose collected letters fill a volume about as big as Hemingway's—I love reading the letters of other writers—made a particular point of handling his correspondence before he began work every day, and plainly it was a trick that worked for him, for he did manage to produce a shelfload of books and even win a Nobel Prize, although, it must be noted, neither a Hugo or a Nebula.

But even so, I think writers less proficient than Steinbeck or Hemingway ought to be cautious about their correspondence loads. In the peculiar world of science fiction, with its astonishing degree of contact between writer and reader and between writer and writer, the potential for getting into brilliant and exhausting exchanges of correspondence is enormous. At the Denver convention a few months ago I gave my address to five or six people, warning all of them that although I'd be glad to continue our discussions by mail, I was a slow and unreliable correspondent. And so I am, though I'm neither slow nor unreliable in any other aspect of my life; but I let the letters pile up, giving quick response only to the ones that say HELP or FOR GOD'S SAKE HURRY or PLEASE SIGN THE ENCLOSED CON-TRACT AND RETURN IT AT ONCE or MY SECONDS WILL CALL ON YOU IN THE MORNING UNLESS. I also have two or three regular correspondents with whom I've been exchanging letters steadily for years, and they get premium treatment, because the value I derive from those correspondences outweighs, to me, the value I might get from putting equivalent energy into turning out more fiction.

But everybody else, including people I like a good deal as well as the total strangers who want favors, get put into the when-I-get-a-chance heap, and for a lot of them the chance never comes. It's a matter of creative survival. I know all too well how easy it is to write letters instead of stories; I also know that the royalty checks on my Collected Letters are going to go to my estate, not to me, and won't help much in paying the bills that also arrive in the morning mail. A word of caution, then, to those who expect writers to reply faithfully to their mail: you may be stealing the next Hugo winner from us all. And to writers who find themselves turning enthusiastically to their correspondence instead of to that overdue manuscript: you may be fooling yourself, but not the rest of us.

One essential technique in handling correspondence should be kept in mind by all writers. I learned it from that cagy old pro, L. Sprague de Camp, decades ago. In the right-hand drawer of my desk I keep, at all times, fifty or sixty postal cards. It's impossible to be very verbose when you answer your mail with postal cards. You save a penny or two on postage, besides, and the cost of an envelope, and all that hard work of licking and sealing the flap. But the key thing is that by dashing off a postcard you fulfill your karmic obligations, you keep the flow of communication flowing, you make your correspondents reasonably happy, and *you can get down to work*. Unless, like Lovecraft, you consider your correspondence your real work and your fiction an incidental matter, that's important to bear in mind.

Long-Term Careers

I f I've started sounding like the Old Man of the Mountain lately, in some of these pieces, it's because I've started feeling that way a lot of the time. There's nothing wrong with my health, so far as I know; but even so, concepts like durability, longevity, and—yes—mortality have been on my mind recently.

The reason is easy enough to figure out. A couple of months from now I'll be celebrating the fortieth anniversary of the first time a professional publication paid me real money for something I had written; and, although I was very young when I began my career and still am a very long way from being the oldest s-f writer in the business, it's hard for me to go on thinking of myself as a kid when I realize that I've been writing this stuff for forty years.

That first professional sale, back in the summer of 1953, was actually an article, not a story. I was an active member of the odd little cult known as science-fiction fandom, then: I published a mimeographed amateur magazine four times a year, wrote scholarly-sounding articles for other amateur magazines, corresponded with my fellow fans, attended local conventions, etc., etc., all the while feverishly submitting stories to the professional magazines of the day and inevitably getting them back. Harry Harrison, a young writer then at the beginning of his own career, had just become editor of a minor s-f magazine called *Science Fiction Adventures*, and he called on me to write a 3000-word piece for him explaining fandom to the general s-f readership.

I was eighteen, about to begin my sophomore year at college. Being asked to write an article for a magazine didn't quite have the same thrill for me as selling a story to one, but it was a start all the same. I did my piece post haste. "The weird and wonderful world of science-fiction fandom is a development unique in the history of fiction," it began. "Science fiction fandom is an outgrowth of that announcement in the December 1926 issue of *Amazing Stories* which proclaimed the institution of a 'Discussions' column to begin the following issue and to provide a place where readers of *Amazing* (a lusty ten-month-old infant of a magazine at the time) could 'discuss scientifiction and their impression of this new literature....'" Harry accepted it just as promptly, and at the World Science Fiction Convention in Philadelphia that September he handed me my payment in person—$30 in cash. (I didn't find out for two more years that he had

[*Amazing Stories*, August, 1993]

advanced the money to me out of his own pocket, bless him, and had had to wait until 1955 to collect his reimbursement from the sleazy guy who was publishing the magazine.)

A few months later I sold an actual story, too—to the Scottish magazine, *Nebula*, for the awesome sum of $12.60, and a novel, *Revolt on Alpha C*, and by the time I got my college degree in 1956 I was supporting myself nicely as a free-lance writer, as I have done ever since. And here I am now looking back at a writing career that spans forty years. What an incredibly long time that is to keep on making up stories about alien worlds and imaginary people and getting paid for it! Forty years! *Forty!*

At the time I made my first sales, back there in 1953, *no one* had been writing science fiction professionally for forty years, because the year that is forty years back from 1953 is 1913, and there were no science fiction magazines in existence then. As I pointed out in that piece for Harry Harrison long ago, *Amazing Stories*, the very first one, came into being in 1926. It was only 27 years old when I began selling stories. So, although I'm still a couple of years short of sixty, I've been on the scene for some 60% of the entire history of magazine science fiction in this country. It's a sobering thought.

Yet whenever I start feeling like Methuselah, I remind myself bluntly that I'm still just a babe compared with the *real* senior members of my profession. Jack Williamson, born in 1908, sold his first story seven years before I was born, and is still working at top form two-thirds of a century later: he had a fine one in *Omni* just a couple of months ago. L. Sprague de Camp is six months older than Williamson; he's been a free-lance writer since 1937 and new novels of his are still appearing regularly. Another of our grand old men is Lloyd Arthur Eshbach, who was selling stories to the pioneering s-f editor Hugo Gernsback in the early 1930s, and who now—age 83—is working on a new trilogy of novels. No longer active as a writer, but senior to them all, is Frank Belknap Long, who is, so far as I know, doing well back in New York at the age of ninety. He published his first fantasy story in *Weird Tales* in 1924, and continued producing them for fifty years or so thereafter. When the Methuselah blues start to hit me around birthday time, I think of Jack and Lloyd and Sprague and Frank, whose writing careers spanned periods longer than my entire life to date and in all but one case are still going strong, and it helps put things in perspective for me.

Another heroic record of continued accomplishment is that of 81-year-old Andre Norton: her first science-fiction story was published in 1947, but she had been writing professionally in other fields for at least fifteen years at that time. And there are plenty of other sterling examples of durability in our field in the sub-octogenarian class. Frederik Pohl, who, like me, got a precocious start (he made his first story sales in his teens and was editing a professional s-f magazine by the time he was twenty), will be 74 years old this year, can look back on a brilliant 55-year-long career, and still gets a splendid new novel into print every year or two. Damon Knight, a friend of Fred Pohl's back in the days when they were mere fans, is still writing too, fifty-some years after selling the first one. Hal Clement, though his contributions are less frequent now, can also look back on more than half a century of magnificent science-fiction.

Coming up on the fifty-year mark are some of our grandest writers. Poul Anderson, a mere 67, has sustained an unbroken record of science-fictional excellence since his marvelous debut story, "Tomorrow's Children," which he sold in 1946. Jack Vance—he's 77, I think—is another with close to fifty years of wonderful work behind him, starting with 1945's "The World-Thinker" and continuing on to his current and memorable *Cadwal Chronicles* series. Arthur C. Clarke, whose debut as a writer (delayed five years by his service in World War II) occurred in 1946, is also still turning out the books, nearly five decades later, despite repeated mutterings about retirement, and his hand seems to have lost none of its skill.

The roster of those who have sustained active careers over forty years is pretty impressive, too. Anne McCaffrey, who surely can't be as young as she seems, sold *her* first story in the same year I did, 1953, and still clings with her full Gaelic vigor to her annual slot on the best-seller lists. Robert Sheckley, Philip José Farmer, Marion Zimmer Bradley, James E. Gunn, Gordon R. Dickson, Algis Budrys, John Brunner, Avram Davidson, and, yes, Harry Harrison, are all older than I am, some by a few months, some by a decade or two, and all began their careers around the same time in the early 1950s. Harlan Ellison, Brian W. Aldiss, J.G. Ballard, and Kate Wilhelm arrived a couple of years later. All of them are still around and going strong.

Of course there are sadder tales to tell. Clifford D. Simak is no longer with us, after nearly sixty years as a writer. (He won a Hugo for Best Short Story when he was 77—now there's a mark to shoot for!) Such great figures of the first Golden Age of Science Fiction, the celebrated John Campbell era of 1939-43, as Isaac Asimov, Robert A. Heinlein, Fritz Leiber, Alfred Bester, and Theodore Sturgeon have left us in recent years, most of them having continued to write virtually right up to the end of their lives. Among those who started writing science fiction about the same time I did and went on to demonstrate not only talent but the ability to sustain it over many years, Frank Herbert, Alan Nourse, and Philip K. Dick are dead, much too young. Those grand old veterans Edmond Hamilton and Leigh Brackett are gone too.

Well, nobody lasts forever. What's astonishing, though, is how many of us hang in there for decade after decade. Science-fiction writers may not be quite as durable as symphonic conductors, but we seem to be pretty good insurance risks, in general. And as I chug along now into the fifth decade of my career, still a mere beginner as things go in our field, I look onward to the sterling examples of Jack Williamson, Sprague de Camp, and Andre Norton, who have been doing wonderful work since about the time I was born (or even farther back, in Jack's case) and whose fingers are probably flying over the keyboards of their computers at this very minute, bringing forth next year's entry in their vast and ever-growing bibliographies. Thinking of them, still at it after all this time, is the best cure for premature intimations of decrepitude that I can imagine.

FOUR

COLLEAGUES

Players on the Team

All too many of the pieces in this section are, I'm sorry to say, obituaries. I came into science fiction as a very young man, just about the youngest writer in the business, which means that in the course of my own normal longevity I've outlived almost everyone who was active in the field as a writer or an editor when I started out. I'm not any happier to see my friends die than anyone else, but I do find one reward, at least, in reminiscing about them: it allows me to give due thanks to those who helped me on the way up, and to make my own affectionate farewells to people I knew, liked, respected, even sometimes loved, over the years. And the group of them constitutes, also, a piecemeal anecdotal history, of a sort, of the American science-fiction world over the past forty-odd years. But I'm happy to say that some of the items that follow are simply appraisals of the work of living writers I admire, or tributes to them on some auspicious birthday.

John Cheever speaks in his journals of reading John Updike's essays on Borges and Nabokov and coming away with the feeling of "the thrill of writing, of playing on this team, the truly thrilling sense of this as an adventure."

Exactly so. *The thrill of playing on this team.* Like so many of my colleagues in science fiction I am by nature pretty solitary, even reclusive, certainly stubbornly independent-minded and individualistic. And yet I have always thought of the group of writers who created the thing we think of as "science fiction" as a team, a collegial unit, a closely knit group of players, and I have felt fierce pride and excitement at being a member of that team. Even after four decades as a science-fiction writer, I still continue to feel the thrill of knowing that I am part of it that I play on the same team as Isaac Asimov, Robert Heinlein, Theodore Sturgeon, L. Sprague de Camp, A.E. van Vogt, Henry Kuttner, Clifford D. Simak, Jack Vance, and the other stellar performers of my youth.

At first, of course, I was just a fan sitting in the bleachers, watching the big stars do their stuff, and scarcely daring to imagine that I would ever be allowed to get down on the playing field among them. That was back in the mid-1940s, when I was just entering my teens, and John W. Campbell's *Astounding Science Fiction* (the ancestor of today's *Analog*) was the arena in which nearly everything of any interest in the science-fiction world was happening, and each month's

[*Asimov's Science Fiction*, November 1994]

issue brought some extraordinary new event. What? Asimov has written a new Foundation story? Wonderful! What? Heinlein is back, after his long silence during World War II? Terrific! What? A three-part serial by L. Ron Hubbard? Will it be as good as *Final Blackout*? And what's this? A new Mutant story by Kuttner? De Camp beginning a new series? Doc Smith finally finishing the Lensman epic? One by one, the top players took their turn at bat, swung their mighty swings, sent the ball far out of sight.

Over the next few years I watched new stars come up out of the minor leagues and move right in alongside my early heroes: Alfred Bester, Robert Sheckley, Frederik Pohl, Algis Budrys, Philip K. Dick, James Blish, James Gunn, Poul Anderson, Cyril Kornbluth, Gordon Dickson, Frank M. Robinson, William Tenn, Richard Matheson. Each had something new and fresh to say, each said it in a distinctly individual manner. Some, like Walter M. Miller, Jr., John D. MacDonald, and Wilmar Shiras, came and went in a hurry, making astonishing debuts and then moving on to other places or other activities. But most of the newcomers stayed around, steadily making their contributions, winning their permanent places on the team.

And I, in time, found myself being allowed down on the playing field at last—more or less as a bat-boy, in the beginning, a kid permitted to rub shoulders with the players but not in any real way part of the team. That was all right. I was eighteen. You don't ordinarily expect to get into the starting lineup at eighteen. It was glory enough for me just to walk through a corridor of the hotel where the Worldcon was taking place and have some well-known writer—Robert Bloch, say, or Harry Harrison, or Lester del Rey—wave and grin and call out, "Hi, Bob," as I went past him.

And then, a year or two later, to get the opportunity to pinch-hit occasionally—to fill a small slot in one of the lesser magazines with a very brief story, because one of the editors (Bob Lowndes, Howard Browne, Bill Hamling) had come up a few thousand words short as he was trying to put the next issue together: that was when I began to think I was actually going to make the team. Which indeed I did, very shortly afterward. Bit by bit it all began to happen: my name on a magazine cover; the lead position in the table of contents; a novel serialized in several issues; a book published in actual hard covers. All those painfully accomplished steps on the path toward success in my chosen profession—things I take for granted now, of course, but of enormous symbolic importance when I was a new young writer.

A member of the team, yes. Taking something that Asimov or

Kuttner or Sturgeon had done, and looking at it in my own way, and giving it some new and original spin. Or contributing plots, ideas, themes, characters, of my own, which perhaps Fred Pohl or Bob Sheckley would look at years later and transpose into stories that were uniquely Pohlian or Shecklesque. For so it goes in science fiction (or so it went, at least, in the much smaller s-f field of the 1950s and 1960s, when it was still possible for the writers to read just about every science-fiction book and story being published, and we all did): we collaborate indirectly, each member of the team adding something to the general pot of concepts and techniques for others to take and use and transform.

Though reading all the s-f that gets published is no longer a manageable proposition, the concept of a common pool of science-fictional conceptualization still exists, and there is scarcely one of us who has not added something to it. Of course, the longer you've been around, the more you've been able to add. These days I often read reviews of books or stories that are described as "Silverbergian" in manner, or hear of some new writer who has come up with an entirely new take on something I did decades ago in *Dying Inside* or *Downward to the Earth*, and—as a former bat-boy on this team—I'm delighted by the notion that somewhere along the way I was able to move into a starring position eventually, and bring off a couple of maneuvers that newer players might want to emulate and absorb into their own bag of tricks.

That, I think, is what John Cheever meant by "the truly thrilling sense of this as an adventure." *We are all in this together*, all of us oddly assorted one-of-a-kind people, working within the common body of material and methods that is science fiction and striving to employ that material and those methods to create something that will extend and amplify what has gone before. I could not have written as I did without having read Kuttner and Sheckley and Dick and Sturgeon and all their illustrious predecessors; Sheckley would not have achieved what he did had not Kuttner shown the way, and Phil Dick had van Vogt (and also the versatile Kuttner) to guide him; and everybody, even Asimov and Arthur Clarke, owed something to Heinlein, and Heinlein would not have been the writer he was but for the pioneering work of H.G. Wells.

A team, yes. You watch the stars strutting their stuff, and then you say, timidly or aggressively according to your manner, "Here, let me take a few swings," and you move into position and have your chance at the big time. The lucky ones—by which I mean, really, the talented and determined and durable ones—actually attain a place on the team, some through genius that simply will not be denied, some through persistence and perspiration, some through wild and inexplicable good fortune.

I wanted nothing more, when I was a boy, than the thrill of playing on this team, and I have had it now for my entire adult life. What an extraordinary pleasure it has been to have such senior writers as Jack Williamson or Isaac Asimov or Sprague de Camp, who had been my idols, become my friends instead! And—as a senior figure myself, by now—I have also enjoyed the counterbalancing pleasure of seeing new young writers try out for the team—Joe Haldeman, George Alec Effinger, Gardner Dozois, Kim Stanley Robinson, Greg Benford, and so many others—and make the grade and turn into valued colleagues and dear friends of mine.

I don't know how it works among professional athletes, but one interesting feature of the team that I happen to belong to is the general absence of professional jealousy, at least between older and newer members of the team. A major-league baseball team, I think, can have only 25 members or thereabouts, and the only way a new man can make the team is for some veteran to lose his job. This tends to make for some discomfort among the established pros as a hot new rookie manifests himself in the pre-season training sessions.

It doesn't work that way in science fiction. No one, so far as I am aware, muttered dark and uneasy thoughts about my prolificity when I appeared on the scene in the middle 1950s and began filling all the s-f magazines at once with my stories. Instead I got sincere and helpful advice, in the early days of my career, from the likes of Lester del Rey and Fred Pohl and Jim Blish and Will F. Jenkins, who might more reasonably have been expected to wonder whether I was going to crowd them off the contents pages single-handedly. And so it has always gone, the older writers welcoming the newcomers, watching their performances with interest, occasionally showing them a thing or two when a corrective suggestion might seem appropriate.

Perhaps those writers who come up around the same time eye each other more balefully, out of fear that they will be surpassed by one of their contemporaries. But I don't recall that it worked that way when I was starting out, when my fellow newcomers included such folk as John Brunner, Harlan Ellison, Brian Aldiss, Michael Moorcock, and J.G. Ballard, and then, a couple of years later, Ben Bova, Ursula Le Guin, and Larry Niven. It seems to me that we maintained amiable collegial feelings at all times.

It may be different in today's more crowded writing world—I don't really know—but somehow I doubt that Stan Robinson loses much sleep over the quality of John Varley's new book, or that Nancy Kress frets unduly that Connie Willis is winning too many Hugos, or that Bruce Sterling keeps count of the number of times that the names of James Patrick Kelly or Walter John Williams appear on the cover of this magazine. I prefer to think that they all are reading each other's brilliant work with high appreciation, as I do, and are responding with sincere applause—the heartfelt congratulation that one member of the team owes another for a job well done, as we all go onward together in the great adventure that is science fiction.

Going to Conventions

There's been a certain elegiac tone to these columns this summer, a hearkening back to earlier times, old memories of the science-fiction field that used to be. Undoubtedly the deaths last year of those two colossi of our genre, Isaac Asimov and Fritz Leiber, were factors that aroused much of that feeling of nostalgia in me; and, as I noted a couple of months ago, 1993 is also the fortieth anniversary of my own first sale to a science-fiction magazine. Fortieth anniversaries do have a way of getting one to look toward the past.

And now another fortieth anniversary is upon me. For this is September, the month of the World Science Fiction Convention; and this year's Worldcon will be the fortieth convention I have attended.

The Worldcon is the great annual family gathering of the science-fiction clan, an assemblage of thousands and thousands of people who care passionately about this strange stuff that we choose to read and write. *Everyone* is there: writers, editors, artists, publishers, book dealers, and, of course, readers—the fans, who are actually the people who organize each year's Worldcon and do the brutal work that makes it happen. In the course of my forty years of Worldcon attendance, I've had a chance to meet and get to know virtually the entire roster of science fiction's great creative figures, from Frank R. Paul, Edmond Hamilton, and E.E. "Doc" Smith of the earliest days of our field down to the promising novices who will evolve into the super-novae of twenty-first century s-f. I can't imagine missing a convention. Through all the ebbs and flows of my career, the thought of *not* going to a Worldcon has never entered my mind.

There aren't many who have attended as many as forty Worldcons. Forrest J. Ackerman, that survivor from the dawn of s-f fandom, is one who has, I know: Forry was at the first one in 1939, and has been at virtually every one since. Probably Fred Pohl (who was excluded from that 1939 convention for political reasons by fiat of its organizers, a notable moment in fan history) has been to more than forty, too, out of the fifty that have been held up to this year. Perhaps there are three or four others. But I must be high up on the list of perennial attendees.

This year's convention is in San Francisco, just across the bay from my home. Ironically, the last time I missed a Worldcon, it was in San Francisco also, in 1954: but I lived on the East Coast then, and as a 19-year-old college student I simply couldn't come up with the

[*Amazing Stories*, September 1993]

funds to take me on that vast journey of 3000 miles across the country. I often wonder what that young Bob Silverberg would say, if he could be told that forty years later he would be driving twenty minutes from his home to attend another San Francisco Worldcon— or that he would be writing about doing it in his regular *Amazing Stories* column.

Images of Worldcons past come floating up out of the memory bank as I look back over those astonishing forty years.

Your first one, of course, is always unforgettable. For me that was the Philadelphia convention of 1953, at the glorious Bellevue-Stratford hotel. I was eighteen; I had just made my first professional sale (and would be paid for it, all thirty dollars, at the convention.) And now, at last, I would attend my first World-con! Staying in a three-room suite, no less.

A suite, you say? How did an impecunious college kid manage that? Where did I ever find the money—a suite at the Bellevue-Stratford must have cost all of twelve or fifteen dollars a night, in 1953—to manage such stately lodgings?

Through entrepreneurial zeal, of course. I teamed up with a fellow fan, a kid from Cleveland, one Harlan Ellison, with whom I agreed to split the bill. Then we offered crash space—couches, chairs, the floor, whatever—to our numerous friends in the fan community, at $5 per night. At least twenty of them signed up. The result was a kind of convention within the convention: our three rooms were packed every night, a stellar array of 1953's great fan figures holding an intense round-the-clock party. As the organizers of the commune, Harlan and I not only got to be the ones who slept in the beds (when we slept at all, an hour or two a night) but wound up paying nothing for our suite and turning a profit of forty or fifty dollars each, besides.

It was a wondrous weekend. I stared in awe at the writers and editors I had revered all through my adolescence—Theodore Sturgeon, John W. Campbell, Willy Ley, Frederik Pohl, Lester del Rey, L. Sprague de Camp, and dozens more—moving like ordinary mortals through the throngs in the lobby. I looked with envy on the hot young writers like Robert Sheckley and Frank M. Robinson, whose names were on the tables of contents of all the magazines, and earnestly prayed to join them there some day. (Which I did; and I formed lifelong friendships with them both, besides.) I mingled with fan friends I had known only through correspondence, and worked hard to live up to my postal reputation for acute wit and erudition. I blurted out my literary ambitions to editors like Harry Harrison and Larry T.

Shaw, and was encouraged by what they had to say, though probably they were just being nice to the lanky, crew-cutted tyro that I was. I watched the very first Hugos being handed out, not even daring to suppose that some day I would be a winner myself. And I went home (by bus, Philadelphia to New York) in a daze of excitement and fatigue, my life forever transformed in a single weekend.

I swore never to miss a Worldcon again. But the next year's convention, I discovered, was in far-off San Francisco, the other side of the continent from me. It might just as well have been on the Moon.

By the time of the 1955 convention in Cleveland, though, I was a prosperous young writer who had made at least a dozen sales to the s-f magazines, on my own and in collaboration with the somewhat more experienced writer Randall Garrett, whom I had met in New York. (At the 1953 Worldcon, Garrett had shown up one night, drunk and disorderly, at the perpetual party in the Ellison-Silverberg suite, and I had shut the door in his face. "Do you know who that is?" Harlan had asked me, aghast. "That's *Randall Garrett.* He's a *pro!*" But I didn't care: we had enough loudmouths in the room as it was. Garrett had no recollection of the incident a couple of years later, when we met, and we hit it off beautifully as collaborators.) Now my stories were all over the magazines. I had graduated with lightning swiftness into the professional ranks. It all seemed pretty much like a dream to me as Garrett led me around the convention, introducing me to the writers who were now my colleagues.

I met Isaac Asimov at that convention, and Fritz Leiber, and James E. Gunn, and Fred Pohl, and Anthony Boucher, and the legendary Bob Tucker, and I don't know how many others of the great. It was an awesome thing to be in their presence, actually chatting with them virtually as an equal at a party where only the inner circle of writers and editors was present. The 1953 convention had been my initiation into the tribe; the 1955 one marked my debut among the pros. I was a figure of some interest to them, I could see: the field then was very small, and *any* prolific new writer was immediately conspicuous. (The total attendance at that 1955 convention, fans and pros together, was all of 380 people, so everyone quickly knew everyone else. Modern Worldcons are ten to twenty times as big.)

I remember the trip home from Cleveland, too: six or seven of us, including Harlan, and Ian Macauley (who would become an editor with the New York *Times,* and jolly Karl Olsen (who still comes to conventions, jolly as ever) and some others, crammed into what I think was Macauley's car for an all-night turnpike drive to New York.

I didn't have a driver's license, then, but everyone else took turns at the wheel, including Karl, who *also* didn't have a license but didn't tell us that until he had run the car up on the center median. We survived.

And went on to 1956, a vast Worldcon in New York. I had sold so many stories by then that my colleagues were looking at me not with curiosity, now, but with uneasiness and a bit of horror. That was the year I won my first Hugo—the award for Most Promising New Author. (I beat out two fellows who were still pretty obscure that year: Harlan Ellison, whose professional career had barely begun, and a guy named Frank Herbert, who had had two or three stories published.) It seemed a very long way from that Philadelphia convention, just three summers earlier.

I vividly remember the sweaty, exciting time just after the Hugo ceremony, as I stood there clutching my shiny trophy and accepting congratulations. Betty Farmer, Philip José Farmer's irrepressible wife, came up to me and gave me a hug; and then she said, "You know, Phil won the same Hugo in 1953. And he hasn't been able to sell a story since.") She was just joking, of course. And he and I both managed to keep our careers afloat thereafter, as did Brian W. Aldiss, the third and final winner, a couple of years later, of the Hugo in the Most Promising New Author category.

I could fill a book, I think, with Worldcon anecdotes. (Some of them would get me sued, I suspect.) The 1957 convention was the first overseas one, in London, and I made my first trip to Europe to attend it. The hotel room cost $2.40 per night, and seemed a little overpriced at that, but we had a wondrous time, all 268 of us from both sides of the Atlantic. (The hotel dining room staff would put out the breakfast cereals in open bowls every night, and would urge us please not to take short-cuts through the room on our way to the bar because it would get dust into the corn flakes.)

1958, and Los Angeles: I got to see California at last, the palm trees and the freeways, little imagining that I'd live there some day. Among those I met for the first time at that convention were Poul Anderson and William Rotsler, now friends of decades' duration; I met Terry Carr there too, and watched him meet the beautiful woman who would become his first wife. (The marriage didn't last long, and, sadly, neither did Terry; but he and I had some wonderful times together before his too-early death at the age of 50.)

1959, 1960, Detroit, Pittsburgh....It was at one of those conventions, I forget which, that I was roaming the halls of an afternoon and came upon Gordie Dickson, Poul Anderson, and Ted Cogswell sitting in a hotel room with the door open, contemplating an entire case of tequila. I was never a drinker on the heroic Dickson-Anderson-Cogswell scale, but I do touch a drop now and then; they invited me in and I helped them dispose of some of it. Quite an afternoon.

And Seattle, in 1961: the con was at a little motel near the airport that year. Robert A. Heinlein was the guest of honor, and gave a party in his room *for the entire convention*, the entire roster of 300 attendees, holding court in his bathrobe, pouring drinks himself, greeting dozens of people by name, an astonishing performance. I began to understand why Heinlein was such a mesmerizing writer: his irresistible fiction was an extension of his own magnetic personality. An extraordinary man; it was a privilege to have known him, and if there had been no Worldcons, I might never have had the chance.

Heinlein was the star again in 1962 in Chicago, materializing unexpectedly as though out of hyperspace in a white dinner jacket to collect his Hugo for *Stranger in a Strange Land*. Conventions were starting to get bigger, now: there were 550 people at the Chicago con, in a two-tower hotel of confusing layout. (One night Harlan Ellison and I somehow missed connections with our friends and found ourselves with no way of discovering where the party we were supposed to be attending was located. We didn't even know which building it was in. So we sat quietly by ourselves on a back staircase for an hour or two, reviewing in wonder the dizzying six-year-evolution of our writing careers, until at last someone we knew came by and told us where to find the gathering we were looking for.)

There was the crazed episode in 1967, another New York Worldcon, where dozens of writers waited forever in the hotel dining room for service, and an angry Lester del Rey dumped an overdue salad on the floor while at the same moment Harlan flung a plate of popovers against the wall. And the next night I led many of the same people to a favorite restaurant of mine where we wound up in a back room next to a garbage can, and waited again for our dinners, waited so very long this time that people whose names would be recognized by you all started to go berserk, and I thought I would be lynched by my own friends. Anne McCaffrey had to quell the raging mob, finally.

I no longer regarded myself as a callow novice amidst a band of demigods, by then. I had been around for a dozen years, and plenty of writers junior to me had entered the field—Roger Zelazny, Larry Niven, Samuel R. Delany, Thomas Disch, and more. I watched them arrive one by one, and remembered how the old-timers had watched me do the same.

Still, I was startled in 1968 when the chairman of that year's Worldcon (it was to be in Berkeley, California) phoned and asked if I would serve as Toastmaster at the Hugo Awards ceremony. The toastmastership is one of the Worldcon's most significant responsibilities, and in those years it seemed invariably to rotate exclusively among a small group of our most distinguished citizens—Isaac Asimov, Anthony Boucher, Robert Bloch. Boucher was to have been toastmaster again at that year's convention, but he had died that spring; and suddenly I found myself promoted into that little group. To me it marked a rite of passage in the Worldcon subculture. (My toastmaster stint at the 1968 convention was exhausting and exhilarating, and I loved every moment of it. In the years that followed I ran the awards ceremony on four or five other occasions, and, I hope, lived up to the standard set by my impressive predecessors.)

That 1968 convention was a bizarre event—marked by widespread drug use, the convention debut of weird 1960s clothing and rock bands, riots near the hotel, all the craziness of that strange era erupting all at once. No one who was there will ever forget that dreamlike weekend.

Nor will I forget the more prosaic convention in St. Louis the following year, but for different reasons. Again, I found myself ascending into realms of s-f achievement that would have sent my adolescent self into paroxysms of disbelief. I delivered the keynote address at that convention; a couple of days later, I was handed another Hugo, for my novella "Nightwings"; and then I was told, right at the end of the weekend, that I was to be Guest of Honor at the following year's convention in Heidelberg, Germany.

To be Worldcon Guest of Honor is, I suppose, the summit of the science-fiction writer's course of accomplishment. I was only 35 years old when my turn came, making me one of the youngest ever—along with Heinlein and Asimov, who were 34 and 35, respectively. What amazed me even more, and left me a little abashed as well, was that at the time of my elevation to the Guest of Honorship, such writers as Clifford D. Simak, Frederik Pohl, Jack Williamson, Ray Bradbury, Alfred Bester, and Jack Vance had never been chosen. (They all got their turns, eventually. But they should have preceded me.)

So many stories to tell, so little space for them....

The 1964 convention in Oakland, where I rose to place a mock bid for a convention the following year at some posh resort in the Virgin Islands, and discovered, to my chagrin, that the attendees were taking the bid seriously and had given me a majority vote on the spot.

(I withdrew in favor of London, the genuine bidder.) The 1975 convention in Australia, where I rose to address Australian fandom for the first time and found myself on the verge of telling an utterly unprintable joke about a wombat instead of offering some profound literary observations. The 1978 convention in Phoenix, where the summer heat shriveled our very souls, and Harlan—Guest of Honor that year—gamely wrote a short story while sitting inside a plastic bubble in the hotel lobby, and sold it to OMNI on the spot. The 1979 convention in Brighton, England, where the British publisher Victor Gollancz gave a party for the convention V.I.P.s at the glorious eighteenth-century Royal Pavilion, and we were each formally announced by a crier as though we were coming into the presence of the Queen. The 1987 Brighton convention, too, where Brian Aldiss, winning a Hugo again after a lapse of a quarter of a century, accepted it by amiably declaring, "You bastards, what took you so long?"

(Which brings to mind the grotesque 1983 Hugo ceremony in Baltimore, which was preceded by a ketchupy crab luncheon where thousands of impatient fans began to bang their spoons on the table, after which everything else that could possibly go wrong did. The winners went away happy, anyway.)

Heinlein once more, presiding over a Red Cross blood drive in Kansas City in 1976: you wanted a Heinlein autograph, you had to donate a pint of your blood. Or Fred Pohl, resplendent in tuxedo, performing tirelessly and brilliantly at four or five functions a day in his capacity as master of ceremonies at the 1989 Boston Worldcon. Or the evening I spent with Isaac and Janet Asimov at the same convention—the last time, as it turned out, that I would ever see Isaac. Or the post-Hugo party at the 1990 con in Holland, where I stood around in a crowded room in the heat of an almost tropically humid evening wearing jacket and tie while accepting congratulations for my newest award until I felt myself beginning to melt, and ran off to my hotel room two blocks away to change into fresh clothing....

The 1991 convention in Chicago, where the glittering block-long bar of the Hyatt Hotel offered grappa at $350 a shot, and where I met Kim Mohan of *Amazing Stories* for the first time. (He bought me a drink. But our first meeting happened to take place in the hotel next door, so I didn't get a chance to put a shot of that grappa on his expense account. Just as well, I suspect.)

And last year, in Orlando, where the elite of science fiction gathered twice a day in the lobby of the elegant Peabody Hotel to watch a parade of ducks....

Forty years. The stories I could tell would fill a book and a half.

And now this year, in San Francisco. Another Worldcon, a new collection of wondrous memories to add to the rich store already laid by. If this is going to be your twentieth or twenty-fifth convention, well, it'll be good to see you again, old friend. And if it'll be your first Worldcon: welcome, stranger! You're in for the experience of a life-time.

Isaac

I suppose he's already finished the first volume of *Asimov's Guide To The Afterlife* and is doing the research for Volume Two, which deals with the Other Place. He's also been having some lively conversations with Shakespeare, Coleridge, and Lewis Carroll concerning aspects of their work that he discussed in books of his own and now wants to ask them a few questions about. After that comes a new robot novel and then the first novel in the Third Foundation series, to be followed by *After Eternity,* a book of speculative essays. And then....

He *has* to be still working, somewhere. It wouldn't be like him, otherwise. But we aren't going to get to read those books ourselves, and that is very, very sad and strange. As is his disappearance from our midst. For half a century he stood at the very center of the science-fiction world, amusing and instructing us at the top of his lungs—and now he's gone. Hard to believe, hard to accept. The magnitude of our loss is incalculable; the reality of it is going to take some time to sink in.

I first set eyes on Isaac Asimov, so far as I can recall, at some minor science-fiction convention underneath the vanished Third Avenue Elevated Railway tracks in Manhattan, somewhere around 1950. He was then just about thirty years old, and already inordinately famous in our little cosmos—the author of the Foundation stories (including the just-published magazine serial "....And Now You Don't," which would become the book Second Foundation), and the first nine of the robot stories, and the Thiotimoline hoax, and, of course, the established classic "Nightfall," which he did when he was only twenty-one. I didn't have much to say to him, at that convention. I was just a high-school kid of fourteen or fifteen—a mere pisher, Isaac would have said—who published a smeary mimeographed fanzine and wrote terrible little half-baked stories and had grandiose and implausible dreams of selling one of those stories to a science-fiction magazine some day. I was very shy and had good reason to be. And there was Isaac Asimov, I*S*A*A*C A*S*I*M*O*V, jolly and extroverted, holding court at high volume and high energy surrounded by the likes of Frederik Pohl, Lester del Rey, Theodore Sturgeon, and Cyril Kornbluth, in that miserable little drafty rented hall under the Third Avenue El. Was I going to walk up to him and stick out my hand and say, "Hi, Ike." (That was what people called him then, Ike. He hated it and finally got everyone to stop.) "I'm Bob Silverberg, and I'm only fourteen years old but I'm going to be pretty famous myself some day, so here's your chance to get to know me right at the start. Maybe I'll let you collaborate with me on a novel or two when I have time." But I wasn't like that—I'm still not much like that—and so I didn't say a word, just stared, thinking, *It's Isaac Asimov. ISAAC ASIMOV!*

(Of course, if my temperament had been more like Harlan Ellison's, say, I'd have marched up to him and said in awe and rapture, "You Isaac Asimov?" And he would have smiled indulgently. And I would have looked him up and down and said, switching in a split second from a look of awe to one of contempt, "Well, let me tell you, I think you're a *nothing*, Asimov." Or so the apocryphal story goes. Harlan claims that what he really said was merely, "You aren't so much." Harlan was like that, then. He's much better behaved now.)

Isaac and I were officially introduced four or five years later, at the 1955 World S-F Convention in Cleveland. He was Guest of Honor at that convention, which made him all the more awesome to me, but by now I had begun my own professional career and my adolescent shyness had begun to melt away. I was sharing a room at the con with Randall Garrrett, a well-known writer of the period with whom I had been collaborating all through 1955, and he was an old friend of Isaac's. (Garrett was, if anything, even noisier and more extroverted than Isaac, and shared his love of Gilbert & Sullivan, outrageous puns, and boisterous behavior.) Randall dragged me up to Asimov and introduced me as that bright young brat who was suddenly selling stories all over the place. Isaac gave me a nice-to-know-you-kid kind of greeting, pleasant but remote. I mentioned that I was a Columbia student—Isaac had gone to Columbia too, fifteen years earlier—and he gave me a closer look. What was this, another precocious Jewish kid from New York who had gone to Columbia and now was selling stories all over the place at the absurd age of twenty? Who did I think I was, I could see him thinking—Isaac Asimov? But he managed a few cordial words, anyway, and I wandered away very impressed with myself for having held the attention of Isaac Asimov for sixty seconds or so.

A year later it was all very different. I was an established professional, a member of the gang (sort of a mascot, actually), a Hugo winner at the preposterous age of 21—and I had just gotten married to an attractive young lady who happened to be an electronics engineer. Isaac was always willing to chat with attractive young ladies who happened to be electronic engineers, and when I introduced her to them he greeted her in a way that startled her considerably and which really ought not to be described in detail in a sedate family magazine like *Amazing Stories*. I had to explain to her that world-famous science fiction writers often did things like that and they weren't to be taken seriously. She was amused....I think.

Isaac and I never really became what could be called close friends—he didn't go in much for having close friends as I understand the term, and his outward mode of uproarious high-spiritedness was too much unlike my own more aloof and melancholy manner for us to establish any real intimacy. But the superficial resemblances of our lives—the precocity, the New York/Columbia backgrounds, the prolificity, even our somewhat troubled first marriages—gave us areas in common that led to a friendship of a sort.

We saw a good deal of each other in the 1960s, sometimes in Boston (where he lived during that decade) but more often in New York. I came to realize that behind his ebullient facade was a man more troubled than joyous, who hid his unhappiness in vast outpourings of work; he discovered, eventually, that behind my gloomy-looking exterior was a man somewhat less anguished than was commonly believed, though often gloomy enough, who *also* used work as an antidote to unhappiness. We enjoyed each other's company; on those rare moments when he and I were alone with each other, we pulled back our public facades a little, though only a little; we argued good-humoredly over this and that and on two occasions in the 1970s had pretty serious disputes, both of which were eventually resolved in a harmonious and mutually satisfactory way. (One sprang from Isaac's incredulity over my statement of 1974 that I was giving up writing forever—he thought that was a damned silly thing for me to be doing, and said so publicly—and the other was a misunderstanding that sprang from his taking seriously a facetious remark of mine about radioactivity.) We exchanged letters fairly frequently after I moved to California; I commissioned a short story from him for a book I was editing and by so doing indirectly got him back to writing novels after a 15-year hiatus; when my first marriage broke up in the mid-1970s he had some useful things to tell me, having gone through something similar himself a few years before. Then came a long period when we had only the most occasional contact with each other; and then, through a series of bizarre twists and turns that neither of us could have anticipated, we wandered into a collaborative relationship in which we produced novel-length versions of his three most celebrated novellas, "Nightfall," "The Ugly Little Boy," and "The Bicentennial Man."

(During the writing of which, I often found myself hearkening back to that time forty years before when I had stared in wonder at the author of "Nightfall," looking upon him as some sort of unapproachable demigod. Now I was working within that story myself as though I were he, inhabiting it, rethinking it, developing it. In a weird way I had not only come to know Isaac Asimov but to *be* him. I'd love to send a memo to my adolescent self about that.)

And now he is gone. His death leaves an immense void in our community. He was, of course, a great writer, and an extraordinarily brilliant man, and a remarkably vigorous and stimulating human being. He was also a singular and unforgettable character, a strictly one-of-a-kind person. We are all of us unique—by definition, Isaac would say—but he was (and may God and Isaac forgive me for this violence against our language that I am about to commit) more unique than any of us. Those of you who knew him will know exactly what I mean. I miss him immensely. May he rest in peace, wherever he is—by which I mean, in his case, may he be writing books up there just as fast as he can.

Heinlein

The word that comes to mind for him is *essential*. As a writer—eloquent, impassioned, technically innovative—he reshaped science fiction in a way that defined it for every writer who followed him. As a thinker—bold, optimistic, pragmatic—he set forth a pattern of belief that guided the whole generation of youngsters that grew up to bring the modern technological world into being. As a man—civilized, charming, resilient in the face of difficulty—he was a model of moral strength and a powerful pillar of support for many who may not even have been aware of his quiet benefactions.

The writing first. He was the most significant science-fiction writer since H.G. Wells. I don't necessarily mean the *best* science-fiction writer: that's too nebulous a term, because one could argue that so-and-so was a superior prose stylist and that so-and-so was unequalled in the dexterity of his plotting and that so-and-so had deeper insight into human character, and so forth. But the three so-and-sos I have in mind, each of whom was able to outdo Heinlein in some aspect of his craft, would, I think, instantly agree with me that Heinlein was one of his masters, was in fact the writer who had done the most to determine his attitude toward the writing of science fiction. Without him, I suspect, most of the classics of modern science fiction would never have been written.

Wells invented the basic form a century ago. Propose a plausible but startling thesis (invaders come to Earth from Mars; traveling backward and forward through time is possible; a clever scientist can reshape animals into a semblance of human form) to begin with. Assemble a cast of sympathetic and clearly depicted characters and drop them into the midst of the crisis. Develop the implications of the thesis by showing the characters struggling with the ongoing crisis. Tell what happens in clear, precise, and unmelodramatic prose. And provide a resolution to the basic story problem that grows convincingly out of the fundamental nature of the situation, the people involved in it, and the way the universe works as best we can understand it.

Within the space of about fifteen years Wells systematically invented nearly all the fundamental science-fiction themes that the rest of us have been exploring ever since, and set them forth in novels so well told that they have retained great popularity among readers everywhere. His example is a towering one: how odd, then, that within

[From *Requiem*, edited by Yoji Kondo, 1992]

a generation science fiction should have become, at least in the United States, the dreary, debased thing that it did.

What happened was that it went in two directions, neither of them good. One school of writers—its apostle was Hugo Gernsback, the founder of the first American science-fiction magazine—produced interminable droning lectures instead of readable stories, retelling the basic Wellsian themes in leaden prose. Bald bespectacled scientists delivered endless yards of arid narrative, festooned with footnotes. The other school—which grew out of the late nineteenth century dime-novel tradition—went in for wild, breathless tales of action and adventure, also using the basic Wellsian canon of plot situations but populating them with mad scientists, beautiful young female journalists, jut-jawed heroes, and other caricatures. Neither kind of writing could hope to appeal to more than the most specialized kind of audience: studious, emotionally retarded men on the one hand, and callow, emotionally undeveloped boys on the other.

In 1937 the leading science-fiction writer of the period, 27-year-old John W. Campbell, Jr., was given the editorship of the leading science-fiction magazine of the time, *Astounding Stories*. Campbell at once proclaimed a revolution. Out with the mad scientists and the lovely imperiled lady journalists; out with the footnotes, too. He wanted writers who knew how to tell a story adults could read without gagging and who believed also that a story should be *about* something. What he wanted, in effect, was science fiction with Wellsian intellectual intensity and with the kind of appealing straightforward prose that any non-science-fiction writer—the contributors to *The Saturday Post*, say—would be expected by his audience to provide.

A number of new writers came forward to meet Campbell's new requirements, and their names are hallowed ones in our community: Isaac Asimov, Theodore Sturgeon, A.E. van Vogt, L. Sprague de Camp, Lester del Rey. But of that whole horde of brilliant beginners, the one who made the greatest impact was the 32-year-old Robert A. Heinlein.

There was so *much* of him, for one thing. His debut came with a short story, *Lifeline*, in the August 1939 issue. Then came another short in November and a third in January 1940—and that one, the remarkable mood-piece *Requiem*, immediately signified a writer of major importance. A month later there was the two-part serial *If This Goes On*—and three months after that the novelet *The Roads Must Roll* and then the novellas *Coventry* and *Blowups Happen*; and Heinlein was only gathering force, for 1941 brought the novels *Sixth Column* and *Methusaleh's Children*, the short novel *By His Boostraps* (under a barely concealed pseudonym), the astonishing innovative novelet *Universe*, and several others, with more to come in 1942 before the exigencies of World War II turned his attention temporarily in other directions.

But it wasn't by volume alone that Heinlein seized command of science fiction. His belief that a story had to make sense, and the irresistible vitality of his storytelling, delighted the readership of *Astounding*, who called for more and even more of his material. John Campbell had found the writer who best embodied his own ideals of science fiction. In one flabbergasting two-year outpouring of material for a single magazine Heinlein had completely reconstructed the nature of science fiction, just as in the field of general modern fiction Ernest Hemingway, in the 1920's, had redefined the modern novel. No one who has written fiction since 1927 or so can fail to take into account Hemingway's theory and practice without seeming archaic or impossibly naive; no one since 1941 has written first-rate science fiction without a comprehension of the theoretical and practical example set by Heinlein.

The nature of his accomplishment was manifold. His underlying conceptual structures were strikingly intelligent, rooted in an engineer's appreciation of the way things really work. His narrative method was brisk, efficient, and lucid. His stories were stocked with recognizable human beings rather than the stereotypes of the mad-scientist era. And—his main achievement—he did away with the lengthy footnotes of the Gernsback school and the clumsy, apologetic expository inserts of the pulp-magazine hacks and found an entirely new way to communicate the essence of the unfamiliar worlds in which his characters had to operate. Instead of pausing to explain, he simply thrust character and reader alike into those worlds and *let communication happen through experience.* He didn't need to tell us how his future societies worked or what their gadgets did. We saw the gadgets functioning; we saw the societies operating at their normal daily levels. And we figured things out as we went along, because Heinlein had left us no choice.

So he transformed everything in science fiction. The readers loved his work, and so did his fellow writers. The transformation became permanent and irreversible: Heinlein's technical standards became the norms by which editors, critics, and writers defined the excellent in science fiction.

As for Heinlein the thinker—

Others in this volume, I suspect, will deal with his position as an inspirational philosopher at the dawn of the age of space. Suffice it here for me to say that he provided a vision of the future that seemed attainable and worth attaining, and that others set about the job of attaining it *specifically because they had had Heinlein's vision to guide them.*

Not that he was infallible. The film *Destination Moon*, which he conceived, demonstrates that. Its 1949 image of a single-stage spaceship built by a private group of entrepreneurs and hastily fired off to the moon ahead of schedule, without any sort of preliminary testing because sheriffs waving cease-and-desist orders are closing in, is preposterously far from the realities of the actual event of twenty years later. So too are the details of the flight, with its frantic mid-course corrections desperately worked out with scratchpad calculations, and the frenzied climactic attempt to shed weight in order to make the homeward liftoff. (Somewhat more melodramatically handled in the movie than in Heinlein's own story version—probably because other writers were called in to give the film more of a Hollywood flair.)

That Heinlein's imagination fell short of the subsequent Apollo Eleven realities is worth noting not only because it shows us the limitations of even the keenest-eyed of seers but also because it illuminates just how much of the first moon flight Heinlein was able to get *right*, twenty years before the fact. He failed to foresee the multi-stage rocket, the vast national effort that the launch would require, the immense technological support system that would be necessary, and, most strikingly, the extraordinary live telecasts of the moon mission itself. But what he did capture was the fundamental essence of the enterprise: the importance of going to the moon, the *look* of the floodlit and gantried spaceship as it makes ready for takeoff, the feel of the voyage itself. We smile at the simplistic aspects of Heinlein's story; we shiver with awe when we consider how powerfully and well he visualized and communicated to us the underlying realities of the enterprise.

And as for Heinlein the man—

I wish I had spent more time with him. We met perhaps a dozen times over twenty-five years: not nearly enough, but for much of the time we lived on opposite coasts, and after I became his near neighbor, only 70 miles away, his weakening health and increasing reclusiveness made it difficult for me to see him. We exchanged letters and phone calls; I regret that there was little more than that.

He was a delightful human being, courtly, dignified, with an unexpected sly sense of humor. I met him first, so far as I can recall, at the 1961 World Science Fiction Convention in Seattle, where he was guest of honor. He amazed everyone there by holding an open-house party in his suite and inviting the entire convention to attend. That would be unthinkable today, when five or six thousand people go to such conventions. The attendance in 1961 was only about two hundred, but it was still a remarkable gesture: Heinlein in his bathrobe, graciously greeting every goggle-eyed fan (and a few goggle-eyed writers) who filed into the room. We struck up a correspondence after that convention. I remember telling him that I had already published seven million words of fiction—I was only 26, but very profilic—to which he replied, "There aren't that many words in the language. You must have sold several of them more than once." And went on to tell me how Isaac Asimov's wife had complained that Isaac worked so hard that all she saw of him was the back of his neck: "Isaac stopped just long enough to point out that they had two children," Heinlein commented. "Then he resumed dirtying paper at his usual smoking-bearing speed. (Come to think of it, you don't have any children, do you?")

On the other hand, when he asked me in 1962 if I was planning to install a bomb shelter in my newly purchased house and I said no, that I'd rather be atomized swiftly rather than live in post-nuclear America, a long, chilly silence ensued. The soon-to-be author of *Farnham's Freehold* wasn't going to look kindly on someone who was willing to admit that there were circumstances under which he'd just as soon not survive. But later he forgave me, and never a harsh word passed between us again—not even when I reprinted his story *The Year of the Jackpot* in one of my anthologies and failed to notice that the printer had left out the all-important last three pages. He was the soul of courtesy as he gently called the horrifying omission to my attention.

A great writer, an extraordinary man, a figure of high nobility: there was no one else remotely like him in our field. Within the science-fiction world there were many who disagreed with him about many things, but there was no one who did not respect him, and there were a good many, myself included, who came close to revering him. It has been hard to grow accustomed to his absence: he has left an immense empty place behind. But his books are still here, and always will be. For those of us who knew him, however slightly, there are warm inextinguishable memories. And even those to whom his very name is unknown feel his presence daily, for he was one of the molders of the world in which we live.

Don Wollheim

O ne of the great figures of American science fiction died last fall, an editor who put his mark on it as indelibly as John W. Campbell or Hugo Gernsback. Their names are legendary; his may not be familiar to you at all. It was Donald A. Wollheim.

Donald who? you ask. Yes, very likely you do. It's a name known mainly on the inside, within the profession.

But consider these things:

Have you ever read a paperback novel by C.J. Cherryh, Marion Zimmer Bradley, Andre Norton, or Tanith Lee? The chances are good that it was published by DAW Books, then. That was Don Wollheim's distinctive publishing company, which bore his initials: Donald A. Wollheim. Since its founding some twenty years ago it has published hundreds of s-f and fantasy novels, most of them the kind of colorful, richly imaginative adventure stories that Wollheim loved, and in that time it has won thousands of new admirers of that distinctively Wollheimian brand of fiction.

Have you ever read a science-fiction anthology? Wollheim edited the first one that achieved mass-market publication: *The Pocket Book of Science Fiction* of 1943, a magnificent collection of classic stories by Heinlein, Sturgeon, H.G. Wells, and others. My impressionable young mind was haunted for days by images out of T.S. Stribling's "The Green Splotches" from that collection. Wollheim edited the first anthology of original s-f too, *The Girl With the Hungry Eyes*, in 1947, with great stories by Fritz Leiber, William Tenn, and other top-notchers of the period.

Have you seen those newfangled double-novel books that Tor has been publishing, the kind that have a novel by Silverberg on one side and one by Jack Vance or Gene Wolfe bound upside-down on the other, so that whichever way you turn it a cover painting faces you? Don Wollheim invented those in 1953, when he was the editor of Ace Books: they were called Ace Double Books. Among the writers who got their first paperback audiences in those back-to-back books were Philip K. Dick, Samuel R. Delany, John Brunner, Leigh Brackett, Poul Anderson, Ursula K. Le Guin, Harlan Ellison, Brian W. Aldiss, and a guy named Silverberg. Over on the reprint side, Ace offered the first paperback editions of Asimov's *Foundation* series, Robert E. Howard's Conan books, and A.E. van Vogt's Null-A novels.

Or—speaking of first paperback editions—have you ever read a

[*Amazing Stories*, June 1991]

fantasy trilogy? The books of Stephen Donaldson, say, or David Eddings, or any one of a hundred others, going back to the ancestor of them all, J.R.R. Tolkien? There was a time when no paperback company published fantasy at all, no one, nobody at all. It didn't sell, they said. There was no public for it. Then Don Wollheim's Ace Books brought out a reprint of *Lord of the Rings*, and the rest is publishing history.

(It wasn't, by the way, an authorized paperback reprint. Wollheim had tried to buy reprint rights to the Tolkien trilogy from its American hardcover publisher, but they turned him down: paperbacks were tacky, they thought. They didn't want to deal with a little house like Ace. Whereupon Wollheim, who had already observed that the hardcover house hadn't bothered to obtain proper copyright protection for the Tolkien books, simply published them without permission. It was a controversial thing to do; but Don Wollheim never minded being controversial. His edition of the trilogy met with such success that the hardcover publisher hastily authorized Ballantine Books to do a legitimate reprint edition of a slightly revised text, and Ace's books went out of print. But without that push from Wollheim, Tolkien would probably never have made it into paperback in this country— and publishers would still be telling each other solemnly that there was no mass-market audience for fantasy novels.)

To continue: have you ever read any of the novels of A. Merritt? C.S. Lewis' *Silent Planet* trilogy? The stories of H.P. Lovecraft? Before Wollheim ran Ace, he was the editor at the pioneering paperback house, Avon Books— and it was there, between 1947 and 1951, that he put the work of those great fantasists into newsstand editions that won wide audiences for these previously obscure writers.

During the Avon years, also, Wollheim edited a quarterly magazine, *The Avon Fantasy Reader*—for which he ransacked the yellowing pages of *Weird Tales*, *Argosy*, and other classic fiction magazines of the 1920s and 1930s, giving new life to the fiction of Clark Ashton Smith, Robert E. Howard, William Hope Hodgson, C.L. Moore, and dozens of others. (He published the occasional original story in it too—such as "Zero Hour," by the young Ray Bradbury.)

Going back still further: his first editing job, in 1941, was to run two low-budget short-lived pulp magazines, *Cosmic Stories* and *Stirring Science Stories*. Perhaps "low-budget" is a little too euphemistic: the contributors didn't get paid anything at all for them if the magazines survived past the first few issues. Since no professionals would write on that basis, Wollheim turned to his friends in the world of

New York science-fiction fandom for his material. His friends at that time included C.M. Kornbluth, Isaac Asimov, Damon Knight, James Blish, and Frederik Pohl, all of them just beginning their migrations from fandom to professional writing. You'll find some of their earliest (if not their best) stories in the pages of *Cosmic* and *Stirring*.

My own debt to Don Wollheim, both as reader and writer, was enormous. The kind of science fiction he most loved—rich in wonder and imagination, depicting in vivid detail sweeping vistas of the infinite—was the kind most likely to appeal to my developing mind when I was eleven or twelve years old. Which was how old I was when I stumbled upon an early Wollheim anthology, *Portable Novels of Science*, in Macy's book department one afternoon not long after World War II. I remember staying up half the night to finish Olaf Stapledon's *Odd John*, which seemed to speak to me personally (as it has to every overbright maladjusted kid who has ever read it); and then I went right on to devour John Taine's *Before the Dawn*, that magnificent portrayal of dinosaur life, and Lovecraft's spooky and wondrous *The Shadow Out of Time*, and by the time I finally dozed off over H.G. Wells' *The First Men in the Moon*, somewhere around two or three in the morning, my soul had been irrevocably altered. A literary virus had invaded it; and it was Don Wollheim who put it there, as he did for an entire generation of impressionable readers who grew up to be the writers you've cherished for decades.

In person he could be difficult: abrasive and passionately opinionated, a fierce ideological combatant, a vehement holder of grudges. Behind the abrasiveness, though, he was actually a shy and likeable man, as his long-time friends can attest; but that wasn't always readily apparent to outsiders. Even within his own circle he made many enemies along the way and he rarely forgave them, and when you visited his office, as I often did thirty-five years ago, he would regale you with accounts of their iniquities and shortcomings in a highly pungent way.

I suppose I was one of those enemies for a while, because, like nearly everyone who dealt with him in his early days as an editor, I ultimately disappointed him by moving on to other publishers. At the beginning of my career, in the mid-1950s, I quickly struck up a relationship with Wollheim and he published many of my earliest novels. We had lunch together many times at a German restaurant around the corner from the Ace office in Manhattan, where I listened in awe as he fulminated about the failings of other editors and writers; now and then I was the guest of Don and his devoted wife Elsie at their book-crammed house in Queens; and whenever I turned in a book, there was always a new contract forthcoming. But eventually my skills matured to the point where I could approach such publishing houses as Doubleday and Ballantine, for whom I could do longer and more complex books than I had been doing for Don (and get paid more, too.) And I suspect that at that point I joined the long list of those who had let Don Wollheim down, and I have no doubt that for a long time thereafter he had bitter things to say about me to anyone who would listen.

But the bitterness, if it was there, was wholly one-sided. I never felt anything but affection for this prickly, difficult, complicated man, and gratitude for all that he had done in revealing the wonders of science fiction to me and in shaping my career. And after a time whatever grudge he may have borne against me went away, and we enjoyed some amiable times together—notably at the 1988 World Science Fiction Convention in New Orleans, where—at least fifteen or twenty years after this high distinction should have come to him—he was Guest of Honor.

His last few years were marred by serious medical problems and his death, at the age of 76, came as a welcome release. We ought not let his passing go unrecognized. For more than fifty years this seriously underrated figure devoted his life and formidable energies to the development of the field we love. He was one of the great shapers of science-fiction publishing in the United States.

Lester

"Cantankerous" is the first word that comes to mind, and then "stubborn," closely followed by "feisty," and then maybe "outrageous." He worked hard at distancing people through calculated outbursts of curmudgeonly vehemence. But there was a heart of gold somewhere underneath all the outer gruffness, and he was deeply loved by those who loved him, of whom I was one. A childless man himself, he played the role of second father to a number of science-fiction writers of my generation, and I counted myself privileged to have been among that group.

I'm speaking of Lester del Rey, who died in May at the age of 77—another of science fiction's grand masters leaving us. Those of you who are relatively new to the s-f world may think of him as the man for whom Del Rey Books—the publisher of so many science-fiction best-sellers by Anne McCaffrey and David Eddings and Stephen Donaldson and Arthur C. Clarke—was named. That is in fact not quite the case. The del Rey of Del Rey Books was *Judy-Lynn* del Rey, Lester's wife from 1971 until her death in 1986, who transformed and expanded the publishing and marketing of s-f books in so startling a way, some fifteen years ago, that the science fiction and fantasy division of Ballantine Books was renamed in her honor. Lester himself remained in the background at Del Rey Books, an active but much less visible participant than his wife, devoting himself chiefly to the company's fantasy line. But certainly his passionate and powerfully held opinions on writing were a mighty force in shaping Judy-Lynn's editorial policies.

His name, by the way, wasn't really "Lester." I'm not sure what it was. I don't think anyone is. The name he accepted as his actual one was, approximately, "Ramon Felipe San Juan Mario Silvio Enrico Smith Heathcourt-Brace Sierra y Alvarez-del Rey y de los Verdes," but whenever some s-f reference source printed some version of it Lester could usually be heard to say that they had gotten it wrong, and it may be that he added or dropped names to the string as it pleased him to do so. The official list always seemed to begin with "Ramon Felipe San Juan Mario Silvio Enrico," at any rate, and then got less predictable from there. When and how the monicker "Lester" was hung on him, I never knew, but he was using it when he began writing fan letters that were published in *Astounding Stories* in the middle 1930s, and that was the byline that appeared on his first published

[*Amazing Stories*, July 1993]

story, "The Faithful," in the April, 1938 *Astounding*. (But he carved any number of pseudonyms out of his collection of given names later on: Philip St. John, John Alvarez, Marion Henry, R. Alvarez, etc., etc., etc.)

Lester was a short, slender, untidy-looking man with a wispy beard, a disarming grin, and a strong, commanding voice. He got your attention immediately and knew how to keep it. I was amazed when he told me once that he stood only five feet three; surely he was the biggest five-foot-three human being on this planet. His voice had much to do with that, but so did his sublime self-assurance. (He carried a business card, for a while, that simply said, "Lester del Rey—Expert." He could offer answers to questions on virtually every subject; sometimes they were even the right answers, but they were always given quickly and confidently. I never saw him at a loss for words, never, not even a moment's faltering.

He was not, I think, a great science fiction writer, and perhaps he knew it, and if he did, it certainly must have pained him; but he let no sign of that pain reach the surface. Very early in his career he wrote a story that became a classic—"Helen O'Loy," 1938: a warm-hearted, realistic robot story, head and shoulders over most of the s-f of that time in its humanity and compassion. But it would win no awards if it were published for the first time today. A number of fine stories followed in the next few years—"The Day is Done," "The Wings of Night," "Into thy Hands," and especially the powerful atomic-energy novella, "Nerves." He was an important figure in the so-called Golden Age days of John Campbell's *Astounding* before the Second World War. But whereas other Golden Age figures—Robert A. Heinlein, Isaac Asimov, Theodore Sturgeon, A.E. van Vogt, L. Sprague de Camp—went on to produce a string of masterly novels and short stories in the postwar era, Lester wrote little of consequence in the fifties, less in the sixties, and then—writing fiction having become a terrible struggle for him—essentially nothing at all.

The problem was, I suspect, that unlike a lot of us he never felt *driven* to write. Writing was just a mechanical skill he had picked up, along with many others—he could just as readily have earned his living as an electrician, a plumber, a mechanic, a typewriter repairman—and he saw it, always, as a craft rather than an art. He wrote his first story more or less to see if he could do at least as good a job as the people who were getting published in *Astounding*, and when he found that he could, he wrote some more. But in the second half of his life he often went a year or two, and sometimes much more than that, without even thinking about writing fiction. Fiction as a concept—assembling words into effective patterns—mattered a great deal to him. But he seemed to feel little impetus to write the stuff himself except when there were bills that needed to be paid, and he left us a surprisingly short list of science-fiction masterpieces for one of such lofty reputation.

Why, then, consider him a grand master?

Partly for the *way* he wrote: his unaffected, down-to-Earth style, a valuable corrective to the melodramatic excess that afflicted so much s-f of the pulp-magazine era. But we value him as much for his influence as an editor and a counsellor to other writers as for the example of his own writing.

Fiercely opinionated, irrevocably convinced of the strength of his grasp of storytelling technique, he imparted his knowledge of narrative technique to a whole generation of writers, myself among them. He edited a significant line of boys' adventure novels in the early 1950s—the famous Winston juveniles—and also, for a little while, a group of outstanding s-f magazines. Before that, he was office manager for a major literary agency for many years. And throughout his entire career he functioned as a mentor, a conscience, an irritating voice of inescapable truth, for all those dozens of fellow writers. He knew what a story *ought* to be—Lester was dogmatic the way Mount Everest is a tall mountain—and he painstakingly shared his sense of craft with any writer who would listen, though he had no tolerance for fools, none whatever, and quickly separated himself from their company, emphatically and permanently, in a way that even a fool was likely to comprehend.

He was about twice my age when we met—I was 19, I think, and he would have been 38 or 39. I was a raw novice and he was a stalwart of the Campbell golden age. But there was no hint of patronization in his attitude toward me: we fell into a friendship almost at once, one writer with another, and it stayed that way for the next four decades. I lost my awe of him pretty quickly, and when we disagreed on something we disagreed loudly and longly, but our disputes were always within a context of love, and there was never any doubt about that. (Not that I ever won an argument with him. No one ever did.)

He could be blunt: usually was, in fact. But always in pursuit of the truth. Perhaps the best advice anybody ever gave me as a writer came from Lester, when I was 22, maybe 23, and had discovered that I could make a lot of money fast by cranking out bang-bang pulp adventure fiction at a rate of thirty or forty pages a day. "You claim that what interests you in writing is mainly to make money," Lester told me. "But in that case you're really operating against your own best interests by knocking out all this junk. You write a story as fast as you can type and you get a penny a word from it *and that's all the money you're ever going to make from it.* It'll be forgotten five minutes from now. But if you were writing at the level of quality that I know is in you, turning out the kind of fiction people respect instead of simply stuff that will sell, you'd be bringing in an income on those stories from anthology sales and reprint editions forever. So even though you tell me that you're strictly a commercial writer, what you're doing these days doesn't make any sense simply on your own dollars and cents basis."

I had never stopped to look at it that way, and his reasoning brought me up short in amazement. In my own way I am just as stubborn as Lester ever was; but within five minutes he succeeded in changing my entire outlook on my work and set me on the path toward writing the books and stories that established me in my real career.

That was his specialty—cutting through somebody's carefully constructed bullshit to reach the carefully concealed realities beneath. I saw him do it again and again. (Nobody ever succeeded in doing it to him.)

His life was full of sorrows. His health was never very good. He outlived two dearly loved wives, both much younger than he was, who died in different but tragic ways. His own writing career was marked by anguish, fruitless effort, and, I suspect, profound dissatisfaction with the work that he did manage to produce, though he would have denied that on his deathbed. But he was tougher than nails, and I never heard him complain about anything. (The closest he came, I think, was after the stroke that took his wife Judy-Lynn away at the age of 40 or so. "I don't have very good luck with my wives, do I, Bob?" is what he said.)

Of all the many deaths that have rocked our field in recent years, I think this one hits me the hardest. Some of those who have gone from us were greater writers than Lester—the names of Heinlein, Asimov, and Leiber jump instantly to mind, and I could extend the list—and many of them were my dear friends, besides. As I've noted, though, it wasn't Lester's writing, particularly, that won him his place in the s-f pantheon, and though he was my friend, I mourn his loss in a way that goes beyond, I guess, the way one mourns a friend's death. *Isaac* was my friend, and I was saddened to see him go. But what I felt on hearing of Lester's death was a sense not of friendship ended but of a family tie sundered. I'm not speaking metaphorically, here. Sure, the science-fiction world is a kind of goofy family, and we all bear a certain kind of kinship for one another. But my feelings for Lester went beyond metaphor. I was one of his sons; he was one of my fathers, with all the complexities and turbulence that such a relationship implies. And I suspect that I won't be the only one who says something like that in the tributes that his death will bring forth.

Campbell, Boucher, Gold

So I was giving out Hugos once again at the World SF Convention last year in Glasgow, and once again it was my pleasure to hand the Best Editor trophy to good old Gardner Dozois, the guiding figure of this sterling magazine, who was carrying off the shiny spaceship for the umpteenth time for his fine editorial work.

Asimov's Science Fiction is now close to twenty years old, and for most of that time, I think, it's been the dominant science-fiction magazine, the place where the creative action has been happening. It's my belief that in its run of nearly 250 issues so far it has published as much great science fiction as any s-f magazine that ever existed. (And I am somebody who has been paying close attention to s-f magazines for almost fifty years, and whose file of back issues goes back a quarter of a century beyond that. Please bear in mind also that I'm not an employee of the magazine or of the gigantic corporate octopus that owns it, simply a free-lance writer who does these columns once a month.) Gardner Dozois has been the editor of *Asimov's* for more than half the magazine's life. Since *Asimov's* is unquestionably one of the great s-f magazines of science-fiction history, shouldn't Gardner therefore be ranked one of the great s-f magazine editors?

Of course he should. Stories from *Asimov's* have carried off a preponderance of the Hugo and Nebula awards ever since Gardner began running the magazine, and have occupied much of the space in the annual Year's Best anthologies, even the ones that Gardner doesn't edit himself. An editor who systematically publishes a ton of great science-fiction stories every year, year after year, certainly should be considered a great s-f editor, right? And so he is, by all of you who keep giving him the Hugo practically every year.

But somehow I find that I just can't rank Gardner among the all-time greats, myself. I have no doubt that he deserves to be listed right at the pinnacle, but somebody else will have to draw up the list. I'm sorry, Gardner. It's a purely personal thing, for me. In my mind there have been only three great s-f magazine editors, and the list is forever closed, for me. Try as hard as I can, I can't make room in my soul for a fourth, even an editor as good as you are. I can't get beyond that imperishable triumvirate—John W. Campbell, Jr., Anthony Boucher, and Horace L. Gold.

Oh, there have been plenty of other important and distin-

[*Asimov's Science Fiction*, September 1996]

guished editors in the seventy-year history of magazine science fiction. Surely Hugo Gernsback, the grand inceptor of it all, was an important editor, and so was Sam Merwin, Jr. when he was running *Startling* and *Thrilling Wonder*, and Larry Shaw of *If* and then *Infinity*, and Robert W. Lowndes of the estimable *Future Science Fiction* and its companions; and such people as Frederik Pohl and Robert P. Mills and Lester del Rey and Ben Bova and Cele Goldsmith, among others, right up to Shawna McCarthy, Gardner's immediate predecessor at this magazine, all turned in memorable jobs as editors in their day. But for me, Campbell, Boucher, and Gold stand alone at the summit.

Why do I put them so far beyond the others—even beyond the formidable Gardner Dozois himself?

Well, for one thing, I was afraid of them.

I couldn't ever be afraid of Gardner. He's a jolly, lovable man, and the worst thing he could ever do to me, aside from sitting on me, would be to turn down one of my stories. I could survive that. (I have, as a matter of fact, though it hasn't been a frequent experience.) But Gardner could never turn to me and say, "I don't really think you have what it takes to be a science-fiction writer, Bob." He could never say, "Your entire life's work is nothing but a pile of second-hand bubblegum, Bob." He could never say, "Have you ever considered getting a paying job, Bob?"

Oh, I suppose he *could* say those things. But I'd know he was just horsing around. (What were my stories doing in so many of his anthologies, if they weren't any good?) And in any case it's too late in my career for Gardner, or anybody else, to utter The Words That Destroy.

I was twenty years old, though, when I first ventured into the lofty realm ruled by Messrs. Campbell, Boucher, and Gold. I was pretty confident, at least outwardly, that I had the right stuff, and that they would eventually make room in their magazines for me alongside the offerings of such folk as Theodore Sturgeon, Isaac Asimov, Fritz Leiber, and Alfred Bester. But I lived in fear of the moment when one of these titanic editors would hold up a manuscript of mine between forefinger and thumb and say, "What is this thing doing on my desk, you arrogant little pisher?"

That was forty years ago. I *was* an arrogant little pisher, and they were the three greatest science-fiction editors there had ever been, and when I dealt with them I felt like the merest peasant trying to get the attention of Zeus or Apollo or Poseidon. Do you understand, now, why

I have trouble putting a nice young guy like Gardner in the same category as those three?

John Campbell was Zeus. He was a big man, six feet tall and over 200 pounds, and he was the greatest s-f writer in the business before I even was born; and then, in 1937, when he was only 27 years old, he gave up free-lance writing to edit the magazine that then was called *Astounding Stories*, and now has become *Analog*. It was while editor of *Astounding* that this tough-minded, domineering man discovered such new s-f writers as Asimov, Heinlein, Sturgeon, van Vogt, and de Camp. The list of his regular writers comprises just about everybody of any importance in the history of science fiction between 1939 and 1952 except Ray Bradbury and Fred Pohl, neither of whom, somehow, ever saw eye to eye with John. For nearly everyone else, though, a sale to Campbell's *Astounding* was your ticket of admission to the club. You might be able to slip a story past any of the other editors, but in order to sell to Campbell you had to do it *right*. John was dogmatic the way potatoes are starchy: not only did he know what went into the making of a good s-f tale, he understood how the universe worked, and if your story violated the laws of the universe, why, he would tell you so, and you crept out of his office wondering why you had ever bothered learning how to type.

I was terrified of him. The first time I sold him a story, in 1955, I was so electrified by the notion of having done it that I couldn't sleep all night. A couple of years later, when I brought myself for the first time to call him "John," I thought I would be struck down by a thunderbolt on the spot. He was that awesome. I went on to sell him dozens more; but I was always amazed to find myself doing so. Even when I disagreed with him, and sometimes I did, I felt awe at the very idea that I could be so bold. (Isaac Asimov felt exactly the same way about John. You could look it up in Isaac's autobiography.)

By the time I began writing for John, he was already an editor in decline, though. His dogmas had fossilized around him, his quirks and prejudices had come to overwhelm his common sense, and his magazine was no longer the center of the action. Two writers whom he had helped to develop were, by the mid-1950s, stealing most of his thunder.

One was Anthony Boucher, the Apollo of my triumvirate—the most elegant and cultivated of men, a charming *litterateur* with a passionate love for cats, opera, detective stories, and the Roman Catholic Church. (I once sent him a story about an opera-loving priest who collaborates with a telepathic cat to solve a murder mystery. Tony was amused, but he didn't buy.) From 1949 to 1958 he was, in conjunction with J. Francis McComas, the founding editor of *The Magazine of Fantasy & Science Fiction*. Where the stolid engineering-oriented Campbell favored profound ideas of cosmic scope with a lesser emphasis on style and characterization, the more elfin Boucher inclined toward writing of greater literary distinction, graceful stories that often were playful or sly or touching. He took from Campbell a lot of writers who yearned to reach for more emotional scope in their work than Campbell felt comfortable with, or whose sometimes dark views of the world were at odds with Campbell's formidable optimism. Campbell had led science fiction away from its pulp-mag heritage; Boucher now drew it onward toward mainstream levels of literary attainment. His circle of writers, like Campbell's, struck me as an exclusive club that I yearned to join.

What I feared, when I showed a story of mine to John, was that he would tell me I couldn't think well enough for him. What I feared from Tony was that he would tell me I couldn't write well enough for him. Tony would never be unkind to anyone—it simply wasn't in his nature—but I knew that in his gentle way he could nevertheless be devastating by implication, and I dreaded it. But I sent him stories anyway, and he sent them back with kind little notes, and eventually, the month I turned 22, he bought one. I had become a member of the club. I sold him a second one a few months later, and then he retired from editing, to the great sorrow of us all. (He was only 57 when he died, ten years later, in 1968.)

And Poseidon, the thunderer? He was Horace Gold, who started *Galaxy* in 1950 and ran it until poor health forced him out about fifteen years later. Gold was a perfectionist—a brilliant, prickly, difficult man, who made you rewrite your stories a dozen times and then rewrote them himself anyway. He drove his writers crazy. In endless lengthy telephone conversations he turned their stories and their psyches inside out. Evidently seeing some talent in me, he appointed himself my conscience, and hammered away at every sign of laziness in my work, every bit of glibness and formula writing. The fact that I was selling stories all over town didn't matter much to him: he insisted that I work to my fullest potential in every line. What a thorn in my side he was! But how enormously valuable his goading was in helping me to reach the level of quality he knew I could attain.

Campbell, Boucher, Gold. Each in his own way helped to form me as a writer and to move me toward maturity as an adult, and so they hold a special place in my life. To me they will always be the great ones, off on Olympus by themselves. Sorry, Gardner. You're doing a top-notch job, and history will rank you with the best our field has ever produced. But no latter-day editor, no matter how good, can move in alongside those three in my mind.

Philip K. Dick: A Premature Memoir

I expected to outlive him, but not by this much. There always seemed to be something extravagant about the way he consumed his life-force: he was burning himself up too fast. It showed in his eyes. He looked at you in an intense and piercing way that seemed also to be warm and loving, as if he was thinking, *I understand exactly what kind of lunatic you are, and I forgive you for your madness and know that you forgive me for mine.* That's an exhausting way to look at someone. That's an exhausting way to be looked at.

We met for the first time at the World Science Fiction Convention that was held in Oakland, California in 1964. I think Phil lived in Oakland, then, or else Berkeley; I was still a New Yorker, though I would settle in Oakland myself a few years later. (I didn't have the faintest idea that any such move was in my future, and I would have scoffed at the very notion.) We had followed parallel paths in our careers—coming up through the penny-a-word pulp magazines, writing dozens of short stories a year, moving on to paperback original novels for advances of a thousand dollars apiece. Phil had been a couple of years ahead of me on the track, and so I had looked to him as a role model. The way to do it, I thought, was to sell a lot of clever little stories to *Future Science Fiction* and *Galaxy* and *Imagination*, and then to move up to Ace Double Novel Books, just as Phil Dick has done. And so I did, although the stories I was writing in those days were hardly to be compared to his: he was doing authentic Philip K. Dick fiction right from the start, while I was just turning out potboilers most of the time.

We liked each other immediately. He offered me some snuff. (He was into snuff back then. Perhaps it was just a passing thing with him, because I never saw him take snuff again, but he was offering it around pretty promiscuously at that convention.) He showed me how to sniff it, and I did, and I sneezed, and Phil smiled, as if to say, *Silverberg may be even faster than I am at knocking out a short story, but he doesn't know shit about sniffing snuff.* In his way he was a very competitive man. Then he turned to his wife of the moment—this was Anne, I think—and said, "There's someone here I want you to meet. This is the great science fiction writer Robert Silverberg."

The great science fiction writer Robert Silverberg. If someone were to introduce me that way now, well, okay, it would make some sense: I'm sitting in front of a six-foot shelf of awards and I can legitimately

[From *Philip K. Dick: The Last Testament*, by Gregg Rickman, 1985]

accept the notion that I hold a significant place in my field. But this
was 1964. Great? Not then, not by a long shot. I had written hundreds
of utterly forgettable stories, a dozen or so decent ones, and maybe
two or three that were really worthwhile. And then I had drifted right
out of science fiction (the first of my retirements) to do books on
archaeology and popular science. I couldn't tell whether Phil was
mocking me with that "great science fiction writer" line, or indicating
basic ignorance of the recent s-f field, or grossly misjudging me, or
just horsing around, or seeing something in my work that even I didn't
see. I still don't know. Perhaps it was all five things at once. God
knows he was capable of holding five or six more or less mutually
exclusive positions at the same time.

I don't think I was a great science fiction writer in 1964—I may
have been on the verge of becoming one, but back then I was still no
more than a competent journeyman pro—but Phil certainly was. He
had already done *Solar Lottery, The World Jones Made, Eye in the Sky*,
a hundred dazzling short stories, and of course *The Man in the High
Castle*. A great writer even then, no question of it. By "great" I mean
that he had virtually from the start pursued the task of setting his
unique vision of the universe on paper, and had done it in a unique
way that I found extraordinarily powerful. Each of us has a unique
vision of the universe, of course, but most of us aren't all that unique
when we write; the world is full of mediocre writers whose product is
dull gray sludge, all of it absolutely interchangeable in every aspect.
That mountain of sludge streaming from typewriters and word pro-
cessors all across the land is a Phildickian image; and he would have
written of it in a uniquely Phildickian way, easy enough to imitate but
not so easy to have invented. You had to be Phil Dick to have invented
that style, dense and fluid simultaneously, the perfect vehicle for
creating his gritty, maddening, wildly funny and tragic worlds.

We stayed in touch, though we were three thousand miles away
and met infrequently. Our career paths diverged. His life was full of
turbulence, and it affected his career; he never seemed to be able to
get off the penny-a-word treadmill, even when he moved up from
paperback originals to hardcover books. We had the same agent; I
asked about him often, and generally the news was that he was in
financial trouble, or having difficulty writing, or breaking up with a
wife, or some such thing. Yet he seemed to remain outwardly cheerful,
no matter how dismal his circumstances became: stoicism, maybe, or
Zen discipline, or just a sense of cosmic irony, I suppose. Meanwhile
my own career was on a steady upcurve. I was back in science fiction,

I was hitting my artistic stride at last, I was doing the work that established my name and obliterated the memory of all those potboilers. I was also, not incidentally, making a goodly lot of money and living the good life, mansion in the finest part of New York, trips to Europe and the Caribbean every year, and so on and so forth. Phil knew all that, and—exaggeration being intrinsic to the Phildickian style—began treating me as though I had the wealth of Onassis. Not only was I a "great science fiction writer"—and now there was some evidence that I really might be—but I was, if you could believe Phil, making hundreds of thousands of dollars a year and sitting on an investment portfolio worth a couple of billion. He wanted to know my secret. "Clean living," I told him. He was never resentful or envious, exactly; I think he simply assumed I had better luck than he did, which in some ways was so. It seemed to him just one of the immutable conditions of the universe that his life was perpetually a mess and mine was in order. Even so, it was hard for us to maintain any kind of real human connection; he was uneasy with me now, and there was a ferocity to his playfulness that grew out of his own anguish. Not that he wished me any less success, but he wanted a little for himself. He was human. For years thereafter he looked toward me wistfully, as if I were cloaked in a nimbus of invulnerability that had been denied him.

But I am no more invulnerable than anyone else, and my share of anguish was coming. The splendid mansion burned in 1968, and when I saw Phil at the s-f convention in Berkeley that summer he was warm and sympathetic. Then I rebuilt the house and went on to a new pile of awards and glories, while he slipped into the deepest financial and emotional troubles of his life, and the contrasts became unbearable for him. So he played with me, in a tense and oddly hostile way, and we were both uncomfortable. In a letter announcing his fifth marriage he asked me to tell people to "send us money and treats and telegrams and other wonderful things that will please us and cause my blood pressure to fall. I feel at this time that it would be very sad for say you or...to be saying 'Gee, you know, if we had sent Phil and Tessa a lot of money, presents, gum, nylons, booze, back around April of 1973 he'd still be alive and writing, and it wouldn't be on our conscience what became of him when he realized no one cared shit about him any more.' I want to spare you that....Make checks payable to the PHILIP K. DICK RETIREMENT FUND and your cancelled check is your receipt because I hear Tessa calling me now to take out the garbage, so I won't be able to write again for a long time." Once we held a long public conversation in fractured Latin in the cocktail lounge of a convention hotel; it was wildly funny, but I would rather have been speaking English with him. I figured he was lost to me. He was a figure out of Gorki's *The Lower Depths* now, and I was moving in a gilded world of Diners Club cards and African safaris. But the wheel turned again; in 1977 I found myself on the shoals of a marital breakup; I wrote to Phil, who was such an expert on those matters, to tell him of my confusions and fears, and he replied with great love, saying "[I] started to cry and I drank what I had of tequila. Now I'm drinking coffee and shaking. Nobody ever was able to say anything to me when I was/have been where you are right now. Some people even said very cruel things, like, 'Well, Phil, how did you manage to fuck it up this time?' Everything hurt anyhow so it didn't make much difference....Here is a hug, and already I did pray, although I believe He knows our needs and will help. I'll keep in touch with you one way or another. Let me say, too: time does heal. It really does. It destroys, too, but it does heal." And afterward such contact as we had was untinged by the little edginess and uneasiness that had sprung up between us during his years of hardship.

Then at last he became successful in the way that the world understands the concept of success; and I think he grew calm within himself at last, though I had little contact with him in those final years; and then he died, at just the wrong moment. (There is a right moment for dying, but Phil hadn't reached it. He had earned, by thirty years of grinding work in dreary poverty, a few years of bright lights and big bucks. And he had earned, too, the chance to write whatever he wanted to write, without the necessity of bringing in androids and Ganymedean slime molds and robot taxis. Though I suspect he was a science fiction writer by innermost nature and would not have attained the greatness in mainstream fiction that he did in s-f, main-stream fiction was what he wanted to write, and in his late fifties he should have had the chance to return to it and see his work published. *Timothy Archer* was all he had time to do; there would have been others.) You may argue that it is better to die at the threshold of worldly success than to go on through it and discover its essential hollowness, but I'm not so sure. Some of that hollowness might have comforted Phil nicely in his later years. You may argue, too, that it is better to die at one's artistic peak than to outlive one's gifts or one's fame, and I suppose it is; but things are never as neat as that. Verdi wrote his greatest operas in his seventies, F. Scott Fitzgerald, after a decade of obscurity and failure, was halfway through what may have been his finest novel when he died, younger even than Phil.

I don't think Phil ever expected the sort of success that was eventually heading his way just when he died. I don't think he expected to live much past fifty, either. In a feverish self-consuming way he poured himself out onto paper and he ran through a confused and tempestuous life, and then he went away. I have no doubt at all that he was a great writer. As I said in a review of *A Scanner Darkly* seven or eight years ago, he may also have been a great man. Like many great men, he was both exhilarating and exhausting to be with. I think that comes through clearly in Gregg Rickman's marvelous and invaluable set of conversations with him. How splendid that those tapes exist and now have been published—so that we hear the very voice of Phil Dick speaking from beyond the grave like some character out of *Ubik*.

He is gone. We still have his books, and now we have these conversations as well. For that, at least, I can be very grateful—not only that I was fortunate enough to know that strange and remarkable man in some slight way, but that he left behind something of himself to which I can return again and again. I miss him keenly. But he is still here.

Philip K. Dick: The Short Fiction

It was the late spring of 1953, and I was eighteen years old and finishing my freshman year of college, and despite a heavy academic load I was writing a short story just about every other week in the hope that if I only wrote enough of the things, one of them eventually would be bought and published by a science-fiction magazine. My real ambition, which to the amazement of most of my friends and relatives I actually would achieve in another few years, was to sell a lot of stories, to see them published in every magazine of the era (*Amazing Stories, Fantastic, Astounding, Galaxy, Fantasy & Science Fiction, If, Future,* and all the rest) and be widely admired for my cleverness and productivity. But as of the late spring of 1953 I had nothing to show for these fantasies except a thick sheaf of rejection slips, and I would have been deliriously happy if just one, *one* of all my many stories could win editorial acceptance somewhere.

Meanwhile a couple of guys six or seven years older than I was were already living the very fantasy that was at the center of my feverish dreams. Coming out of nowhere, they suddenly were appearing on the contents pages of just about every science fiction magazine from the classiest to the pulpiest, turning out an astonishing stream of bright, lively, original short stories at a rate of one every two weeks or so. I admired and envied them both inordinately. One of them was Robert Sheckley and the other was Philip K. Dick. I know how prolific they were because I kept a little list of all their stories, by way of reminding myself of what it was possible to accomplish if only you were quick-witted enough and hard-working enough and talented enough. Sheckley had six stories published in 1952—his first year—and followed them with twelve more in the first half of 1953. Dick announced himself with four in 1952 and published *seventeen* in the first six months of 1953, seven of them in June alone, on his way to a total of thirty that year.

I was paying attention to their feats. Boy, was I ever paying attention.

Sheckley and the even more prolific Dick were of special interest to me because my own ambitions revolved about quantity as well as quality. I wanted to be a good science-fiction writer, yes, but also I sensed in myself some peculiar quality of discipline or energy or simple manic fervor for writing that would permit me to be more than usually productive. Henry Kuttner, that great and now largely forgot-

[*Amazing Stories Anthology*, 1996]

ten s-f writer of the 1940s, was one of my idols, in part because Kuttner was so prolific that he found it necessary to use fifteen or twenty pseudonyms to conceal the full volume of his output. (And the quality of Kuttner's work did not seem to be impaired by the speed with which he turned it out.) Dick and Sheckley were Kuttneresque figures to me, versatile and inexhaustible. Their stories, too, seemed to me to show the influence of Kuttner's approach to writing fiction, which was another reason for my admiration. Kuttner's approach struck me as a very fine approach indeed, and anyone who employed Kuttner as a model was likely to find a sympathetic reader in me.

The dark side of being a swift and efficient writer who can write and sell a short story every week or two is that that very productivity engenders the suspicion that the work of such writers is glib or superficial, whereas the work of writers who labor interminably to produce a sparse and slender *oeuvre* often is regarded as profound mainly because of its rarity. This is as true outside the science-fiction world as within it, and many a prolific writer (Charles Dickens, William Shakespeare, John Updike, Joyce Carol Oates, Irwin Shaw) has had to struggle against that subtle unwillingness to accept the fact that some writers can perform consistently well at a fast pace of production.

I was, naturally, fascinated and thrilled by Dick's astonishing everywhere-at-once debut as a science-fiction writer. When an editorial blurb such as this accompanied one of his stories ("The Preserving Machine," in the June, 1953 *Fantasy & Science Fiction*, edited by Dick's friend and mentor Anthony Boucher) it was only too easy for me to drift into a pleasant adolescent daydream in which my name replaced Dick's as the subject of the encomium:

> "In November of 1951 Philip Dick sold his first story (to *F&SF*, we may add proudly), and within a very few months thereafter he had established himself as one of the most prolific new professionals in the field. By now he has appeared in almost every science fiction publication—and what's most surprising, in each case with stories exactly suited to the editorial tastes and needs of that particular publication: the editors of *Whizzing Star Patrol* and of the *Quaint Quality Quarterly* are in complete agreement upon Mr. Dick as a singular satisfactory contributor. Joining with them, we consider this latest Dick precisely *our* kind of story: gently witty, observant and pointed, with a striking new idea attractively blending science and fantasy."

But the sheer volume of Dick's early short fiction operated against him, too. Certainly there is a condescending tone to this 1956 review by the critic Damon Knight of Dick's first novel, *Solar Lottery*:

> "Philip K. Dick is that short story writer who for the past five years or so has kept popping up all over with a sort of unobtrusive and chameleonlike competence....Entering and leaving as he does by so many doors at once, Dick creates a blurred impression of pleasant, small literary gifts, coupled with a nearsighted canniness about the market—he writes the trivial, short, bland sort of story that amuses without exciting, is instantly saleable and instantly forgettable.
>
> "The surprise of a book like *Solar Lottery* from such an author is more than considerable."

Solar Lottery, as Knight goes on to demonstrate, was in fact a superb novel, so vividly told and inventively constructed that Knight was flabbergasted to find that the author of all those "trivial" stories had been capable of writing it:

> "Dick states his premises, shows you enough of his crowded complex world to give you your bearings—and then puts away his maps and charts for good. You are in the world of the bottle and the Quizmaster, the Hills and the legal assassins, and you see the living surface of it, not the bones....
>
> "Then there's the plottiness...each new development not merely startling—anybody can startle—but startling *and logically necessary*. This is architectural plotting, a rare and inhumanly difficult thing; and who in blazes ever expected Dick to turn up as one of the few masters of it?"

Who in blazes, indeed? Certainly not Damon Knight, who at least in 1956 was mysteriously unable to see the promise inherent in Dick's sparkling early stories or to recognize the technical storytelling skill that permitted Dick to turn those stories out with such speed. But within a couple of years, years in which the seemingly indefatigable Dick published novels with the same relentless rapidity as he had offered short stories—two books in 1957, three in 1958—even Knight found it necessary to concede that "at his intermittent best, Dick is still one of the most vital and honest working science fiction writers." Phil Dick would, of course, go on to produce a whole bookshelf of extraordinary novels—*The Man in the High Castle, Do Androids Dream of Electric Sheep, Ubik, The Three Stigmata of Palmer Eldritch, Martian Time-Slip*, and ever so many more—and by the time of his premature death in 1982 would be considered one of the great modern masters of the genre.

But let's keep the focus on those early stories, the ones that seemed to be winning Dick at the outset of his career a reputation for little more than facility and excessive willingness to please editors, rather than examining yet again the famous works of his later years.

Were they all as "trivial" and "bland" as Knight, taking his first critical look at Dick's work forty years ago, believed?

Consider "Impostor," one of the seven Dick stories of June, 1953. (It appeared in John W. Campbell's *Astounding Science Fiction*, the most highly regarded of the old science fiction magazines.) Spence Olham is the protagonist: a high-ranking weapons-research expert in an era not too far in the future when Earth is under attack by invaders from Alpha Centauri. Olham, wearily working to design some sort of device that will allow beleaguered Earth to strike back at the so far invincible outworlders, finds himself suddenly arrested by a security official who accuses him of being an alien spy. He tells the bewildered Olham that the invaders have infiltrated Earth's defensive bubble with a humanoid robot whose task it is to destroy a particular human being and take his place. "Inside the robot," Olham is told, "was a U-bomb. Our agent did not know how the bomb was to be detonated, but he conjectured that it might be by a particular spoken phrase, a certain group of words. The robot would live the life of the person he killed, entering into his usual activities, his job, his social life. He had been constructed to resemble that person. No one would know the difference....The person whom the robot was to impersonate was Spence Olham."

Olham is informed that he will be taken off to an isolation camp on the Moon, where he will be disassembled so that the bomb within him can be rendered harmless.

It's quite clear to Olham—who just a little while before has been discussing vacation plans with his wife—that some terrible mistake has been made. He knows that he isn't an alien humanoid robot; and we know it too, because Olham is the highly sympathetic and quite recognizably human character through whose viewpoint all this is being told. En route to the Moon he envisions the terrible fate in store for him: "There were men in the building, the demolition team, waiting to tear him to bits. They would rip him open, pull off his arms and legs, break him apart. When they found no bomb they would be surprised; they would know, but it would be too late."

Desperately the terrified Olham escapes from his captors when

they reach the Moon by pretending to be the very robot they suspect him of being and bluffing the security men into believing that
the bomb within him is about to go off. They flee in panic, and he
returns to Earth alone aboard the ship in which they had brought
him to the Moon. Olham contacts his wife and urges her to locate
the staff doctor of his weapons project, who will be able to conduct
tests proving that he is human. Tense chase scenes follow, as security officers pursue Olham into a forest near his home, where he has
gone hoping to find the actual alien robot aboard its crashed spaceship. The security men close in just as—to his great relief and ours—
he finds the wrecked ship. The robot, badly burned, is on board.
Olham has managed to demonstrate in the nick of time that he is
an authentic human being.

The security officers, apologetic now, are still congratulating
Olham on his miraculous last-minute escape from peril when one of
them, taking a close look at the charred robot, sees a bloody knife
sticking out of the "robot's" chest. What they had taken to be a robot
is in fact the murdered body of the real Spence Olham. And then—
Dick's stunningly economical final few lines:

> "This killed him," Nelson whispered. "My friend was
> killed with this." He looked at Olham. "You killed him with
> this and left him beside the ship."
>
> Olham was trembling. His teeth chattered. He looked
> from the knife to the body. "This can't be Olham," he said.
> His mind spun, everything was whirling. "Was I wrong?"
>
> He gaped.
>
> "But if that's Olham, then I must be—"
>
> He did not complete the sentence, only the first phrase.
> The blast was visible all the way to Alpha Centauri.

Dick's setup is marvelously elegant. Not only does the pitifully
misunderstood protagonist turn out to be the alien robot after all,
but the very words of stunned acknowledgment of the fact that he
utters are, in fact, the previously coded signal that will detonate the
bomb within him. In "Impostor" we see not only the first statement
of the overriding obsessional theme that would make Dick famous—
How can we trust our perceptions of reality?—but also his enormous
skill, here at virtually the beginning of his career, at putting a story
together.

This early mastery did not go unrecognized even then, despite
the uneasiness that Dick's prolificity caused in those first years in

critics like Damon Knight. Dick's "Impostor" of 1953 has turned up in a dozen or more anthologies or more over the years, beginning with Groff Conklin's *Science Fiction Terror Tales* in 1955, Edmund Crispin's *Best SF 2* the following year, and, among many others, a book called *The Metal Smile*, published in 1968 and edited by—yes, Damon Knight.

Among those who applauded Dick's work right at the outset and learned quickly to search the magazines for more of it was, as I have already said, the young Robert Silverberg. Like any number of would-be writers before me, I was then in the stage of ferociously studying How It Is Done, and the spectacular debut of Philip K. Dick (and also that of Robert Sheckley) in 1952—53 had caused me to give those two writers particular attention. Compare Ray Bradbury's remarks, written in 1948, about one of his own special literary heroes, Theodore Sturgeon: "Perhaps the best way I can tell you what I think of a Theodore Sturgeon story is to explain with what diligent interest, in the year 1940, I split every Sturgeon tale down the middle and fetched out its innards to see what made it function. At that time I had not sold one story, I was 20, I was feverish for the vast secrets of successful writers." What Bradbury was doing to Sturgeon's stories in 1940, I was doing to those of Dick and Sheckley thirteen years later. Sturgeon, by then, was too great a master for me to hope to equal, but there was some reason to think that I could, with enough study and practice, reach the level of accomplishment that these two bright new writers had managed to attain, and I studied each new story of Dick and Sheckley with infinite care.

Dick had caught my eye right away, before anyone knew how prolific he was going to be, with his very first story: "Beyond Lies the Wub," in the July, 1952 issue of *Planet Stories*. That magazine was the pulpiest of all the science-fiction pulps, famous in its time (and still cherished now by cognoscenti) because of the utter wildness and woolliness of the action-adventure space-opera stuff that it published. (Writers of the caliber of Sturgeon, Bradbury, Leigh Brackett, Isaac Asimov, and Poul Anderson loved to write for it. I wish it had lasted long enough for me to have had a chance.) Dick's "Beyond Lies the Wub" is the story of a spacegoing transport ship, one of whose crewmen has somehow acquired a huge pig-like Martian beast called a wub. Food starts to run short aboard the ship and the captain announces plans to have the wub butchered and served. But as he is telling the ship's cook to figure out how best to prepare it, the wub unexpectedly speaks up:

"I think we should have a talk," it says. "I'd like to discuss this with you, Captain, if I might. I can see that you and I do not agree on some basic issues."

The unexpected tone of wacky solemnity—in the pages of a magazine where aliens customarily were hideous fanged killers with beady eyes and glittering scales—told me instantly that I had found something unusual.

The captain feels that he has found something unusual, too. He beckons the wub into his office and they discuss the situation. The wub is telepathic and highly intelligent. "We are a very old race," it tells him. "Very old and very ponderous. It is difficult for us to move around. You can appreciate anything so slow and heavy would be at the mercy of more agile forms of life." The wub explains that it lives by eating plants, mostly. "We're very catholic. Tolerant, eclectic, catholic. We live and let live. That's how we've gotten along." It is aware that the captain wants to have it cooked, and it can quite understand his desire to do so. "You spoke of dining on me. The taste, I am told, is good. A little fatty, but tender. But how can any lasting contact be established between your people and mine if you resort to such barbaric attitudes? Eat me? Rather you should discuss questions with me, philosophy, the arts—"

This, in *Planet Stories*?

The debate goes on. The captain points out that the ship's food supplies are unfortunately quite low and the wub's meat is needed. The wub is sympathetic but unwilling; it suggests that everyone on board draw straws to see who is to be eaten. Which is not what the captain cares to do. Some philosophical discussion between the wub and the crewman who is its actual owner follows—"So you see," the wub says, "we have a common myth. Your mind contains many familiar myth symbols. Ishtar—Odysseus—" The conversation is interrupted by the captain, who still has his mind on food; in the end the outcome is unhappy for the wub, but Dick has a diabolical little sting at the end of his tale that implies that the unfortunate alien has had the last word after all.

A few months later came "Roog," in *Fantasy & Science Fiction*—the first story Dick had ever sold, though several others had reached print ahead of it. There were aliens in this one, too—roaming through a suburban neighborhood. The dogs spot them first:

"Roog!" the dog said. He rested his paws on the top of the fence and looked around him.

The Roog came running into the yard.

It was early morning, and the sun had not really come up yet. The air was cold and gray, and the walls of the house were damp with moisture. The dog opened his jaws a little as he watched, his big black paws clutching the wood of the fence.

The Roog stood by the open gate, looking into the yard. He was a small Roog, thin and white, on wobbly legs. The Roog blinked at the dog, and the dog showed his teeth.

"Roog!" he said again.

Unfortunately the dogs are the only ones who can see them. And, though they shout "Roog! Roog!" in increasing alarm, the dull-witted humans all about them simply wonder why the dogs are barking so much. So the invasion proceeds.

A singular mind was at work in these little stories. And the stories never struck me as bland or trivial in the least. Quickly I learned to look forward to each new story by Philip K. Dick.

And, as we all came to see, there would be plenty of them. Why was Dick so prolific? In part it was the sheer exuberance of his magnificent imagination that brought all those stories forth in such a great rush. He had read science fiction since he was a boy—a lonely, insecure, ill-adjusted boy—and his head teemed with the marvels that A.E. van Vogt, Henry Kuttner, Robert A. Heinlein, and the rest of the great writers of the so-called Golden Age of Science Fiction had put there. Now his own variations on their themes came flooding freely out. Once he had sold "Roog" to Anthony Boucher—a munificent $75, close to the top rate for science fiction in those days—Dick devoted himself with furious energy to writing. "I began to mail off stories to other s-f magazines," he recalled in 1968, "and lo and behold, *Planet Stories* bought a short story of mine. In a blaze of Faust-like fury I abruptly quit my job at the record shop, forgot my career in records, and began to write all the time. (How I did it, I don't yet know; I worked until four each morning.) Within the month after quitting my job I made a sale to *Astounding* (now called *Analog*) and *Galaxy*. They paid very well, and I knew that I would never give up trying to build my life around a science fiction career."

But of course those magazines *didn't* pay very well, except per-haps by the standards of the record-store clerk that Phil Dick had been when his writing career took off in 1953. The best that any writer could hope for from a science-fiction magazine, back then, was the three cents a word that the top magazines paid. Three cents a word for a story like "Impostor" is $180. Not bad, maybe, for a story written in two or three days, at a time when Dick could rent a small two-story house in Berkeley, California, for just $27.50 a month. But what about the stories that trailed off into incompletion, or the ones that no editor wanted to buy, or the ones that had to be sold to the bottom-rung magazines at half a cent a word payable on publication six months or a year after acceptance? It was, actually, a life of poverty that Dick had chosen for himself, a life of cheap ramshackle rented houses and ground horsemeat for dinner. Things grew better for him later on, but never very *much* better. The irony of Phil Dick's career is that the big movie sales, the international fame that came to him when *Blade Runner* and *Total Recall* were filmed from his work, the reissues of his novels in a dozen countries, the flood of income from a myriad sources, all happened after his death at the age of 54, thirteen years ago.

And so he wrote all those short stories, for love and for money, a great deal of love and not very much money. Then, exhausted by the need to come up with a brilliant story idea every few days, year in and year out, he turned to writing novels—for a thousand dollars each, in those days. It was a tough life. It wore him down and, I think, eventually it killed him.

The story that is reprinted here is one of a number that he sold to *Amazing Stories* during that early period of dazzling short-story production. *Amazing*, in 1953, had come out of a long period of dreary decline, transforming itself from a shabby pulp magazine to an elegant little slick publication with handsome cover paintings and color illustrations, then unheard of in a fiction magazine, inside. The old pulp *Amazing* had largely been staff-written by hacks; the new slick one featured material by the best science-fiction writers of the time, Robert Heinlein, Theodore Sturgeon, Ray Bradbury, Arthur C. Clarke, Henry Kuttner, Walter M. Miller, Jr. It was in the fourth of these slick *Amazings* that the name of Philip K. Dick appeared on the contents page, just below those of Kuttner and Miller, with a deft little piece called "The Commuter," and two issues later he was back again with this one.

How I stared at those beautiful issues of *Amazing Stories*, forty-odd years ago, and dreamed of being published in one myself some day! How I longed to follow the route of Philip K. Dick, seven years my senior, and find my own stories listed there along with those of his and Sheckley's and Kuttner's! With mounting pleasure—and, I admit it freely, no little envy—I watched the career of Philip K. Dick unfold from story to story and then blossom out into the novels that would win him his real fame; and later, much later, when my own career had begun in a way rather like Dick's, I came to meet him and to get to know him and count him among my friends. Our lives diverged eventually—his became increasingly dark and troubled, plagued by messy personal entanglements, money troubles, and steadily worsening health—and toward the end I felt little envy for him indeed, though my admiration for his work remained undimmed. He seems to me today one of the greatest of all science fiction writers, both in the short story form and as a novelist. His artistic influence is readily visible in the themes and approaches of many of today's most celebrated s-f writers, especially in book form. I think his superb short fiction is no longer as well known as it deserves to be, and I direct your attention to it wherever you can find it—starting right here.

James Tiptree, Jr.

The critic John Clute, in his introduction to the wonderful collection of stories by "James Tiptree, Jr." that Arkham House published in 1990 under the title of *Her Smoke Rose Up Forever* and which you should certainly buy immediately and read, because Tiptree was one of the great masters of modern science fiction, has this to say about a certain much-discussed introduction to a previous Tiptree collection that I wrote nearly two decades earlier:

> "In 1975, in his introduction to Tiptree's *Warm Worlds and Otherwise*, Robert Silverberg gave voice to a biocritical speculation about the author which has since become famous. 'It has been suggested that Tiptree is female,' he wrote, 'a theory that I find absurd, for there is to me something ineluctably masculine about Tiptree's writing.' Given human nature, it's unlikely many of Silverberg's readers could have failed to enjoy the discomfiture he must have felt in 1977 when Tiptree's identity was uncovered, and there is no denying that what he said was both inapposite in its self-assurance and culture-bound in its assumption that an artifact of language...was inherently sexed, so that only a biological male could utter it. This was surely careless of Silverberg."

What this is all about, for those who come in late, is the revelation in 1976 that the mysterious person who for the previous eight or nine years had been writing superb science fiction under the name of "James Tiptree, Jr."—and whose easy familiarity with such "masculine" matters as guns, airplanes, the interior workings of automobile engines, and the military/espionage world seemed to indicate that he was, as I put it in my celebrated introduction, "a man of 50 or 55, possibly unmarried, fond of outdoor life, restless in his everyday existence, a man who has seen much of the world and understands it well"—was, in fact, a 61-year-old retired psychologist named Alice B. Sheldon, very much female.

Well, I certainly looked silly, didn't I! But—contrary to my good friend John Clute's assertion—I felt very little 'discomfiture,' only surprise, and some degree of intellectual excitement. For what the Tiptree affair had done was to bring into focus the whole issue of whether such things as "masculine" and "feminine" fiction existed. This is what I had to say in an unabashed afterword to my Tiptree introduction when *Warm Worlds and Otherwise* was reissued four

[*Amazing Stories*, March 1993]

years after Alice Sheldon had confessed to being the author of those "ineluctably masculine" Tiptree stories:

> "Just before Christmas, 1976, came a letter in the familiar blue-ribbon typing, hesitantly confessing that 'Tiptree' is the pseudonym of Dr. Alice B. Sheldon, and hoping I would not be too upset about having gone so far out on a limb with my insistence on 'Tiptree's' maleness. Quite a surprise package....
>
> "Okay: no shame attaches. She fooled me beautifully, along with everyone else, and called into question the entire notion of what is 'masculine' or 'feminine' in fiction. I am still wrestling with that. What I have learned is that there are some women who can write about traditionally male topics more knowledgeably than most men, and that the truly superior artist can adopt whatever tone is appropriate to the material and bring it off. And I have learned—again, as if I needed one more lesson in it—that Things Are Seldom What They Seem. For these aspects of my education, Alli Sheldon, I thank you. And for much else."

I never met the woman who wrote the Tiptree stories, though as the editor of the *New Dimensions* series and other projects of the 1970s I published a number of her finest stories. We corresponded, on and off, for about fifteen years. Since "James" is a male name and the Tiptree stories were not only crisp, tough, conventionally "male" in voice but also indicated a much deeper knowledge of machinery and politics and the military world than many unquestionably male writers (Robert Silverberg, for instance) have, I had no reason to think that this reclusive, much-traveled, knowledgeable Tiptree person was anything but what "he" seemed to be.

Alli Sheldon herself, be it noted, *never* in any way claimed to be a man to any of her many correspondents. She simply never said she wasn't, and left us to draw our own conclusions. And occasionally dropped in an artful half-truth to keep us bamboozled.

For example, in a letter to me of June 8, 1974, she noted that I had written my last letter to her on the back of a piece of my wife's stationery, and so, she said, "I read the first part of your letter under the impression I was hearing from her. In fact, I shaved and applied lotion before continuing."

Very tricky. Men, of course, are not the only members of the human species who shave; but shaving is, nevertheless, an act that is more commonly associated with men than with women, perhaps because the part of the body that men customarily shave is more visible than the parts women shave.

But notice also that Tiptree talks about feeling that it would be appropriate *to shave and apply lotion* before continuing to read a letter that seemed to come from my wife, which could easily be construed as a macho male's amiable way of saying that he would want to look his best in the presence of such an attractive woman as he understood my wife to be. (In the same paragraph, though, "Tiptree" provided, if I had only had the wit to see it, a huge hint in the other direction. My wife in 1974 was not the Karen of modern times but Barbara, an electronics engineer with a training in physics, very much the prototype of the liberated woman; and Tiptree, citing Barbara's reputation as a formidable scientist who also happened to be female, said, "She is, if you want to know, one of my chief inducements to forsake anonymity, the other being U.K. Le Guin." I was free to interpret that as meaning that if Tiptree came out of hiding he would have the chance to meet those two remarkable women—something a man might very well want to do; but in hindsight it also appears to be saying that the success of those two women in attaining intellectual achievement and public acclaim despite the handicap of belonging to the "second sex" was almost inspiring enough for the author of the Tiptree stories to admit that she, too, was a woman.

I assume that Alli Sheldon felt she would somehow be at a disadvantage if she submitted her stories with a female by-line. In fact she was wrong about that: such women as Kate Wilhelm, Joanna Russ, Ursula Le Guin, Anne McCaffrey, and Marion Zimmer Bradley were already quite prominent in s-f when the first Tiptree stories began to appear. But also, I think, the masquerade in false whiskers was a kind of stimulating game to her, a facet of her complex, quirky personality. And certainly she carried it off brilliantly.

Eventually a Baltimore fan named Jeffrey D. Smith, through clever sleuthing, uncovered the Sheldon identity behind the Tiptree stories. In December, 1976, she admitted the truth to a small group of people like me whom she felt she might have offended by allowing them to persist in their error. ("Honour, or something, compels me to do something after which I fear I may have lost a deeply valued friend," she wrote me, and confessed the truth about herself, saying, "It hasn't been a put-on or attempt to take advantage, it just grew and grew until 'Tip' became me.") And when I replied that I was more amused than angered, she wrote back to say, "Thank God. Jesus with what trepidation I opened your letter....When I saw how thick it was I thought, Here it goes. Two pages of telling me what a shit I am; all gone forever.")

I suppose I *could* have been annoyed. She had seen my infamous introduction proving that she was male before it was published, and let it appear in print. (Her comment to me on it after reading the manuscript was, "Just read your intro for that Ballantine thing. Jesus god, man. I won't go on about looking over my shoulder to see who in hell he's *talking* about....The organization and clarity of the thing is a bit boggling. It conveys the picture of a mind so lucidly, effortlessly informed that on request it turns out indifferently a flawless essay on the lepidoptera of Mindanao or the political theories of Apollinaris Sidonius." Not a hint from Tiptree there that my lucid and well-informed mind was completely in error about the writer I was discussing.)

After all this time, one basic issue remains: Was Alice Sheldon/James Tiptree a writer who was so well informed about traditional man-stuff like guns and armies and machinery that she crossed the boundary that separates men's fiction from women's fiction, or is that boundary in fact nonexistent? As you form your own opinion, bear in mind that we are talking about a woman who was born in 1915, and that even in the world of the 1970s, not all that long ago, men were the ones who did most of the rough, tough things that Alli Sheldon wrote about with such apparent expertise. The lines have blurred since then; the stereotypes have begun to break down.

I *still* think that Ernest Hemingway wrote like a man and that Jane Austen like a woman, and that there are discernible differences both in style and in content. (Don't tell me about the yearnings toward androgyny that have surfaced in Hemingway's posthumously published work: he still sounds like a man to me.) So, the Tiptree episode notwithstanding, I suppose I still haven't fully learned my lesson.

In the very collection that I prefaced was the powerful feminist story "The Women Men Don't See." The title tells it all. I chose to interpret it as the work of a man with great insight into the difficulties women face in our culture. Stupid of me, in retrospect. I let myself be snookered by the first-person-male narration and forgot to listen to what was really being said.

Or consider, if you will, Tiptree's classic "Houston, Houston, Do You Read?," which was published after I wrote my introduction and won all the awards in sight. It's a superb story. The male sex has become extinct and the women are doing just fine by parthenogenesis, and then three men out of the past turn up out of a time-warp.

They act like boobs, generally. They can't help it, poor things: they're men, after all. And the cool, competent women of that future world know what to do with them. I like to believe that if I had been able to read that cruel, magnificent story before I had written that 1975 piece on Tiptree, I would have thought twice about proclaiming the "ineluctable masculinity" of its author. Maybe a man *could* have written "Houston, Houston." But certainly I don't think so. Am I in trouble all over again?

Roger and John

The deaths last summer of Roger Zelazny and John Brunner knocked two giant holes in the science-fiction firmament. They also caused me considerable personal sorrow. And, in an incidental way, the two deaths happened to provide a vivid illustration of the meaning of the word "tragedy" in its classical literary sense. For—as I'll explain in a moment—one death seems to me to have been truly tragic, and the other not tragic at all, but rather simply a damned shame.

Both men had had long and significant careers as writers; both met relatively early deaths. Zelazny, who died of cancer on June 14, 1995, was 58 years old. His first professionally published science-fiction story appeared in 1962. Brunner, who succumbed to a massive stroke at the World Science Fiction Convention in Glasgow, Scotland, on August 25—the first time, by the way, that a writer has died at a Worldcon—was 60. His earliest published work of science fiction, apparently, was the pseudonymous novel *Galactic Storm* by "Gill Hunt," which was issued in 1952, when he was only eighteen.

Of course the loss of these two great writers so much before their time was a lamentable thing for those who love science-fiction and fantasy, who revered their work, and who hoped yet to see further masterpieces from them; and of course I am among that group. But what struck me so particularly hard about these two events, only about ten weeks apart, was something much more private. The fact that both men were within a year or so of me in age, Roger a bit younger, John a few months older, naturally provided me with intimations of my own mortality. But—beyond that—I took their passing virtually as I would deaths in my own family. It is not simply the authors of *Lord of Light* and *Stand on Zanzibar* and *This Immortal* and *The Whole Man*, but Roger and John, that I mourn.

I have never had much of a family life. I had neither brothers nor sisters, and by choice I have had no children. My few actual relatives live on the other side of the continent from me and I have little contact with them. And so I have tended to turn the world of professional science-fiction writers and editors into a surrogate family for me. I have had, along the way, surrogate fathers like Lester del Rey, and surrogate uncles like Fred Pohl and Isaac Asimov and Harry Harrison, and surrogate brothers like Harlan Ellison and Joe Haldeman and Barry Malzberg and my agent, Ralph Vicinanza; and a few surrogate

[*Asimov's Science Fiction*, March 1996]

sisters also. I have a whole host of surrogate cousins and nieces and nephews as well. And so I regard my colleagues not as competitors or rivals whose successes threaten me, but rather as kinsmen for whom I have the warmest of affection. I cheer them when they win awards; I offer comfort when things go badly for them. When one of them seems to have done something annoying or irritating or foolish, as members of your family will invariably do, my reaction is always tempered by love. And when one of them dies—especially when the death comes well before it should—it is a harsh and sometimes devastating blow.

Roger and John were my friends for decades. I first met John at the World Science Fiction Convention in London in 1957, and Roger at the Cleveland convention nine years later. They were very different men and my friendships with them were different from each other in many ways, but in their different ways those friendships were strong and loving ones, and to have them ripped away from me so suddenly and so soon is a difficult thing to face.

I said above that their deaths, for me, illustrate the difference between a tragedy and a damned shame. Let me try to explain.

"Tragedy," in modern times, has become an overworked and even debased word. We read about the tragic outcome of a schoolyard brawl or some barroom quarrel, or about a tragic traffic accident, or the tragic failure of some team to win the championship that it seeks. We hear about the tragedy of Bosnia, the tragedy of the environment, the tragedy of AIDS, this tragedy and that one. These are all serious matters, and for the people directly involved they surely seem tragic indeed. But none of them is a classical tragedy in the literary sense, a tragedy in the way that the ancient Greek playwrights understood the meaning of the term.

To the Greeks, a tragedy was a very specific thing: the story of a man (or sometimes a woman) of great capability and attainment and ambition, who attempts great things and ultimately fails in his attempt, overreaching himself and losing all because of some inherent and fundamental flaw in his character. The very thing that drives him to his greatness will eventually and unavoidably bring him down. His downfall and defeat are instructive; and the onlookers, the audience at the drama, experience a catharsis, and go from the theater purged of the feelings of pity and fear by having vicariously lived through the tragedy of the hapless tragic protagonist.

One of the best known of tragic figures is Sophocles' Oedipus—a man of kingly bearing and nobility of soul, whose tragic flaw is his hot temper. En route to the city of Thebes, Oedipus becomes embroiled in a quarrel with a stranger at a crossroads, and kills him, unaware that the other man is in fact the father from whom he has long been separated, Laius, the king of Thebes. He continues on into the city, and in short order not only replaces Laius as king but marries Laius's widow, Queen Jocasta—again, unaware that she is his own mother.

The gods, appalled by the misdeeds of Oedipus, however unknowing they had been, send a plague down on Thebes. Angrily Oedipus vows to find out who is the villain responsible for the city's difficulties, and perseveres in this effort until he learns, to his own horror, that the man he must punish is himself. Whereupon he blinds himself and resigns his kingship, and goes forth as an outcast into the world, wandering in poverty until he attains the forgiveness of the gods and redemption many years later.

Or consider Agamemnon, the great leader of the Greek army that went off to make war against Troy. He is so proud, so utterly determined to achieve victory in the war, that he unhesitatingly sacrifices his own daughter Iphigenia when a soothsayer tells him that the girl must be slain in order for the Greeks to have success against the Trojans. In the modern world it is Iphigenia who might seem to be the tragic figure, but to the Greeks she was merely incidental to the story; it is mighty Agamemnon around whom the tragedy centers, for he will be brought down in the hour of his triumph years later upon his return to Greece, when his vengeful wife Clytemnestra murders him for having given their daughter up for sacrifice.

And then there is the demigod Prometheus, who looks down upon the hapless primitive race that is mankind, and takes pity upon them and, in contravention of the direct commandment of Zeus, teaches them the use of fire and the other arts of life. Prometheus, stubborn and rigid, implacably driven by the demands of his own conscience, sees himself as having no choice but to defy Zeus; but Zeus, the new and still insecure king of the gods, is equally implacable in his punishment of Prometheus' defiance, and chains him to a rock for all eternity, setting an eagle to pluck forever at his liver.

Shakespeare understood the nature of tragedy too. He gave us the lordly Macbeth, whose flaw was that he is unable to say no to his ferocious wife, and the valiant Othello, who is vulnerable only to whispered innuendos of his wife's infidelity, and the regal Lear, who foolishly thinks that his eldest daughters love him, and many another such tragic figure.

And what do Lear and Othello and Macbeth, Prometheus and Agamemnon and Oedipus, have to do with Roger and John?

This: that the life and death of one of these men fulfills the requirements of classical tragedy, and one does not. One lived a happy life, a man successful virtually from the start in all that he attempted and greatly beloved by all who knew him, and at a particularly joyous time of his life was cruelly picked off in a random way by a malevolent twitch of a few cells within his own body. His death was a sad thing, a great loss, a cause for lamentation—a damned shame. But the other man, after setting equally high goals for himself and attaining equally great things, was cast down from those heights midway through his days by circumstances partly of his own making, and found himself forced into a lonely, embittered existence that ultimately damaged his health and shortened his life. His fall from grace was truly tragic.

Roger was the happy man who led the happy life. He wanted from boyhood to be a writer; his poetry and fiction appeared in his school literary magazines, and often won prizes. By the time he was twenty-five he had begun what was to be a dazzling career in science-fiction, and within a year had published the astonishing novella "A Rose for Ecclesiastes," which brought him his first Hugo nomination, widespread acclaim, and a place in the definitive anthology *The Science Fiction Hall of Fame*. When the Nebula awards began in 1965, Roger, still only 28, won two the very first year, for the novella "He Who Shapes" and the novelet "The Doors of His Face, the Lamps of His Mouth." A year later he had his first Hugo, for the novel "....*And Call Me Conrad*," and a long string of further Hugos and Nebulas would follow, most recently the Hugo in 1986 for "24 Views of Mount Fuji" and in 1987 for "Permafrost." His novel *Damnation Alley* became a movie; his lengthy "Amber" fantasy series has had enormous popularity with readers since its inception in 1970.

His personal life was just as serene a succession of triumphs. After a brief early marriage about which he rarely spoke, he married Judy Callahan in 1966. The marriage, which produced three wonderful children, always struck me as enviably stable and happy; and when, to my great surprise, Roger and Judy separated a few years ago, he settled into a new and obviously satisfying relationship with Jane Lindskold, whom he was planning to marry at the time of his death. In Santa Fe, New Mexico, where he had settled in 1975 in a lovely house overlooking the city, he had a close and supportive circle of friends, and wider circles of friendship beyond, for he was a gentle and charming man whom it was impossible to dislike. And then, suddenly, at the apogee of this admirable life, came the cancer that killed him within a year.

John, too, had had a fast start to his career. Prolific, energetic, he filled the science-fiction magazines of the late fifties and early sixties with superb stories by the dozens, and made an early mark in the novel with such titles as *Echo in the Skull* and *The Hundredth Millennium*. His early work was always competent and professional, and sometimes a good deal more than that; but when he was about thirty he found his mature voice, and gave us a string of significant books like *Squares of the City* and *The Whole Man*, and then in 1969 the huge and masterly *Stand on Zanzibar*, which brought him his first and only Hugo award. He seemed to build on that triumph in the years immediately following, with such important and well-received books as *The Jagged Orbit* and *The Sheep Look Up* and *The Shockwave Rider*, in which he invented the concept of computer viruses at a time— 1975—when the computer concept itself was still largely unfamiliar to most people. He was only about forty then; and it appeared that he was staking a claim for himself in the science-fiction world as a natural successor to the aging titans, Heinlein, Asimov, Clarke.

It was not to be. Something went wrong in John's life.

He was a more than usually complicated man—a prickly perfectionist, sometimes sharp-tongued, always certain of the correctness of the positions he took, generally (though not always) with good reason. As the critic Peter Nicholls aptly put it at the convention where John died, "John Brunner was a clever, generous, difficult man and not all that easy to love. The interesting thing is that so many of us did."

His manner—suave, aristocratic, erudite—bothered some people. His wit and brilliance often proved alienating. He had many friends, but in time he began to make enemies, too, and some of them were powerful ones. There were fellow writers who disliked him and did him disservices. He fell easily into friction with editors who displeased him or agents who failed to fulfill his high expectations.

Perhaps the critical moment of transition for John from successful writer to tragic figure—the true tragic overreaching that ultimately shattered him—was his decision, about 1975, to write a massive historical novel set in nineteenth-century America, a book called *The Great Steamboat Race*. It was a book of a type remote from anything he had done before and very much unlike anything that John's readership—the fans of *Stand on Zanzibar* and *The Sheep Look Up*—

were expecting. He worked on it for five terrible years, from 1976 to 1981, during which time the editor who had purchased the book and the agent who had arranged its sale both died. The effort cost John a prodigious amount of energy and undoubtedly weakened his health; and, because he did no other work during the time he was writing it, it became an enormous drain on his finances. Then the massive thing finally appeared, in February of 1983, and it failed utterly. It sank from sight and left no trace. He was never the same again. When he came to the U.S. in the summer of that year, as guest of honor at the Baltimore Worldcon, he seemed weary and shaken, and told me that most of his books were out of print and no publisher seemed interested in taking on his future work.

Another great blow fell in 1986, when his wife Marjorie died. She was considerably older than John, and had been failing for some time; but her death, nevertheless, had a shattering impact on him. I saw him on two occasions in Europe in the autumn of 1987; he was then only 53 years old, but he looked like an old man.

From then on all paths led downward for John. Marjorie's death caused problems for him that took him away from his writing for months at a time. His worsening health—he had a genetic predisposition toward hypertension and strokes—called for medications that interfered with his concentration, a terrible circular trap, further damaging a tottering career. He married again a few years ago, but the marriage was a troubled one. He began to seem like a lost soul, haunted, despondent. In an astonishingly sad convention speech a couple of years ago, he spoke openly of the collapse of his career and expressed the hope that some publisher might offer him proofreading work to do as a way of paying his bills. As I said in a eulogy I delivered for him at the convention where he died, his sudden death may have been a welcome release from an ever more difficult life. And yet—it was the final tragic twist—I understand that not long before he died John had resolved to embark on a major new novel, one that he hoped would restore his position in our field and replenish his depleted savings. In order to write it with a clear head, though, he had to stop taking the medicine that controlled his high blood pressure—a decision which surely must have been a contributing factor to his fatal stroke.

So we lost two of our finest writers almost simultaneously last summer, and I lost two old friends, and we were provided with a sorry literary lesson in the meaning of tragedy to boot. John Brunner's long sad decline from his early greatness, marked as it was by bad choices and bad luck and bad health and culminating finally in the thunder-bolt from the jeering gods that brought him down at a science-fiction convention, is as close to a true classic tragedy as we can have in this godless age. Whereas Roger Zelazny, happy all the way, was by a bitter irony interrupted prematurely in the serene progression of his sunny life—a melancholy thing, greatly to be regretted; but (as Roger him-self, a student of classical drama, would surely agree) nothing that Sophocles or Shakespeare could have used as the substance of a great play.

Zelazny: This Immortal

Near the back of the August, 1962 issue of *Fantastic*, a minor science fiction magazine that has been defunct for many years, there appeared a two-page story by an unknown author that began with these startling paragraphs:

> When he was thunder in the hills the villagers lay dreaming harvest behind shutters. When he was an avalanche of steel the cattle began to low, mournfully, deeply, and children cried out in their sleep.
>
> He was an earthquake of hooves, his armor a dark tabletop of silver coins stolen from the stars, when the villagers awakened with fragments of strange dreams in their heads. They rushed to the windows and flung their shutters wide.
>
> And he entered the narrow streets, and no man saw the eyes behind his visor.

Vivid, immediate, idiosyncratic. "When he was thunder in the hills"—a bold use of metaphor in an era when such flamboyance had become unfashionable. "The villagers lay dreaming harvest"—an unusual syntactical choice, a small grammatical connective chopped away to great effect. "Silver coins stolen from the stars," "fragments of strange dreams in their heads"—an immediate touch of wonder and eeriness. "No man saw the eyes behind his visor"—romantic, melodramatic, instantly conjuring us into the world of Sir Lancelot or perhaps Scheherezade. The author's name was Roger Zelazny; he was twenty-five years old; in the first few lines of his first published story he had announced his presence and defined his method.

Now consider this opening passage from an equally brief story by the same new writer, *Passion Play*, published the same month in *Fantastic's* undistinguished companion magazine, *Amazing Stories*:

> At the end of the season of sorrows comes the time of rejoicing. Spring, like the hands of a well-oiled clock, noiselessly indicates the time. The average days of dimness and moisture decrease steadily in number, and those of brilliance and cool begin to enter the calendar again. And it is good that the wet times are behind us, for they rust and corrode our machinery: they require the most intense standards of hygiene.

A different manner, this: cooler, more controlled, much less given to rhetorical flourish. There are no overt metaphors, and the one

[Introduction to the Easton Press edition, 1986]

simile ("Spring, like the hands of a well-oiled clock," has a certain schoolboy earnestness about it.) Yet notice the measured power and subtle scansion of that opening sentence, "At the end of the season of sorrows comes the time of rejoicing." There is a medieval weight to the statement, "And it is good that the wet times are behind us," which is at once balanced and corrected by the remainder of the sentence, with its playful notion of proper "hygiene" for machinery. Anyone paying close attention to these two little stories—and I doubt that very many people did, other than Cele Goldsmith, the enterprising young editor who accepted them for publication—might well have suspected that they were receiving the first notice of the arrival on the scene of a master of the storytelling art and a master of prose technique. No one, I suspect, made that observation about Roger Zelazny in 1962.

But all through 1963 his work continued to appear in *Amazing* and *Fantastic*, gradually gathering some attention; and in November of that year he moved to the much more widely read *Magazine of Fantasy & Science Fiction* with the astonishing and powerful novella *A Rose for Ecclesiastes*. No one failed to notice that one. It was nominated for the Hugo award—the Nebula trophy had yet to come into being—and was quickly snapped up by several anthologists. A few years later, when the Science Fiction Writers of America nominated the best s-f short stories of all time for its Hall of Fame, *Ecclesiastes* was one of the twenty-six chosen—and the sole representative of what was then the modern era of science fiction. It might have been possible to overlook those remarkable but inconspicuous earlier stories; but after *A Rose for Ecclesiastes* there could be no doubt of the place Roger Zelazny was going to make for himself in the science-fiction world.

(Curiously, Zelazny revealed a decade later that *Ecclesiastes* was actually written a year or so *before* his first professional sales. Zelazny's friend Thomas Monteleone, in his 1973 University of Maryland M.A. Thesis on Zelazny's work, makes it known that Zelazny had been slow to offer the story for publication because he thought its scientific inaccuracies would draw embarrassing criticism. So it would appear that Zelazny's distinctive style and narrative methods were fully formed even in his early twenties.)

His progress in the years just following *Ecclesiastes* was astonishing. 1964—a year complicated by many personal misfortunes for the young writer—saw him publish a handful of minor stories and one major one (*The Graveyard Heart*); but 1965 began with the publication of his long and complex novella, *He Who Shapes*, and a few months later brought the impressive novelet, *The Doors of His Face, the Lamps of His Mouth.* In that year the Science Fiction Writers of America first instituted the Nebula award, and Zelazny was voted two of the five trophies given out for 1965, one for *He Who Shapes* and the other for *The Doors of His Face.*

Doors also was a Hugo nominee, though it fell short of winning the award when the 1965 Hugos were handed out at the World Science Fiction Convention held in Cleveland in September, 1966. By way of consolation, though, Zelazny picked up a Hugo at that convention for another work—his third award-winner of the year. This was the novel—his first—that had been published in *Fantasy & Science Fiction* issues of October and November 1965 under the title of *...And Call me Conrad,* and reprinted in expanded form by Ace Books shortly afterward as *This Immortal.*

It was an awesome performance, this outburst of award-winners. Zelazny seemed to be everywhere at once, and never less than brilliant. I think no writer of the time, with the possible exception of the equally individual and gifted newcomer Samuel R. Delany, was discussed and analyzed with such intensity by his peers. No one with any sense thought of studying Zelazny's work with an eye toward imitating it, since his voice was so unmistakably his own that anyone adopting his method would manage to produce nothing more than pastiche, at best. But the propulsive manner of his storytelling and the vigor and gusto of his style were worth careful consideration by anyone who hoped to stay in the thick of things in that exciting, experimental time.

This Immortal, as its Hugo award indicates, received quick recognition. (It shared the award, actually, with Frank Herbert's *Dune*—and it is a measure of Zelazny's immense popularity with the audience at that early stage of his career that his book managed to achieve a tie with Herbert's already celebrated blockbuster.) The book had its flaws, hardly surprising when one considers that is was its author's first: but it had virtues, too, extraordinary ones. In the context of the science fiction of its period it was, in fact, a revolutionary work.

Algis Budrys, discussing it in the December, 1966 issue of *Galaxy,* quarreled somewhat with the novel's resolution. ("The immediate problem in the book—the relationship of Earth to Vega—is solved too neatly. It's perhaps fitting that a novel largely concerned with the Aegean view of life should solve its major complication with a god from a machine, but it's bad practice nevertheless.") But Budrys called the book "extremely interesting and undeniably important" all the same, praising its charm, its swiftness of pace, and in particular its optimistic outlook at a time when most young science-fiction writers were given to bleakness: "*This Immortal* is based on thoroughly understood, inexhaustible engagements with one's own grasp....[Conrad] seems to understand that disaster is Man's lot. He also understands that struggle is Man's lot, and so though he may rage at heaven, and go into a killing fit when he hears that an earthquake has killed his beloved, he keeps this event separate in his mind from his duty." Although Budrys referred to Zelazny's use of ancient myth as "actively regressive in a number of senses"—it foretold that hankering for bygone days among science-fiction readers and writers that eventually led to the 1980s boom in medieval fantasy—he distinguished *This Immortal* from several other much-acclaimed science fiction works of the day because of Zelazny's underlyingly positive approach to problem-solving.

Another significant critic of the day, Judith Merril, whose approach to science fiction was often intensely political, found the book not merely "regressive" but downright reactionary. "Zelazny's response to the common feeling of myth-loss," she wrote in the December, 1966 issue of *Fantasy & Science Fiction*, "is an attempt to refurbish the old forms of positing a devolutionary process (radiation-induced) in which the figures of ancient Greek mythology reappear 'naturally': not so much the new-wine-in-old-bottles of the usual old-myth-justification or sword-and-sorcery as an attempt to decant the old stuff into new ones." Thus she thought is was "an impressive disappointment: impressive for its poetry, its technical skill, its occasional philosophical insights and character asides; disappointing as a novel, both in conception and structure."

For all these harsh strictures, though, Merril did note the revolutionary nature of the style and treatment: "Alternately intensely-intimately-tender and tough-hard-boiled in mood, essentially introspective in tone, much more preoccupied with personal moralities and ethics than group mores or behavior, the treatment is very close to the Hammett-Chandler school—something rarely attempted and much less often realized, in any variety of s-f. And as was sometimes true of Hammet, and almost always of Chandler, the writing itself covers all varieties of excellence, from glib to superb."

Between them, these two contemporary reviews, I believe, go to the heart of the matter. Budrys singles out the staunch and unyielding willingness of the immortal Conrad Nomikos to grapple with any and all obstacles, never once retreating into depression or defeat; but such a world-view would be mere conventional pulp-magazine heroics but for the singular manner, now flip and now lyrical, in which Conrad's nature is communicated to us by the first-person narrative. We see Conrad not simply as a gallant Captain Future superman doing battle for Earth against the Vegan hordes, but as a complex, pragmatic, plausible human being: a superman, yes, but a likeable and realistic one. It is no small accomplishment to tell a Superman's story in the first person and make it sound even halfway plausible; and Zelazny, I would argue, goes rather more than halfway.

This Immortal, as Algis Budrys and Judith Merril pointed out in the year of its publication, falls something short of perfection as a novel. But perfection is not always a prerequisite to enjoyment, and in fact perfection of a certain kind—that of stony elegance—may sometimes interfere with enjoyment. Enjoyable is surely what *This Immortal* is. But its casual, offhand narrative tone, its cheerfully subliminal erudition (consider the cannibal chieftain who cites Joseph Conrad and J.G. Frazer virtually in the same breath), its lively and good-natured incorporation and recomposition of the cliches of pulp adventure fiction, make it an astonishing and refreshing deviation from the conventions of science fiction. Even the best science fiction: how staid, how ponderous, most of the classic novels of the field tend to sound, matched against Zelazny's breeziness! Only Alfred Bester, in his two great novels *The Demolished Man* and *The Stars My Destination*, and Robert A. Heinlein in some of his more unbuttoned first-person stories, have managed to approach the gusto of the Zelazny style. But they only approach it.

> *"You are a Kallikanzaros," she announced suddenly.*
> *I turned onto my left side and smiled through the darkness.*
> *"I left my hooves and my horns at the Office."*
> *"You've heard the story!"*
> *"The name is 'Nomikos.'*
> *I reached for her, found her.*
> *"Are you going to destroy the world this time around?"*
> *I laughed and drew her to me.*
> *"I'll think about it. If that's the way the Earth crumbles—"*

Off and running. And he never stops.

Harlan

I haven't updated any of the essays in this book, preferring instead to leave them in the context of their times, append the dates of original publication to each one, and assume that you will understand that over the course of ten or fifteen years things do change, magazines go out of business, people get older and eventually die. You can readily enough figure from the date on the next piece that its subject is no longer "a couple of years past 40," as I say he is here. But I do want to note that the number of his marriages now totals five, and the fifth marriage now, to the estimable Susan, has lasted longer than the first four put together. Practice makes perfect, I guess.

We met for the first time in the summer of 1953, at the World Science Fiction Convention, which was held at Philadelphia's Bellevue-Stratford Hotel. (Yes, the same hotel that went out of business in 1976 after the outbreak of a mysterious lethal blight among the American Legion. I wouldn't be at all surprised if some fan at *our* convention had salted the place with spores of the 23-Year Plague.) Our previous contacts had been by mail and telephone, but I had heard descriptions of him from a mutual friend, and I spotted him almost the instant I walked into the hotel. He was the little guy in the center of the crowd, doing all the talking and obviously holding his audience in the palm of his hand.

"Ellison?" I said. "Silverberg."

He said something snide out of the corner of his mouth, and a deep and strange friendship was born.

He was about nineteen, then, and lived in Cleveland. I was a trifle younger, and lived in Brooklyn. We were both fans, then, who published fanzines. Mine was dignified, quiet, and serious, full of sober articles on the history of science fiction. Harlan's magazine was gaudy, flamboyant, enormous, and raucous, with vociferous headlines calling attention to sensational exposes of the science fiction world's soft underbelly. ("The mad dogs have kneed us in the groin again" was a classic Ellisonism of the era.) By your fanzines ye shall know them, I guess; we were of very different personalities, and what we published reflected that. I suppose we really had only one important thing in common in 1953: a passionate desire to be writer. A science-fiction writer, specifically.

Two Ellison episodes of the 1953 convention remain clearly with

[*Fantasy & Science Fiction*, July 1977]

me after almost a quarter of a century. One occurred on the convention's last night. A certain obscure fan from New York had taken offense at some remarks of Harlan's, and had journeyed to Philadelphia that Monday for the purpose of "getting" him, bringing along a pair of brawny goons for support. The sinister-looking trio—leather jackets, slicked-back hair, all the totems of the teenage hood of the time—converged on Harlan in the lobby. Any sensible man would have vanished at once, or at least yelled for help. Harlan? Sensible? He stood his ground, snarled back at his much bigger adversaries in a nose-to-nose confrontation, and avoided mayhem through a display of sheer bravado. Which demonstrated one Ellison trait: physical courage to the verge of idiocy. Unlike many tough-talking types, Ellison is genuinely fearless. He wins some and he loses some—I can think of a couple that he lost spectacularly—but he never backs off.

The other significant incident took place at the banquet of that convention. The toastmaster (Robert Bloch? Isaac Asimov?) broke into the flow of routine banquet schticks with a special announcement of interest to anyone in the audience who knew Harlan Ellison. (And that was just about everyone, even though he'd been involved in the world of s-f fandom only a couple of years at that time.) Harlan, he said, working in collaboration with another gifted young fan named David Ish, had sold a short story called *Monkey Business* to Anthony Boucher's *Fantasy & Science Fiction*. A beaming Harlan rose to take a bow and the grand ballroom of the Bellevue-Stratford rang with applause. As a would-be writer myself, still waiting for that first letter of acceptance, I felt a certain tincture of envy mixed with my admiration. But the announcement was a bit premature. Harlan and Dave hadn't quite sold *Monkey Business* yet; they had merely *submitted* it. In due time Tony Boucher read it and rejected it, doubtless with great courtesy, but a courteous rejection is still something short of a sale. To Harlan's eager imagination it had seemed that a story so good was certain to be sold, and he had begun telling people that weekend that he *had* sold it. Which illustrates a second Ellison trait: a hunger for literary success so powerful that it dissolved the fine but vital distinction between fact and fantasy.

For a long time, all of Harlan's literary triumphs were of that same illusory nature. In December of 1953 he came to New York and visited me at Columbia University, where I was then a sophomore. My roommate was out of town, and he stayed with me at the one-room apartment I shared just off-campus. In a pizzeria on Amsterdam

Avenue we discussed our dreams of future professional success. In my case the future had already begun, for in the few months since the Bellevue-Stratford convention I had sold a couple of stories and even a novel, *Revolt on Alpha C.* Harlan, too, had "sold" a novel—a 27,000-word juvenile called *Starstone*, which, aided by a recommendation from Andre Norton, he had sold to the prestigious Gnome Press. Only it wasn't so. Harlan was anticipating reality again, and ultimately reality failed him.

He went back to Cleveland, and I didn't hear much from him for over a year. In such time as I could spare from my classes I pursued my writing career with sporadic success, getting a few more short stories published and a second novel rejected. In the spring of 1955 Harlan reappeared in New York, this time to stay. He rented a room on the floor below mine and set up a literary factory—desk, type-writer, paper clips, postage box, dictionary and other reference books, white typing paper, yellow second sheets, memo file, and all the other paraphernalia of our trade. Everything was fastidiously arranged, each item in its proper place. Another Ellison trait: he is neat. His private life may sometimes be a shambles, his schedule of obligations may be running seven months late, but his physical surroundings are always meticulous, even now when he lives in a sprawling Los Angeles house splendidly jammed with books, records, paintings, artifacts, and miscellaneous memorabilia.

The summer of 1955 was a long, hot, brutal one for Harlan. He took a job in a Times Square bookstore to cover his expenses, and spent his nights at the typewriter. But he didn't sell a thing. There was the famous time when he told me that he had a crime story "90% sold" to *Manhunt*—for so he had been told by an editor of that once-celebrated hard-boiled-fiction magazine. But in fact *Manhunt* never bothered to look at unagented manuscripts, and Harlan's story turned up in the mailbox the next day bearing a printed rejection slip. Getting the last 10% of that sale had been too much to manage.

A few weeks later Harlan swaggered into my room and proudly declared, "You'll be pleased to know that I hit Campbell today, Bob." I had an immediate vision of the towering John Campbell sagging to the floor of his office, blood spouting from his impressive nose, while a triumphant Harlan stood over him stomping the great editor's cigarette holder and nasal inhaler into ruin. But no: "to *hit*" an editor is or was writerese for selling him a story, and all Harlan meant was that he had just cracked the toughest and most demanding of science-fiction markets, *Astounding SF.* He hadn't, though.

So it went for him, one imaginary sale after another in a hellish summer of frustration and failure. That I was now selling stories at a nice clip did not improve Harlan's frame of mind, for our friendship always had a component of rivalry in it. When Randall Garrett moved to New York and settled in the apartment hotel where Harlan and I lived, he swiftly went into collaboration not with Harlan, the thwarted amateur, but with Silverberg, the successful new pro: another wound for Harlan to endure. Other s-f people, not writers but fans, also settled in what was fast becoming a kind of crazy commune on West 114th Street, and some of them treated Harlan's desperate boasts of imminent professional success with harsh contempt. The summer became a nightmare for him. Rejected by all editors, mocked and teased by his friends, he clung somehow to his goal and banged out an immense, bloated, preposterous novelet called *Crackpot Planet*. He sent it off to one of the upper-level magazines of the day, *If*, and then went back to Cleveland to visit his family.

Now I had read most of Harlan's stories that summer, and many of them seemed of full professional quality to me. There was one called *Glowworm* that struck me as a bit on the bombastic side but alive with vivid images and eerie intensity, and there was one called *Life Hutch* that I thought was an altogether tight and neat little puzzle story that wouldn't have disgraced the pages of John Campbell's *Astounding*. Those two had been rejected all over the place, and I couldn't understand why. But *Crackpot Planet* was, I felt, a true dog, an absurdity, a mess, and I told him so. Harlan shrugged. Not worth the postage to send it to a magazine, I said. He shrugged again. And went to Cleveland.

A couple of weeks passed. I checked his mailbox regularly, and forwarded anything of interest—rejection slips, mostly—to him. One day I looked in the box and there was a letter from *If*. They were buying *Crackpot Planet*, all 17,000 silly words of it.

I wasn't Harlan's first sale. By this time Larry Shaw had bought *Glowworm* for his new magazine, *Infinity*, and a sleazy yellow-journalism magazine had purchased a serious article Harlan had done on kid-gang life, distorting it out of all recognition when they published it. But those two sales had been to friends of Harlan's, and so perhaps were tainted by personal sympathies. The sale to *If* had been coldly professional: a story sent off to a strange editor in another city, an acceptance coming back. Harlan was in.

There was no stopping him after that. By the end of 1956, he was selling at least a story a week, and in the subsequent couple of decades he's never had much difficulty persuading editors to buy his wares. His early work was awkward and raw—a weird compound of Nelson Algren and Lester del Rey, in which he managed to absorb the worst features of each, meld them, add liberal dollops of Hemingway, Walt Whitman, Ed Earl Repp, and Edgar Allan Poe, and top off everything with a wild melange of malapropisms. (As of 1955 he wasn't sure of the difference between "decorum" and "décolleté.") But there was a core of throbbing excitement within all that verbal non-sense, and the inner power remained within him as the outer junk sloughed away with maturity. And so came the stories that won him his flotilla of Hugos—*Repent, Harlequin, The Beast That Shouted Love, I Have No Mouth*, and the rest—and so came the fiery, passionate essays, and the savage and eloquent contemporary fiction, the best of which you can find in his book *Love Ain't Nothing But Sex Misspelled.* Out of that cauldron of an imagination came such stuff as *Pretty Maggie Moneyeyes*, with that elegant last line that may be the best single moment in all of Ellison's thousands of stories. Out of it, too, came the novella *A Boy and His Dog*, which was submitted to me for *New Dimensions* circa 1969 and which I rejected with a two-page-sin-gle-spaced catalog of its faults, and which went on to win a Nebula and become a motion picture, and which I would reject all over again, maybe with a three-page letter, if it came to me tomorrow. Shows you how much *I* know.

But I don't really want to talk about Harlan's stories here. You can find the stories on your own; what you can't find, unless I give it to you, is such knowledge as this: I saved Harlan's life twice. (Blame him on me, folks.)

The first time was in 1955, and probably doesn't really count, because what I ostensibly saved him from was suicide, and Harlan is one of the least suicidal human beings I know. But he was deeply depressed—this was during the time of 90% sales and instant rejec-tion slips—and talked darkly of jumping out the window of his third-floor apartment. I was living down the hall. I nodded and indicated his bookcase. "Be sure to leave the door unlocked when you do it," I told him amiably. "You've got some stuff here I want to read." He shut the window.

In the summer of 1956, he and I attended the first Milford Science Fiction Writers' Conference, held at a ramshackle resort on the Delaware River not far from the homes of Damon Knight, Judith Merril, and James Blish, the organizers of the meeting. Most of the demigods of the field were there—Ted Sturgeon, Cyril Kornbluth, Phil

Klass, Kate MacLean, Fred Pohl, and who-all else—and we were by many years the youngest and most brash of the writers present. One sunny afternoon, while most of the demigods were discussing the problems demigods have, Harlan and I went down to the river for a swim. Boldly we set out from shore, and rapidly we found ourselves being swept toward Philadelphia or perhaps Cuba by an inexorable current. We began to struggle toward a sand flat midway across the river; and, as we swam, I glanced over at Harlan and saw that he was in very serious difficulties indeed.

Which was odd. Harlan is a short, compact man of considerable muscular strength. (I found that out a few years later, when I tried to duck him in a Seattle swimming pool and ended up under water myself.) I'm a head taller than Harlan, but I'm a slender and not notably brawny man. Why he was having so much trouble with the current that day, while I was making my way fairly easily in it, I don't understand. But he seemed to be at the end of his endurance. I looked toward shore and caught sight of Judith Merril and a few other workshoppers; I waved to them, trying to indicate we were in trouble, and they blithely waved back. (Perhaps they understood the message and were exercising the most effective form of literary criticism.) Since none of them budged toward the water, it was all up to me, so I swam toward Harlan, grabbed him somehow, and hauled him through the water until my feet were touching bottom. It was half an hour or so before he felt strong enough to leave the sand flat for the return journey. Later that day, some of the demigods soundly rebuked me for my heroism, but I have only occasionally regretted saving Harlan from drowning.

In the autumn of 1956 Harlan married, right before my very eyes. (I have attended three of his four wedding, missed the fourth only because I was out of the country, and I suppose will go on attending his weddings year after year until death do us part.) He and his bride settled on Manhattan's West Side in what was then a pleasantly old-fashioned apartment house and which probably by now is a pestilent tenement. I recall dropping in one Saturday morning to find a crater a yard wide in the kitchen wall: Harlan, in preparation for an African safari that never came about, had picked up an elephant gun at a bargain price, and, proudly waving it about, had blasted open the wall and nearly made himself a widower all in one glorious discharge.

Instead of going to Africa, Harlan went to Fort Dix. I know of no one, except perhaps myself, less capable of accepting the disciplines of the United States Army, but Harlan was drafted in 1957 and spent two years in the service, stationed mainly in Kentucky. For most of that time he was to the Army like unto a thorn in a lion's paw, a mariner in the belly of a whale, but the bewildered organization found no way of ridding itself of him, nor he of it, and he served a full tour of duty, managing somehow to produce two of his infrequent novels while in uniform.

We lost touch with each other for some years thereafter. He lived briefly in New York, drifted on to Chicago to work as a magazine editor, went from there to Hollywood. We saw each other only at science-fiction conventions or on his occasional business trips to New York. He was changing, growing up slowly and reluctantly but steadily, establishing himself as a writer in many fields, building a new life for himself in California. He had always been outspoken, energetic, vociferous, the center of attention in any group, a wonderful stand-up comic, a mimic, a song-and-dance man, but in the early years much of this extraordinary extroversion had been a mask for desperate insecurities, as though he believed that no one would be able to hit him if he were only fast enough and funny enough. During the California years, something new came into him, a sense of confidence, of acceptance of self, of new assurance, so that his hyperkinetic manner and his lunatic humor no longer seem like defenses, but merely his natural mode of communication. He still has his areas of insecurity, sure, but he knows that he has shaped precisely the life he wanted to shape, that in his world he is a star, that when he wakes in the dark hours of the morning and asks himself what he has accomplished he can give himself answers, and not depressing answers.

Harlan is a couple of years past 40 now. He lives on a ridge in the hills overlooking Los Angeles, in a house so crammed with fascinating objects that it is a work of art in itself, and he is a busy man, leaping from telephone to telephone as he oversees an intricate array of publishing projects, movie deals, lecture dates, and such. We see each other often, for the oddities of destiny have brought me to California too, and though our houses are 400 miles apart there is more contact between us than there was for some years when we both lived in New York. We are each other's yardstick, in a way, for we have had one another to watch, to study, to wonder at, for a quarter of a century, since late boyhood, and, having shared our fantasies of what we wanted our adult lives to be, we know exactly where we have achieved what we dreamed of achieving, and where we have gone beyond what we dared to dream, and where we have fallen short.

I could tell you much more. I could fill this magazine with Harlan stories. (So could anyone who has been around him for long, but I've been around him longer than anyone else.) I could tell you of Harlan and the Chinese waiter, Harlan and the birdbath, Harlan and the Winnemucca whorehouse; I could tell you of the time Harlan slew the nine-foot-tall paratrooper with a single glance, of the time he nearly caused a break in diplomatic relations between the United States and Brazil, of the time he almost provoked a famed New York restaurateur to drown him in a butt of ketchup. But soft: we are observed, and some of these stories ought not to be shared with utter strangers. Another occasion, perhaps, and I'll set them down for your delight.

Enough for now to say that he is a phenomenon, a wonder, and let that sum it up. If there were one more of him on this planet, the continuum itself would not be able to stand the strain of it. But how pale and drab the lives of many of us, myself certainly included, would have been, had there been one Harlan less.

Theodore Sturgeon

It was saddening to be around him the past ten years or so, because I felt that he had outlived his own talent and I didn't want to give him any hint that I felt that way. But I see now, looking back over the pattern of his life, that I wasn't entirely right. Even though he wrote very little fiction of consequence after 1962's *When You Care, When You Love*, even though he maneuvered his way through the remaining 23 years of his life with promissory notes, fancy dancing, and endless reiteration of potent insights that had turned into desperate cliches, those 23 years were not at all a waste. He was very much a presence, even as the helpless giant that he had become. As book reviewer, as lecturer, as patient and loving teacher of young writers, as inspirational figure casting a warm and benevolent aura, he managed to play a powerful and valuable role in the world of science fiction at large, even though those of us who saw him at close range knew that he had somehow lost his own way.

No question that he was a giant. He brought things to science fiction that had never been there before: eloquence, passion, a love for life, and a fiery poetry that found its natural expression in prose. When hardly more than a boy he scattered wondrous stories by the double handful through John Campbell's *Astounding* and *Unknown*, forty-odd years ago. *Microcosmic God* is the one that has had the most attention, but there were others. Then came the stories of the later 1940's, in which he wrestled with pulp-magazine formulas and came out the winner, and then, suddenly, at the beginning of the 1950's, he rose above the frameworks of magazine fiction entirely and out came that fantastic decade-long deluge, *The Dreaming Jewels* and *More Than Human* and *The Touch of Your Hand* and *Saucer of Loneliness* and *To Here and the Easel* and *A Way of Thinking* and *Granny Won't Knit* and *The Man Who Lost the Sea* and on and on—simply listing the titles brings back in me that exhausting, awesome, dizzying sense of the man's profligate productivity that I felt all during that decade.

And after that, nothing much: some fine short stories, but not as wondrous as those before, and not the novels that were locked somewhere within him. Eventually we realized that the work he had done in the forties and fifties was his work, and now it was done, and that was all there would be. Sturgeon the lecturer, Sturgeon the reviewer, was what we had now. Would that he had been able to practice what he preached; but what he preached was so awesome that

[*Locus*, June 1985]

no mortal could have lived up to it, and he was (though we didn't want to believe it) as riddled with flaws as the rest of us. He wrote wonderful singing joyous stories, a great many of them, and though I wish that there had been even more, I know we need to be grateful for the ones that exist. He was writing in six colors when everybody else was content in black-and-white; he gave us a full orchestra in symphonic splendor when all the rest were picking out their tunes on off-key spinets. Long ago, a very young Ray Bradbury compared the very young Sturgeon to a puckish troll lurking beneath a bridge, not a bad image. But I have another, out of Shakespeare. He was our Ariel. And if he had a little Caliban mixed into him, so much the better: Ariel could be insufferably ethereal now and then, whereas Caliban had some earthy virtues about him that could have benefited even an airy sprite.

In his quiet way he worked an immense transformation on science fiction. Now the process of measuring his full impact can begin.

Jack Vance: The Eyes of the Overworld and the Dying Earth

Of all the ephemeral science-fiction magazines that fluttered in and out of existence in the early 1950's—there must have been fifty of them, few surviving as long as twelve months—one of the most transient was Damon Knight's *Worlds Beyond*. It made its appearance in the late autumn of 1950, a small, neat-looking 25-cent magazine printed on rough pulp paper, published some excellent short stories, including several that have become standard anthology items, and expired with its third issue. Actually, it was virtually stillborn, for its owners, Hillman Publications, killed it a couple of weeks after the first issue was released, as soon as the preliminary sales figures had been received and found wanting. The second and third issues were distributed only because they were too far along in the production process to halt.

The first issue of *Worlds Beyond* offered many fine things—C.M. Kornbluth's *The Mindworm*, John D. MacDonald's *The Big Contest*, reprint of classic fantasies by Graham Greene, Philip Wylie, and Franz Kafka, and some short, trenchant book reviews by editor Knight, harbingers of his later brilliant critical essays. But for me, adolescent science-fiction reader with head buzzing with dreams of distant tomorrows, the most exciting thing of all was the advertisement on the back cover, blue type on yellow background, heralding a novel by Jack Vance called *The Dying Earth*:

> Time had worn out the sun, and earth was spinning toward eternal darkness. In the forests strange animals hid behind twisted trees, plotting death; in the cities men made constant revel and sought sorcery to cheat the dying world.
>
> In this dark and frenzied atmosphere Jack Vance has set his finest novel, *The Dying Earth*, a story of love and death and magic and the re-discovery of science. Through this time, fabulously far from now, wander men and women and artificial creatures from the vats, driven by fear, lust, and the ever-present need for escape.
>
> One episode from Jack Vance's astonishing novel is printed in this issue of *Worlds Beyond* under the title, *The Loom of Darkness*. If you enjoyed this excerpt, you won't want to miss *The Dying Earth*.

I found threefold joy in that announcement. For one thing, it

[*Introduction to the Gregg Press edition*, 1977]

promised an ambitious new series of original science-fiction novels in paperback format—after the Vance book would come Isaac Asimov's novel *Pebble in the Sky*—and that was heady news, for the infant American paperback industry had not yet gone in for science fiction in any significant way, and an increase in the skimpy supply of my favorite reading matter was something to greet with enthusiasm. (It may seem hard to believe today, but in 1950 each new s-f novel was an *event*.) Then, too, the far-future setting of *The Dying Earth* held a special attraction for me. One of the first works of science fiction I had discovered was H.G. Wells' *The Time Machine* (1895), and I had been so captured by the vision in that book's closing pages of the last days of earth, that forlorn snow-flecked beach under a black sky lit by a ghastly blood-red sun, that I had searched through all the science fiction I could find for comparably powerful glimpses of the eons yet to come. Olaf Stapledon had met that need in me, and H.P. Lovecraft, and Arthur C. Clarke, and still I remained insatiable for knowledge of the end of time, and this new novel seemed likely to feed that strange hunger. And, lastly, I rejoiced because the author was Jack Vance, for whose voluptuous prose and soaring imagination I had lately developed a strong affinity.

In 1950 Vance had been writing science fiction only a year or two longer than I had been reading it; we were both newcomers. His first published story, *The World-Thinker*, had appeared in the Summer 1945 issue of *Thrilling Wonder Stories*, a gaudy-looking pulp magazine that ultimately became far less tawdry than its outer semblance would lead one to think. Magazine science fiction in 1945 was pretty primitive stuff, by and large, and so too was *The World-Thinker*, a simple and melodramatic chase story; but yet there was a breadth of vision in it, a philosophical density, that set it apart from most of what was being published then, and the novice author's sense of color and image, his power to evoke mood and texture and sensory detail, was already as highly developed as that of anyone then writing science fiction, except perhaps C.L. Moore and Leigh Brackett. A brief autobiographical note appended to the story declared, "I am a somewhat taciturn merchant seaman, aged twenty-four. I admit only to birth in San Francisco, attendance at the University of California, interest in hot jazz, abstract physical science, Oriental languages, feminine psychology." The magazine's editor added that Vance had been in the Merchant Marine since 1940, was serving somewhere in the Pacific, and had been torpedoed twice since Pearl Harbor.

Over the next few years a dozen or so Vance stories appeared, most of them in *Thrilling Wonder Stories* and its equally lurid-looking companion, *Startling Stories*. There was nothing very memorable among them—nearly all were clever but repetitive and formularized tales of intrigues of one Magnus Ridolph, a rogue of the spaceways—but it was clear that a remarkable imagination was at work producing these trifles, for even the most minor story had its flash of extraordinary visual intensity and its moments of unexpected ingenuity. Would Vance ever produce anything more substantial, though? Finally, in the spring and summer of 1950, came two long and impressive Vance works. *Thrilling Wonder* offered the novella "New Bodies for Old," and a few months later *Startling* published his first novel-length story, "The Five Gold Bands." The first was a conventional adventure story in form, but the prose was rich with dazzling descriptive passages, sometimes to the point of purpleness, and the science-fiction inventions—the Chateau d'If, the Empyrean Tower, the technology of personality transplants—were brilliantly realized. "The Five Gold Bands" was even more conventional, a simple tale of interstellar treasure hunt, but it was made notable by its unflagging pace, the lively assortment of alien beings with which Vance has stocked it, and the light, sensitive style. Obviously 1950 was the year of Vance's coming of age as a writer, and *The Dying Earth* was a book I eagerly sought. The eleven-page slice published in the first number of *Worlds Beyond*, a delicate tale of wizardry and vengeance, whetted my appetite with its images of decay and decline, tumbled pillars, slumped pediments, crumbled inscriptions, the weary red sun looking down on the ancient cities of humanity.

"At your newsstand now," that back-cover ad in *Worlds Beyond* proclaimed, but where was the book? On the dark and snowy winter afternoons I searched the paperback racks of Brooklyn for it, but saw no sign of it or of any other Hillman Publications books. A second issue of *Worlds Beyond* appeared, still advertising *The Dying Earth*, and still the book was impossible to find. Eventually—it may have been the last week of 1950, or perhaps it was just after the turn of the year—a friend gave me a copy that he had bought somewhere. It was the first chaotic winter of the Korean War, and paper supplies were tight, distribution channels confused; Hillman Publications had killed its paperback line, like *Worlds Beyond*, almost at the moment of conception; only a few thousand copies of *The Dying Earth* had gone on sale, in scattered regions of the country. The book, a shabby little item printed on cheap paper, with a crude, blotchy cover, was from the day of publication one of the great rarities of American science fiction. I treasured my copy; I treasure it still.

And yet I found the book obscurely disappointing. It was not a novel, I quickly saw, but rather a story sequence, six loosely related tales set against a common background, with a few overlapping characters to provide continuity. (Mysteriously, the first two stories were reversed, so that the central character in the opening chapter was a woman who is not created until the second chapter. This defect, which I assume was the publisher's error, has been corrected in later editions.) The loose-jointed structure didn't trouble me unduly, although I would at that time have preferred a more orthodox pattern with the familiar magazine-serial format of beginning, middle, and resolution; but what disturbed me was the discovery that the book was not truly science fiction at all, but fantasy.

What I wanted, in my literal-minded way, was absolute revelation of the far future. Wells, in *The Time Machine*, had meticulously described the climatic and geological consequences of the heat-death of the sun; Stapledon, in *Last and First Men* (1930), has proposed an elaborate evolutionary progression for mankind over the next few million years. But Vance showed no such concern for scientific verisimilitude. A truly dying Earth would be a place of thin, sharp air, bleak shadows, bitter winds, and all humanity long since evolved beyond our comprehension or else vanished entirely. But, though there are some strange creatures in Vance's world, his protagonists are mainly humans much like ourselves, unaltered by the passing of the millennia. Here is Liane the Wayfarer:

> His brown hair waved softly, his features moved in charm and flexibility. He had golden-hazel eyes, large and beautiful, never still. He wore red leather shoes with curled tops, a suit of red and green, a green cloak, and a peaked hat with a red feather.

And here is the world Liane inhabits:

> There was a dark blue sky, an ancient sun....Nothing in sight, nothing of Earth was raw or harsh—the ground, the trees, the rock ledge protruding from the meadow; all these had been worked upon, smoothed, aged, mellowed. The light from the sun, though dim, was rich, and invested every object of the land, the rocks, the trees, the quiet grasses and flowers, with a sense of lore and ancient recollection. A hundred paces distant rose the mossy ruins of a long-tumbled castelry.

The stones were blackened now by lichens, by smoke, by age; grass grew rank through the rubble—the whole a weird picture in the long light of sunset.

Liane wears medieval garb; the narrative action of *The Dying Earth* is largely a series of encounters among sorcerers; ruined castles stand at the edge of meadows. This is not science fiction. It is a continuation of the work of Scheherazade by other hands, a *Thousand Nights and a Night* romance of never-never land. To Vance, the dying Earth is only a metaphor for decline, loss, decay, and, paradoxical though it may sound, also a return to a lost golden age, a simple and clean time of sparse population and unspoiled streams, of wizards and emperors, of absolute values and the clash of right and wrong. If I failed to appreciate *The Dying Earth* when I first encountered it, it was because I had asked it to be that which it was not. I admired the music of the prose and the elegance of the wit, the cunning of the characters and the subtlety of human interactions; but it was something other than science fiction, except maybe for the sequence titled "Ulan Dhor Ends a Dream," and science fiction of the narrowest sort was what I sought.

The first edition of *The Dying Earth* disappeared and became legendary almost at once; Hillman Publications turned to other things, and no more books came from it, not even the promised Asimov novel; and Vance, perhaps expecting nothing more from the publication of his first novel than he had received—that is, a small amount of cash, prestige in exceedingly limited quarters, and general obscurity—went on like a good professional to other projects. *Startling* and *Thrilling Wonder* remained congenial markets for him over the next few years, and his narrative skills grew ever more assured, his style more dazzling, his mastery of large forms more confident. Now he worked almost entirely in the novella and the novel, with such magazine stories as "Son of the Tree," "Planet of the Damned," "Abercrombie Station," "The Houses of Iszm," and the immense odyssey "Big Planet." In 1953 came a novel for young readers, *Vandals of the Void*, and the ephemeral paperback publication of his earliest long story, "The Five Gold Bands," as *The Space Pirate*. By 1956, when Ballantine Books issued what may be his supreme accomplishment in science fiction, the powerful novel *To Live Forever*, Vance's position in the front ranks of science fiction was manifest. He had achieved no great commercial success, for his work was too "special," increasingly more dependent on a resonantly archaic, mannered style and a cultivated formality of manner, to win much of a following among the casual readers of paperbacks, but it was cherished by connoisseurs, and his popularity with the science-fiction subculture known as "fandom" was considerable. His novella, "The Dragon Masters," which had much the flavor of *The Dying Earth*, brought him his first Hugo award when it was published in 1962. The same year *The Dying Earth* itself was reissued in paperback by Lancer Books as part of a "limited edition" series of classic reprints. This second edition would go through several printings in the 1960s.

That Vance would choose to set another novel in the actual world of *The Dying Earth* came as a surprise, however. Except for the early Magnus Ridolph stories he had never been a writer of sequels or linked series of stories,* nor were any of his novels related to any other by a common background as are, say, many of the books of Robert A. Heinlein or Poul Anderson. And *The Dying Earth* was fifteen years old, a work out of a distant era of Vance's career, when *The Magazine of Fantasy and Science Fiction* unexpectedly announced in its issue of November 1965 that it would begin publication the following month of the first of five novellas in the same setting as that celebrated book.

Over the next eight months the stories appeared, in this order;
"The Overworld," December 1965.
"The Mountains of Magnatz," February 1966.
"The Sorcerer Pharesm," April 1966.
"The Pilgrims," June 1966.
"The Manse of Iucounu," June 1966.

And later in 1966 the complete work was published in paperback form as *The Eyes of the Overworld* by Ace Books, the small but enterprising house that had previously brought out most of the fine adventure stories that Vance had written for *Startling* and *Thrilling Wonder* in the early 1950s. *The Eyes of the Overworld* included all five of the *Fantasy and Science Fiction* novellas plus a sixth, "Cil," that had not been used by the magazine. There were minor differences between the magazine versions and the book: the chapter known as "The Mountains of Magnatz" had been heavily and clumsily rewritten for the magazine to repair the damage done by the extraction of "Cil" from the fabric; small explanatory passages required by the magazine stories had combined two of Vance's chapters under one title, so that in fact the book had seven episodes all told.

The new book was not so much a sequel to *The Dying Earth* as a companion. None of the characters of *The Dying Earth* are to be found in *The Eyes of the Overworld*, though a few historical figures such as

---

* In recent years he has become quite fond of the multi-volume novel.

the sorcerer Phandaal are mentioned in both. There are references in *The Eyes of the Overworld* to some of the geographical features of *The Dying Earth*—the cities Kaiin and Azenomei, the Land of the Falling Wall, the River Scaum—but most of *The Eyes of the Overworld* takes place far beyond the Realm of Grand Motholam, in an entirely new series of strange places. The bizarre quasi-human creatures of *The Dying Earth*, the deodands and erbs and gids and such, do recur, and their presence among the fully human folk of the era is at last given some explanation; but mostly the world of *The Eyes of the Overworld* is created from new material. It is impossible to tell how the events of one book are related in time to those of the other, though the same feeble red sun illuminates both.

Structurally, too, the books are different. Both are episodic, but *The Dying Earth*'s six sections are virtually self-contained, each with its own protagonist. Characters recur from episode to episode—Turjan of Miir, Liane the Wayfarer, the synthetic girls T'sais and T'sain, the sorcerer Pandelume—but only occasionally do they interact across the boundaries of the episodes, and most of the chapters could have been published in any order without harm to the book's effect. Not so with *The Eyes of the Overworld*. Here all is told from the point of view of a single protagonist, a typically Vancian scamp named Cugel the Clever, and indeed *Cugel the Clever* appears to have been the author's original title for the book. The structure is that of the picaresque novel—the cunning rascal Cugel moves across a vast reach of the dying Earth, getting in and out of trouble as he goes—but the individual episodes are bound together by a theme as old as Homer (for Cugel is trying to get home). His task is defined, and the entire pattern of the novel made plain, in the opening sequence: Cugel overreaches himself by attempting a burglary at the manse of the magician Iucounu, is apprehended, and is sent by way of penance under compulsion on a difficult quest in a remote land. We know at once that Cugel will find that which Iucounu has ordered him to obtain, will undergo great hardship and tests of cleverness as he struggles to return to his homeland with it, and in the end will try to outsmart the magician and exact a vengeance for all he has suffered. Whereas *The Dying Earth* as a whole is plotless and subtle in form, *The Eyes of the Overworld* carries a rigid skeleton beneath its picaresque surface.

Where the books are one is in the texture of the world that encloses them. *The Eyes of the Overworld*, like *The Dying Earth*, is a covert fantasy of the medieval. The first few pages bristle with artifacts of the fourteenth century A.D.—a public fair with timbered booths, amulets and talismans, elixirs and charms, gargoyles, a gibbet, a pickled homunculus. Cugel, in his wanderings, eludes archers and swordsmen, halts at an inn where wine-drinking travelers gather to trade gossip by the fire, joins a band of pilgrims bound toward a holy shrine. This is not the glittering clickety-clack world of science-fiction gadgetry. We might expect to meet Robin Hood in it, or Merlin, or Godfrey and Saladin, Tancred and Clorinda, but never Buck Rogers or Captain Kirk. Mysterious monsters prowl the planet, yes, flesh-gobbling deodands and dread ghouls, but they are only the analogues of gryphons and basilisks; they are aspects of the past, not the future. Everything in the world of these two novels of the remote future is old and mellowed, as, indeed, would medieval Europe be if it had survived intact into our own time, which is essentially the fantasy that drives Vance's imagination in these books. A sickly red sun dangles in the sky, said to be soon to go out, but the author is only pretending to be writing about the end of time. His dying Earth is moribund because *from his viewpoint* it is ancient, buried in the past, although he would have us believe he writes of a time yet unborn.

It is a perilous world, where enemies lurk everywhere and strike almost at random, and the chief activities of its denizens are theft, incantation, and chicanery. Power is all. No one lives at peace here, for danger is constantly at hand. The stories, ingenious and seductive, are built almost entirely out of conflicts; the war of wits, the contests of sorcerers, the ferocious struggles of rival rogues; and while conflict has been a wellspring of fiction since at least *The Illiad* and *The Odyssey*, it also in this case reveals a singularly bleak world-view made more palatable only by the elegance of the prose in which it is set forth and the unfailing courtliness with which the murderous beings of the dying Earth address one another.

That courtliness is an essential part of Vance's style. Cugel, having battered a sinister cannibal into serving as his guide, urges the creature to hurry, saying, "Why do you delay? I hope to find a mountain hospice before the coming of dark. Your lagging and limping discommode me." And the deodand replies, "You should have considered this before you maimed me with a rock. After all, I do not accompany you of my own choice." It is not the traditional language of magazine science fiction. And in another scene, wherein Cugel cruelly destroys a sentient crustacean that had annoyed him, the courtly manner is even more pronounced. "Why did you treat me so?" the dying shell-man asks faintly. "For a prank you have taken my life, and I have no other." to which Cugel replies, "And thereby you will be prevented from further pranks. Notice, you have drenched me to the skin." A curse is pronounced upon him by his victim, and Cugel responds in a manner that any experienced reader would instantly identify as that of Jack Vance: "Malice is a quality to be deplored. I doubt the efficacy of your curse; nevertheless, you would be well-advised to clear the air of its odium and so regain my good opinion."

If the tone of such exchanges owes nothing to the pulp magazines in which Vance first found publication, the prose technique is equally alien to that of Messrs. Asimov, Heinlein, or Clarke. A privately published pamphlet of 1965, Richard Tiedman's *Jack Vance: Science Fiction Stylist*, the most perceptive essay yet written on this author, suggests John Ruskin, Clark Ashton Smith, and Lord Dunsany as the chief influences on Vance's prose style. Certainly there is much of the ornate, congested approach of Smith in the early Vance, and the deftness of Dunsany, and the passionate pre-Raphaelite purpleness of Ruskin, though Vance's characteristic restraint and coolness temper excess. The two Dying Earth novels provide an instructive lesson in the evolution of style, for the first is unabashedly romantic in a way that the second, written by a far more experienced and time-sombered man, is not. Consider this passage from *The Dying Earth:*

> The light came from an unknown source, from the air itself, as if leaking from the discrete atoms; every breath was luminous, the room floated full of invigorating glow. A great rug pelted the floor, a monster tabard woven of gold, brown, bronze, two tones of green, fuscous red and smalt blue. Beautiful works of human fashioning ranked the walls. In glorious array hung panels of rich woods, carved, chased, enameled; scenes of olden times painted on woven fiber; formulas of color, designed to convey emotion rather than reality. To one side hung plants of wood laid on with slabs of soapstone, malachite and jade in rectangular patterns, richly varied and subtle, with miniature flecks of cinnabar, rhodochrosite and coral for warmth. Beside was a section given to disks of luminous green, flickering and fluorescent with varying blue films and moving dots of scarlet and black. Here were representations of three hundred marvelous flowers, blooms of a forgotten age, no longer extant on waning Earth; there were as many star-burst patterns, rigidly conventionalized in form, but each of subtle distinction. All these are a multitude of other creations, selected from the best human fervor.

Vance has never lost his love of the feel and taste of colors, of the color of textures, and no book of his is without such passages of sensuous excess; but they have become more widely spaced in the narrative flow, and his raptures more qualified, as in this comparable passage from *The Eyes of the Overworld*:

> Cugel approached warily, but was encouraged by the signs of tidiness and good husbandry. In a park beside the pond stood a pavilion possibly intended for music, miming or declamation; surrounding the park were small narrow houses with high gables, the ridges of which were raised in decorative scallops. Opposite the pond was a larger building, with an ornate front of woven wood and enabled plaques of red, blue and yellow. Three tall gables served as its roof, the central ridge supporting an intricate carved panel, while those to either side bore a series of small spherical blue lamps. At the front was a wide pergola sheltering tables and an open space, all illuminated by red and green fire-fans. Here townsfolk took their ease, inhaling incense and drinking wine, while youths and maidens cavorted in an eccentric high-kicking dance, to the music of pipes and a concertina.

The Dying Earth is, possibly, the more sophisticated work technically; its rolling structure seems a more delicate mechanism than *The Eyes of the Overworld*'s neatly calculated symmetries. *Eyes* is a single unified construct, heading forward from its earliest pages toward an inevitable end and the inevitable final ironic twist; one admires the perfection of Vance's carpentry, but it seems a lesser achievement than the relaxed and flowing pattern of *The Dying Earth*, which more fully portrays an entire culture from a variety of points of view. Cugel the Clever is an appealing rogue, but one misses the innocence of some of *The Dying Earth*'s characters and the sublime skills of others.

Nevertheless the book is a worthy companion for the classic earlier novel: enormously entertaining, unfailingly ingenious, richly comic, a delightful fantasy now published in durable form for the first time. *The Dying Earth* has only recently attained hardcover publication for the first time too, albeit in a limited edition that may already be unobtainable. Taken together, they are two key works in the career of this extraordinary fantasist. Nor are they necessarily their author's last visits to the mysterious world of the reddened sun. Vance, now in his late fifties, is still an active writer and a sly one, much given to surprise. In the October 1974 issue of *The Magazine of Fantasy and*

Science Fiction he offered without preamble a new exploit of Cugel the Clever, "The Seventeen Virgins," unconnected in content with *The Eyes of the Overworld*. Since then, no more in that vein; but a new Dying Earth book may at this moment be in gestation. I suppose I could telephone Jack Vance, who is my neighbor here in California, and ask him of his plans for Cugel, but that would spoil the surprise, and, in any case, he would probably offer me only some cunning evasion. Like the sorcerers who inhabit the dying Earth, Vance is not one to tip his hand without good reason.

Jack Williamson

This is the opening paragraph of a science fiction story that was published in 1928:

The Metal Man stands in a dark, dusty corner of the Tyburn College Museum. Just who is responsible for the figure being moved there, or why it was done, I do not know. To the casual eye it looks to be merely an ordinary life-size statue. The visitor who gives it a closer view marvels at the minute perfection of the detail of hair and skin; at the silent tragedy in the set, determined expression and poise; and at the remarkable greenish cast of the metal of which it is composed, but, most of all, at the peculiar mark upon the chest. It is a six-sided blot, of a deep crimson hue, with the surface oddly granular and strange wavering lines radiating from it—lines of a lighter shade of red.

And this is the beginning of a story published in 1947:

Underhill was walking home from the office, because his wife had the car, the afternoon he first met the new mechanicals. His feet were following his usual diagonal path across a weedy vacant block—his wife usually had the car—and his preoccupied mind was rejecting various impossible ways to meet his notes at the Two Rivers bank, when a new wall stopped him.

The wall wasn't any common brick or stone, but something sleek and bright and strange. Underhill stared up at a long new building. He felt vaguely annoyed and surprised at this glittering obstruction—it certainly hadn't been here last week.

And the third story, which appeared in 1978, starts like this:

The office intercom grunted.

"Olaf?" It was Sakuma, head of Northcape Engineers. "Clients for you. A couple of motherworlders, pretty fresh to Medea. Want a research station built. I told 'em you could do it."

"Where?"

A silent second.

"Listen to 'em, anyhow," Sakuma said. "They're serious. Well funded. We've talked about the risks, and they're still determined. They want to see Farside—"

[*Amazing Stories*, November 1988]

Much of the stylistic history of modern science fiction is encapsulated in these three excerpts. The first story ("The Metal Man," *Amazing Stories*, December 1928) starts in a clear, quiet way, undramatic but suggesting wonders to come: rather British in tone. The second ("With Folded Hands") exemplified the slick, efficient style of the postwar *Astounding Science Fiction*, where it appeared in the July 1947 issue: strangeness dropped down in the commonplace world of bank loans and weedy lots. And the third ("Farside Station," written for Harlan Ellison's *Medea* anthology but first published in the November, 1978 *Isaac Asimov's Science Fiction Magazine*,) is very much up-to-date in manner, fast-paced and clipped.

Different as they are from one another, these lead paragraphs have two things in common. One is that they all get their stories moving quickly and encourage the reader to want to know what happens next. The other is that they all were written—over a fifty-year period—by Jack Williamson. Who is still at it today, a decade after his superb *Medea* story appeared, and whose sixtieth anniversary as a science fiction writer we commemorate with this issue of *Amazing Stories*.

Sixty years of first-class science fiction?

Consider that a while. Calvin Coolidge was President of the United States when Williamson's first story was published. Isaac Asimov was not quite nine years old. Roger Sheckley and Philip K. Dick had just been born. Robert Zelazny, Harlan Ellison, Algis Budrys, and Robert Silverberg were all still some years in the future. Radio was new; television was science-fiction; movies were silent. And Jack Williamson—born in Arizona, not yet a state of the Union in 1908— had just sold his first story.

Simply to plug away writing publishable fiction for sixty years would itself be an extraordinary record of persistence, even if the work were only mediocre. But when the Science Fiction Writers of America gave Jack Williamson its Grand Master trophy in 1975—the second such award to be given, Robert A. Heinlein having received the first—he was not being honored merely for endurance. Over the decades Williamson has created an astonishing body of classic science fiction. What reader has ever forgotten the rollicking *Legion of Space*, first published more than fifty years ago? The powerful, brooding werewolf story, *Darker Than You Think*, of 1940? The chilling masterpiece of the robot takeover, *With Folded Hands*, and its 1948 sequel, *The Humanoids*?

And so much more. The *Seetee* series, science fiction's first exploration of antimatter. The soaring, visionary *Starchild* books written in collaboration with Frederik Pohl. The great adventure story *Golden Blood*. And then, too, *The Reign of Wizardry, The Power of Blackness, Manseed, Lifeburst*—on and on and on. All of it written with vigor, power, constantly renewed inventiveness and insight. His writing has grown with the years. His work is always fresh, always new, always at the forefront of the field. No one could possibly have been able to tell that "Farside Station" in *Medea* was the work of a seventy-year-old writer. No one could possibly guess that the stories he will publish this year are the work of an eighty-year old. In the late 1970's, at a time when most s-f writers half his age were still clinging defiantly to their typewriters, Jack Williamson had already switched over to a word processor. He is the *youngest* sixty-year veteran anyone could imagine.

He doesn't *look* young, this tall, shy, gangling man who has spent his life under the Southwestern sun. You can see his years in the stoop of his shoulders, now, and in the folds and creases of his skin. But you need only spend ten minutes talking with Jack Williamson to feel the youthful openness of his restless, inquiring mind and the resilience of his indomitable spirit. And you need only read a few lines of any of his sixty years of science fiction and fantasy to know that you are in the presence of one of the world's great storytellers. He's a splendid writer and a warm, wonderful human being. It's been a privilege to know him and a delight to read him. He honors us by his presence in our midst. This Sixtieth Anniversary Jack Williamson *Amazing* is only a small token of acknowledgement for all that he has achieved.

City: Clifford D. Simak

He was a stocky, white-haired middlewestern newspaper editor when I knew him, a man of gentle mien with twinkling eyes and a warm smile and a calm, unpretentious manner. Since he tended to write stories set in the world he knew best, which was that of Wisconsin in the 1920s, it was easy to think of him primarily as a folksy, homespun kind of writer, science-fiction's own cracker-barrel philosopher. The ostensible setting of his fiction might be the eightieth century, or a parallel universe, or a strange world of some other galaxy, but somehow, in one way or another, it was always fundamentally Wisconsin in the 1920s there, a world of farmers and dogs and fishing-holes and rocking-chairs on the porch. And so it was all too convenient to categorize Clifford D. Simak's work as mere nostalgic rhapsodizing for a time of lost innocence— simple, gentle fiction by a simple, gentle man. *City*, his most highly regarded novel, is the best evidence I know that this is a vast oversimplification.

In understanding Simak, it might be useful to consider the career of another American writer with whom he has more than a little in common: Robert Frost. Frost celebrated the vanished world of rural New England in straightforward, unadorned, colloquial verse, telling apparently artless little tales of hired men and mended fences and crows shaking snow out of hemlock trees. Those who wanted to see in Frost's work only the cheery countrified affirmations of an American bumpkin-bard saw only that and nothing more, and for a long time he was popularly regarded by casual readers as a cheerful spinner of the sort of verse often found on greeting cards; but those who were willing to take a closer look at his poems discovered that behind the Currier-and-Ives surface lay a cold, clear-eyed vision of the fullness of life, realistic and uncompromising even unto the ultimate darkness and bleakness.

So too with Simak. He was, by my unvarying experience and that of his other colleagues, a genuinely good and kindly man, benevolent and lovable, a thoroughly *nice* person. (Frost, so I understand, was not quite as nice.) And he did, in his fiction, recapitulate again and again his woodsy boyhood world, so different from the one most of us have experienced. "We hunted and fished," he once wrote, "we ran coons at night, we had a long string of noble squirrel and coon dogs. I sometimes think that despite the fact my boyhood spanned part of the first and second decades of the twentieth century that I actually

[*Introduction to the Easton Press edition*, 1996]

lived in what amounted to the tail end of the pioneer days. I swam in the big hole in the creek, I rode toboggans down long hills, I went barefoot in the summer, I got out of bed at four o'clock in the morning during summer vacations to do the morning chores. For four years I rode a horse to high school—the orneriest old gray mare you ever saw, and yet I loved her and she, in her fashion, loved me. Which didn't mean she wouldn't kick me if she had a chance. And before high school I walked a mile and a half to a country school (one of those schools where the teacher taught everything from first grade through eighth.)"

Which didn't mean she wouldn't kick me if she had a chance. A little touch of country realism, that. Simak never is afraid to express sentiment, but he is no sentimentalist; the country boy learns early that life is real and life is earnest, and that after the rich crops of summer come the inevitable cold blasts of autumn's winds and the silence of the winter snows. Those who go to his fiction—the best of it, anyway—for bland reassurance are likely to come up against disturbing surprises. *City* is a prime case in point.

Simak was born in 1904 in Millville, Wisconsin, where his father, a native of a town near Prague, had built a log house and established a small farm. After high school he held a succession of miscellaneous jobs before joining a small-town newspaper, the Iron River *Reporter* of Iron River, Michigan, in 1929. Swiftly he rose to become its editor; then he moved along to Spencer, Iowa in 1932 to edit the Spencer *Reporter*, and when that paper was bought by a larger chain his employers moved him to a series of jobs as editorial troubleshooter for various small newspapers in North Dakota, Missouri, and Minnesota. Seeking greater journalistic challenges, in 1939 he found a job on the copy desk of the much larger Minneapolis *Star*, and he rose steadily through the paper's hierarchy until in 1949 he attained the post of news editor, a position he would hold until 1962, when he was named science editor of the Star and its companion paper, the Minneapolis *Tribune*.

Reading had been an important part of his life from his first years, and an early fascination with the science fiction of Jules Verne, H.G. Wells, and Edgar Rice Burroughs led him, by 1927, to become a regular reader of the pioneering science-fiction magazine, Hugo Gernsback's *Amazing Stories*. Like many science-fiction readers, he soon decided to try his hand at writing stories of his own as a part-time avocation. His first, "Cubes of Ganymede," was submitted early in 1931 to T. O'Conor Sloane, the scholarly octogenarian who had replaced Gernsback at the helm of *Amazing Stories*. Sloane accepted the story but somehow never notified Simak of the fact, nor did he get around to publishing it; evidently it languished forgotten in the magazine's files until 1935, at which time Sloane returned it as obsolete. It never did see print.

Simak had better luck with his second story, "World of the Red Sun," which Gernsback published in the December, 1931 issue of his new magazine, *Wonder Stories*. Over the next couple of years Simak wrote a handful of other stories for the primitive science-fiction magazines of the day. Those early stories were undistinguished items with names like "Hellhounds of the Cosmos" and "Mutiny on Mercury," but they displayed a considerable gift for science-fictional conceptualization and they were notable also for Simak's clear, precise, straightforward narrative style.

Even as a hobby, writing science fiction in that period was an unrewarding pastime: the magazines paid poorly and slowly, the editors were often capricious and limited in their tastes, the troubled circumstances of Depression-era publishing made it a matter of chance that any magazine would survive long enough to publish the material it had accepted. (And payment was generally made only on publication.) Simak drifted away from writing fiction and not until 1937, when the vigorous and iconoclastic John W. Campbell became editor of *Astounding Stories*, the most successful of the three existing magazines, did he return.

Simak found Campbell's uncompromising rationalism and his no-nonsense approach to the craft of fiction very much to his own taste. He became a frequent contributor to Campbell's retitled *Astounding Science Fiction* during that magazine's robust Golden Age, a period when Campbell was introducing such new writers as Robert A. Heinlein, Isaac Asimov, Theodore Sturgeon, L. Sprague de Camp, and A.E. van Vogt to his readers, creating an astonishing revolution in the nature of magazine science fiction.

Although, because his stories were relatively few and far between, Simak was never considered a first-magnitude star of Campbell's magazine in the same way as Heinlein or van Vogt, he nevertheless quickly became one of the most important members of the Campbellian circle of writers. He introduced himself to Campbell's readers with three short stories within five months, "Rule 18," "Hunger Death," and "Reunion on Ganymede." (An adolescent reader named Isaac Asimov didn't like "Rule 18," and wrote to Campbell to tell him so. When Asimov's letter was published in the magazine, Simak sent a letter to the teenager, politely asking him for further details of what he felt was wrong, so that he might improve his work. Asimov, amazed, re-read the story, discovered that he had misinterpreted Simak's subtly understated technique as incompetence, and apologized, thus starting a correspondence between the two that would last for many decades. As he entered into his own writing career, Asimov unashamedly and openly imitated Simak's literary approach.)

After those initial stories came a three-part serial, *Cosmic Engineers*, a space epic that blended the grandiose high-tech mode of such established *Astounding* favorites as E.E. Smith and Campbell himself with his own uncluttered and direct narrative approach. He followed it over the next five years with a group of competent but unspectacular stories at intervals of four to seven months, earning himself a solid place in the second rank of Campbell's contributors. The down-home manner of his writing and the resolutely unflamboyant nature of his themes, though, led his work to be consistently underestimated by the readers.

And so, when a short story called "City" appeared in the May 1944 *Astounding*, it was received in most quarters with indifference. The ho-hum opening lines—"Gramp Stevens sat in a lawn chair, feeling the warm, soft sunshine seep into his bones"—promised nothing more than amiable folksiness, and as the story unfolded, setting forth a prediction of a re-ruralized United States of the near future and making much use of phrases like "danged fool" and "that dadburned lawn mower," it seemed to deliver just that. Campbell's readers gave it a disappointing fourth place in their monthly review of the issue's contents.

But two months later came a sequel, "Huddling Place," that carried the premise of its predecessor into new and unsuspectedly somber territory, as Simak demonstrated that one of the consequences of the dismantling of American urban life would be a crushing sense of agoraphobia. "Huddling Place," when the ratings came in, finished in second place, behind the opening installment of Raymond F. Jones's powerful and popular novel, *Renaissance*. And when "Census," the third segment of what now was obviously going to be a continuing series, appeared in the September 1944 issue, it too finished a strong second behind another installment of *Renaissance*. Campbell's readership—in the main, a fastidious and knowledgeable group of sophisticated science-fiction readers—had quickly come to see that Simak had something special under way.

Four more stories followed at irregular intervals, until what had become known as the "City" series came to its apparent end in the December, 1947 *Astounding* with "Aesop." By then the series had traveled an immense distance from its deceptively underplayed opening, and Simak had unveiled a startling melange of robotics, immortality, extraterrestrial exploration, and parallel-world mysticism, all stemming in unforced sequence from his original premise of a decentralization of urban civilization. "Aesop" finished first in its issue's reader ratings, topping even the current installment of E.E. Smith's long-awaited novel, *Children of the Lens*.

The tale was told, or so it seemed, and that was that. In those days, when the concept of paperback books was just becoming established and science fiction in hardcover form was entirely the province of a few undercapitalized private presses, virtually all magazine science fiction—even the work of Heinlein and Asimov and Bradbury—was doomed to immediate oblivion, surviving only in the yellowing files of pulp-magazine collectors. When Simak unexpectedly added an epilog to the "City" series—"The Trouble with Ants," four years after the publication of "Aesop"—it was an event of interest mainly to those collectors. (The fact that the story appeared not in *Astounding* but in a mediocre contemporary, *Fantastic Adventures*, caused no little discussion at the time. Plainly Campbell had rejected the story—but why? Simak, questioned many years later about it, replied, "What I remember him writing was that he thought we had enough of the series. So I took him at his word. I never argue with an editor. He has a perfect right to turn down a story." But other writers, less kind-hearted than Simak or perhaps more knowledgeable about Campbell's philosophical quirks and prejudices, have speculated that the real reason for the rejection was Campbell's unwillingness to publish a story so barren of hope for Earth's human inhabitants. Passively handing the planet over to the ants would never have been an idea palatable to Campbell. Or perhaps Campbell felt that the story formed too inconclusive, as well as too bleak, a finale for the famous series. Simak may have felt that way too: two decades later he wrote a second epilog to the series, fittingly entitled "Epilog," as a contribution to a book of original stories by Campbell's regular authors that was published in Campbell's honor, a couple of years after the great editor's death in 1971. In it he explicitly resolved much that had been left unsaid at the completion of the original 1944-51 group of stories.)

City did not, of course, remain hidden in crumbling pulp-magazine pages forever. The private-press science-fiction publishers assiduously mined the classics of Campbell's *Astounding* all during the early 1950s, bringing forth Heinlein's "Future History" novels and Asimov's "Foundation" books and Smith's "Lensman" series and much else; and 1952 it was the turn of Simak's "City" stories, artfully assembled into chronicle form by means of a group of brief prologs by supposed canine editors of the ancient tales, and published by Gnome Press, one of the foremost specialist houses of the day. Many other editions have followed over the years, and *City* is generally considered to be one of the greatest science-fiction works of its era. (In 1953 it received the International Fantasy Award, the most significant science-fiction/fantasy literary award at that time, as the best science-fiction novel of the year, and it has been included in virtually everybody's hundred-greatest-science-fiction book list ever since.)

But is it, I wonder, really science fiction? Certainly it is no ultra-realistic "hard-science" novel. Simak attempts little in the way of extrapolative thinking, and such as there is has long since been rendered obsolete by events. His profound nostalgia for a vanished America led him, in the opening story, to show how the world of circa 1823 could be recreated by way of post-World War II technology—hydroponics, atomics, cheap private planes leading to a withering away of urban culture by the late twentieth century. That did not happen, nor is it likely to. He gives us, also, such oddities as an experimental starship essentially being designed and built by one man, and hints at the possibility of the heritability of acquired characteristics, something that surely he (and Campbell) knew was not merely an unorthodox scientific concept but a disreputable one.

No, I think Simak had something other than extrapolative prediction in mind. What he has given us is a poetic fantasy of an imaginary time that he must never seriously have expected literally to come to pass, a steadily deepening vision of an ever stranger future Earth. He is writing about the loss of community in a world altered by technology, and the strange manifestations of the communal spirit that might emerge once our present mechanistic society has been swept away by the forces we have set in motion. His folksy opening, Gramps and his "dadburned" lawn mower, widens and widens until a breathtaking personal vision of futurity is revealed, informed on every page by the deep compassion that was integral to Clifford D. Simak's character, but innately pessimistic as a view of humanity's future on Earth. *City* is no humanistic hymn to the enduring spirit and worth of the human race. Far from it.

"The series was written in a revulsion against mass killing and as a protest against war," Simak declared, many years afterward. "The series was also written as a sort of wish fulfillment. It was the creation of a world I thought there ought to be. It was filled with the gentleness and the kindness and the courage that I thought were needed in the world. And it was nostalgic because I was nostalgic for the old world we had lost and the world that would never be again....I made the dogs and robots the kind of people I would like to live with. And the vital point is this: That they must be dogs or robots, because people were not that kind of folks."

And so, surprisingly, it turns out that the literary masterpiece of this warm and good and loving man is basically an excursion into misanthropy—the quiet cry of someone who has lost patience with his own species. We see mankind—focused, for simplicity's sake, through the single family of the Websters—making a series of decisions, often disastrous ones, that cumulatively obliterate our history, our culture, everything familiar, and even, eventually, our ties to Earth itself, so that we abandon the planet to sentient dogs, to wise old robots, to mutant supermen, and—finally—to the ants.

"Desertion," which has been reprinted many times as a stand-alone story, is the key story here. It relies on what is essentially magic—the conversion of humans and even dogs at the flip of a switch into an unimaginably alien life-form—to make powerful points about the nature of humanity, of perception, and even the man/dog relationship. The dark, haunting final lines of that story—embedded as it is virtually at the center of the book—give the lie forever to the legend of Simak as a simple, artless celebrator of the epoch of the old swimming hole. There are certain flaws of execution in *City* that Simak would, I'm sure, gladly have acknowledged. But to pay much attention to them is to miss the point. *City* is a rich and powerful and disturbing novel, as well as a work of singular beauty and remarkable visionary power, the finest book of one of the greatest of the pioneering science-fiction writers of the Campbellian Golden Age.

FIVE

TODAY'S WORLD

The Power of Words: One

I worry a lot about matters of grammar, syntax, and linguistic evolution—
not a surprising preoccupation, for a writer. Herewith, to begin this section,
a sampling of a good many pieces I've done on the subject.

Warning: The material that follows contains words formerly considered to be unprintable. This column is rated X, or U, or PG, or something like that.

"Oh, shoot!" the little old lady cried, as she dropped one of the many parcels she was carrying. Gentleman of the old school that I am, I picked it up and handed it back to her.

"Oh, shoot!" the five-year-old boy in the park yelled, a couple of minutes later, as his San Francisco 49ers cap went sailing away in the autumn breeze. Somebody else's mother caught it as it rolled past her, dusted it off, and handed it back to him.

These two individuals of very different demographic groups would probably be surprised to learn that they were committing the act of *euphemism* in public, but that's exactly what they were doing. The little old lady may or may not have been aware—probably she was—that what she was really exclaiming was "Oh, shit!" in a form considered appropriate, once upon a time, for well-bred Americans, "shit" as an interjection being an expression of annoyance or disappointment, and "shoot" being the sanitized version of that disagreeable word. The five-year-old boy, most likely, had no idea that what he was saying had any meaning whatever, other than as a way to indicate annoyance, and he was not yet old enough to realize that a simple change of vowel would transform his innocent "Oh, shoot!" into something more bothersome to adult ears. Give him another year for that, I figure.

What power a single letter has! A harmless word can be rendered potent with the tiniest of shifts!

I came late to my understanding of "Oh, shoot!" because I grew up in New York City, a place where even fifty-odd years ago such nice-nelly euphemisms were looked upon as quaint, or, to be more accurate, contemptible. It wasn't until I had begun to mingle with well-bred folk from places like Illinois and Wisconsin and Ohio that I learned about that phrase, and even then I thought at first that it was just some curious regional mispronunciation.

I found out about a different single-letter euphemism during my

[*Asimov's Science Fiction*, November 1995]

very short career as a writer of Westerns for a pulp magazine called *Western Action* in 1956. I was so injudicious as to have a sheriff refer to the recently apprehended villain as "this here bastard." To my surprise it came out in print as "this here *bustard*."

A bustard is a large, impressive game bird related to the crane. A bastard is a child born out of wedlock. Puzzled by the change, I asked my editor, the amiable, scholarly Robert W. Lowndes, about it. He reminded me that *Western Action* and its sister pulp magazines were part of a large group of publications of which the best known and most profitable was *Archie Comics*. The readership of Archie was very young; and the publisher didn't want to offend the mothers of his readers by arousing the suspicion in them that he was publishing smut on the side. So vile words like "bastard" had to be replaced by "bustard" in the Western pulps to protect the integrity of the big moneymaker.

Is anyone fooled by these little changes? Of course not. Then why bother to make them? Because words are magical; words have incantatory power; and, as any practicing magician knows, it is necessary to get the incantation *absolutely right* if you want it to work. An error in a single syllable, nay, a single letter, will result in a nullification of the spell or even a completely unintended (and usually catastrophic) result.

So the nice old lady knows that no one will look askance at her for saying "Oh, shoot," but she'd certainly raise eyebrows if she used the underlying incantation instead. The publisher of Archie knew he was safe from outraged mothers if he shunned the horrifying "bastard" in favor of the virtually identical, but incomprehensible, "bustard." And so on. Our popular speech is full of such stuff. "Darn," "goldarn," "heck," "gee whiz," "holy gee," and "doggone" all came into being as expletives that skirted the powerful mojo contained in such words as "damn," "God damn," "hell," "Jesus," "Holy Jesus," and, apparently, "Dog on it." "Son of a gun!" or "S.O.B." soften the ferocious impact of "Son of a bitch!" Et cetera.

Of course, things are much rougher these days, languagewise, and new euphemisms have come into use as new unprintables get closer to print. "Asshole" is still considered to be something of a dangerous word, and until recently it never made it into newspapers and popular magazines even in expurgated form. But lately I've begun seeing it in the papers in the form of "a--hole," which looks as odd to me as "bustard," and which in no serious way conceals the underlying vulgarism. The a--hole is the part of the body that the shoot comes out of, I guess. (The cognate word "butthole" doesn't seem to be unprintable at all—there's some sort of, ah, musical group around here called the Butthole Surfers who get their unlikely and, I would think, obscene name in the paper all the time, and then, too, we have Beavis and Butthead, who have failed to attain the obscurity that they really ought to have.)

A curious use of hyphenated purification turned up in my local newspaper, the San Francisco *Chronicle*, in 1973, when a lengthy and abstruse French movie called "The Mother and the Whore" played here. San Francisco in the 1970s, as you may have heard, was not exactly as chaste as Dubuque, but nevertheless our delicate newspaper persisted in forcing the theater advertising this movie to refer to it, bewilderingly, as "The Mother and the W----" I suppose that if the local university had been doing a production of John Ford's classic seventeenth-century play, "'Tis Pity She's A Whore," it would have had the same treatment. (I've always regarded "whore" as rather a tony sort of word. In the schoolyards of Brooklyn when I was a boy we pronounced that word "hooer," and *hooer* has ever since seemed to me quite a shocking item, whereas *whore* is elegant, posh, the preferred drawing-room version of the term.)

Taboos, of course, come and go. As recently as 1948 Norman Mailer found it necessary to spell the familiar term for copulation as "fug" in his novel of World War II, *The Naked and the Dead*. A few years later James Jones, in his war novel, *From Here to Eternity*, was able to use the full four-letter form in all its awesome immensity. "Fuck" still isn't widely seen in newspaper copy, but it's pretty doggone ubiquitous everywhere else and whatever shock value it once had is goldarn well eroded by now. (Though I was startled to see, in Paris a couple of years ago, posters everywhere promoting a movie called "Fucking Bernard." The word is foreign to the French and not taboo there, but it was odd to see it all around town in letters a foot high, all the same. The movie will need some other title, I suspect, if it ever plays here, unless things are changing even faster than it currently seems.)

The magical powers of the "unprintable" words has long been fascinating to me. A quarter of a century ago I examined some of our little inconsistencies of usage in my novel *The World Inside*, which takes place in the year 2381, and in which a young historian ponders the oddities of our era, and particularly the restrictions that twentieth-century people placed on words, in this passage:

"A phrase leaps out of a supposedly serious twentieth-century work of social criticism: 'Among the most significant developments of the decade was the attainment of the freedom, at last, for the responsible writer to use such words as *fuck* and *cunt* where necessary in his work.' Can that have been so? Such importance placed on mere words? Jason pronounces the odd monosyllables aloud in his research cubicle: 'Fuck. Cunt. Fuck. Cunt. Fuck." They sound merely antiquated. Harmless, certainly. He tries the modern equivalents. 'Top. Slot. Top. Slot. Top.' No impact. How can words ever have held such inflammatory content that an apparently penetrating scholar would feel it worthwhile to celebrate their free public use? Jason is aware of his limitations as a historian when he runs into such things. He simply cannot comprehend the twentieth century's obsession with words. To insist on giving God a capital letter, as though He might be displeased to be called god! To suppress books for printing words like c--t and f--k and s--t!"

That novel of mine was serialized in *Galaxy*, one of the leading s-f magazines of the era, and the passage I have just quoted was printed without editorial objection, four-letter words and all, in the July, 1970 issue. Evidently my 24th-century historian's ruminations on the harmlessness of our ancient obscenities caused some static among the readership, though, because just a few months later *Galaxy* ran Robert A. Heinlein's novel *I Will Fear No Evil*, in which Heinlein, then 63 years old, allowed himself for the first time in his life to use a few of the formerly unprintable words right at the end of his book. The passage in question was a joyous and grateful hymn to the pleasures of love, and this is precisely how it appeared in the December, 1970 issue of *Galaxy*, only five months after my own meditation on verbal censorship:

> "Thank you, Roberto, for letting me welcome you into my body. It is good to touch— to f---, be f---ed."

Which is to be f---ed indeed. Oh, shoot, I thought, reading that in 1970: we have lost the battle already. But in fact the battle goes on and on, as taboos come and go. I'm not entirely sure which side I'm on myself any more, as former vile obscenities bubble on the lips of darling babes. I know how idiotic the verbal taboos are, and yet I am starting to regret the coarsening of taste that has come with our liberation almost as much as I would regret (and oppose!) an attempt to compel us to return to the hecks and goldarns and shoots of yesteryear. A complicated subject, by cracky!

The Power of Words: Two

A few months back I wrote about the power that "unprintable" words hold, even at a time when the taboos that make them unprintable are breaking down—how, even in this perhaps excessively liberated era, people still pay homage to the incantatory power of the terrible words by using such euphemisms as "shoot" in speech and "a--hole" or "f---" in print instead of coming right out and employing the actual and literal items.

I mentioned also my surprise, when visiting Paris a couple of years ago, at seeing conspicuous ads for a movie called "Fucking Bernard" on posters all over the city. That reminded me that words that are terribly shocking in one language often are totally innocuous in another. And now comes another reminder of the infinity of semantic distinctions on this small but complex planet, in the form of a piece in the New York *Times* about words that are taboo in Japanese newspapers and on Japanese TV. In this case, the taboo words aren't obscene, either here or in Japan: they are words that have come to be deemed insensitive to the feelings of the unfortunate—that is, words we would call "politically incorrect" to use. But the Japanese list has plenty of surprises for Americans, even after our own exposure over the past ten years or so to the well-meant but fuzzy-minded euphemisms of the political-correctness people.

For instance, according to the manual of 162 forbidden words issued by the giant TV Asahi network, "Research Materials on Word Usage," the word *mekura*, meaning "blind," must never be used. TV Asahi wants its newscasters to refer instead to a "person with seeing disability," which sounds like good old American political correctness jargon to me, except that this is one that I don't think is taboo even here. I don't know why the Japanese are so troubled about using "blind"—it strikes me as a useful and non-insulting one-word way of saying "person with seeing disability"—but perhaps the explanation lies in the metaphorical transformations that "blind" has acquired. My dictionary gives "without the sense of sight" as the primary meaning of *blind*, but when I get down to the secondary meanings, I discover "lacking in intellectual, moral, or spiritual perception," followed by "purposeless," and then by "acting without intelligence or conscious-ness," and so on down to "closed at one end," as in a "blind" alley.

I suppose that those who are hypersensitive to the feelings of others are troubled by the possibility that if we speak of Stevie

[*Asimov's Science Fiction*, June 1996]

Wonder or Helen Keller or Jorge Luis Borges, say, as "blind," we may appear to be calling them "lacking in intellectual, moral, or spiritual perception." Perhaps the same pejorative set of secondary meanings for "blind" obtains in Japanese as it does in English, though, because it seems to be a really offensive term in Japan these days. TV Asahi won't let anyone use the Japanese equivalent of "blind alley," either, and a rubber stamp, which the Japanese call a "blind stamp," has to be called "a seal placed without thinking" on the air. One Japanese talk show, Papepo TV, will actually superimpose the character that means "forbidden" over the face of any guest who utters a word that's on the proscribed list—visual as well as audible bleeping!

I'm not convinced that such niceties are really necessary, though I am willing to concede certain points to the politically correct—for example, that a word like "dumb," which has two meanings of which one is most uncomplimentary, isn't ideal for describing people with hearing disabilities. But in general I think they go too far in the direction of sensitivity, and the Japanese, evidently, have been going farther still.

We have been taught of late to speak of epileptic "seizures" instead of "fits," but in Japan even the word *tenkan*, which simply means "epilepsy," is now the target of criticism. The Japanese Epilepsy Association (which I suppose has another name for itself in Japanese) wants people to speak of "persons of paroxysmal cerebral problems" instead.

This particular euphemism has recently caused problems for a well-known Japanese science-fiction writer, Yasutaka Tsutsui, who wrote a story about thirty years ago in which a robot policeman ordered a driver out of his car after detecting erratic brain waves coming from him. When the story was reprinted last year in a language textbook, the epilepsy association complained that the incident might encourage the view that people with unusual brain waves—including epileptics—should be hospitalized. The offending passage was deleted from the textbook, and Tsutsui, declaring, "Fear rules in Japan!" vowed never to write again. "Cleansing literature won't improve understanding," he said.

TV Asahi's list of newly *verboten* words in Japan includes *hage*—"bald"—and *chibi*—"short"—and *busu*—"ugly woman"—and *kichigai*—"crazy." The usual politically-correct euphemisms must be employed instead—"mentally handicapped person," and such. *Urenokoru*, which means "unsold merchandise," can't be used because it's also a slang term for "unmarried woman." *Shizoku*, a term referring to the samurai class, is forbidden because it implies approval of the class system. And so forth, an ever-increasing list that quickly wins acceptance (superficially, at least) in fundamentally conformist Japan. Whether these pious circumlocutions have actually succeeded in getting anybody to think nicer thoughts about bald, short, ugly, blind, or involuntarily unmarried people is, of course, a different question, and I suspect you know what my answer to it would be.

A specifically Japanese verbal problem has to do with the group of people known as the *burakumin*, a low-prestige caste in officially classless Japan. The burakumin caste goes back hundreds of years, to a time when rigid class distinctions did in fact play a powerful role in Japanese society. It was created to include all those who engaged in "polluted" occupations—those who butchered animals or handled leather, for example, and beggars, and—well, entertainers, those vulgar folk who juggle or sing or write science-fiction for a living.

The caste system in Japan was formally abolished in the nineteenth century, and officially there are no such people as burakumin any more. In fact, though, the caste still exists at least in the minds of the Japanese. Because burakumin generally have low incomes and low educational levels, they are regarded with distaste by Japanese of the officially nonexistent higher castes, who sometimes go to the extent of hiring private investigators to determine whether their prospective mates might be tainted by burakumin blood. (Thus, since intermarriage between burakumin and Japanese of other classes is rare and burakumin have no one to marry but each other, the existence of the despised burakumin caste is permanently perpetuated.)

In the 1970s the burakumin themselves attacked this problem by urging that the term itself not be used—hoping, I suppose, to blend into Japanese society more effectively by eliminating all public reference to themselves. One result of this successful campaign was to proscribe, at least in formal usage, all sorts of peripheral burakumin-associated words. One can no longer use the word *eta*, an insulting term meaning "polluted," or *tosatsujo*, "slaughterhouse," because these might remind people of the burakumin. Thus, when a newscaster spoke of the drug violence turning American city streets into a "slaughterhouse," he was roundly rebuked. One does not speak of slaughterhouses; one speaks of "meat processing facilities," a term not as easily applied to the troubled neighborhoods of our land.

The burakumin have achieved their goal so thoroughly in the new politically-correct Japan that publishers and broadcasters now automatically suppress all use of their name. But the burakumin have discovered that disappearing totally from public discussion is not always a beneficial thing for downtrodden people. No word may be used in print or on the radio that suggests to people that such folk as burakumin ever existed, but that doesn't mean that their lot in Japanese society has gotten any better: unmentionable or not, they *still* remain a group whom members of more fortunate castes look down on. One example of this surfaced a couple of years ago when Michael Crichton's novel *Rising Sun* was translated into Japanese. A woman in Crichton's book, half black and half Japanese, speaking of herself as an outcast in Japan because she is of mixed race and has a deformed arm, compares herself with the lowly burakumin. The Japanese publisher, unwilling to use the dreadful word, edited the passage out—thereby, incidentally, glossing over the fact that the burakumin are still there, and still an oppressed class.

Thus the burakumin have learned an ironic lesson in the suppression of words: their own campaign has made them utterly invisible, to their own disadvantage. The ultimate paradoxical effect has been that the Buraku Liberation League, a group they founded to combat the discrimination against burakumin that still quietly goes on in Japan, was unable to advertise books calling attention to their plight because the books' own titles used the forbidden word that describes them. And when the same organization asked that the passage in the Crichton book be restored, the publisher refused.

Meanwhile, we over here in the science-fiction field blithely send our space explorers out to alien planets equipped with semantic converters that efficiently translate Earth-speech into Rigelian or Betelgeusean, and vice versa. Which is very convenient not only for the explorers but for the people who make up the stories about them, but I wonder just how easy it's going to be for the programmers who design those semantic converters to make them work properly. As we have learned in the era of political correctness, it's only too easy to give offense through the use of words that sound innocent to us but are scabrously offensive to somebody else. It'll probably be a good idea to equip those thought-converters with an automatic disclaimer phrase to begin every conversation—something like "Please forgive me if I inadvertently transgress against your verbal sensitivities." That may do the trick—except if we run up against a culture for whom asking forgiveness for unintended offenses is so mighty an insult that it calls for an immediate lethal response. Words are such mighty things that you never can tell that will happen when you begin unleashing them in all their terrible, if inadvertent, power.

Gourmet to Go

Words are the tools of my profession, just as scalpels and lasers are those of a surgeon, and chisels and saws are those of a carpenter. (Though I suppose carpenters are also using scalpels and lasers these days, and surgeons, probably, chisels and saws!) But one big difference between my profession and those others is that whereas a surgeon's tools, or a carpenter's, are safely stowed away in their containers when not in use, mine must be stored right out in public, where anybody at all can come along and blunt their cutting edge.

What I mean by that is that I have no exclusive rights to the words I use; and if other people choose to misuse one, in such a way that the misuse is eagerly picked up and accepted as correct usage by the population in general, I have lost the use of that word myself. I can no longer be certain, you see, that if I use it properly I will be properly understood.

Consider "fortuitous." It means *accidental*. It doesn't mean fortunate, or, at least, it didn't until a few years ago. "*Fortuitous*" and "fortunate" both have the same Latin ancestor, *fors*, which meant "luck." But two Latin derivations emerged from *fors*. One was *fortuitus*, meaning "accidental" or "casual," and the other was *fortunatus*, meaning "happy" or "lucky." But because the English word "fortuitous" somehow sounds grander and more erudite than "fortunate," people started, fifteen or twenty years ago, to use it to have the same meaning as the similar (but different) word.

Where does that leave me, the writer? Suppose I use "fortuitous" correctly, in its pure sense, and tell you that just as my hero and heroine were about to enter the hotel where they were to spend their long-postponed honeymoon, the fortuitous arrival of an old friend caused them to hesitate in the street just long enough to be squashed flat by a 500-pound safe that fell on them from a neighboring forty-story. "Fortuitous?" you say in wonder. "What's so god-damned fortuitous about that?" But of course it was—purely fortuitous as I understand the word. You happen to understand it differently; and, as a result, I can't use it at all any more.

Or consider this, from a recent scholarly article on Roman history I happened fortuitously to read yesterday:

> "With few exceptions, no Roman ruler ever failed as completely as did Gaius Messius Quintus Decius. This pen-

ultimate loser had been granted the title 'Traianus' by the
Roman Senate...."

Huh? *Penultimate* loser? Who was the ultimate one, then? "Penultimate" means *next-to-last*. The prefix pen in that word comes from the
Latin *paene*, "almost." Something *penultimate* is almost last the way a
peninsula is almost an island. But half-literate people who like their
words to make a big noise have decided that "penultimate" is simply
a more impressive way to say "ultimate," and I see it used that way all
the time. "Ultimate" isn't ultimate enough for them; so they intensify
their statement with the orotund "penultimate." Hapless educated
man that I am, I don't know which meaning to expect, the one that
stems from a comprehensible Latin root, or the new free-floating one.
Nor, if I use the word myself, can I expect my readers to understand
what I'm talking about. ("He fired his penultimate shot; and then he
fired the one after that." Come again, Silverberg?)

Or consider the word "gourmet." Comes from the French; means
"a lover of fine foods." (To be distinguished from *gourmand*, a French
word meaning "glutton.") Naturally Americans began almost immediately to confuse "gourmet" with "gourmand," as we so often do
with words we think sound alike. (Cf. "flaunt" and "flout.") But a
subtler process of linguistic corruption has been at work here, too.
First we turned "gourmet" into an adjective meaning "very fine," as
when we refer to a "gourmet" restaurant when we speak of one that
serves food that gourmets might like to eat, or "gourmet" food to
describe the food that gourmet restaurants serve. But now, I see, the
adjective has turned back into a noun in English—a noun that doesn't
mean, as it originally did, a consumer of fine food, but rather the food
itself. Just the other day I noticed a newspaper advertisement for a
shop that sells take-out food. "GOURMET TO GO," was the headline.
Took me a while to figure out what it meant. If I use "gourmet" in a
story now, how long will it take you to figure out what *I* mean?

But mine are only the problems of a mere peddler of pseudo-sci-
entific fables. Our society's contemporary habit of verbal imprecision
causes much greater difficulties when it is the vocabulary of science
that is getting messed around with. Science is a precise business.
Methods and results must be described accurately if they are to be
reproduced; and the reproducibility of results is essential to scientific
advance. Which is why scientists, when they can, use the language of
mathematics in discussing their work.

But for purposes of explaining their work to the public at large they are required to use the language of that public, modified by such new technical terms as are necessary. And that can lead to trouble, for using words in scientific discussions is something like using hedgehogs as croquet balls: words get up and move around as they please. Our society has the greatest velocity of concept-transmission in human history, and the faster a new concept moves from mind to mind, the more quickly it seems to become garbled and ceases to be available for its original functions, to everyone's great loss. Some cases in point:

Clone. In genetics, a clone is the collective term for all the descendants of a single individual that has been reproduced by asexual propagation—a plant, say, that has been extensively multiplied through the taking of cuttings. But when the notion of "cloning" human beings came to public attention in the 1970s, the word quickly shifted meaning: it refers now not to a *group* but to an *individual* whose genetic coding is identical to someone else's: "Isn't she gorgeous? I wonder where I could find a clone of her!" Are you saying that you want ten of her, all alike? No, not at all. But the biologist who uses the word to describe a specific population of mutated giant amoebas will be unable to get laymen to understand what he means.

Negative feedback. "Feedback" is the means by which a self-regulating system keeps itself operating correctly. A thermostatically controlled heating system constantly monitors room temperature so that it can turn the furnace on whenever the temperature falls below the desired level. What reaches the thermostat is quantitative information: the amount of departure from the desired condition. It can be expressed as a negative quantity: "We are minus three degrees from optimum in here." Technically, then, what the thermostat is getting is negative feedback, which is useful stuff, allowing an automatic-control system to correct an undesirable situation. *Positive* feedback would therefore be the kind of information that increases a system's deviation from the optimum, i.e. an undesirable thing. But when the whole feedback concept passed into public use this subtle distinction was lost. "Positive" is good, right? "Negative" is bad. So now we have the concepts of "positive feedback"—i.e., praise, constructive criticism—and "negative feedback," which is grumbling, hostility, general obstreperousness. And the old cybernetic concept of negative feedback as the key to automatic regulation goes down the drain. Another good tool lost.

Paranoid. A psychological term describing a clinical mental state marked by delusions and pathologically overintense suspiciousness;

but in common usage today it merely means "very uneasy," always taking the preposition *about*, as in, "I am paranoid about getting my rent increased next month," or, "She is very paranoid about spilling red wine on her white carpet." This is a sad and silly trivialization of a useful clinical term. Using "paranoid" so casually robs us of a way of characterizing true paranoia (Hitler, Stalin, Lee Harvey Oswald).

Nuke. Not a technical term, but a corruption of one, *nuclear*, as in "nuclear reactor" or "nuclear weapon," from *nucleus*, the core of the atom. The popular slogan "No more nukes!" may thus be taken to mean either "Stop building nuclear power plants!" or "End the threat of atomic warfare!" This blurs a distinction that some thoughtful people would like to make: there are those who see atomic bombs as nasty dangerous things but who regard properly designed nuclear power plants as beneficial to humanity. Lumping both into the class of "nukes" creates emotionally potent confusion, probably not by accident, and makes it easy to argue that the nuclear power plant across the bay is likely to turn your little suburb into Hiroshima or worse if someone throws the wrong switch.

What is demonstrated by these examples, and others that no doubt could be added, is that the wondrous vitality of language carries certain built-in risks. The advance of knowledge requires the creation of new technical terms, and these, if they are vivid enough and powerful enough, pass swiftly into popular use. But the conceptual need they meet in popular speech is not precisely the one for which they originally were coined; and soon they are transformed or deformed in a way that invalidates their primary sense. If one person thinks negative feedback is useful and another views it with alarm, the phrase has become an instrument of confusion instead of communication. It seems an inevitable process of decay—a case of the power of entropy working even on the ultimate anti-entropic weapon, language itself. And so we will go on and on, looking for positive feedback among our clones and getting paranoid about nukes, while useful meanings shift and blur without our noticing what is taking place. Me, I'm off to Chez Maurice to calm my nerves over some gourmet French food, since I am, fortuitously, the penultimate gourmand.

The International Language

I had my first demonstration of European linguistic virtuosity in 1960, at a restaurant on the Promenade des Anglais in Nice, where the head waiter greeted each guest in that guest's language. Usually he could guess the right language to use before the new guests had even spoken—from the cut of their clothes, I suppose, or haircut style, or the shape of their noses. I was one of his rare mistakes: he hailed me in French, perhaps because even in 1960 I wore a neat little goatee, and that must have looked French to him. (Beards were so rare on Americans in 1960 that children would turn to stare at me in the streets. That changed a few years later.)

I watched in awe as he moved from table to table, exchanging a bit of Italian with one set of diners, Spanish with another, German with a third, Portuguese (perhaps) with a fourth, and English (after I had admitted the truth) with me, while continuing all the while to issue instructions in French to the rest of the restaurant's staff. Coming as I did from the resolutely monolingual United States, I was deeply impressed.

I can make myself understood pretty well in Italian, can conduct basic tourist transactions and inquiries in Spanish and French, can manage a few dozen words of German, all of which puts me ahead of most Americans abroad; but I don't regard myself as fluent in any of those languages. Wherever I go, and I've been to a lot of places, I try to learn at least how to say "please" and "thank you" and "where is the toilet?," and in Turkey last year Karen and I got very good at explaining in pidgin Turkish that our car had a flat tire; but basically I conduct myself in English wherever I go, supplementing it where appropriate with Italian or a bit of Spanish or French, and generally I am understood. English is the language of Earth. In our tales of the future, we science-fiction guys often tend to have Earthmen speaking something called "Terran," but the election has been held, the results are in, and "Terran" is in fact going to be English. Forget about Esperanto.

It's already happened. I don't mean simply that hotel clerks and taxi drivers have learned English in order to be able to communicate with obstinately monolingual tourists from the United States. I mean that people of various nations and languages are using English to communicate *with each other*, because it's the only language they have in common.

[*Asimov's Science Fiction*, July 1996]

In the Scandinavian countries, English long ago became mandatory for elementary-school instruction, and most people in Sweden, Norway, and Denmark speak it with great ease. The same is true in the Netherlands. A logical move: these are small European countries that speak obscure languages which few foreigners care to master, and if they are going to communicate easily with the other countries with whom they do business (and they are all active mercantile nations) it's a good idea to master an internationally useful tongue.

So English has become the language in which the Dutch speak to Russians and Norwegians talk to Greeks. The efficiency of knowing English has become apparent in recent years even to the speakers of less esoteric European languages—German, Italian, even French, which English has displaced as the international means of communication, just as French had displaced Latin. Everywhere, nowadays, you will find people who have nothing in common linguistically except a knowledge of English talking to one another in that language.

Aboard a ferry traveling in the Greek islands ten years ago, for example, I listened with fascination as a little group of young Swedish, French, and German travelers who had just met aboard the boat carried on an animated conversation in variously accented English. A couple of years ago in a Prague restaurant I overheard a Czech businessman discussing a real-estate transaction with a Turk—in English, of course. Again and again in Spain, Italy, and Turkey I have seen local tour guides delivering English-language lectures on archaeology or art to groups of Japanese tourists; since the tour leaders all know English already, and most Japanese do also, it has not proven necessary for the guides to bother learning Japanese. So it goes, around the world.

But the Terran language that is emerging out of English is not going to be much like the English we speak in San Francisco or Chicago or Boston. Any American who has been to England already knows that American English and English English not only sound different, they differ greatly in vocabulary. (A New Yorker who enters a London "subway" isn't going to find any trains, only an underground passage; what he really wants is the "underground," which Londoners often call the "tube." As for the New Yorker's "tube," that's the Londoner's "telly," right?) If the two main English-speaking countries of the world, after only two and a quarter centuries of political separation, already speak two widely differing forms of the language, what sorts of Englishes are going to evolve in Asia, Africa, and South America among people whose primary linguistic background is something else, over the next few hundreds of years? And though speakers of those Englishes may be able to understand each other, will we be able to understand *them*?

Colloquialisms are a big part of the problem. Ours, of course, baffle many foreigners, even those who know conventional English well. Taking the words at their literal meanings can lead one into dire semantic trouble. "So you're getting the hang of doing business in English now?" an American asks the Japanese director of an automobile company in Prague. "I am getting hang?" he replies, mystified. Nor does his English-speaking Czech staff have much of a clue. "Means...I depend on it?" one asks. "I'd like to have it?" guesses another. "I'd like to stop it?" a third surmises.

Consider the conversation-stopping effects of all the sports metaphors we pepper our speech with—"slam dunk," "judgment call," "game plan," "home run," and so forth. (What about that vivid phrase, "peppering" our speech?) What is a non-native speaker to make of "highbrow," "looney tunes," or "funny farm?" How are they supposed to decipher the special grammatical structures of our younger life-forms? ("I was like, 'Come off it,' and then he goes, 'Hey, chill out, babe....' ")

Worse yet, regional Englishes spoken only by those who use English as a *lingua franca* (and there's a wonderful semantic mishmosh!) are emerging, causing new sorts of difficulties. An English linguist named Alan Firth, who is studying these problems at the University of Aalborg in Denmark, offers this transcription of a conversation (in English, more or less) between a Danish exporter of cheese and an Egyptian importer in Cairo:

"So I told him," the Egyptian says, "not to send the cheese after the, the blowing in customs."

The Dane, not understanding, replies cautiously, "I see, yes."

"So I don't know what we can do with the order now."

Now the Dane is worried. "I'm not, er, blowing, er—what is this, too big or what?"

"No," says the Egyptian. "The cheese is *bad*. It is, like, fermenting in the customs' cool rooms."

"Ah! It's gone off!"

"Yes, it's gone off."

So communication is achieved. But it requires a very careful procedure. The Dane doesn't have any way of knowing that what the Egyptian means by the "blowing" in Cairo customs is the sniffing of the cheese to see if it's all right. But when the Egyptian finally explains that the cheese is bad, light dawns for the Dane (see how metaphor pervades everything we say!) and he cries out that the cheese has "gone off." The Egyptian might well think he's saying that the cheese has exploded; but since the universally comprehensible word bad has been uttered in a timely way, the Dane now knows about what "blowing" means to the Egyptian, the Egyptian knows what "gone off" connotes for the Dane, and—now that they both get the ticket, so to speak—they can proceed to do business. "Purists may turn in their graves as they murder the English language—and get their deal," Professor Firth observes. "It may be risky to not quite understand," he says, "but there's something to lose by saying you don't. The skilled communicators know when it's OK. Once you get the contract, you go back, clear things up—and 5,000 tons of cheese are on their way to Egypt." Or, as an English-speaking Czech factory manager puts it, "One of the things we all have in common is we all speak poor English. We get by on what we have." And what they have, though it may not be the Queen's English or even the President's, is English enough to allow disparate peoples to communicate with relative ease all over the world.

As foreigners assemble Englishes of their own, and as those home-grown varieties establish themselves in different regions of the planet, the parent tongue itself will undergo a certain amount of pushing and pulling. It always has. It began as a Teutonic language and absorbed heavy input along the way from the Norman French (who were of Scandinavian origin but spoke a Latin-derived language) and then from all the rest of the world. The global Terran that will emerge from English may cause some problems for those who regard English as their mother tongue. "Natives must understand," says Franciszek Grucza of the Warsaw Institute of Linguistics. "They say, 'This is our language, not yet yours.' I say it's not true. English is not the language of American or British natives only. This is our language too." And it will undergo some very strange metamorphoses indeed on its way to becoming the planetary lingo.

Or the interplanetary one. In one of my favorite s-f stories, James Blish's "Common Time," a spaceman making a faster-than-light voyage meets the beadmungen, spacefaring aliens who tell him, "We-they pitched that the being-Garrard with most adoration these twins and had mind to them, soft and loud alike. How do you hear?"

And once Garrard realizes that the beadmungen are speaking to him in English, he replies, "I pitch you-them to fullest love." And so it will go, as we and the beadmungen speak English to one other amongst the celestial spheres.

The Fragmented Global Village

When the Tylenol-poisonings story broke last fall, I found myself in a peculiarly isolated position. For I had never heard of Tylenol; and yet everybody about me seemed to be thoroughly familiar with the drug.

Two factors were responsible for my ignorance. One is my reluctance to use medication except in case of dire need. When dire need arises, I take an aspirin. (I *have* heard of aspirin.) My aspirin consumption is about three tablets a year; with that sort of medical background, I have no real reason to be familiar with newer and better pain-killers. The second thing is that I rarely watch commercial television, and, when I do, I invariably tape-record the programs and use my fast-forward control to zip me through the commercials instantaneously when I play my tapes. So I had never been exposed to a Tylenol commercial. I found out about the drug and the poison scare the same way: from my daily newspaper.

No, I don't watch network TV news, either. But almost everyone else does, it seems—because surveyors found, a few weeks after the poisonings, that an astounding 99% of the American public knew about the story. Newspaper readership isn't that high—I am constantly amazed to discover that friends of mind simply don't read them. So it must have been the 11 o'clock news that spread the word about Tylenol so efficiently.

About the same time as I was discovering these things, my local newspaper ran a political cartoon that left me puzzled—because I had no idea who the man in the drawing was. I showed the cartoon to a friend, who expressed surprise that I didn't recognize the Republican candidate for Senator in this year's election. But I didn't. I follow the news in the papers and on the radio, not on television—and I wouldn't have recognized the Senatorial candidate, or the Gubernatorial one either, for that matter, of either party, if I had bumped into him at the post office. Yet the newspaper automatically assumed that all Californians would know what the cartoon meant: everyone watches TV news, right?

Which set me thinking. Apparently we have all entered the era of the global village that Marshall McLuhan was talking about a few years ago; we are all hooked into a nationwide data-disseminating network; everybody gets the same set of inputs every night (except for a few mavericks like me who are bored by network news programs,

[*Amazing Stories*, May 1983]

and wait for the morning paper.) So everyone knows what the Commissioner of the National Football League looks like, and the Secretary-General of the United Nations, and the director of *Raiders of the Lost Ark*. (Except me.) Ten million Americans watch *Wall Street Week* every Friday and rush to call their brokers, first thing Monday, with orders to buy or sell the stocks that are discussed. Everyone knows who the hero of the World Series was, and how high he threw his glove when the game was won. And so on.

The terrible unanimity and conformity of the national psyche that results from this nationwide electronic communion has been much discussed for decades, of course. The dreary impact of having one hundred million people wondering who shot J.R.—a mania that spread to Europe and gave the global village a few extra suburbs for a while—is awesome to contemplate. But I offer a bit of extrapolative thinking that contains both hope and confusion. This nationwide cathode-ray conformism is about to fall apart, throwing Americans out into a cruel night of mysterious independence of experience. I think the TV networks are in their last decade; and when they go, so too will the community that orbits them.

Cable TV is already fragmenting the audience. Independent channels come snaking into town from halfway across the state, bringing unfamiliar inputs. Some of these cable stations are shipped from much greater distances, via satellite relay—notably that Atlanta channel that turns up on everybody's set. But cable is only the beginning of the upheaval.

There's the video recorder, too. It greatly expands the availability of television programming, and bring with it a vast range of choices that compete with the standard network items of prime time. You don't *have* to watch the evening news, now; you may find yourself watching the movie you taped at three that afternoon, while you were at the office. Or last year's Superbowl, if football is your dish. (It isn't mine.) Slipping a cassette into the slot completely removes you from the structured grasp of the networks—and from those Tylenol commercials, too.

Finally, direct satellite transmission is just around the corner. The way the entrepreneurs tell it, we'll hook up a three-foot-wide antenna, costing a few hundred dollars, that will snare for us any number of broadcasts from the satellites hovering overhead (and thank you, Arthur C. Clarke!) Anywhere up to a hundred channels may become available, from all over the world—meaning that we can keep our video recorders busy soaking up twelve or fifteen hours a day of non-network programming, enough to satisfy the most addicted of videophiles without ever having once to switch to CBS.

When all that happens—and it will, doubt it not—one of the least endearing aspects of American life will disappear. The transmission of instant clichés ("at this point in time") or the latest grammatical blunders ("fortuitous" taken to mean "fortunate") will be greatly impeded. The circulation of wearisome catchphrases ("Go for it!" "Sock it to me!" "Would you believe—") will be severely diminished. Your fellow workers will not all be discussing Johnny Carson's program when they show up at the office in the morning.

I don't mean to postulate Utopia. Network TV will not be replaced by a dazzling diet of Shakespeare, Mozart, and Tolstoy. The stuff streaming in over the cables or pouring down from the satellites will probably mostly be the same old junk, or perhaps brand new species of junk. But the point is that people are going to be watching all sorts of *different* kinds of junk, and they're not going to have the same community of information any longer. In the fragmented global village of the 1990's, people may actually have to tell each other the news; and despite the acceleration of data transfer that has steadily been going on all this century, and which is not going to relent, some degree of swiftness in communication is going to vanish with the breakdown of the big television networks. I think that may be a good idea. Within a matter of days after the Tylenol horrors, dozens of diligent freelance creeps were making their way through our drugstores, dropping sinister contaminants into packages of eyedrops and headache pills and whatnot. In a nation less harmoniously unified by electronic media, such ghastly fads may be a little slower to catch on.

Political Correctness, One: Minority Hypersensitivity

I have never thought of myself as particularly bigoted. I do have certain residual and practically innate attitudes that I acquired as a result of having grown up as a white male American of middle-class background, and I have some distinctly reactionary political notions that evolved in me during an adult life spent largely in the upper tax brackets. But I also belong to what was not very long ago a severely persecuted religious minority, and I'm not much given to racial or cultural prejudices; live and let live has been my general rule. On the other hand, I'm also a writer. I populate my stories with, among other entities, blacks, Jews, homosexuals, Protestants of Anglo-Saxon ancestry, women, Armenians, Turks, and Marxists. When some member of one of those groups behaves less than nobly in one of my stories, I've never regarded it as an attack on that group in general, since I've considered myself to be writing about individuals.

Hence my surprise when I received an issue of *Gay Community News*, a Boston paper, that contained a lengthy discussion of my use of prejudicial stereotypes. The item was actually an account of the Boston World S-F Convention of September, 1980, at which I was master of ceremonies, and the report on my performance began pleasantly enough with a description of me as "a writer we have long respected both for the brilliance of his writing and his long dedication to using unusual cultures, including gay culture, in his fiction." A footnote amplified on my various excellences as a writer, but then went on to observe:

> "Sometimes, however, Silverberg's use of minorities is questionable. He relies on cartoon figures. In the novel *Dying Inside*, he has a gang of jive-talking black basketball players beat a man unconscious. Another novel, *The Book of Skulls*, has a gay character, Ned, who is purely vicious and evil. Ned triggers the suicides of three other gay men, who all happened to have loved him. With this book, Silverberg is whipping gays with a double whammy—we're shown as being either horrible, self-centered monsters or death-wishing sadsacks.
>
> "On one hand, Silverberg's use of minority characters can be almost called commendable—he is showing us that we do not live in an all-male, Anglo-Saxon, lily-white world. However, the manner in which he uses minorities raises many questions."

[*Amazing Stories*, November 1981]

The main question that comes to my mind out of all this is what impact minority hypersensitivity is going to have on creative artistry in science fiction. More than most other forms of category fiction (westerns, mysteries, gothics), s-f is read by people who are emotionally or physically disadvantaged in some way, and those people, in our field, tend to be highly articulate. If gays, blacks, women, Jews, Armenians, or whatnot start screaming about prejudice every time a member of their group is shown in less than favorable light, a kind of minority tyranny will insure that all villains are going to be WASP Republicans, and all our black characters will be as noble as Uncle Tom, all our gays as serene as Plato. That may make for virtuous social behavior but it makes for lousy fiction, and we already have a sufficiency of that. (Besides, the WASP's may start complaining too.)

The humorlessness of the minorities is an understandable sensitivity. When one has been subjected to irrational abuse for decades or centuries or millennia, one gets a little testy about it. (One also learns to get over that, after a while. The gays right now are as grouchy about their image as the blacks were a decade or two ago, the Jews somewhat earlier, et cetera. No minority ever fully relaxes its guard, but eventually its members learn to stop being so touchy where it doesn't count.)

And—minority sensitivities or no—*it is not the job of the artists to be nice to people.* We are not social workers. We are not therapists. We are not crusaders. We are tellers of tales, inventors of fiction. What we offer is not comfort but vision. Not all the visions are cuddly ones. There is a substantial segment of the science fiction audience that *wants* cuddly visions, and is getting them in movies. (Cf. *Close Encounters of the Third Kind, Star Wars*, et cetera, et cetera, where nobody ever gets seriously hurt and emotional conflict is purely on the eighth-grade level.) Fine. Their needs should be met too. The creator of non-cuddly art has enough problems, though, without having to worry about whether he's offending minorities. Homer offended minorities. Proust offended minorities. Joyce offended minorities. Write to them, if you like. Leave me alone.

I replied to *Gay Community News* somewhat sadly that I thought their remarks about me were "wrongheaded and unfair," going on to say, "In the old days before gays had come out and become a political force, one of the most delightful aspects of them, for me, was their sense of humor, that is, their awareness of the absurdity of everyday life and their clear-eyed perspective on contemporary nonsense. (A bit of a stereotype too, I must add.) Evidently when one is politicized one loses some of one's balance, for a lot of what comes out of the gay community now strikes me as humorless, dour, oversensitive, and just plain silly....

"The remarks on my own writing, though generally complimentary, annoy me where I'm accused of relying on 'cartoon figures,' as when I have a gang of jive-talking black basketball players beat a man unconscious, or where I portray a gay character as 'purely vicious and evil.' With your help I now realize that in the real world no blacks ever commit violence and all homosexuals are people of the most saintly character, and I'll endeavor not to portray them otherwise in future work lest I deviate into stereotypes again. I thank you for this valuable corrective sermon: one of my goals as a writer is to portray character with honesty, and I would not want to distort anything by departing from approved modes of minority behavior. Incidentally, the footnote remark is the first comment I've had from the gay community in any way critical of *Book of Skulls*. Jeez, folks, try to remember how to laugh! At yourselves first, then at the rest of the universe."

Perhaps it's a matter of timing. When Hitler's minions were stuffing Jews into the ovens at Buchenwald, it was not the appropriate moment to talk about Jewish moneylenders and landlords, Jewish noses, Jewish accents—only Jewish intelligence, Jewish stoicism, Jewish culture. Gays, having been ostracized by all right-thinking straights for so long, have now begun to emerge as respectable human beings in some parts of our society for the first time, and they will hear nothing said against any of their kind right now. So too with women, so too with Chicanos, so too with—well, fill in the blanks yourselves.

Well and good. Putting aside racism and sexism is part of our growing up as a civilization, and long overdue. But the writers of science fiction—at least, this one—are not going to be agents of the revolution. We reserve the right—at least, I do—to call 'em as we see 'em. Stories are still about conflicts; people in conflict are imperfect people; some of the guys with flaws are going to be gay. If members of minorities don't care for such realism, let them clean up their acts. After all, nobody writes stories about macho Zen monks who lie and cheat and rape and loot. (I think.)

Political Correctness, Two:
Redskins and Bloody-Nosed Aliens

It will be spring or early summer when you read this, but such are the exigencies of publishing deadlines that I'm writing it on an autumn morning, midway through that long limbo of grim holiday cheer that runs from Halloween to New Year's Day.

The interminable holiday season is not without its rewards, though, for the observer of modern cultural trends.

From Arlene Hirschfelder, for example, who is an education consultant with the Association on American Indian Affairs in New York, comes a plea for an end to what she sees as the exploitive use of Native American imagery in American popular culture. "It is predictable," she writes. "At Halloween, thousands of children trick or treat in Indian costumes. At Thanksgiving, thousands of children parade in school pageants wearing plastic headdresses and pseudo-buckskin clothing. Thousands of card shops stock Thanksgiving greeting cards with images of cartoon animals wearing feathered headbands. Thousands of teachers and librarians trim bulletin boards with Anglo-featured, feathered Indian boys and girls."

Ms. Hirschfelder finds this objectionable—as she does the use of such names as "Indians," "Redskins," "Braves," and "Chiefs" for sports teams. She sees all this as an affront to the Native American people. "This image-making," she asserts, "prevents Indians from being a relevant part of the nation's social fabric."

The naive response might be to say that it is the very use of these images that *keeps* the Indians part of our nation's social fabric, by reminding us that before our ancestors came to this land it was inhabited by a very different people of strikingly different culture and physical appearance. But no, that's not what Ms. Hirschfelder means by "relevant." The Halloween costumes and other playful bits of pseudo-Indianism conceal, she says, "the reality of high mortality rates, high diabetes rates, high unemployment rates. They hide low average life spans, low per-capita incomes and low educational levels. Plastic war bonnets and ersatz buckskin deprive people from knowing the complexity of Native American heritage—that Indians belong to hundred of nations that have intricate social organizations, governments, languages, religions and sacred rituals, ancient stories, unique arts and music forms."

She has a point of sorts here. Certainly many American Indians

[*Amazing Stories*, July 1988]

today lead bleak, difficult lives, as do members of many other groups who do not belong to the dominant ethnic majority of the nation. And it is instructive for all of us to remember that the way that dominant ethnic majority came to have possession of the land now included in mainland USA was to evict the Indians from most of it by a combination of force and chicanery, in a long and bloody one-sided struggle. We took what we wanted and gave them very little except rum and infectious diseases in return, and when the job was done we penned the survivors up in what amounted to concentration camps.

Nevertheless, Ms. Hirschfelder's righteous wrath descends, I think, too late and on the wrong target. She fails to understand that history is one thing and myth is another, and that although myth generally evolves out of history it takes on a life of its own that cannot be extinguished so long as the culture that brought it into being endures. Many of our ancestors (not mine, as it happens, nor Ms. Hirschfelder's) took part in a determined campaign of genocide against the American Indians. It is not a pretty part of our history, and while I feel no personal guilt over it I do regret the destruction of the fascinating cultures that fell before the conquering Europeans. But in the process of that act of genocide certain mythic images were generated here. They hold real power for our secularized and largely tradition-free children. They are not entirely negative ones, either: most of us grow up thinking of the Indians as noble savages, primitive but dignified, who fought a desperate losing battle against the encroachments of a grubby band of pioneers. That is as much a stereotype as any other, but it seems to me not a disgraceful sort of myth to have attached to one; and if our children tend to keep it alive with their peace-pipes and tomahawks, their bow and arrows, their buckskin leggings, well, so be it. It is the only history we have here, after all. And abolishing it will do not one damned bit of good for the unfortunate Native Americans who struggle against poverty, alcoholism, and tuberculosis in odd corners of our land. What earnest but misguided folk like Ms. Hirschfelder fail to see is that if we wipe our Indian stereotypes completely from our repertoire of folk imagery, it will become even easier for us to forget all about those unhappy survivors of an ugly genocide who still dwell among us. At least so long as the kids run around with tomahawks and feathered headdresses they still have some idea that there was once another race here before us.

Meanwhile, elsewhere on the holiday front, I am informed that this year's Christmas toys run heavily toward the gross and ugly. From one major toy manufacturer comes Sammy Sneeze, a hideous plastic monster. "Squeeze Sammy Sneeze," the placard informs prospective purchasers. "Alien blood pours from his nose!"

And another company offers the Dissect-an-Alien Playset, which contains a visitor from another world whose twelve internal organs can be pulled out and reinserted like pieces in a three-dimensional jigsaw puzzle. For that extra little touch of realism the organs are covered with realistic "glow-in-the-dark alien blood."

Then there is the G.I. Joe Space Station, a $200 item armed with Star-Wars-like gadgets that can destroy any life-form the universe might send this way. A squadron of interplanetary Rambos guards Earth against nasty outsiders in this impressive gadget.

Here, I think, is fertile territory for someone like Ms. Hirschfelder to explore. The American Indians have already lost their war against the Europeans; it won't be of any help to them now to ban toy tomahawks or to make the Washington football team find a new nickname. But the aliens aren't here yet. We still have a chance to instill in our children proper loving attitudes toward our green-skinned many-tentacled friends from space. Such vicious toys as the G.I. Joe Space Station and the Dissect-an-Alien Playset are programming today's young ones with a needlessly hostile outlook toward unfamiliar life-forms. This may lead to unfortunate violent incidents when aliens do begin to arrive on our world. And if we start dissecting the first visitors from space just to see if their organs really do glow in the dark, they may answer back with undesirable belligerence. A word to the wise ought to be sufficient—and those American Indian headdresses that our kids wear ought to be useful reminders. The next time a war between widely differing cultures is fought in North America, *we* may be the ones who end up on reservations.

Political Correctness, Three: Geezer Ruminations

One winter day in 1990 the Wall Street Journal, a newspaper which runs a good deal of feature material that has no visible relationship to the world of high finance, published an amiable piece by James P. Sterba under the heading, "Goodbye Geezer Groom?" It concerned Mr. Sterba's difficulties in obtaining his favorite hair tonic, Vitalis V7, which he had used for decades to slick down his hair, but which was beginning to become unavailable in recent years as a result of product "improvements."

If ever there seemed was a harmless little piece, incapable of offending the most fierce of politically correct sensibilities, it was Mr. Sterba's pleasant nostalgic lament for the hair-goop of his boyhood. Or so I would have thought. But no: a few weeks later the Journal's letter column published in its letter column this screed from Lyda Maxwell Smayling of Minneapolis, which I take the liberty of quoting in its entirety:

> "Use of the word 'geezer' was a shocking departure from the Journal's customary concern for the sensitivities of minorities. The stigmatization of older, rural men by the pejorative 'geezer' was an appalling breach of journalistic responsibility.
> "The Journal is careful to avoid street-language epithets in characterizing the racial, religious and ethnic minorities making up the majority of the population of New York City— rural, elderly men deserve the same consideration."

"Geezer" a politically offensive word? An affront to the sensitivities of minorities? Its use in the hallowed pages of the Wall Street Journal a shocking departure from concern, an appalling breach of journalistic responsibility? At first I thought the letter was a spoof. But as I stared and stared and stared at it, I realized that Ms. Smayling very likely is absolutely serious. She is outraged by Mr. Sterba's casual use of the slurring epithet "geezer" to describe a group of older men that includes, among others, Mr. Sterba himself. She is quick to take up cudgels against the offensive term and its offending users. She will protect the denigrated geezers of the world from further mockery of that sort, just as—I am quite sure—she would denounce the use of such terms as "chick," "spade," "fag," or "yid," should she encounter them in print anywhere.

[*Amazing Stories*, September 1990]

I don't know. I just don't know.

I myself probably qualify as a geezer—not by Ms. Smayling's definition, since I'm not rural, but very likely anybody who attended his first science-fiction convention 40 years ago and was already in high school at the time would be regarded as a geezer by a good 68% of today's population. I'm also unquestionably a yid; I'm married to a lovely chick who's also a yiddess; my next-door neighbor is a spade (he drives a Rolls-Royce, incidentally; his other car is a Mercedes); my closest business associate is a fag. I don't often use these terms for them, of course, and on those rare occasions when I do, it's understood to be in the loving way that people who know each well will do it. I wouldn't call a stranger any such thing. I probably wouldn't call a stranger a geezer, either. But until Ms. Smayling raised my consciousness, I would never, never, NEVER, have classed "geezer" as being offensive in the way that the other epithets I've just been tossing around undeniably are.

The problem here is that people of such staunch political correctness as Ms. Smayling, in their zeal to see to it that nobody's feelings get hurt in any way, are bringing about a revolution in our way of speech that will, if carried to its inevitable extreme, reduce our language to kindergarten mumbo-jumbo. (There! I'll get angry letters from kindergarten students, or more likely their teachers!)

Among the victims of these crusades are writers of science fiction, who, like other science fiction writers, try to reproduce the rhythms of actual human speech in their work. "Geezer," I see now, goes on the forbidden list. "Drunk" is probably objectionable to somebody, who wants us to call such folk "alcohol-intolerant persons." There are no more "fits," only "seizures." No more "morons" or "dopes," just "learning-disabled people."

I understand the theory of it all. We don't want to be cruel to the unfortunate. But writers do owe some debt to reality, too. People do use these terms. Maybe only villains do, but would Ms. Smayling and her ilk object if we put perjoratives in the mouths of villains, at least? (" 'By darn, I'll wipe out every geezer in the commune,' cried the swaggering young punk.") Perhaps not. But I resent having these nice-nelly limitations put on me as a writer, and I definitely think things are getting out of hand when "geezer" joins the list of forbidden words.

Where will it end?

As it happens, the fine science-fiction writer Connie Willis has already answered that question for me, in an elegant satiric story called "Ado." You can find it in the January 1988 issue of our esteemed competitor, *Isaac Asimov's Science Fiction Magazine*.

Connie Willis is nobody's idea of a rebel. You will not see her with punk hair or black-leather jeans, you will not hear her utter four-letter words, you will not find her wearing cocaine spoons for earrings. Connie Willis is a Nice Person. But nice persons too are concerned about all this humorless mealy-mouthed censorship—that's the word, *censorship*—that the virtuous would like to impose on us for the sake of improving human nature. Connnie's story "Ado" concerns the attempt of a high-school teacher to stage one of Shakespeare's plays. *Othello* and *The Merchant of Venice* are quickly discarded—offensive to minorities. Half a dozen more, led by *Taming of the Shrew*, are scrapped for being sexist. *Macbeth* has witches in it—might upset the people afraid of Satanists. And so on and so on, until only *Hamlet* is deemed sufficiently politically correct.

But then—one paragraph will do—

"The National Cutlery Council objects to the depiction of swords as deadly weapons. 'Swords don't kill people. People kill people.' The Copenhagen Chamber of Commerce objects to the line, 'Something is rotten in the state of Denmark.' Students Against Suicide, The International Federation of Florists, and the Red Cross object to Ophelia's drowning.' "

And so on. You get the idea.

It's not the writer's job to worry about offending people. It's the writer's job to tell the truth as he sees it—and to use the words that fit the tale.

So be it, Ms. Smayling. Your well-meaning crusade puts you on the side of the devil, as far as I'm concerned. Lord help us all if "geezer" becomes some kind of evil agist epithet. So says this geezer, at any rate.

I'd Like to Talk to You, Robert

This is not an era in which traditional courtesies are thriving, a matter which seems to be of concern only to geezers like me. (Although there is some interest on the part of the politically correct in maintaining courtesy to geezers, as readers of this column a couple of issues back will recall.)

A case in point is this business of casual use of first names.

Maybe it's not happening all around the country the way it is here. I live in California, which has always prided itself on its informality. A few weeks ago, at dinnertime, I picked up the telephone and heard a cultured male voice say, "I'd like to talk to you about making a contribution to the San Francisco Symphony, Robert."

Robert?

I'm a subscriber to the Symphony. Now and then I do make contributions to worthy causes, and I suppose the Symphony qualifies as one of those. But why does the Symphony think it's good policy to solicit contributions from strangers on a first-name basis? Or is that something it does only when calling science-fiction writers? Would it address the 78-year-old widow of some rich local industrialist as "Jane" or "Martha" while trying to extract dollars from her? Or the industrialist himself, if he's still among us: would he be "Jim" or "Phil?"

I'm afraid I wasn't very courteous in my reply. I told the cultured-sounding solicitor that I didn't like being solicited by telephone at dinnertime and that I especially didn't like being called "Robert" by strangers looking for favors from me. Then I hung up.

Afterward, ruminating over the incident, I found myself wandering into a curious byway having to do with this whole first-name business, which is that I don't even like being called "Robert" by my friends. "Robert" is my professional first name. It's the name I was born with, and the one I use on my stories. My friends call me "Bob." They've been doing that for more than forty years. I like it. (My first few stories were actually published under the byline of "Bob" Silverberg, before an older hand told me it sounded a little too casual.) Nobody who has known me more than ten minutes calls me "Robert," except for a few extremely inattentive people. Whenever I hear myself addressed as "Robert" I know that it's some stranger presuming on a relationship that doesn't exist.

And a lot of other science-fiction writers have the same quirk, or some variation on it. I was surprised, thinking about it for a time, how complicated this naming business really is.

The writer whose books appear under the byline of "Samuel R. Delany" is "Chip" to his friends, never "Sam" and certainly not "Samuel." He's very patient when people call him "Sam," but he doesn't like it. Edward John Carnell, the great British science-fiction editor of years gone by, was "Ted" to everyone—a common British diminutive of "Edward." Chelsea Quinn Yarbro is addressed as "Quinn," never as "Chelsea." A. Bertram Chandler, the Australian science fiction writer, was "Jack" among intimates, though at some point people began calling him "Bert." Not *Bertram*, ever. Another "Bert" of some time back was H.J. Campbell, the British writer and editor. ("Bert" was short for "Herbert" in his case.) And R.A. MacAvoy, who doesn't have to worry about being called by her first name by strangers who have read her books, because she hides it behind those initials, is "Bertie" to her friends, derived from "Roberta."

The preferred nomenclature can change. John Varley used to be "Herb" to his close friends—Herbert is his middle name, I think—but lately I've heard him spoken of mainly as "John," even by people who know him quite well. Isaac Asimov once had a nickname, but he loathed it, and said so whenever it was used, and eventually almost everyone forgot it. Robert A.W. Lowndes, the editor and writer, is "Doc" to his friends of the 1940's, "Bob" to people like me who met him a decade or so later. I never asked him why the nickname changed; and I never called him "Doc," either. Another "Doc" was E.E. Smith, Ph.D. His first name was Edward, but he kept that pretty much to himself. Within the science-fiction world he was universally "Doc"—he wanted it that way—and I suppose outsiders such as symphony solicitors would have had to call him "Dr. Smith.")

Some writers are so fond of their nicknames that they turn them into real ones. Jack Vance's birth certificate reads "John Holbrook Vance," but he writes as "Jack" and everyone calls him that and I wouldn't be surprised if he uses "Jack" as his formal first name on contracts and tax returns and such. His son's name is John also, but he's known as "John," which makes things simpler around the Vance household.

There are s-f writers who never much mind being called by nicknames, or even, as I do, prefer it. I think here of "Bob" Sheckley, "Fred" Pohl, "Hank" Kuttner, "Ted" Sturgeon, "Phil" Dick, "Jim" Blish. And then there are some who are never called by nicknames even where easy possibilities exist: David Brin, David Hartwell, James

White, Arthur C. Clarke. No Daves, Arts, or Jims in that bunch. (Like Asimov, Clarke once did have a nickname, not "Art," but it wasn't entirely a flattering one and after a time it passed into general oblivion.)

Randall Garrett was "Randy" for a long time, but eventually got tired of the sniggering implications of the nickname and let it be known that he wanted only his formal first name used. Most of us tried our best. In a somewhat similar way, Charles N. Brown, the publisher of *Locus*, weary of being confused with a comic-strip character, would rather be "Charles" than "Charlie," and perhaps he's succeeding at it; but I have thirty years of practice at calling him by the nickname and I'm not doing a good job of making the transition to "Charles."

And then there's the case of Robert A. Heinlein. He was "Bob" to his friends for decades. When I met him in 1958 that was what everyone called him, and he was still signing his letters that way a few years later: I just checked my files to make sure. But somewhere along the way he turned into "Robert," apparently because his wife Ginny liked the sound of it better, and Ginny Heinlein is the sort of person who tends to get what she wants. As a "Robert" who'd rather be addressed as "Bob," I didn't find it came naturally to me to transform Heinlein from a "Bob" into a "Robert." So I went on calling him "Bob," which really wasn't proper any longer, and he suddenly started calling me "Robert," which wasn't appropriate either, and we muddled around with this first-name business for five or ten years before agreeing that neither of us really cared which version of our name the other used. Eventually I got the hang of calling him "Robert" and he managed to remember that I was still "Bob" and all went smoothly thereafter.

F.M. Busby has a first name, but he doesn't like it. He answers to "Buz" among friends. Strangers, like solicitors for the Seattle Symphony, are forced to call him "Mr. Busby," because they don't know what else to use. (I do, but I'm not telling.) "Spider" isn't Spider Robinson's first name any more than "F." is Buz Busby's, but the symphony fund-raisers up Vancouver way where he lives probably don't dare call him "Spider" when they phone him at dinnertime. (I know his real name, too, but I don't plan to let the Vancouver Symphony in on the secret.)

One who doesn't have to worry much about this whole nicknames business is Poul Anderson. "Poul" is not a name that lends itself to nicknaming. On the other hand, it has other drawbacks.

Nobody can pronounce it correctly—midway between "pole" and "pool," is what I was once told, but his wife says something close to "puhl," and presumably she knows—and it's very often misspelled as "Paul," besides. I suppose that's what the San Francisco Symphony panhandlers call him when they phone; and, because Poul is an innately courteous man, he neither hangs up on them nor corrects them nor reproves them for gratuitous use of his first name, or some semblance thereof. But life would have been simpler for him if his Norse progenitors had named him "Hans." It's not as mysterious or memorable as "Poul," but it's easier to pronounce, hard to misspell, and not readily adaptable into a nickname. Of course, an earlier Danish writer, fairly well know, had had the same first name, which might have caused some trouble for *our* Hans Anderson when he was starting his career, even if they spelled their surnames slightly differently. But the future author of *The High Crusade* and *The Boat of a Million Years* could have used his middle name to distinguish himself from his famous predecessor.

Hans William Anderson. Not a bad name for a science-fiction writer. I guess we'd call him "Bill."

Gold Doesn't Smell

The cities of our nation have been overrun by hordes of street people—and street people, by definition, live in the streets, which usually means that they tend to excrete in the streets as well. This development has caused an obvious and disagreeable problem for the housebroken portion of the population, leading to the obvious solution: a system of readily available mechanized public toilets.

Such devices are already in operation in many European cities, and not just for street people. They are attractive, even elegant, items, as this inveterate tourist will testify.

I conducted my own field research on the subject a couple of years ago in Paris upon experiencing a moment of metabolic crisis along the fashionable Avenue de l'Opera. There were no cafes in sight, only dignified shops where I would feel abashed to seek succor; but then, to my immense delight and relief, I found myself in front of a sleek tubular structure that had something of the appearance of the nose cone of a space vehicle, just before me on the spacious sidewalk. My command of French, though uncertain at times, was easily equal to the task of decoding the instructions. I dropped a coin in the slot, a franc or two, and a sliding door silently unfurled before me, and I entered a small, clean, brightly lit chamber, a glorious little temple of high-tech elimination, from which in due course I emerged, at the touch of a button, into the sunny splendors of a Parisian afternoon.

Nothing is keeping our cities from installing these magnificent 1990s-style donnickers except 1990s-style domestic politics. One problem that immediately arose here was that of wheelchair access, required by law. I certainly would not deny the right of wheelchair-bound people to toilet facilities, but the troublesome fact is that making the street johns available to them creates a number of technical problems, not the least of which is that the facilities need to be expanded in diameter to a point beyond the capacity of most American metropolitan sidewalks. (There are other issues as well to deal with, considering the automated nature of these devices and the handicapped nature of the handicapped person who might inadvertently become trapped inside one.)

Evidently these difficulties are on their way to being solved in New York City, where, so I understand, trials of four or five different types of automated street toilets are now under way and an ultimate choice is soon to be made. Across the country in San Francisco,

[*Asimov's Science Fiction*, May 1995]

though, the process is entangled at the moment in an uniquely San Franciscan dispute having to do with putting advertising placards on the outsides of the cubicles. The French company that makes the things has handsomely offered to supply the City by the Bay with a couple of dozen of them free of charge, in return for nothing more than the right to sell ad space on them. This proposal was doing well in municipal governmental circles until someone discovered that the manufacturers were apt to turn a *profit* on their generous donation this way. The profit motive is not regarded benignly by some very vocal San Franciscans, and revelations of potential money-making caused the gift to be voted down by the indignant Board of Supervisors, leading to an acrimonious public debate that is still going on. (The Frisco streets aren't getting to smell any sweeter, meanwhile.)

No doubt, the need being as urgent as it is, we will ultimately get our Parisian-style mechanical privies out here in California. At least we have overcome our inherent American puritanism to the point of being able to discuss openly the fact that living organisms periodically rid their bodies of waste matter; the discussion now has come down merely to little contemporary niceties of political necessity. In the Old World, where the processes that Americans quaintly hide behind such terms as pee-pee and doo-doo have always been taken for granted as the facts of life that they are, this is all handled in a much simpler way, and has been for thousands of years.

Roman cities were particularly well provided with public latrines, as you can see today when you visit the ruins of Pompeii or Herculaneum, or, in fact, almost any excavated ancient site in Italy. Inevitably you will come across an elaborate marble cacatorium in the center of town—ten or twenty stone seats lined up in a row, separated by raised ledges that often are decorated by sculptured figures of dolphins or sea-serpents. These were highly public latrines indeed, gathering-places where one met with one's friends, traded gossip, made business connections. Above the seats were niches that in ancient times held statuettes of the appropriate gods—Stercutius was the Roman god of ordure, Crepitus the god of convenience—to whom small offerings were made by the users of the facility. The walls of these establishments were adorned with bright frescoes or stuccoed reliefs and the ubiquitous Roman fountains.

As a rule the Romans didn't have elaborate toilet facilities within their own homes, though. They used basins and chamber-pots, which servants would empty from apartment-house windows into street drains outside. This sometimes had unfortunate consequences for passers-by, as the satirist Juvenal observed—"Clattering, the storm descends from heights unknown"—and eventually receptacles were placed on street corners in the hope of discouraging this air-borne dumping.

The Emperor Vespasian, who ruled from 69 to 79 A.D., was a thrifty and pragmatic sort who greatly increased the availability of these receptacles in Rome, and not only imposed a tax for their use but turned a profit for the public treasury by selling their contents to farmers for fertilizer and to wool-fullers as processing chemicals. He set up a number of new public latrines also. Vespasian's elder son, the future Emperor Titus, found all this a bit tacky and told the old man so, but Vespasian replied that he saw nothing wrong with deriving revenue from such a source. Pulling out a gold coin, he held it under Titus' nose and observed that gold doesn't smell, even when it comes from a urinal.

Vespasian thus won a small measure of immortality—for public urinals to this day are known as *vespasiani* in Rome and as *vespasiennes* in Paris. At least one of Vespasian's original installations is still in use in the Roman district of Trastevere. (But how the good emperor would be amazed by the washroom at the Ristorante Pietro Valentini, just off the Piazza Navona, where water flows automatically when you put your hands under the faucet, soap likewise comes magically from the soap dispenser, and hot air from an automatic hand-dryer! Would charges of sorcery have been leveled at the proprietor of such a facility in Imperial Rome?)

Undoubtedly the politicians who run our cities will, in the fullness of time, bring public urban sanitary facilities at least up to the level that Vespasian's Rome attained two thousand years ago. We can look forward, sooner or later, to automated conveniences that will meet the needs not only of our homeless population but even of ordinary taxpayers, who also have bladders and bowels. But is any thought being given, I wonder, to the problems that will arise some day when extraterrestrial visitors are wandering the streets of New York and San Francisco as tourists?

This is not, at the moment, a matter for our elected leaders to consider. But science-fiction writers probably should be thinking about it a little. It's very likely that aliens *will* excrete—but how? (Stanley G. Weinbaum dealt with the question all the way back in 1934, in his classic short story "A Martian Odyssey." The first human explorers of the red planet discover a row of pyramids in the Martian desert fashioned from small hollow bricks of silica—which turn out to be the fecal matter of a Martian life-form with a silicon-based body chemistry. Twenty years later, Sam Moskowitz ran an alchemical variation on the Weinbaum theme in "The Golden Pyramid"—his Martian explorers found a critter that ate lead, transmuted it to gold with the aid of an atomic pile in its belly, and brought forth neat pyramidal golden turds.

But those were aliens on their home turf. I can't recall, off hand, many stories that deal with the difficulties aliens will encounter when they try to perform their natural bodily functions while traveling on Earth. (Fritz Leiber did do one called "What's He Doing in There?" about a visiting Martian who goes into his host's bathroom and doesn't come out for hours. But it turns out the traveler from parched Mars is simply taking a bath. Are there others?)

What I should do, I suppose, is consult the indefatigable anthologist and expert on all things science-fictional, Martin Harry Greenberg. Marty is the editor, after all, who put together such specialized collections as *The Future I* (first-person stories), *The Future in Question* (stories with question-marks in their titles), and *The Science Fiction Weight Loss Book*. Yes, Marty would know, if anyone does. Why, it's altogether probable that he is, even as I speak, already hard at work on *Galactic Restrooms*—or will it be called *LooFantastic*?

Struldbrugs

Whiile Gulliver is visiting the kingdom of Luggnagg, he is asked by a member of the royal court whether he has seen any of their "*Struldbrugs*, or *Immortals*. I said I had not, and desired he would explain to me what he meant by such an appellation applied to a mortal creature. He told me, that sometimes, though very rarely, a child happened to be born in a family with a red circular spot in the forehead, directly over the left eyebrow, which was an infallible mark that it should never die. The spot, as he described it, was about the compass of a silver threepence, but in the course of time grew larger, and changed its color; for at twelve years old it became green, so continued till five and twenty, then turned to a deep blue; at five and forty it grew coal black, and as large as an English shilling, but never admitted any further alteration. He said these births were so rare, that he did not believe there could be above eleven hundred *struldbrugs* of both sexes in the whole kingdom...."

Gulliver at once cried out, "Happy nation where every child hath at least a chance for being immortal! Happy people who enjoy so many living examples of ancient virtue, and have masters ready to instruct them in the wisdom of all former ages! But happiest beyond all comparison are those excellent *struldbrugs*, who being born exempt from that universal calamity of human nature, have their minds free and disengaged, without the weight and depression of spirits caused by the continual apprehension of death."

If he had been so lucky to be born a *struldbrug*, Gulliver told himself, he would have devoted his first two hundred years of life to amassing great wealth and mastering all the arts and sciences; and then he would spend the rest of eternity serving as "the oracle of the nation," "forming and directing the minds of hopeful young men," and engaging in lofty philosophical colloquies with a set of companions chosen from his own immortal brotherhood. But why, he wondered, were none of these wise beings present at the court, sharing the wisdom of their great age with the king? Perhaps they found the court too vulgar and hectic a place, and passed their time in some more rarefied abode.

But reality, as usual, failed to match Gulliver's lofty fantasy. The *struldbrugs*, he was told, were indeed exempt from death—but not from aging. By the time they reached eighty, "they had not only all the follies and infirmities of other old men, but many more which arose

[*Amazing Stories*, July 1992]

from the dreadful prospect of never dying. They were not only opinionative, peevish, covetous, morose, vain, talkative, but uncapable of friendship, and dead to all natural affection....Envy and impotent desires are their prevailing passions.... At ninety they lose their teeth and hair, they have at that age no distinction of taste, but eat and drink whatever they can get, without relish or appetite. The diseases they were subject to still continue without increasing or diminishing. In talking they forget the common appellation of things, and the names of persons, even of those who are their nearest friends and relations. For the same reason they never can amuse themselves with reading, because their memory will not serve to carry them from the beginning of a sentence to the end." Because of the changes that time works in all languages, they become unable, after a few hundred years, to communicate with anyone but their own kind.

Eventually Gulliver meets a few *struldbrugs*, and is appalled by their hideous appearance and the misery of their condition: "The reader will easily believe, that from what I had heard and seen, my keen appetite for perpetuity of life was much abated. I grew heartily ashamed of the pleasing visions I had formed, and thought no tyrant could invent a death into which I would not run with pleasure from such a life." The *struldbrugs* are one of the most terrifying inventions of Jonathan Swift's classic novel—which is surely one of the masterpieces of science fiction.

But when we turn from *Gulliver's Travels* to yesterday's newspaper we find life imitating fiction; for here is the case of 85-year-old John Kingery of Portland, Oregon, who was abandoned in his wheelchair at a dog racing track in Post Falls, Idaho, wearing bedroom slippers and a sweatshirt that said "Proud to be An American." In his hands he held a bag of diapers. A note pinned to his chest said that his name was "John King" and that he was suffering from Alzheimer's Disease. As was true of Gulliver's *struldbrugs*, he was able to reminisce about his youth, and to speak amiably about farms and farming; but he could not remember his name or where he came from. Eventually he was identified by administrators of a Portland nursing home, who recognized him from a photo in the paper, and he was flown back to Oregon clutching a teddy bear in his hand, utterly unaware of what was going on around him.

John Kingery's daughter had checked him out of his nursing home about ten hours before he was found in Idaho. Presumably his family could no longer bear the strain or financial burden of caring for him. "Granny dumping" is what this is called, according to a spokesman for the American Association of Retired Persons. "Not a day goes by when a hospital emergency room somewhere in America doesn't have a case where some elderly person has been abandoned, usually by the children." And a survey by the American College of Emergency Physicians found that some 70,000 people were abandoned in this manner during 1991.

It does not appear to be against the law in Idaho to abandon an elderly person unable to care for himself, though it is in Oregon. Abandoning dogs or children, though, is illegal in Idaho.

So we have *struldbrugs* of our own. They are an enormous problem for their families. And—in an era of constant medical advances—their number is increasing all the time.

Consider a case that strikes closer to home for me than that of John Kingery. My wife Karen's grandmother is 92 years old. She lives in a retirement home in Florida; her daughter lives nearby and visits her frequently. For the past decade the old woman has been in a steady mental and physical decline, to the point where she seemed barely aware of her surroundings. Early in 1992 it became apparent that she would not live much longer. Her family thought it best to transfer her from the retirement home to a nearby hospital, where she could receive whatever specialized care she might require during the last few weeks of her life.

No abandonment was practiced here. Karen's mother has been a model of daughterly concern during her mother's long descent into old age. On checking her into the hospital, though, she suggested to the hospital authorities that her mother's comfort ought to be made a higher priority than her mother's continued survival. Care for her, yes; but not to the point where the old woman's mere husk was being sustained in some weird kind of mechanical quasi-life.

"Oh, no," the hospital authorities replied. "We can't take her on that basis. We'll make every effort to keep her alive indefinitely, and if that's not acceptable to you, take her to some other hospital."

Yes, of course. The Hippocratic Oath, to which all medical practitioners for the past twenty-five centuries have subscribed, declares, "The regimen I adopt shall be for the benefit of my patients according to my ability and judgment, and not for their hurt or for any wrong. I will give no deadly drug to any, though it be asked for me...." An honorable philosophy; but note also the admonition of the nineteenth-century poet Arthur Hugh Clough:

Thou shalt not kill; but needst not strive
Officiously to keep alive.

Karen's grandmother, supported by all the formidable technology of 1990s medicine, has now spent three months in the hospital where she was supposed to have died within a matter of days. She weighs 75 pounds; she has little notion of where she is; in her last rational statement she indicated that she was quite willing to see her long life come to its end. But daily miracles are performed to prevent that. The cost of all that is formidable. The taxpayers—*you*—are paying it. To the hospital, Karen's grandmother is a valuable asset, a productive profit center. Small wonder that the doctors strive to keep her alive.

Over the next thirty years, there will be a quintupling of the number of Americans over the age of 85—to a total of 15 million. In the same period the number of Alzheimer's Disease victims is expected to triple, reaching 12 million by the year 2020.

Gulliver's Luggnagg, a small kingdom, had only eleven hundred *struldbrugs*. We are the mightiest nation on Earth and we do everything on a much grander scale. But sometimes—all too often, it seems—it becomes necessary to ask if we really understand the implications of some of the things we do. The times cry out for a successor to Jonathan Swift.

When Empires End

Sometimes great empires *do* go out of business in something like a voluntary way. I remember when the far-flung British Empire was dismantled after World War II: first India was cut loose, and then the African colonies (Kenya, Tanganyika, Nyasaland, and such) and finally even the small Caribbean islands, known only to winter vacationers and stamp collectors—Grenada, St. Kitts, Dominica, St. Lucia, etc., etc. Eventually the whole world-wide aggregation of possessions, put together so laboriously during the eighteenth and nineteenth centuries, had been turned loose, filling the U.N. with exotic new members and turning Great Britain once more into a minor island nation living on its imperial memories and trying to contend with the flood of ex-colonial peoples who had taken up residence in the former mother country.

The end of the British Empire was dictated by external forces— the impoverishment of Great Britain by two world wars, making it unable to contend with the rise of nationalist fervor among the colonial peoples, so that it became more sensible to let the colonies go than to try to hang on to them. Still, it was very much a voluntary withdrawal when we compare it with the behavior of imperial aggregations of the past, which more often than not engaged in desperate terminal struggles to survive. (Cf. the Seleucids of Syria, the Mongols of the Khanate, the Third Reich, etc., etc.)

But the British Empire at its most flagrantly imperialistic was a relatively benign affair, not much given to wholesale massacre and brainwashing of the subject populations. Now, though, the Evil Empire itself has struck its flag and dissolved itself peacefully—the vast and loathsome Soviet Union, after seven decades of imposing the cruel hoax of its unproductive political ideology on the peoples of the Russian heartland and on their unwilling neighbors to the west, has simply dried up and blown away. It is an extraordinary development in modern history, which very few prophets indeed had foreseen.

The problem, of course, is that Communism simply didn't work: by destroying economic incentive, it ensured the gradual impoverishment of those who lived under it, thus requiring totalitarian political methods in order to keep its advocates in power. Dictatorial governments may hang on in the short run, but eventually their innate shortcomings create such havoc that the consent of the governed is withdrawn—as in Nero's Rome, in France in 1789, in Romania in

[*Amazing Stories*, March 1992]

1989. The great achievement of Mikhail Gorbachev was to realize that the consent of the governed in the U.S.S.R. and its satellites could no longer be maintained by force, and so he resolved to lift the force—whereupon the people, untrammeled at last, discarded not only their leaders and their economic system but the structure of their nation itself.

The interesting thing about these startling events, from the standpoint of the science-fiction connoisseur, is that it took only seventy-four years for Leninist-Stalinist Communism to fall apart. Most of our great empires have lasted somewhat longer than that: the Roman, for instance, had five or six pretty good centuries, beginning with Rome's conquest of the Hellenistic world in the second century B.C. and continuing on through Constantine's division of the empire in the fourth century A.D. The Byzantine Empire that succeeded it lasted for a thousand years, with some interruptions. The great imperial dynasties of China held sway over much of Asia for an even longer period. The Terran record seems to be held by the Pharaonic Egyptians, who managed to sustain a coherent political system for close to three thousand years, again with a few interruptions. (For most of that time, though, the Pharaohs ruled over a compact and culturally homogeneous territory, what we would call a kingdom rather than an empire.)

But the grand and glorious Evil Empires of science fiction (and even the good ones) tend to survive much longer than that. The durability that is ascribed to them in our classic novels ranges far into the High Metaphoric.

Consider the empire that Frank Herbert created in *Dune*. I am indebted to Will McNelly's formidable *Dune Encyclopedia*, certainly the most impressive secondary work of science fiction ever constructed, for giving us a historical chart that views most of what we regard as history as falling under the First Empire, founded by Alexander the Great and enduring in various permutations for close to five thousand years, covering our entire era and then some. Then two periods of instability, known as The Empire of a Thousand Worlds and the Age of Ten Thousand Emperors, disrupted it for a period of some 45 centuries until the Wars of Reunification (lasting 2500 years!) led to the Empire of Ten Thousand Worlds and the First Golden Age. Yet even that was only the dawn of the real imperial period, and Herbert's chronology mounts on through dynasty after dynasty for an additional *twenty thousand years*. Herbert is dealing, in other words, not with plausible realities but with sweeping poetic hyperboles. A shrewd observer of political trends, he knew as well as anyone that the structures of human society are unlikely to endure in recognizable form for more than a dozen generations or so. But the grandeur of his vision led him to expand his time-frame to cover not mere centuries but whole bushels of millennia. He wasn't writing political history: he was writing science fiction of a splendidly mega-lomaniacal scope, with profoundly entertaining results.

A.E. van Vogt's Isher empire, which dazzled us all forty years ago but now has fallen into some obscurity, was a robust precursor of Herbert's great realm. *The Weapon Shops*, first of the two volumes, takes place in the 48th century of the Isher dynasty, when the beautiful Empress Innelda rules all the inhabited worlds of the galaxy. The sequel, *The Weapon Makers*, continues the tale of the struggle between the Isher rulers and the secret underground movement known as the Weapon Shops—a struggle which itself has been going on for thousands of years.

How cheerfully we science-fiction writers toss around the millennia and the light-years! Isaac Asimov's *Foundation* novels span thousands of years—the earliest of the books opens in Year 12,020 of the Galactic Era—and the empire over which his monarchs reign covers so many worlds that the total number is quite literally uncountable. Asimov knows better than to ask us to accept this fiction at face value—as did I, writing of the giant planet Majipoor in *Lord Valentine's Castle* and speaking of a political system that had endured without significant change for fourteen thousand years. As Brian Aldiss said in an essay on galactic empires in 1976, "You can, in other words, take these stories seriously. What you must not do is take them literally. Their authors didn't. There's a way of reading everything."

Empires that embrace a thousand solar systems are untenable concepts. Unless the imperial army is big enough to establish garrisons everywhere, the citizens of the far-flung realm will simply ignore the diktats coming from the capital, and the empire will exist in name only. And empires that last for a hundred centuries virtually unchanged are equally implausible. The human race is too volatile, too impatient: systems evolve, polities mutate. Nothing has ever stayed the same on our world for more than a few generations; to expect a dynasty to settle in for three or four thousand years is to venture into pure fantasy.

So we see from the collapse of the U.S.S.R. Lenin's great vision of a worldwide socialist empire failed in a mere eight decades. (Outdoing Hitler's Thousand-Year Reich, though, by quite a bit.) The imperial headquarters at the Kremlin eventually could not make its grasp hold even in nearby Latvia and Lithuania and Estonia, let alone on the worlds of Betelgeuse IX. The people of the former Soviet Union have had a brutal lesson in the way economics works; and we who cherish the grandiose dreams of science fiction, watching the events abroad in fascination and amazement, have had a useful reminder of what a magnified and highly intensified version of the real world it is that science fiction gives us.

The Revenge of History

As the long agony of the former Yugoslavia goes on and on, my thoughts turn to the ancient and bloody history of the place. There are principles working themselves out in this small tormented land that are worth careful consideration by those of us who like to write of the destinies of imaginary galactic empires—principles of historical karma, of the unyielding grip of the dead hand of the past.

Consider how the nations we now call Serbia and Croatia came into being:

Like virtually all of Europe from Britain and France to the shores of the Black Sea, they once were part of the Roman Empire. The Romans had absorbed the central and coastal region of Yugoslavia—the modern-day Croatia—as early as 155 B.C., after a long series of wars against the native Illyrian people. They gave the area the name of Dalmatia, imposed the Roman legal system on the Illyrians, and established Roman-style cities and towns for colonists who came over from nearby Italy.

The interior territories—not only modern-day Serbia, but regions in what now are Hungary and Austria, extending as far north as the Danube—came under Roman attack in the reign of Augustus, beginning about 35 B.C., and in the time of Augustus' successor Tiberius the area was organized into the Roman province of Pannonia. From the beginning of Roman Imperial times, therefore, the neighboring districts now known as Serbia and Croatia were under separate administration, though the populations of both places were quite similar, mainly Illyrians with some Roman settlers mixed among them.

As the increasing size of the vast empire made central administration an unwieldy proposition, the city of Rome itself lost its primary position as the seat of government. It became not at all unusual for emperors to emerge from provincial backgrounds. Several generals of Pannonian birth reached the imperial throne in the middle years of the troubled third century; and a native of Dalmatia, the powerful Diocletian, took command of the empire in the year 285, ruling vigorously for the next twenty years. Diocletian, the first to experiment with dividing the far-flung empire between several jointly ruling emperors operating out of different capitals, chose Dalmatia for his seat of rule, building a great palace for himself on the coast that still exists in the Croatian city of Split.

[*Amazing Stories*, October 1993]

Constantine the Great, who eventually emerged as Diocletian's successor, made various attempts to reunite the empire under his sole control; but that proved impossible. By 395 the realm had been permanently divided into eastern and western empires, the eastern with its capital at Constantinople and the western based at Ravenna in Italy. And please take careful note of this important fact:

The boundary between the two empires ran right through what would one day be Yugoslavia. Dalmatia—the modern Croatia—became part of the Western Empire. Pannonia—including what is now Serbia—was assigned to the Eastern Empire. And thereby hangs our tale; for the two regions experienced vastly different fates in the centuries that followed.

During those centuries wandering armies of barbarian tribes—Huns, Goths, Slavs, and many more—rampaged across Europe, bringing the old Roman regime down in ruins. The Western Empire, which had taken in most of Britain, France, Germany, Italy, and central Europe, was overrun and entirely destroyed. The Eastern or Byzantine Empire, which ran from the Danube on into Syria and Egypt, fared much better, but it lost control of many of its European provinces, among them Pannonia, which fell first to the Huns, then to the Goths, then to a tribe called the Avars.

The shrewd Byzantine Emperor Heraclius, seeing that he was unable to stem the barbarian tide, formed an alliance with certain tribes that he regarded as friendly, and encouraged them to drive out the troublesome Avars. About 635, with Heraclius' backing, a Slavic tribe called the Croats took possession of the old Roman province of Dalmatia. About the same time, Heraclius supported the entry of a closely related group of Slavs, the Serbians, into what had been Pannonia.

Even so, the boundary line that had divided the two halves of the Roman Empire continued to exert its force. Under Constantine the Great, Christianity had become the official imperial religion; but bitter doctrinal disputes in the fourth and fifth centuries had led to the establishment of mutually hostile Western and Eastern branches of the Church with differing liturgical practices and theological beliefs, one acknowledging the authority of the Bishop of Rome—the Pope—and the other under the control of the Patriarch of Constantinople.

The Slavic Croats, strongly influenced culturally by the old Roman populace of the Dalmatian coast, gave their allegiance to the Roman Catholic Church. They said their prayers in Latin and those of them who were literate used the Latin alphabet. Their cousins next door, the equally Slavic Serbs, accepted the teachings of the Orthodox Eastern Church; they prayed in Greek, the official language of the Byzantine Empire and its Church, and used the Cyrillic alphabet, made up of Greek letters with special adaptations for Slavic sounds. Linguistically, genetically, culturally, the Serbs and the Croats had originally been very similar indeed. But a fluke of history had brought one group into the Eastern sphere of influence and the other into the Western, and that little accident of territorial distinction has survived now for fourteen centuries, leading directly to today's Yugoslavian tragedy.

The histories of both peoples from that point on are shot through with violent episodes. The Serbs, because their territory lay to the east of that of the Croats, struggled for centuries against Byzantine domination. Finally they established an autonomous Serbian kingdom in the twelfth century as Byzantium weakened under increasingly severe Turkish attack.

But the Serbs themselves came up against the Turks in the fourteenth century, and in 1459—a few years after they had finished off the tottering remnants of the once-glorious Byzantine Empire—the Turks annexed Serbia. The Serbs would remain under oppressive Turkish rule for the next 345 years, breaking free at last in 1804 and managing through many complexities to maintain their independence throughout the nineteenth century. (Bosnia, a piece of the old Roman province of Pannonia lying between the Serb and Croat territories that had also been settled by Slavic Serbians when the Roman Empire collapsed, was likewise conquered by the Turks. Unlike the Serbs of Serbia, who largely retained their Greek Orthodox Christianity, most of the Bosnians converted to Islam under Turkish pressure—thereby lighting another fuse stretching into the twentieth century.)

As for the Croats, whose coastal territories looked westward into Roman Catholic Europe, they established a prosperous maritime kingdom in the tenth and eleventh centuries, but involved themselves in a war with their powerful rivals the Venetians and were greatly weakened. During the Middle Ages they were dominated now by the Hungarians, now by the Venetians. Like the Serbs, they came under Turkish attack, losing some of their territory to them. But with the aid of Austria-Hungary, which had emerged in the sixteenth century as a successor to the old Western Roman Empire, they were able to avoid falling to the Islamic conqueror. The price of their freedom was to swear allegiance to the Austro-Hungarian Emperor, Ferdinand I, in 1527, and for the next four centuries the Croats remained largely under Austrian domination, interrupted by a period of French control in Napoleon's time.

During all these difficult times, migrations of fleeing peoples took place that resulted in pockets of Serbian settlement within Croatian territory, and the mixing of Croats into the Serbian lands. This, too, would make for trouble later on.

The whole intricate regional situation exploded early in the twentieth century, when a struggle between Austria and Turkey for control of Bosnia led to the outbreak of the First World War. In the aftermath of that chaotic struggle, the huge Austrian and Turkish empires both were dismembered by the peace treaty of 1919, and a host of newly independent nations appeared on the map of Europe—Czechoslovakia, Poland, Austria, Hungary, and something called the Kingdom of Serbs, Croats, and Slovenes, which soon afterward re-named itself "Yugoslavia."

And of what, exactly, was this country called "Yugoslavia" consti-tuted?

Why, of Roman Catholic Croatia, and Greek Orthodox Serbia, and Moslem Bosnia, plus assorted other adjacent fragments of the ancient Roman provinces of Dalmatia and Pannonia. How neat, how convenient, to tuck them all into one charming little country!

But geographical proximity means nothing when great cultural chasms separate kinsmen. The Orthodox Serbs detest the Catholic Croats; the Croats loathe the Serbs. When Hitler and Mussolini carved Yugoslavia into autonomous protectorates in 1941, the Serbs and Croats once more found themselves living in separate countries, and the Croats, unhindered suddenly by the imposed patriotism of a central Yugoslavian government, turned on any Serbs they could catch and massacred them with astonishing ferocity. Thousands, perhaps hundreds of thousands, of Serbs perished in Croatian con-centration camps. The triumph of Yugoslavian Communism restored some measure of stability in 1946; but when the Communist regime fell apart a generation later, it was the turn of the Serbs to take revenge on the Croats. (And, meanwhile, these two peoples, still adhering to their rival branches of Christianity, both pounced on their other neighbors, Moslem Bosnians.)

Those who yearn for quick and easy solutions in this struggle should bear in mind that the problem was created as far back as A.D. 395, when the Roman Empire was split into two realms, and was intensified soon after when Christianity underwent bitter schism, with the dividing line of these fissures cutting across the Balkan peninsula and separating what has become the land of the Serbs from the land of the Croats. That split has been unmendable ever since, with bloody results today as Serbs and Croats vent their age-old and long-repressed hatreds on one another. Creators of imaginary future histories take note: when the galactic empires are formed, unpredictable forces will come into play that will dominate the history of the universe for thousands of years thereafter—and the warring worlds of A.D. 10,993 may look back in anguish at decisions made in the remote and half-forgotten fifth or sixth millennium that will prove forever impossible to undo.

Holocaust Deniers

Who controls the past," George Orwell told us in *1984*, "controls the future: who controls the present controls the past." And so the Party that dominates the world of Orwell's nightmare vision constantly revises history for its own benefit. "If the Party could thrust its hand into the past and say of this or that event," Orwell's Winston Smith observes, "*it never happened*—that, surely, was more terrifying than mere torture and death."

The evil empire on whose sinister premises of information control Orwell based his unforgettable parable has collapsed of its own dull-witted malevolence. At last, at long last, the oppressed citizens of the Soviet Union withdrew their consent from their malign government, and—in one of the great unlikely happenings of human history—it simply went away. But the fundamental principles of thought control on which the Soviet Union was built are older than Stalin, older than Marx. They were with us in the days of the Pharaohs; they will be plaguing us still in the days of the Great Galactic Confederation. They are at work right this minute in the United States.

I'm referring to the ongoing effort to deny that the Holocaust—Hitler's campaign of extermination against the Jews of Europe during World War Two—ever took place. At the core of this program of Orwellian disinformation is a band of neo-Nazi fanatics who live in the dark and twisted hope that the goals of their great martyred leader will some day yet be realized. Which is something that I doubt very much will happen, any more than it did the first time it was attempted. Still, there's cause for uneasiness here. What brought Hitler to power in 1933 was a mixture of German gullibility, ignorance, muddled patriotism, and a powerful component of resentment over the harsh terms imposed on Germany at the end of what we now call World War One. What is fueling the growing success of the Holocaust deniers is the robust and ever-increasing component of stupidity that seems to be becoming an American national characteristic.

Six million people—mainly Jews, but also Gypsies, homosexuals, marginal people and undesirables of all sorts—died in the Nazi death camps in the early 1940s. That shouldn't really be a debatable point. We have motion-picture documentation of the liberation of these prisons by Allied troops, showing the emaciated survivors in their camp uniforms, the gigantic mounds of corpses stacked like firewood, the incinerators and gas chambers where the endless mass

[*Amazing Stories*, Winter 1994]

murders were carried out. We have the records of the German high command, authorizing "the final solution to the Jewish problem," as the extermination program was euphemistically called. We have the presence still among us today of living witnesses, people who actually endured years in Auschwitz or Buchenwald or Dachau and bear the tattooed concentration-camp identification numbers on their arms. The immense fact of the German extermination program of the 1940s looms in world history like a dark mountain.

And yet—and yet—

A few months ago it was announced that a Roper Organization poll of 992 American adults and 506 high school students, interviewed in October and November of 1992, revealed that 22 percent of the adults and 20 percent of the high school students thought it seemed possible that the Holocaust had never happened. Twelve percent of the adults and 17 percent of the high school students said that they weren't able to answer the question—that they had so little information about the event that they weren't in a position to tell whether it had or hadn't happened.

What does that mean? If the Holocaust—which took place only a few years ago, relatively speaking—is already so beclouded in our minds that one fifth of us aren't even sure it occurred, then what about the Roman Empire? Did it ever exist, or were the ruins we see in Europe and Africa all faked by Mussolini to bolster Italy's grandeur? For that matter, did Mussolini ever exist? When? Why? And what about Italy itself? Why does a high-school boy in Cleveland or Milwaukee have to believe there is such a place? No one he knows has been there. Mere photographs, and even the claims of supposed witnesses to the existence of an actual far-off country by that name, may not be convincing enough.

When we come down to the issue of sufficient proof, we stumble on ancient philosophical problems. What is sufficient? What is proof? Is there any way of proving that the world is billions of years old? If I tell you that the world was created in a single moment last Tuesday—complete with fossils, ruins, history books, and our individual memories of the week before last—is there any way that you can prove me wrong?

But formal logic is one thing, and the testimony of those who suffered in Auschwitz and still live among us is something else.

"What have we done?" asked Elie Wiesel, who survived both the Auschwitz and Buchenwald death camps and received the Nobel Prize for his books about his experiences there. "We have been working for years and years. I am shocked that 22 percent—oh, my God."

Actually, it should be no surprise that the high school students in that poll were vague on the subject of the Holocaust. It took place, after all, in their grandparents' time, which is prehistory to them. How many of them, I wonder, know whether the Civil War happened before or after the two World Wars, or if it happened at all? How many could name the Presidents of the United States in order from Roosevelt to Bush? Or even those from *Carter* to Bush? A survey taken recently at Ivy League colleges showed that three quarters of the students questioned were unable to identify the author of the phrase, "government of the people, by the people, and for the people" as Abraham Lincoln, and that half of them could not provide the names of their state's two Senators. (Can you?) We *expect* ignorance from the young, these days; we are astounded when they know that Switzerland is a country in Europe, or that Montana is west of Ohio.

But the *adults* in that poll who had their doubts about the Holocaust's reality—many of them 60 years old, or more—

Something more sinister than mere ignorance is at work here. We are entering Orwellian territory. History is being rewritten by people with agendas. Just as certain "scholars" have begun to tell us that the Pharaonic Egyptians were black-skinned people, in defiance of all historical evidence, just as only last year Christopher Columbus was transformed from a hero into a villain by revisionist "historians," so too do we have in our midst a little group of covert Nazi sympathizers who are attempting to further their racial and political views by taking advantage of American gullibility to befog the historical record of the Holocaust.

For example, a group calling itself the Committee for Open Debate on the Holocaust has declared that "the figure of six million Jewish deaths is an irresponsible exaggeration" and asserts that the gas chambers at the Nazi prisons were used merely as "life-saving" fumigation chambers in which lice and other pests were removed from the clothing of the prisoners. The ovens in which hundreds of thousands were roasted alive are turned, by these Holocaust deniers, into "crematoria" for the bodies of internees who died of disease. And why were Jews being interned by the Nazis in the first place? Simply as defensive tactics, we are told, to prevent these enemies of the German state from perpetrating acts of sabotage, just as in the United States at the same time citizens of Japanese ancestry were being rounded up and placed in detention camps.

(I should add, for the benefit of the history-impaired, that we really did round up and imprison Japanese-American citizens during the Second World War, in a shameful and over-emotional reaction to the surprise Japanese attack on our fleet at Pearl Harbor. But the resemblance to the German death camps ends there.)

The Holocaust revisionists, when they first emerged in the 1970s, were widely dismissed as crackpots in a class with those who insist that the entire United States space program, up to and including the landings on the moon, was a hoax. But they have persistently pushed their ideas into prominence, arguing that "different perspectives" on great events have a right to be heard, and getting relatively little opposition at a time when "multiculturalism" and "tolerance of minority views" are trendy educational notions. And in this strange era, where Presidential candidates campaign on television talk-shows and issues of great public moment are decided by polling the ignorant, those who argue that no Nazi extermination program ever happened have succeeded not only in being heard but in getting a fifth of the Roper Organization's poll sample to believe that they may have a case.

They have no case, say I. They are malicious liars, twisting the facts in the hope of sanitizing the monstrous deeds of their idol, Hitler, and laying the groundwork for new purges of inconvenient opponents of their ideas. And they say, No, no, we are merely trying to get at the truth.

What is truth? asked jesting Pilate, and would not stay for an answer. If half the population is hopelessly ignorant and the rest of us are willing to give a fair hearing to anybody who demands one, no matter how blatantly foolish or downright evil their point of view, and if anyone's opinion is as good as the next guy's, what chance is there for the survival of civilization? I say that the Holocaust happened, that Italy actually exists at this moment, that a bearded man named Abraham Lincoln was President of the United States a century and a half ago. You reply that I can't prove any of that; and there the discussion has to end.

But if no one believes anything, and no one knows anything much, everything is cast into doubt. *Everything.* Which allows those who are immune to doubt to impose their will on their goofier and more tentative-minded neighbors. We have entered the era, it seems, of the universal *reductio ad absurdum*, where nothing is permanently true, where every fact is subject to complete revision. "All that was needed," says Orwell, "was an unending series of victories over your own memory. 'Reality control,' they called it; in Newspeak, 'double-think.' "

Yes. Orwell had it right, forty-five years ago. Who controls the past controls the future.

Coming Attractions

As this dizzy century spirals toward its welcome close, the newest zone of kinkiness that has popped out among us involves cigarette smoking. So says my trusty informant on matters of social change, *The Wall Street Journal*, whose fearless reporters check up on all sorts of cutting-edge phenomena for me now that I am not really a cutting-edge kind of guy myself any more.

According to the *Journal*, a whole new genre of cigarette-porn movies has emerged in video-cassette form. "Smoxploitation films" is the generic term for these items. Typical of the form is the 30-minute video called "Paula," in which a young blonde woman wearing a strapless gown and a black hat with a veil slinks into view, lights a cigarette from a candle, takes a deep drag or two, and blows some smoke rings. After a time she switches over to a cigarette holder, and smokes some more.

That's it. She doesn't strip. She doesn't make lewd or suggestive remarks. She just stands there and smokes. Smokes provocatively, maybe; smokes voluptuously; but, still, all she does is *smoke*. If you want the privilege of watching Paula puff, it'll set you back $34.95. Apparently it's worth it, to those who find such things worthwhile. "She is a fabulous smoker," says the reviewer in *Smoke Signals*, a monthly newsletter that keeps watch over artistic endeavors of this sort. "As the video progresses, she does quite a few outstanding slow nose exhales."

Other torrid smoxploitation items reported on recently by *Smoke Signals*, which operates out of the hotbed of deviant social behavior that is Providence, Rhode Island, include "Smoky Kisses" (two women sharing a cigarette) and "The Two Sides of April" (drab unprepossessing girl bares her true seductive nature when she lights up.) The actresses—many of whom aren't smokers in real life, and say that they get pretty glassy-eyed and green around the gills after a long grim day before the camera—are trained in such arcane technical skills as the "snap inhale," which requires them to release little bursts of smoke from their lips and then to gulp them down, and the "French inhale," in which they blow smoke out of their mouths and draw it simultaneously into their nostrils. "The exhale is very important," notes one smoxploitation-film expert.

The smoke-film aficionados who write for *Smoke Signals* also assay Hollywood movies for their nicotine content. A review of "Mad

Love," starring Drew Barrymore, points out with displeasure that although Ms. Barrymore smokes throughout the movie, and "there are many deep inhales," the director doesn't bear down hard on the best moments of the smoking, and, besides, "the exhales aren't great."

The tone is very much like that to be found in those blurry little magazines that provide quick summaries of the high points of the latest pornographic films. But there's no pornography to be found in the smoxploitation genre—at least, not pornography of the old-fashioned kind that involved healthy young unclad folks enthusiastically Doing It before the camera. Nudity is utterly taboo in these movies. We don't even get lingerie shots. The fans don't want any such stuff. Watching fully-dressed girls smoke is the be-all and end-all of smoxploitation. What sells the videos, says Edward Luisser, a major producer of smoking videos, is "the look, the attitude, the mannerism of smoking. It's not so much the sexuality as the erotic allure, the hint of mystery."

What we have here, in fact, is a brand new kind of fetishism, a specialized kind of erotic behavior that omits the stuff that most of us think of as erotic and substitutes the passion and fervor that arises from watching a pretty woman suck combustion products into her lovely and irreplaceable lungs. The linkage between smoking and sex is old stuff in the films—anyone who's seen movies of the 1930s and 1940s can cite any number of tensely erotic scenes involving slinky actresses, square-jawed men, and wisps of curling smoke. But the smoking seems to be *replacing* sex in these new videos. "Smoking is the fetish of the '90s," declares Dian Hanson, the editor of a fetish magazine called *Leg Show* that says it has a circulation of 250,000. "Anytime something becomes widely condemned and taboo, it will be eroticized," says Ms. Hanson, who tries to work smoking scenes into her magazine's photographs every month. Nor are *Leg Show* and *Smoke Signals* the only, ah, sites where this fascination prevails. The Internet folks can drop in at "alt.sex.fetish. smoking" for impassioned discussions of famous women who smoke, and other hot topics.

You don't have to be a smoker, apparently, to want to watch smoking videos. The pleasure is said to come from thinking about the rebellious and defiant nature of women who are so free of inhibition and social restraint that they are willing to flaunt on video their defiance of today's taboo against lighting up. They are engaging in wild and crazy stuff, in the context of the no-smoking 1990s, and that makes them exciting. Go figure.

I'm a life-long non-smoker myself, who has always found the habit nasty and isn't turned on by people who practice it. And as I read about all this latest manifestation of modern-day creepiness (or so I see it) in the *Journal*, what came immediately to my mind is the scary, brilliant story called "Coming Attraction" by the late Fritz Leiber, one of the greatest of all s-f writers, published all the way back in 1950. (You can find it in my anthology *The Science Fiction Hall of Fame*, classic stories chosen by vote of the Science Fiction Writers of America.) Leiber's story, nearly half a century old now, was a good thirty years ahead of its time in its depiction of the dark and strange thing that our end-of-the-century world has become. Though something as inherently innocuous as getting kicks from sitting around watching films of women smoking is mild by comparison with many of the things Leiber imagined in "Coming Attraction," it nevertheless would have been an appropriate companion to the other forms of decadence that made the story so memorable.

The Leiber story takes place in New York of the near future—Leiber doesn't specify the date, but my guess is that he meant it to be thirty years or so later than the time of the story's creation—which is to say, about fifteen years in our own actual past by now. It opens fast. "The coupe with the fishhooks welded to the fender shouldered up over the curb like the nose of a nightmare. The girl in its path stood frozen, her face probably stiff with fright under her mask. I took a fast step toward her, grabbed her elbow, yanked her back....The big coupe shot by, its turbine humming."

It's a vile time, all right. Roving gangs of juvenile delinquents are everywhere. Their cars have fishhooks on them to skewer pedestrians, and leave huge clouds of black smoke behind them as they make their getaways. Women wear masks in the street, but often leave their breasts bare. They also go in for affixing razor-sharp metal caps to their fingertips, so that a slap or a caress is likely to draw blood. (Some of the kinkier men wear masks too—the newest kind of cross-dressing.) The most popular sport is man/woman wrestling, using big, strong women and small wiry men. The most familiar plot in hard-boiled crime novels is the one in which two female murderers go gunning for each other. Nightclubs are dim places glowing blue, where what would later be called go-go girls dance non-stop, naked except for their masks. Popular music—and remember that Leiber was writing in the era of Perry Como and Bing Crosby—is pretty much what you'd expect: "There was a band going full blast in the latest robop style, in which an electronic composing machine selects an arbitrary sequence of tones into which the musicians weave their raucous little individualities."

Things get darker and darker, and eventually, after a brawl in a night-club, the narrator pulls the mask from the face of his new companion, the girl whom he had rescued from the fishhook car. "I don't know why I should have expected her face to be anything else. It was very pale, of course, and there weren't any cosmetics. I suppose there's no point in wearing any under a mask. The eyebrows were untidy and the lips chapped. But as for the general expression, as for the feelings crawling and wriggling across it—

"Have you ever lifted a rock from damp soil? Have you ever watched the slimy white grubs?"

I should point out that Leiber needed an atomic war as the rationale for the changes that brought about the sinister society depicted in "Coming Attractions." He tells us about radioactive hell-pits in downtown Manhattan and shows us the stump of the Empire State Building and mothers carrying mutant children through the streets. That was all a plausible enough scenario in 1950. But we didn't need Soviet megatonnage detonating in our cities to bring us the music, drugs, dress, and body-piercings of our time. We managed to reach the decadence and all-out creepiness of Leiber's future America all by ourselves, a voluntary cultural evolution, without such explosive help from outside.

Fritz Leiber, were he alive today, would not be at all surprised to hear that the high-minded movement that has virtually driven cigarette smoking from public America has led directly to the desire, on the part of some citizens at least, to stare with delight at the spectacle of delectable videotaped women practicing snap inhales and slow exhales. The eroticization of the forbidden was something that Fritz Leiber understood very well. I wouldn't be at all surprised, in fact, to find some casual reference to something very much like the smoxploitation videos somewhere in one of his actual stories. The really sad thing, I think, is that "Coming Attraction" doesn't even seem shocking any more. Why should it? We see analogous horrors every day and take them for granted.

It's a weird time, isn't it, folks? You and I, of course, are still leading clean, wholesome lives amidst all the cultural detritus of the bizarre and freaky late 1990s. We don't wear masks in the street, we don't try to slice up pedestrians with the sharp hooks welded to the fenders of our cars, and we don't go to blue-lit night-clubs to listen to ghastly discordant music. We don't smoke, either, and we don't get thrills from watching young women dragging deep. We are nice folks, you and I, not in any way kinky.

But the crazy stuff that's going on all around us, as the century winds down—

Oh, Fritz! Oh, Jesus!

SIX

A Few Personal Items

The Books of Childhood

In recent years I've been reassembling the books I loved in my childhood some fifty years ago—an enterprise born not simply of nostalgia but from deep curiosity about the narrative material that went into the forming of Robert Silverberg, writer. For surely what we read in childhood makes the strongest impressions on us, leaving ineradicable imprints that, so I believe, recur in the work of any creative artist throughout his life. And now, with hundreds of stories and an uncountable number of books behind me, I'm trying to learn something about the source from which that seemingly inexhaustible flow of narrative has come.

So I've been prowling the rare-book dealers, and consulting catalogs, and cudgeling my own memory to try to reconstruct my reading preferences of the late 1930s and early 1940s. A ferociously retentive person like me would be expected to have the books of his childhood still on hand, I suppose, but in fact many of them were books I never owned in the first place, because I was such a dedicated user of the Brooklyn Public Library. (When I returned to Brooklyn a few years ago I revisited my ancient library branch, naively thinking some of those books would still be on the shelves, but of course they had been read to tatters long ago and replaced by the favorites of a newer generation.) As for the books I did own, some are still in my possession but most were destroyed in the fire that swept through my house in 1968. I made notes at the time on what was lost (and in some instances kept the charred copies) and that has helped me greatly in this job of reclaiming the past.

I'm not talking, incidentally, of the standard children's books that everyone in my era read—*Tom Sawyer*, *Huckleberry Finn*, *Alice in Wonderland*, *Through the Looking Glass*, *Lamb's Tales from Shakespeare*, *Peter Pan*, *Just So Stories*, *The Arabian Nights*, and such. I read all of those, of course—read them dozens of times—but what I've been looking for are the more esoteric things, the ones that went particularly into the shaping of the science-fiction writer that I was to become.

In fact I should have become a fantasy writer, I guess, because what particularly preoccupied me in those early years were books of myths and legends. I have some of them on the desk before me now: Padraic Colum's *The Children of Odin*, a retelling of the Norse myths, and an obscure little pamphlet called *The Heroes of Asgard* by A. and

[*Amazing Stories*, April 1992]

E. Keary dealing with the same body of material (my original copy, water-stained but intact) and Colum's *The Adventures of Odysseus and the Tale of Troy*. And also, a really esoteric one, Helen Zimmern's *The Epic of Kings*, which draws on the great Persian epic of Firdausi, and which after years of searching I have only recently managed to find again. How they filled my mind with wonders, those books! Loki and the Fenris wolf, Audhumla the primordial cow, Odin at Mimir's well, the tale of the Volsungs, of Sohrab and Rustem, of the injudicious Kai Kaous and the noble Kai Khosrau, the death of Achilles, the wanderings of Odysseus—I dreamed of them, I embroidered on their plots in my mind, I longed to enter their world in actuality. Images from those Norse and Greek myths still course vividly through my mind and I can find their correlatives in my own writing; but I have transmuted them all to science fiction instead of producing new adventures of the Aesir or the heroes of Troy. Most likely the primary reason for that is that I came to maturity at a time when fantasy was an unpublishable category and science fiction a thriving and expanding operation, and I wanted what I wrote to see print.

But there is another reason. I was exposed at the same early age to the s-f virus, which had the same mythic power for me, and which, apparently, affected me even more deeply.

For instance, here is my copy of *The Complete Works of Lewis Carroll*, the Modern Library edition, which I see from my father's inscription was given to me when I was not quite eight years old. The first 271 pages of this 1293-page volume are given over, of course, to the two Alice novels, which show signs of having been read and read and read. But the trail of fingerprints and eyetracks indicates that I went right on to the next two novels, *Sylvie and Bruno* and *Sylvie and Bruno Concluded*, books that no one else I know has ever mentioned reading. I don't know what category they fall into: not quite fantasy, not really science-fiction; but there is a weird logic to them that makes them seem almost like parallel-world stories, since they take place in a sort of England, but not any England we would recognize. What Lewis Carroll achieved in these two little-known books was a variation on the free play of fantasy that we see in *Alice* or *Looking Glass*, but it is a down-to-earth kind of fantasy that has more resonance with science fiction. Beyond them in the huge volume is "The Hunting of the Snark," and some other poems, and then, in the back, an astonishing bunch of conundrums in logic and other mystifications that had a profound effect on my childish mind although I was unable even to begin understanding what their author was talking about. It was Lewis Carroll's rigorous, orderly, and logical exploration of the utterly incomprehensible, I think, that helped me to understand what science fiction (as opposed to fantasy) is all about.

A couple of other discoveries about the same time pushed me toward science fiction. The Buck Rogers comic strip, for one—I dimly remember a Sunday page, circa 1941, in which aliens with red puckered faces came swarming over a sea-wall while Buck and his companions tried to push them back. And then, in 1942, *Planet Comics*—embodying a glorious vision of the spectacular interplanetary future that left me hungry for more of the same, and led me on and on until at last by the age of ten I had found H.G. Wells and Jules Verne and my destiny was set in stone forever. (I tried, a couple of years ago while attending a convention of comic-book collectors, to find the issue of *Planet* that had so spun my mind into orbit. I was willing to pay the staggering sum being asked for issues of that vintage. But I couldn't seem to recognize, in the crudely drawn pages of the issues I saw, the particular splendors that had illuminated my mind nearly half a century before. Perhaps the ink had faded; or perhaps I was looking at the wrong issue.

Here is another book of my childhood that sent me in still another direction as a writer: Walter de la Mare's marvelous fantasy *The Three Mulla-Mulgars*, a curious tale of the adventures of three highly intelligent monkeys who set out across the heart of a fantastic Africa to find the golden land from which their father had come. (It's a wonderful book, and I say so not merely because I see it through the eyes of the child who loved it: I re-read it yet again a few months ago and was as profoundly moved by its beauty and mystery as I had been when I was nine.) Images out of that remarkable book have been turning up in my own science-fiction books for decades; I usually recognize them for what they are after the fact, and smile, and leave them there as an homage. There are passages in my newest novel, *Kingdoms of the Wall*, that owe their power to my decades-old recollections of *The Three Mulla-Mulgars*. So be it. No writer invents everything from scratch; our imaginations are billion-piece mosaics fashioned from everything we have ever experienced, including all that we have ever read. But also de la Mare led me circuitously to write an immense historical novel; for his monkeys encounter, midway through their jungle odyssey, a stranded Englishman named Andrew Battell, with whom they become involved for two or three chapters. About 1965 I discovered quite by accident that Andrew Battell had really lived; and, stumbling upon the text of Battell's own journal, which surely de la Mare had used in writing his novel, I resolved to retell his story myself, and eventually did so in my immense historical novel, *Lord of Darkness*, which is nothing else than my imagined version of Andrew Battell's autobiography. I tip my hat to Walter de la Mare again and again throughout its 559 pages, but only someone who has read *The Three Mulla-Mulgars* would know that, and I have never met anyone else who has.

I am pleasantly aware, as I forage through the reconstituted library of my childhood, that books I have written are part of other people's store of images and recollections. Again and again I hear that someone's first novel was one of my early books for young readers— *Revolt on Alpha C*, say, or *Lost Race of Mars*. So the cycle goes round and round. We read, we absorb, we transmute, and we offer new stories for new readers, who will eventually recycle our own work into tales for the readers of generations to follow.

In darker moments I wonder whether today's young readers— brought up on *Teenage Mutant Ninja Turtles* instead of *Heroes of Asgard* and *The Children of Odin*—will produce fables and fantasies of their own with any value whatever. Garbage in, garbage out, as they say. But I want to think that I'm wrong: that the myth-making function of mankind is eternal, and that there will always be powerful new stories growing out of powerful ancient ones, no matter what debasements of popular culture may thrive in the marketplace. In any case, it's not my problem. I won't be around to see what the writers born in 1985 will be writing forty years from now. And if I don't care for what has been produced in the interim, well, I can always go back and re-read *The Three Mulla-Mulgars* or *Sylvie and Bruno* or *The Epic of Kings* one more time.

The Books of Childhood, Continued

Graham Greene, again: I have long found his essays and novels a source of wisdom and inspiration. This comes from his autobiographical essay, "The Lost Childhood":

"Perhaps it is only in childhood that books have any deep influence on our lives....In childhood all books are books of divination, telling us about the future, and like the fortune teller who sees a long journey in the cards or death by water they influence the future."

Greene was speaking in particular of how the books he had read in his own distant childhood in Edwardian England had sent him on the path toward becoming a writer, and had even shaped the *kind* of fiction he would choose to write. But not only writers, he says, are set on their paths by their early reading.

"I was safe as long as I could not read," Greene tells us. "The wheels had not begun to turn—but now the future stood around on bookshelves everywhere waiting for the child to choose—the life of a chartered accountant, perhaps, a colonial civil servant, a planter in China, a steady job in a bank, happiness and misery...." We are stamped irrevocably in our childhoods, he says; the impressions we receive then determine the years ahead. And he offers as one epitome of that idea the startling lines from AE's poem "Germinal"—

In ancient shadows and twilights
Where childhood had strayed,
The world's great sorrows were born
And its heroes were made.
In the lost boyhood of Judas
Christ was betrayed.

Exactly so. In every childhood there is a moment when a door opens and lets the future in—and very often it is a book that provides that moment.

A month or two ago, I spoke of the books in my own childhood that did that for me—retellings of Norse and Persian legends and the poems of Homer, an obscure novel by Lewis Carroll, and a wonderful fantasy by Walter de La Mare, among others. But I didn't speak in any particular way about the science fiction books that I stumbled upon some forty-five years ago that sent me spiraling off into the orbit that

[*Amazing Stories*, October 1992]

has defined my life's career. I mentioned some Jules Verne and H.G. Wells, yes, but only in passing.

I have the actual books on my desk before me now—five of them, treasured artifacts of my childhood. Here is Verne's *Twenty Thousand Leagues Under the Sea*, in an undated and virtually anonymous edition published by "Books, Inc." I suspect it was given to me in 1943 or 1944. I had no idea, of course, that it was science-fiction; I was not to hear that phrase itself for another couple of years. But I knew, as I read it over and over, that it was a magical tale of adventure that relied not on witchcraft and the supernatural but on a clear-eyed comprehension of the real world. Verne's crisp technical descriptions ("Besides other things the nets brought up, were several flabellariae and graceful polypi, that are peculiar to that part of the ocean. The direction of the Nautilus was still to the southeast. It crossed the equator December 1, in 142 degrees latitude; and on the fourth of the same month we sighted the Marquesas group....) provided so plausible a texture of verisimilitude to my science-oriented mind that I took it quite for granted when Captain Nemo made a side trip to visit the sunken ruins of Atlantis in his submarine. Verne's underwater tour of the world showed me our planet as a place of marvels populated by hordes of extraordinary creatures. Somehow, unawares, I learned the distinction between fantasy and science-fiction even then, and my mode of writing was determined in that moment, years before I even knew I was going to be a writer.

Then here is Donald A. Wollheim's *The Pocket Book of Science Fiction*, first of all paperback s-f anthologies. The copyright date is 1943, but my edition is a 1947 printing, and that must be when I discovered it and eagerly paid my twenty-five cents. Ten stories, here; one of them was by H.G. Wells, whom I had already discovered in the public library. (I had read *The Time Machine*, at least, by 1946, though it would be years before I owned a copy myself.) I knew Wells's name was a mark of quality in this peculiar kind of literature for which I already knew I had a predilection; but I discovered other writers in Wollheim's anthology, too—someone named Theodore Sturgeon, and Stanley G. Weinbaum, and Robert A. Heinlein. I wasn't sure how to pronounce Heinlein's name, but his whacky fourth-dimensional story, "—And He Built a Crooked House," gave me immense pleasure. So did Sturgeon's powerful "Microcosmic God," and Weinbaum's joyous "A Martian Odyssey." And then there was T.S. Stribling's long, mysterious "The Green Splotches," which I now know to be a classic early s-f story by a once-famous mainstream writer.

My head reeled with wonders. I was thrown into a fever of excitement. My yearning for the world of the distant future was so powerful that I could taste and touch and smell it. Off I went to the book department at Macy's, and stumbled at once into *Portable Novels of Science*, edited by—Wollheim again! In it was Wells' *First Men in the Moon*, and John Taine's epic of time-travel and dinosaurs, *Before the Dawn*, and Lovecraft's spooky *The Shadow Out of Time*, and above all Olaf Stapledon's tale of super-children, *Odd John*, which seemed to speak directly to lonely, maladjusted, high-I.Q. twelve-year-old me.

The damage was completely done. Not content to read these stories, I had to recreate them in my own words. I started writing imitations of the stories that had most moved me in Wollheim's second book: fragmentary Lovecraftian visions of the far future, time-machine epics replete with Mesozoic scenery, moody tales of the emotional problems of young supermen. I have no idea where any of these things are today—no doubt they would enliven somebody's doctoral thesis on my life and works. But I scribbled away with enormous energy, reliving the stories I had come to love by paying them the sincerest form of flattery.

I had thought all along that I was going to be a scientist when I grew up, by the way. A paleontologist, most likely, or perhaps a botanist. And so I was startled, one day in 1948, when a school adviser who had spoken recently to my father said, "Your parents seem to think you're going to be a writer. Do you think that's so?"

I was astounded. A writer? It had never crossed my mind! "I'm planning to go into science," I told her in bewilderment. But apparently I was the only one who hadn't seen the obvious. That day was a pivotal one in my life—one of those profound Greenian moments when the future reaches toward a child and engulfs him. I have never forgotten the confusion in which I said to myself, "They think I'm going to be a writer? Are they serious? *Could* I be a writer? Am I a writer already? Maybe I am." And the mechanism began to tick in me. Paleontology's loss was science-fiction's gain, that day in 1948—for, now that the suggestion had been openly made, I embraced it as though it was what I had had in mind all along. Which very likely I had.

The next two books confirmed the addiction and thrust me further along the path. One was Groff Conklin's *A Treasury of Science Fiction*, with stories by Heinlein, Arthur C. Clarke, L. Sprague de Camp, Murray Leinster, Jack Williamson, and a good many more of my future demigods. (And one great story, "Vintage Season" by the pseudonymous "Lawrence O'Donnell," to which I would write a sequel, forty years later.) Hardly had I plumbed the depths of the Conklin anthology when I found another and even more astonishing book, the classic Healy-McComas *Adventures in Time and Space*, which dazzled me beyond repair with Heinlein's "By His Bootstraps" and del Rey's "Nerves" and Hasse's "He Who Shrank" and van Vogt's "Black Destroyer" and de Camp's "The Blue Giraffe" and a passel of others that I read until I knew them virtually by heart. (Among them was one called "Nightfall," by someone with the odd name of Asimov. I lived long enough to help turn that one into a novel. You live long enough and the strangest things happen to you.)

What those two anthologies told me, other than renewing my belief that science fiction was a wondrous thing that expanded my fledgling mind toward the infinite, was that there was such a thing as science-fiction magazines. Cannily I looked at the copyright lines of the stories in the books and found their names: *Amazing Stories, Planet Stories, Thrilling Wonder Stories*, and above all *Astounding Science Fiction*, where perhaps 75% of all the stories I had most admired had originated. I rushed out and bought them—and began to buy back issues too—and neglected my homework to read them late at night—and sent the editors my crude and pitiful little stories—

And—well—my parents were right. Evidently I was thinking of becoming a writer. Before me on my desk are the five books that did it to me. As Graham Greene put it, the future had been standing around on bookshelves everywhere waiting for this child to choose. And choose it I did, in a double sense of the word. Once I had those five books in my possession my future was determined, and it was to be a future of science-fiction writing.

The process never stops. Books did it for Graham Greene; books and s-f magazines did it for me. Somewhere, right now, someone as young and impressionable and alert-minded as I was in 1947 is picking up this glossy issue of *Amazing* and staring at it in growing excitement and curiosity. And in that moment of mounting wonder was the winner of the Hugo Award for 2032 A.D. decided.

The Oakland Fire

Thinking fast is a good idea when disaster comes, but sometimes the best thing is not to think too much at all. And so when the sky turned black over Oakland midway through a lovely golden autumn morning, just five days ago as I write this, I didn't spend a lot of time pondering which of my possessions I preferred to save if the fire that had suddenly begun to rage five or six miles north of me should reach my neighborhood, as was beginning to seem altogether possible.

Of course, I've had some practice at this kind of thing. In 1968, when I still lived in New York City, fire came from nowhere at four in the morning on a February night and drove me out into 12-degree weather. I had very little time that night to gather things, or even my wits; so just about all I took with me was the manuscript of the book I was working on and one little ancient Roman glass bowl that I found particularly precious. I didn't even bother to grab the ledger in which I keep irreplaceable business records. Instead of trying to pack up the four cats and various kittens of the household, I chased them all down to the basement, four stories below the fire itself, and shut them into a room where I thought they'd be safe. That turned out to be dumb, because one of the first things the firemen did was to open that room, letting cats loose into the house. As it happened, all the cats survived the fire anyway, and so did many of the possessions that I had left behind, though the house itself was a total wreck. And I found the ledger a few days later in the ruins of what had been my office.

This time, when the alarms began to go off in the distance and that terrible plume of smoke fouled the sky, the *first* thing I did was corral the cats—different ones, 23 years later—and pack them into their carriers. Then I got the business ledger, with 23 more years of notations in it, and the little box of backup disks containing my current story and the financial records I had just finished transferring to my new computer. The computer itself I left behind, along with a houseful of treasures. My wife Karen and I loaded what we had chosen to take into the car, turned the car around in the driveway to be aimed outward for quick departure, and spent the next hour and a half hosing down the roof of the house while the fire drew closer. At half past three in the afternoon the helicopters came overhead, bellowing evacuation orders for our entire neighborhood, and we joined the outward migration. As I passed through the house and the separate building that is my office, locking things and setting burglar alarms, I did find myself wondering whether I would ever see any of this again. But that was as much speculation as I allowed myself. There are times when it's best not to do a lot of thinking.

We took refuge over the hills, ten miles away (it seemed like worlds away) at the home of our friend Jim Benford, who is Gregory Benford's twin brother, and his wife Hilary. And there we stayed through the frightful night of October 20, compulsively watching the terrible scenes on television as the lovely hillside town where I have lived for the past twenty years underwent trial by fire.

Conditions couldn't have been better for a major conflagration. Not only has Northern California undergone a drought for the past five years, but the *normal* climate of the California coast gives us long rainless summers, and we had had virtually no measurable precipitation for six full months. There had been an atypical hard frost the previous December, leaving many trees in the eucalyptus forests of the high ridges with clusters of dry dead leaves. And October is usually the warmest month of the year for us: the temperature that morning was in the high eighties. A weird and troublesome easterly wind was blowing out of the hot, dry interior of the state instead of the cool ocean breeze that usually sweeps across the Bay Area.

So when a brush fire that somehow had begun in the hills the day before—and supposedly had been extinguished—came back to life Sunday morning and got out of hand, disaster was inevitable. The parched trees and dry grassy meadows of the hills went up immediately; the lovely wooden houses in the initial fire zone were ignited within minutes; and then, as trees exploded into flame, great firebrands were lifted aloft and carried hundreds of yards by that deadly east wind, down into the heavily populated residential regions below the hill area itself. You probably know the rest of the story, though not as well as we do. By daybreak at least two thousand homes had been destroyed; whole neighborhoods had been obliterated; an enviably beautiful landscape had been transformed into a thing of horror.

Karen and I were among the lucky ones. The fire was brought under control a mile north of our house. At nine the next morning the evacuation area for our immediate neighborhood was lifted, and we said goodbye to Jim and Hilary Benford and set out, badly shaken but immensely relieved, for our house. Because the fire zone blocked the ten-minute direct route between the Benford house and ours, we came home the long way around, a trip of more than an hour; but eventually we were there to see that the place had gone untouched. We unpacked our bewildered cats, wandered around thankfully to visit our possessions, and tried to put some of the nightmare behind us.

Most other members of the Oakland hills science fiction community came through, as we did, with nothing more than a bad scare. Charles Brown's hilltop house, where LOCUS is published, was well outside the danger zone. The canyonside house that Jack Vance built with his own hands and where he and his wife Norma have lived for more than forty years was closer to the blaze, but went unharmed; Jack's son John defied the evacuation order and spent the night in the house to guard it, and when I spoke to him by phone that evening he said that glowing embers were floating by but that no fires had started nearby. Poul and Karen Anderson, who live on the other side of the hill in Orinda—also menaced in the early hours of the fire—were all right also. The most remarkable story involved the house on Broadway Terrace where Terry Carr and his wife Carol lived for many years, and which Carol still occupies. The fire came as far south as Broadway Terrace, wiping out everything along the north side of the street. But Carol's house is on the south side; and the next day we discovered that it was still there, utterly unscathed along with five or six of its neighbors in the midst of the awesome destruction. And on the Berkeley side of the fire, where the Hotel Claremont (site of the 1968 World Science Fiction Convention) was threatened but ultimately was saved, the house known as Greyhaven, inhabited by Marion Zimmer Bradley's brother Paul, agent Tracy Blackstone, and writers Diana Paxson and Jon DeCles, also came through, despite early rumors that it had been lost. On the other side of the ledger was the destruction of the house where my first wife Barbara—who had suffered through that 1968 fire with me—lived. It was in the zone where the blaze broke out, and must have been incinerated in the first moments of the event. (Barbara herself was out of town at the time or her life might well have been in danger.)

Now a few days have passed, and things slowly return to normal for those of us who escaped with nothing more than a few hours of fright, while those who were more closely touched by calamity begin the long, numbing process—which will take a year or more, and in some senses will never be at an end, if my 1968 experience is any guide—of rebuilding their interrupted lives. Already new utility poles are being erected in the disaster area, electric and telephone service is being restored, and crews with chainsaws and jackhammers are starting to haul away debris. In a few weeks wildflowers will begin to bloom atop the ashes; by spring the first new houses will be under construction.

The area where we live is one of the most beautiful in the world. We have the sea nearby; we have hills and mountains; we have a vast blue sky above us most of the year, clear air, months on end of brilliant sunshine. The winters are mild and the summers are gentle, so that our weather is a kind of perpetual springtime. Few of us are talking about moving away, despite all that we have been through in recent years.

But we have been through a great deal here. There has been a drought, in an already dry climate, for the past five years. There was a terrifying earthquake in 1989. 1990 brought us a hard frost, which wiped out cherished gardens decades old and harassed our fertile agricultural regions. And now this fire, which has left so frightful a scar on our lovely hills. It makes one uneasy about what may come next; it eats into one's reserves of resilience. Our friends back east ask us why we don't move to some safer place.

And yet—and yet—

A day or two after our fire there was a great earthquake in India. Last summer the Philippines struggled to cope with the effects of a huge volcanic eruption. Just yesterday I read a newspaper account of another eruption, in the Chilean Andes on August 12, that has buried a section of Patagonia five times the size of Connecticut in volcanic ash, threatening the economic welfare of an enormous region of Argentina. And of course I could go back through the roster of historic eruptions, floods, earthquakes, hurricanes, and all the rest.

So what is the lesson to derive from the fire that roared through my pretty neighborhood last Sunday? That the San Francisco Bay Area, lovely as it is, is too dangerous for human habitation, and that we should all move somewhere else, someplace safer?

No. The real conclusion to draw from what has happened here is something that we already know in the abstract from having read about Pompeii or the Bangladesh floods or the San Francisco earthquake of 1906, but which does not become completely real until it strikes closer to home. And that is that there may be safer places than this one, but that no place is really safe. We who inhabit the planet Earth live on the shoulders of an indifferent giant. At any moment he may choose to shrug or even simply twitch, and hurl us to destruction. It's a wonderful planet, and I don't know of a better one to live on. But even its most beautiful regions are places of peril, and though we like to think of ourselves as the masters of the world, we need to remember that we are only its tenants and the terms of the lease can be altered, without our consent, at any time.

Dreams

L ast night I dreamed that Isaac Asimov, just before he died, had
decided to make a voyage into space. At NASA's invitation he went
up in the space shuttle and beamed a message of joy and wonder and
hope to the Earthbound rest of us.

It was a lovely and touching dream. There was Isaac miraculously
resurrected by my sleeping mind, grinning out at me from the
television screen, his famous side-whiskers looking more formidable
than ever under the gravity-free conditions. I listened to him describing in glowing terms the way the Earth looked to him from orbit, and
telling us how happy he was that he had managed to make this one
journey aboard a spaceship, here at the very end of his life.

It was, of course, a wildly implausible dream, even as dreams go.
Isaac Asimov would have been the last person on this planet to get
aboard a spacegoing vehicle. Arthur C. Clarke would have accepted the
invitation, certainly, if only they had asked him while he was still a lad
of 70 or so. Robert A. Heinlein very likely would have gone. Frank
Herbert, certainly. But Isaac? *Isaac?* Don't be silly. Isaac was the world's
worst acrophobe. A roller-coaster ride that he took when he was
nineteen drove him into paroxysms of panic. He made a grand total of
two airplane trips in his life, both times under military auspices during
his World War II service, and they had such a powerful effect on him
that he studiously avoided air travel for the next fifty years. And though
he lived on the 33rd floor of a Manhattan apartment building, he did
his writing in a room with drawn blinds, facing a blank, windowless
wall. A 30-foot trip in a cherrypicker to light a ceremonial lamp for a
Jewish holiday at a rabbi's request once reduced him to a state of
near-paralysis. No, Isaac was not your basic astronaut kind of guy, and
the thought of him sitting aboard a space shuttle waiting for the
moment of lift-off makes *me* break out in a cold sweat.

But dreams don't have to make sense. That's the best thing about
them, so far as I'm concerned. By day I am (or try to be) a coolly
rational person, lucid of intellect and single of mind, who pursues a
logical course through life with better than average success. Once I hit
my pillow, though, anything goes—hours and hours of free-form
improvisation, utterly unfettered by any sort of logical necessity. In
my dreams, rivers can flow uphill. Cats can fly. (Sometimes, so can I.)
And Isaac Asimov not only lives again, but is capable of taking a trip
aboard the space shuttle and telling us what fun it is.

[*Asimov's Science Fiction*, June 1995]

I love it. It's like an effortless movie show every night.

I try to remember my dreams—the best ones, at least. I tell them to my wife when *she* finally wakes up, a couple of hours farther along in the morning than I do. I tell them to my agent. Sometimes I even jot them down and eventually make use of them in my fiction. I have generated perfectly good short stories out of dreams ("Good News from the Vatican," for example, the one about the robot who is elected Pope, which won me a Nebula in 1972) and on at least one occasion I've assembled an entire novel out of whatever it was that I happened to dream the night before.

The one thing I don't do, usually, is to try to figure out what my dreams "mean." So far as I'm concerned, dreams don't have to mean anything. (I'm sorry, Dr. Freud. In your line of work dreams may be the direct key to the patient's problems, but in my sort of business dreams can be accepted simply as the raw material of fiction without the need for close interpretation. They are bulletins from the unconscious that a writer can treat as dictation from himself to himself, and they will make such sense as is appropriate to the story into which they are mortared. Ursula Le Guin once wrote an essay about her Earthsea books called "Dreams Must Explain Themselves," and the title of that essay nicely expresses my basic position on the subject. Soothsayers and psychoanalysts may need to figure out the true meaning of people's dreams, but I don't: I simply have to find some appropriate *narrative* use for them in the course of some science-fiction or fantasy project, and, if my storytelling sixth sense is working properly, the dream will explain itself within the context of the story as things unfold.)

I was delighted to discover, just a few days before my Isaac dream, that Graham Greene, one of my favorite writers, also paid close attention to his dreams, and in fact kept a diary of them. (A volume of them, covering his dreams between 1965 and 1989, was published posthumously by Viking in 1994 under the title, *A World of My Own: A Dream Diary.*) In that book we see Greene seeing himself taking a boat journey to Bogota with Henry James (not much fun for Greene), undertaking a spy mission to Nazi Germany and thrusting a poisoned cigarette up Joseph Goebbels' nostril, and holding conversations with Oliver Cromwell, Fidel Castro, and Alexander Solzhenitsyn, among others. This very heterosexual man also has a homosexual encounter in his sleep with the master spy Kim Philby, commits both robbery and murder, and meets a talking kitten. A strange and fascinating person was Graham Greene, and his dreams, not very surprisingly, are shot through with the dark, vivid illuminations that made his novels such rich things.

Reading Greene's book of dreams, I was fiercely envious, because my own dreams have been pretty lively ones too and I have let all too many of them go to waste, beyond hope of recovery now. I have never kept a dream diary, or, for that matter, any very detailed diary of my waking life. (Isaac did, and built his three huge autobiographical books around it. Knowing Isaac, I doubt that he jotted down very much about his dreams, though.) Except for those dreams that immediately cry out to me that they can be converted into usable fiction, which I note down early in the morning or once in a while in the middle of the night, I allow them to vanish, and most of them evaporate quickly as the day arrives. (Some stay with me, of course, for years or even decades. Those, I know, are the Important Ones, and you can bet that I have employed them, sometimes more than once, in my writing.)

My most frustrating dream experience—and I wonder if it is one that other writers have had—recurs for me every three or four years. I dream an entire novel. It is a book that—in my dream—I have just finished writing, and now I am re-reading the manuscript before sending it to the publisher; and I lie there in my sleep, turning each page, avidly reading and admiring every word, while one part of my dreaming mind makes note of the fact that I am reading a novel that in reality I have not actually yet written. I remind myself sternly to commit the entire book to memory so that when I awaken I can begin setting it down immediately on paper. It is, of course, a magnificent novel, my best work by far. And, of course, when I awaken I can't remember a single syllable of it, only the fact that I have had That Dream again. (Though once I was able to bring back from one version of this dream some half dozen words that had been embossed on the manuscript page in bold calligraphy. They were not, unfortunately, words in any language that I or anybody else understands.)

But, as I said a few paragraphs ago, I have been able to develop stray images and events that I remember from dreams into stories and even books. (So too did Graham Greene, according to the introduction to his dream diary.) And one time I did indeed put a whole novel together out of eight weeks' collected dreams.

This was *Son of Man*, which I wrote in a kind of white heat in December, 1969, and which was published by Ballantine Books in the summer of 1971. That was a time, some of you may recall, when many of the finest minds of our nation were entering altered states of consciousness with the aid of psychedelic drugs, and *Son of Man* was intended to be a kind of psychedelic adventure in the very far future—surreal, dreamlike, alogical. I did not, incidentally, write it while I was in any sort of drugged state myself. I wrote it the way I have written everything else, sitting down with a clear mind after breakfast and doing a regular daily stint, same time every day, no chemical additives of any kind whatsoever employed while I'm on the job.

But I did transcribe my dreams, and they were grand and glorious ones. There was wondrous feedback between book and dreams throughout the time of writing, and as I got deeper and deeper into the strange novel, the dreams got stranger too, kicking the next day's work into an even higher energy state of strangeness. This is a sample passage, chosen at random:

"He looks. What appears to be a river is gushing from the hole in the side of the mountain. But the fluid that pours out is misty and intricate, carrying in itself a multitude of indistinct shapes. Steam accompanies the dark flow. Patterns form and degenerate within this white halo: Clay sees monsters, pyramids, ancient beasts, machines, vegetables, crystals, but nothing lasts....No two objects are alike. Unending inventiveness is the rule here. He sees a shining spear of a beast go careening end over end, and a thick snaky worm with luminous antennae, and a walking black barrel, and a dancing fish, and a tunnel with legs. He sees a trio of giant eyes without bodies. He sees two green arms that clutch each other in a desperate and murderous grip. He sees a squadron of marching red eggs. He sees wheels with hands. He sees undulating carpets of singing slime. He sees fertile nails. He sees one-legged spiders. He sees black snowflakes. He sees men without heads. He sees heads without men...."

And so on in a blaze of visionary craziness for 213 pages. I would gladly quote the whole thing to you here. It was a once-in-a-lifetime book, emerging via a direct pipeline from my unconscious mind. That it made some sort of sense to others at all was sheer luck; and evidently it did, because in its time the book had plenty of readers, though its time seems to be over now.

Nor do I often have dreams like that these days, and more's the pity. But the dreams still come, and sometimes they are very strange, as my Isaac dream testifies. It was good to see him last night, and I would be pleased to see him again tomorrow night, whether he's broadcasting from space or simply coming across the hotel lobby to greet me at this year's s-f convention. Or maybe he'll be sitting in the row in front of me on the plane the next time Karen and I go to Europe. (" 'Isaac,' I said, 'You're three years dead!' 'I never died,' said he.")

Anything can happen, you know, once head hits pillow.

A Science-Fiction Garden

Six or seven years ago, after two decades as a professional science-fiction writer, I found myself terminally tired of fooling around with androids, star ships, and bug-eyed monsters. The royalties on my books were coming in nicely, I was drawing nifty dividends from some good investments, and my mortgage was paid off. And so I came to one of those apocalyptic decisions: I walked away from my career. To my agent, my publishers, my friends, my readers, and anyone else within earshot I loudly announced that I was giving up writing "forever."

As it happened, "forever" lasted about five years. Then an item called *Lord Valentine's Castle* wandered out of my typewriter, and somehow I found myself back in business. That's okay. If my mind wants to change itself, who am I to argue with it?

But people ask me a lot of questions about the five years of my retirement. "Didn't you write *anything*?" *Well, letters and checks.* "Weren't you *bored*?" *Not for a moment.* "But what did you do all that time."

Well, among other things, I planted a garden.

Plenty of good precedent for that. The Roman general Cincinnatus was summoned from his garden to be dictator. After he conquered the Aequians and saved his country, he resigned his office and went back to his garden. And Voltaire's Candide, after suffering every imaginable calamity, married his beloved and settled down to cultivate *his* garden. Thomas Jefferson, when he wearied of politics, carried out all sorts of horticultural experiments at Monticello.

But the garden I planted was a science-fiction garden.

I live in Northern California, in a region where the climate is not exactly tropical but is certainly benign. The temperature almost never goes below freezing and hardly ever rises above 85. So, I chose the sort of plants most closely akin to my sensibility and taste—that is, the freaky, grotesque, bizarre ones, the ones that look as though they'd strayed off the set of *Star Wars*.

The first thing was a cactus garden, naturally—a weird assortment of spiny, murderous, angular monstrosities that look like a sampling of the flora of Betelgeuse XI. Here's a Peruvian Cleistocactus that's a lot like a furry phallus six feet long. (If I ever catch it mating with the bumpy, prickly Lobivia clump nearby I'm going to run like hell.) Here's an Opuntia that looks like a bunch of Mickey Mouse ears

[*Heavy Metal*, January 1981]

minus the mouse. Here's the creeping devil of Baja California, the sinister Machaerocereus, that snakes along the ground, rooting as it slithers. It would slither all the way to Canada if the climate were right. And this, gobbling up territory like an extraterrestrial invader—that's the gorgon's head Euphorbia out of South Africa, with clusters of fleshy green projections that could have come to my garden straight out of your favorite s-f writer's baddest of trips. I tell you it's weirdsville down there, a spaced-out botanical Twilight Zone of creepies, crawlies, eeries, and ghastlies. A lot of them are wickedly armed, but they won't bite you unless you bite them first—except for the jumping cholla along the border of the garden, which sometimes makes preemptive strikes. (I keep my distance.)

After the cacti came succulents—some leafy, some gnarly, some goofy, all of them strange. They don't run as heavily to nasty spines as the cacti do, but they make it up with even more peculiar forms. I know they come from mundane places like Madagascar and Mexico and Brazil, but their zonkoid shapes and menacing, reptilian textures make it easy to believe that they evolved on worlds where humanoid sacrifice is the Saturday-morning custom and blue green blood flows freely on the high altars. And after the succulents, bromeliads—jungle dwellers, that in nature live perched precariously on tree limbs, feeding themselves by collecting dust specks and frog droppings and mosquito eggs in the little pools of water at their centers. Which led me easily onward to carnivorous plants: grinning green jaws waiting for unwary bugs. And from there—

It was just like writing s-f. I picked the strangest cast of characters I could find, arranged them in an artistically satisfying way, and turned them loose to do their thing, while I sat back and wondered how it would all turn out. I didn't miss my career for a moment. Planting this oddball garden satisfied all my creative hungers. It kept me out of mischief, gave me a powerful sense of oneness with the universe, mightily amused my neighbors, and taught me a great deal about botany and horticulture. There was even a powerful philosophical point in it for me. After having spent my whole life in the creation of extraterrestrial weirdness, I was learning anew that Earth is strange enough. No need to go chasing off to Xfuz VII and Hklplod III—our own little planet, having given us euphorbias and tillandsias and lobivias and billbergias and all the other botanical wonders that provide me daily with such delight, is an incredibly bountiful source of the goddamnedest thrills and chills there are.

And then my acre of land was full, the job was done, and my

creative hungers were still tickling me. So I unretired, and there was *Lord Valentine's Castle*, and I filled its landscape with all the plants of my own garden. Slightly modified, of course—the bromeliads have teeth, and some of the succulents have eyes. Call it artistic license—or is it just cross-pollination?

Why I Wrote a Sequel After All

Among the things I like to eat are breast of wild duck done very rare, veal with chanterelles, and fiery Indian curries. Quite high on the list of things I'd rather not eat are my own words. But one can't always choose one's own ideal diet; and if one makes statements in public, one not infrequently finds oneself required eventually to dine on those statements later on. You are now about to witness such an act of verbal ingestion. I would sooner plead guilty to inconsistency than to dishonesty; and, having committed a whopper of an inconsistency in these very pages, I intend to—well, bite the bullet—and anticipate all the mockers and jeerers by doing the mocking and jeering myself.

This is what I wrote, a couple of years ago, for the March 1982 issue of *Amazing*, in speaking of the current proliferation of sequels, trilogies, and other multi-volume enterprises in science fiction:

> "What about Silverberg, now at work on *Majipoor Chronicles*. It is not, I insist mildly, a sequel to *Lord Valentine's Castle*, since it involves a host of other characters and takes place at earlier periods of Majipoor's history....I would be very much surprised to find myself writing a true sequel to *Lord Valentine's Castle*—the idea dismays and depresses me—and even though you might point out that I also found myself surprised to be writing LVC in the first place, I'm fairly confident that it won't happen. I can't bear the notion of trundling out Carabella and Deliamber and Valentine and the rest of that crowd for another set of adventures. They had their moment on the stage; I'm done with them forever."

A very final statement, even as final statements go. It ranks right up there with "If nominated I will not run, if elected I will not serve," and "As of the book I've just finished, I intend to retire forever from writing science fiction." I admire its firm vigorous unswerving finality. And I suppose I admire my own ability to leap deftly out of the corners into which I've so thoroughly painted myself. For, as it happens, I've just completed a novel (I write this in July of 1983) called *Valentine Pontifex*. Even those few folks who have not yet read *Lord Valentine's Castle* are apt to guess that the new book has some connection with that one. Those who are familiar with LVC, such as John Provo of Fredericksburg, Virginia, were able with no great difficulty to jump to the conclusion that *Valentine Pontifex* must be an actual sequel to *Lord Valentine's Castle* as soon as they saw the announcement of the new book in *Locus*. Mr. Provo was kind enough to write me about it, pointing out that I had elaborately and emphatically told the readers of *Amazing Stories* that I wasn't going to write any such book, and wondering what was going on. (He did say he'd read the new book even if it did turn out to be a mere sequel.)

And in truth what I have done is write a real sequel—not some sort of peripherally connected book, but an out-and-out continuation of the story—to *Lord Valentine's Castle*. I have indeed trundled out Carabella and Deliamber and Valentine and all the rest of that crowd for another set of adventures, though I swore I was done with them forever. I told you quite solemnly that the idea of doing such a book dismayed and depressed me, and I meant it. But there it is stacked up before me, 521 pages of neatly word-processed manuscript. At this very instant the galley proofs are winging westward from New York toward me. By the time these words are in print the book will be on sale. Actually and literally have I done this thing of writing the sequel I said I wouldn't write.

Ah, Silverberg, how come, how come?

For money, you say instantly. Too easy an answer. There will be, of course, a substantial improvement in the Silverbergian balance of payments as a result of my having written that book. But I am not so hard pressed for funds that I needed to take on a project I had publicly described as dismaying and depressing, merely to keep the plumber's bill paid and the larder well stocked with breast of wild duck. Besides, I'd be well enough paid for any novel I chose to write just now; I didn't necessarily have to make one more foray into Majipoor. (Do you think Isaac Asimov *needs* to write a new robot novel, or a fifth Foundation book, to keep the dollars flowing? Do you think Frank Herbert's newly finished fifth *Dune* novel was his only way out of the poorhouse this year?)

Money is part of it, sure. But what finally tipped me toward writing the book I said I wouldn't write was a sense of unfinished business, a nagging little itch at the back of my mind.

When I wrote *Lord Valentine's Castle*, I was emerging from years of retirement as a writer: I meant to do just that one book and scuttle back to my garden. The book had two main plot-threads: the struggle of Valentine to regain his throne, and the struggle of the suppressed and outcast Metamorph aborigines of Majipoor to regain their planet. I took the first of those themes through to a resolution; I left the other

418 A Few Personal Items

wholly unresolved. Obviously I was setting myself up for a sequel, and a flattering number of readers wrote to me to ask what happened next. But I had no intention of dragging myself back over the same familiar ground just to tell the story of the Metamorph uprising: no challenge in that for me, no creative zing, just a filling-in of the dots.

But I had built something else into LVC in an offhanded way—a minor character, a small irreverent boy—who seemed to demand more attention in a later work. Several sharp readers asked me if I meant to write about him. And also I had, in singlemindedly telling the story of Valentine's return to the throne, sidestepped a lot of science-fictional questions about Majipoor: how does this world really *work*, how did it evolve its particular set of customs and laws, what is its total life like? I had concentrated on one small group of characters, leaving much of the vast background unexplored.

So I wrote *Majipoor Chronicles*, using the boy Hissune as the focus through which I could examine various aspects of Majipoor over a period of thousands of years. It wasn't a sequel to LVC; it was a companion, a commentary, a book apart. And as I wrote it I admitted to myself, finally, that I still had unanswered questions to deal with. I had not examined the inner workings of the Majipoor monarchy. I had not explored the contradiction inherent in trying to be both a king and a pacifist. I had not grappled with the implications of the genocidal crime on which the benign and cheerful civilization of Majipoor had been founded. The more I thought about it, the more I began to see LVC as only half a book. It didn't require a sequel so much as it did a completion; by showing only Valentine's return to the throne, but not his efforts to meet the responsibilities of that throne, I had told a fairy-tale, not written a science-fiction novel. And so *Valentine Pontifex* became inevitable.

There it is in bookstores now. In the most accidental of ways I have committed a trilogy, swearing all the way that I had no plan to do any such thing. Mea culpa, mea culpa: but the creative process doesn't always work in neat logical paths, and neither do I.

Was it dismaying and depressing to write the book, as I had feared? Well, yes, in some places it was: for chapters at a time I was unable to cut loose in a freshly inventive way, but was confined to utilizing backgrounds and characters that were already familiar to me. At those times I would rather have been marching onward through new terrain. But then there was the joy of picking up a theme in the first book that had been mere decoration there, and coming to understand its relevance to the real story, and amplifying and developing it as though I had planned all along to do just that: serendipitous discoveries, and delightful ones. And I had a sense, too, of coming to grips with the inner natures of the characters in a way that the somewhat stylized and romantic nature of the first book had not allowed. So the book proved to have artistic rewards for me after all. If I made myself look silly by writing something I had publicly forsworn, so be it: I have looked silly before, and I probably will again, but I have no regrets for have written it. For all my distaste for sequels as a general concept, and all my personal dislike for returning to old territory, the third Majipoor book—like the second—gradually became necessary for me to do, which I had not at all anticipated. So Silverberg, of all people, has produced a trilogy despite his frequently expressed scorn for multi-book books. Better to look silly than to ignore the inner voice that gives the orders, say I.

And will I return to Majipoor a few years from now for yet another novel?

I doubt it very much. But don't hold me to it, okay?

Introduction to "Sundance"

Having included essays on the work of such writers as Philip K. Dick, Jack Vance, Clifford D. Simak, and Roger Zelazny in earlier sections of this book, I conclude it with an analysis of a story of my own— "Sundance," first published in 1968— that provides in a very few pages some significant insights into the way I go about constructing a piece of fiction.

On the surface, there appears to be a transaction taking place between the artist and the audience, and that transaction has the form of an elementary quid-pro-quo deal: I make or do something for your pleasure, you look upon my work and are pleased, you pay me for the time I expended on your behalf. Almost any sort of "entertainment" involving doer and spectator can be viewed in terms of that transactional relationship: the roster of hirelings encompasses writers, actors, painters, football players, sculptors, composers, musical performers, stage and film directors, and a long list of others.

But the deeper we look into the psychology of the artist—or the psychology of the spectator—the more clearly we see that artistic effort is only coincidentally transactional in nature. Artist and audience are on separate trips, and the point at which they meet in order that the spectators may pay the price of admission is only one brief flashing intersection on two otherwise independent journeys. Consider the very different things that a short story "does" for the person who writes it and the one who reads it. These are some of the benefits the writer gets from the creative effort:

> Satisfaction of the shaping impulse, that seemingly universal human drive to reduce entropy, to bring order out of randomness, form out of chaos.
>
> Codification of the writer's own thinking in the cognitive sphere through the organization and development of the ideational substructure of the story—a factor typical of science fiction, in which conceptual rather than emotional material often lies at the story's heart.
>
> Emotional catharsis derived from transfer of some aspect of personal experience, perhaps painful, from recollection to artistic manifestation.
>
> Development of technical skills through exploration of form and possible extensions of the possibilities of form.

The reader, on the other hand, may obtain some or all of these benefits from a story:

[*From Those Who Can*, edited by Robin Scott Wilson, 1973]

A moment of encapsulation in a "pocket universe" drawing him away from the problems of real-world existence: fiction as escape.

Esthetic response to form and style: the pleasure of experiencing a well-made verbal object.

Acquisition of vicarious experience: learning something from a story, perhaps of a technical nature (operations of the stock market, theories of linguistics, effects of psychedelic drugs, methods of sexual intercourse) of perhaps in some more general field of human relationships.

Stimulation of thought: reflections evoked by the story, leading to conclusions not explicit in the text.

There is, of course, a good deal of overlapping in these two groups of categories, and neither writer nor reader ever separates them as neatly as I have done here. The point is merely that the satisfactions a writer gets from writing only occasionally intersect the satisfactions a reader gets from reading.

"Sundance," which I wrote in September, 1968, is a good example of this. It pleased me when I wrote it, and pleases me now: I think I like it best, out of my hundreds of short stories. After a slow start, it has come to please readers too: when awards were handed out for the best science fiction stories published in 1969, a different story of mine received a trophy, but since then "Sundance" has been reprinted eight or nine times, and its career as an anthology piece appears to be just beginning. I am the last person in the world who could tell you what values "Sundance" has to a reader, but I can tell you quite precisely what it achieved for its author in the way of esthetic and emotional satisfaction.

It did not, for instance, give me the special science-fictional delight of creating or developing ideas. One of science fiction's highest values for me as reader is its inventiveness: the putting forth of some new notion, or the recombination of old ideas into dramatically vivid new form. Heinlein achieved that for me "Universe," the multi-generation-starship story; Clement did it in *Mission of Gravity* and Blish in "Surface Tension"; Asimov accomplished it in his robotics stories and novels. All of these are works that methodically exhaust all the implications of an unfamiliar concept. In my own writing I think I've come closest to achieving that in the urban monad stories collected under the title *The World Inside*. But there are no unfamiliar concepts in "Sundance." The central action is the extermination of an abundant animal species by humans who have uses of their own for the territory where that species is dominant. Hardly an original notion: all I have done has been to transfer to another planet the extermination of the American bison in the nineteenth century. Merely using an alien setting does not, however, give the story much validity as science fiction, since there is nothing so alien about the setting I devised as to make it *fundamentally* different from Nebraska or North Dakota; only when I add the possibility that the beasts being slaughtered on that world may in fact be an intelligent species with a rich cultural heritage does the story begin to take on some speculative attributes. Even then I am offering nothing new. And when I make my protagonist an American Indian who is part of the slaughter operation, and thus is compelled to recapitulate the tragic experience of his own race, I provide only an extra level of irony, not any true conceptual insight.

So the material that generates the story is—to me—pretty unpromising stuff. I yoke together a transplanted Western (Buffalo Bill in the Zilch Galaxy) and some currently fashionable radical sentiments (We Sure Gave the Injuns a Raw Deal) to create—what? A tract proving that the expansionist imperialist United States is going to repeat in space all its crimes of the recent past? A little nugget of agitprop that gives the enlightened reader a quick hot flush of righteous indignation? Well, maybe. No doubt "Sundance" can be read, and has been, for its "relevant" political sentiments. No doubt my own anti-imperialist bias and sympathy for the fate of the Plains Indians (and the bison) gives the story thrust and intensity. But I see little value in writing tracts warning against crimes that already have been committed, or even crimes yet to come; my stories may occasionally have politico-ideological content, but never a primary political intent.

What was I up to, then, in "Sundance?" For one thing to get inside the mind and soul of a human being—Tom Two Ribbons—who is manifesting the long-term effects of the destruction of his ancestral culture and who is unable to escape the pain of that destruction even on another planet. But on another level I was after two main things:

> An exploration of ways to dramatize subjective, ambiguous perceptions of reality.
> An exploration of the feasibility of shifting grammatical person within a short story.

Those are both technical aims—matters of literary carpentry. I wanted to see if it was possible for me to tell a story in which the events-as-narrated do not necessarily coincide with the events-as-they-really-happened, and in which the events-as-they-really-happened are withheld as irrelevant. I also wanted to see if I could shift from third person to first, and even to second, without causing fatal discontinuities of structure. The second aim would merely have been a virtuoso stunt, self-contained and irrelevant to the needs of most readers, if I had not integrated it with the first, producing this more refined statement of technical purpose:

To dramatize a shifting, subjective perception of reality
by means of shifts in grammatical person.

Any situation might have let me do this. I chose the bison-Indian parallel because the implied genocidal myth carried its own built-in emotional charge, and a story in which my goals were so abstract, so technical, needed all the emotional intensity I could provide. Whether actual genocide was taking place on that planet was unimportant to me, indeed was outside the scope of the story: what mattered was Tom Two Ribbons' perception, perhaps inaccurate, that such a crime was being committed. A careful reading of the story shows that the action remains ambiguous to the end: not only is the reader uncertain that the aliens really do have intelligence of a human level, but there is some doubt that an extermination is in fact in progress. Since I was not writing an oh-the-horror-of-it-all sermon, the "real" situation did not concern me. What did was the presentation of Tom Two Ribbons' fluctuating emotional states. To do this I set up these structural propositions:

First-person sections would describe Tom Two Ribbons' subjective perceptions of events.

Second-person sections would allow the author to speak directly to Tom, laying down basic narrative situations and providing the concluding statement of ultimate ambiguity.

Third-person sections would render the reality-perceptions of other members of the expedition and show Tom interrelating with those members. I would use present tense when Tom is with them, to heighten the sense of ambiguity, and past tense when Tom is absent from the scene, since his absence removes the feeling of shifting, feverish uncertainty.

I did not always follow this somewhat mechanical scheme; some of the second-person passages, I now see, might well have been told in the first person, and some of the third-person material might have been shifted to second person; basically, though, I think I was consistent to my structural program and that it aided me in bringing off the effect of developing the disintegration of a personality. But a structural program would not have been enough. Having devised my framework, having conceived the character of Tom Two Ribbons, having worked out the basic situation of conflict involving the alien beings, I still had a big job ahead: orchestrating the story, giving it texture and density and color, providing the reader with sensory data to keep him reading on through shift after shift of perception.

Here a strong sense of setting was necessary to keep the story from becoming a mere abstraction, a series of empty postures. Placing the story on another planet gave me a good opportunity for this sort of exterior decoration; giving the aliens a ritual that included the ingestion of a hallucinogenic plant allowed me an even better way of making the story vivid.

One way to describe an alien planet is to drop into the matrix of the story a solid lump of specifications: "Planet X, the ninth of sixteen worlds orbiting the blue-white star Q, had an atmosphere composed of This and That, a diameter So Big, and a gravitational pull That Heavy. There were five continents, and the one on which our story is laid was located in the south temperate zone." Stuff like that gets published all the time. I've written my share of it. Such a passage has the virtue of giving the reader all the background data in one place, for quick reference. It has the drawback of turning that data into a disposable unit that can be excreted from memory before the page is turned. In "Sundance" I had no special intention of creating a novel and ingenious new planet, of the sort that Hal Clement or Larry Niven or Poul Anderson might dream up; that's a noble sport, but it would only interfere with the real business of this particular story. All I wanted was a sense of alienness. So in the first paragraph you encountered a "green-gold sunrise." It isn't Earth. A few paragraphs on, I offer a life-form with low-phylum bodily organization, high-phylum intelligence. More alienness, and, not incidentally, the potential for some misunderstanding by the characters of these creatures' true scope. Two pages farther on come some small creatures—a "spider-analog spinning its asymmetrical web" and a small turquoise amphibian, and after another page comes a note on the weather cycle, from dry weather to foggy. Bits of texture continue to surface until a respectable feeling of density has been achieved: the sun is hot, the grasslands are sweet with gases exhaled by the towering photosynthetic spikes of the oxygen-plants, there are streams and rivers, and yet—and yet—how few words were needed to provide that sense of density! A sensory jab here, a sensory nibble there, a splash of color, a nip of fragrance—yet nowhere in the story is there any information about the size and mass of the planet, its periods of rotation or revolution, the inclination of its orbit, the distribution of its continents. Stories set on Earth, mundane stories about Indians and bison, manage to achieve effects of density of setting without telling you any of those things; why then do it for that alien world, when repeated brief strokes can convey the desired effects?

But there is one place where I pile on the effects, calling on every weapon in the sensorium to make the setting concrete. This is the passage beginning, "They sing now, a blurred hymn of joy," in which Tom Two Ribbons dances with the aliens (or thinks he does), eats their sacred hallucinogenic plant, and experiences that confusion of the senses known as *synesthesia*. I appeal here to taste, touch, smell, sight, and hearing, loading the story with sensory data for 1400 words, more than a quarter of its total length. This is the climax of the story, though it comes in the middle, another technical experiment. (There is a secondary climax, recapitulating the imagery of the first and developing it by introducing members of Tom's family, just before the story ends.) The sensory overload of that 1400-word scene defines the psychological setting of the story, just as another writer might use overload techniques to define his geographical setting. The place where "Sundance" unfolds is the interior of Tom Two Ribbons' mind, and, although I was content to outline the planetary geography with a minimum of data, I provide a wealth of interior data, psychological data, to make the climatic scene as immediate as I can. *And the sensory details are scrambled.* Sunset is perceived as the ringing of leaden chimes, the wind is a swirl of coaly bristles, the scent of the aliens' bodies is fiery red. Setting reinforces the inner drama. Tom Two Ribbons' psychological disorientation surfaces as hallucinatory synesthesia at the moment of his communion with the alien beings whom he identifies with his own ancestors. (Do the aliens themselves experience synesthesia when they eat the plant? The story doesn't say.) What might have been mere decorative detail in another story is intrinsic to theme here. Which is why a writer's dry-as-dust experiment in jiggling with grammar turns out to be the story "Sundance" is. It was a difficult story to write. It was an exciting story to write.